MW00396310

The Confessions of
SOCRATES

R. d. Prendergast.

THE CONFESSIONS OF SOCRATES

© 2017 by R. L. Prendergast

This book is a work of fiction. Although based on historical individuals,
events and cultural ideas, the story is entirely the product of the author's
imagination. Any resemblance to individuals, living or dead, is either
fictional or purely coincidental.

For information about special bulk purchase discounts for sales
promotions, fundraising or educational use, please contact:
Dekko Publishing at sales@dekkopublishing.com

Published in Canada by Dekko Publishing, Edmonton, Alberta, Canada.

Library and Archives Canada Cataloguing in Publication
Prendergast, R. L., 1970-, author
The Confessions of Socrates / R.L. Prendergast.
Issued in print and electronic formats.
ISBN 978-0-9784548-7-6 (hardback)
ISBN 978-0-9784548-9-0 (paperback)
ISBN 978-0-9784548-8-3 (eBook)
I. Title.
PS8631.R45C66 2017 C813'.6 C2016-906591-X
C2016-906592-8

www.RLPrendergast.com

Edited by Marion Hoffmann and Deborah Lawson
Cover art by Roseanna White Designs

Printed and bound in Canada

Printed on 100% post-consumer recycled paper

BOOKS BY
R. L. PRENDERGAST

NOVELS

The Impact of a Single Event
Dinner with Lisa
The Confessions of Socrates

CHILDREN'S BOOKS

Baby, Please go to Sleep

The Confessions of

SOCRATES

❧

R. L. PRENDERGAST

For my son Markus Tana —
May your life be an adventure.

Love, Dad

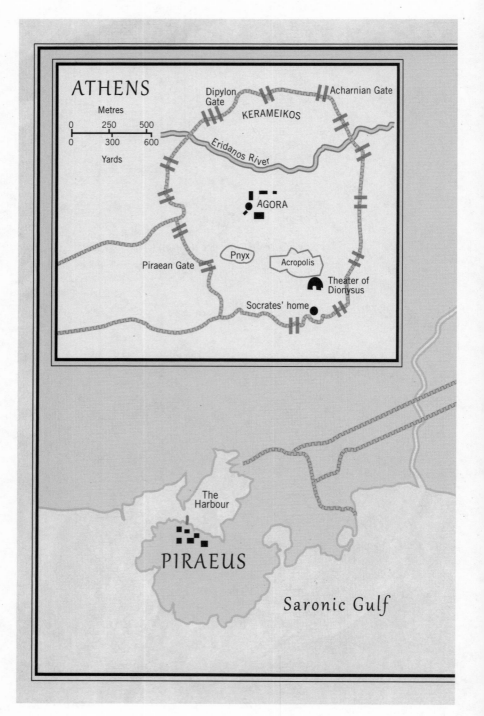

ATHENS

Eridanos River

North Long Wall

South Long Wall

Ilissos River

ATHENS and PIRAEUS
400 B.C.E

Kilometres

0   1   2   3

0   1   2

Miles

N

x

THRACE

MACEDON

Amphipolis

Hellespont

Mount Olympus Potidaea
▲

Troy

Aegean Sea

PERSIAN
EMPIRE

THESSALY

Sardis

Clazomenae

Athens

Island of Samos• •Mycale

Miletus

Island of Delos

Pylos
• • Sparta
Sphacteria

Island of Rhodes•

GREECE 400 B.C.E

Kilometres

0   160

0   100

Miles

N

Socratic Writings Discovered

September 28, 2016

ATHENS, GREECE — In the course of excavating a Greek site in Thebes recently, archaeologists uncovered what was at first thought to be a small tomb. Measuring four feet deep, four feet wide and five feet long, the tiny room contained an amulet, a painted cup, bronze armour, iron weapons and 10 sealed ceramic jars. After carefully exploring and investigating the site, archaeologists removed the artifacts and took them to an undisclosed location.

"We are extremely excited by the find," said Dr. Helena Stais, the lead researcher for the project. "Modern Thebes is built directly above the historical site, making it difficult to reconstruct an accurate history of the ancient city. We believe this discovery might shed new light on some long-standing questions concerning dates and places."

To their astonishment, however, the archaeological team soon found their discovery was even more significant than they had realized.

"The objects in the room were very well preserved. The stone slab that we lifted out in order to get into the room had clearly not been moved since it was put in place originally. The ceramic jars, called amphora, are remarkable; each one is decorated with detailed paintings of Eros, the ancient Greek god of love," Dr. Stais reported. "Of all the objects, the jars and their contents are the most valuable find."

The sealed amphora were found to hold 29 papyrus scrolls. Carbon dating has revealed the papyrus, a thick, paper-like material, to stem from about 400 BCE, making it the oldest Greek papyrus ever discovered. This alone endows the scrolls with major historical importance.

After the scrolls had been carbon dated, the team began translating the nearly pristine documents. And when the translators identified the author, it quickly became apparent that the scrolls would be of global significance.

"I will never forget," said Dr. Stais, "when one of my associates uttered the words, 'I think this was written by Socrates,' and the hair rose on the back of my neck."

Until that point, historians had believed that Socrates, the Greek philosopher, had never written anything himself. All that is known about the man — if, indeed, he even existed — has been attributed to second-hand references by the philosopher Plato, the historian-soldier Xenophon and the comic playwright Aristophanes.

The papyrus scrolls are now confirmed as authentic, written by Socrates as he sat in his jail cell, awaiting execution. The Greek Minister of Culture has stated that the scrolls are of such worldwide interest that transcriptions will be made public as soon as possible.

One translator, on condition of anonymity, has said that many people will not be happy with what was found. "The world has a certain idealistic vision of Socrates," he explained. "But what we have found so far is a flawed human being who struggled with life, as we all do. I believe the world will be forced to re-evaluate its view of this revered historical figure."

DAY 1

M Y DEAREST FAMILY,
I have been sentenced to death. But undoubtedly you already know this. I hope Crito managed to convey the news gently, before you could hear it from the rabble shouting it in the streets.

This is not the outcome I foresaw when I walked to court this morning. I had no idea my trial would become such a sensation. How difficult it is to remember now that I had hoped the minimum 200 jurors would appear, so that my case would be heard speedily and I could put this trouble behind me. Instead, a full jury of 500 citizens showed up and thousands more gathered outside the court to watch. *All the more to witness my victory*, I thought, as I strode smugly to the front of the court. This arrogance — the conviction that nobody was more capable in an argument than I — blinded me to the dangerous nature of my opponents. I will not make that mistake again.

I profoundly regret the anguish my death will cause you. Had the trial been held a day earlier, my execution would have been carried out at sunset today. But the Delia festival began this morning with the sailing of the sacred ship, and the city must, by law, remain pure until its return. If history is any indicator, my execution will be carried out about a month from now.

Although I am relieved there can be no executions until the ship returns from the Island of Delos, this delay will only prolong your grief. And during that time you will suffer in a manner I can only imagine. I am like the limb that has turned gangrenous and must be amputated. If I were to die immediately, there would be pain for you, yes, but the pain would then be done with. As it is, the delay in carrying out my sentence can only serve to make your situation even more difficult to endure.

This is not the first time I have awaited my end. In fact, it's the fourth time. The difference is that the other threats to my life occurred on the battlefield. Shoulder to shoulder, I stood with my companions, our spears poised and ready, anticipating the call to advance on the enemy. I knew I might die. At the same time, though, I was always able to cling to the hope that if we remembered our training, we — I — would survive the onslaught of javelins, swords and stones. On the battleground, the chance for survival always exists.

This time it's different.

The jailer will come to my cell at sunset. I will be freed from my chains, at which time I hope I will be allowed to say my final farewells to a few friends. Much as I desperately yearn to see you all again, my dearest family, I hope you will be well away from Athens by then.

The jailer will then inform me it is time for the poison. A servant will bring a cup of hemlock and hand it to the jailer, who will hand it to me and bid me to drink it. I will be forced to raise the cup to my lips and swallow its contents. If the hemlock is prepared properly, my feet will lose sensation quickly. The poison will first affect my legs and then move upward to my heart.

Adjoining this cell is the room where I will die. I have a morbid need to inspect the room, but the chains around my ankles do not allow me to move far from where I sit. Although I cannot enter it, I can see that the cell is small, with a single narrow window near the ceiling. If I strain hard enough, letting the chains bite into my flesh, sometimes I even glimpse a few clouds through the window. In the centre of the room is a small stone bath in which they will wash my dead body.

The cell I am in at the moment is windowless, and only as long as I am tall. The air here is cool day and night, so it makes no sense that I feel as if I were suffocating — as if I were wearing a Corinthian helmet on a scorchingly hot day, my face surrounded by hot bronze. Ants, spiders and beetles move about the dirt floor, paying me no more attention than they would a stone in their way. If they could speak, what would they say? Perhaps, "He will be gone soon enough. For now we must go around him."

Many names are carved into the cell walls. As I trace my finger over the ones I can reach, I ask myself, "Who were the people who spent their last days in this cell? What were their alleged crimes? Did they scratch their names on the stone to leave their mark on the world? To be remembered?" If so, I understand. Ever since I was a child listening to tales about the heroes of old, I have wanted what they had. I want respect. I want glory. I want fame. I want to be known for my courage, boldness and brilliance. I want to do something that will resonate through the course of history, something that will make my name shine so brightly that the passage of time will not dim its fire. I want to be remembered forever. So very, very much, I want to be remembered.

I worry even more about your safety than about my imminent demise. I greatly fear that those who plotted the trial and the sentencing may not be satisfied with my death alone — that their wrath may extend to you. I did what was requested of me, what I knew to be my only option. I can only hope that the men who put me here will keep their promise and let you be. I hope, quite desperately, that my actions will keep you safe when I am gone.

I long for information. I close my eyes and strain to catch something — anything — pertaining to my situation. Yet all I hear are complaints from the other prisoners, and the jailers' demands for silence. I am not allowed visitors, lest I try to escape. If only my jailers understood that their concerns are unfounded, that I intend to remain here until the end. It is the only way.

My dearest family, I am not ready to die. I'm not ready to move on. Unbearable sorrow fills me at the thought of relinquishing all my plans for the future. I looked forward so much to seeing you boys finish your journeys toward manhood. To seeing you married. To holding your sons and daughters in my arms. So many tormenting thoughts go through my mind. What agony it is, Xanthippe, to know I shall never again feel your hair against my cheek as you rest your head on my shoulder. To realize, my dear sons, that I will not experience the joy of hearing your laughter. Birthdays will take place without me and the seasons will change without my knowledge. How I yearn to do something to prevent my death. But I cannot. You must believe me when I plead with you to forego any attempt to save me. I am determined to see out my end. You must also believe that my death will be your salvation.

Know that you are the joy and beauty of my life. I love you all.

DAY 2

I WOKE IN THE middle of the night to the sound of shuffling feet and the creaking of my cell door. I held my breath, certain that someone was entering my tiny room intending to either stab me in my sleep or cave in my head with a stone. Then an oil lamp was lit, revealing the messenger who came to me last night with ink, papyrus and a note from you. Relieved, I let out a long breath and composed myself. He relayed your messages to me and, to my delight, brought more writing materials.

Two things have not changed since last night. I still love you all dearly and I still will not deviate from the course set before me. Do not attempt to secure my freedom, no matter how tempting you may find the idea, for I am determined to see out my sentence. You must understand that the men who put me here will harm you if I do not. Our messenger will provide you with the evidence of their intentions.

I am horrified about the dog; it is unconscionable that my accusers could have killed him so brutally. Yet the fact that they stooped to such an unnecessary act makes it even more crucial that you leave Athens at once. Your lives are in danger! My accusers are vicious men and cannot be trusted. They may well renege on their agreement to let you be, even though they should know I will keep my end of the bargain.

I believe it would be best for you to go to Thebes. You boys will find work there. And since Thebes is allied with neither Athens nor Sparta, you will be safer in that fiercely independent city than anywhere else.

I have received the food you cooked. Thank you. It doesn't appear to have been tampered with, although I ate sparingly, anticipating it might be. Now that I have only a short time left to me, I don't wish to reduce the length of my life more than I can help.

I feel sorry for the poor souls who are in prison with me. They, too, are due to be executed. And like me, their sentences have been commuted until the ship returns from Delos after the Delia festival. But at least one of them, from what I can tell by listening to snatches of the guards' conversation, has no one to bring him meals; there may be more like him. A month without eating! This poor soul may starve to death before his execution. By the way, please don't send such extravagant fare.

During the day it seems very quiet outside. As a free man, there wasn't a day that I didn't walk past the prison. Each time I passed, I saw someone bemoaning the fate of a husband, brother or father and trying to communicate through the stone walls and high, narrow windows. Now that I am a prisoner, I occasionally hear a guard outside the walls yell, "Clear out!" This leads me wonder whether one of you is out there, trying to speak to me. Are my accusers so worried that I will plan an escape that they forbid anyone who knows me to even loiter outside the prison?

As you know, our beloved Diotima suggested — no, commanded! — that I write about myself, insisting there are things you boys will want to know about me when I am gone. She, at least, has fully accepted that I will not leave this place alive. I agree you might benefit from knowing more about your father — not because I have any great wisdom or knowledge to pass on to you, but because I may have done things or made errors that you may be able to avoid.

What Diotima asks of me is much more difficult than it sounds. Although I know how to write, it is not a method of communication I particularly enjoy. Without voice and hands to give emphasis to my meaning, the written word can be misinterpreted all too easily. Language is far more *how* we say things than *what* we say. Clarity would be ensured if I could sit with you and tell you my thoughts, but since I do not believe I will see you boys again, writing is my only option.

I wonder what you would wish to know about me. I imagine you would be interested in the kind of things I would have liked to have known about my own father, dead now these many years. There is so much I did not know about him: the battles he fought in; how he met my mother; his time at the academy; his friends; anything at all about his childhood. Above all, I would have liked to have known something of his thoughts and feelings. What made him happy? What did he fear? What did he regret? Why did he live his life the way he did? He never shared these things with me. Perhaps this is the way it is between fathers and sons. Thinking about it, I realize how little I have shared with you boys. Men are supposed to show strength and confidence at all times. Fear, sorrow and intimate feelings are usually kept well hidden.

So let me start with what is, for me, more important than anything else: know and remember how much I love you boys, your mother and Diotima. The five of you have brought me great joy and happiness. It is you who make leaving this world so difficult.

Know, too, that I am neither the man I claimed to be nor the man I wanted to be. The reputation I cultivated does not represent the person I truly am. And therein lies the difficulty — how do I explain myself? I don't believe I can do this easily or quickly. It may be best to tell you stories, from the beginning, as I would have liked to have heard them from my own father.

My early childhood comes to me in chunks of memory, like pictures painted on the side of a vase or scenes carved onto a wall. I hold in my mind an image of my mother, dipping a sea sponge in a jug of water and washing me down. "This will cool you," she says, as she gently wipes my forehead, arms, legs and chest.

I recall terrible nightmares and intense pain, in spite of my mother's gentle touch. I woke often from sleep, screaming in fear, and my mother would soothe me with her soft voice. My panic would dwindle for a moment, only to be replaced by a great discomfort. The bones in my right arm felt as though they protruded through my skin, and the right side of my face burned. I wept from the pain. My mother, an experienced midwife, was knowledgeable in the ways of reducing the pain of child-birth. She would hold a cup containing some liquid to my lips, and bid me swallow. I did so, and then I slept.

After all this time, I still remember that cup beside my bed. I can see it now very clearly. Vivid. Real. As if I were five years old again. The cup is reddish-brown and has an image of Eros painted in black on its side. The God of Love is leaping, holding a flute in one hand. I attempt to reach for the cup but cannot move my hands, no matter how hard I try. I ask my mother why I cannot move. She leans over me and smiles. Her eyes are dark and warm and kind. Her smile is meant to be reassuring, but something lurks beneath the surface: worry and helplessness, emotions I understand now, as a parent, but did not understand then.

My mother massages my limbs and pleads with me to stir my body to action. "You must try again," she says calmly. My arms do not obey my commands, nor do my legs. With great effort, I manage to wiggle a finger of my right hand. The movement sends stabbing pains up my arm and I howl in agony. Once again, my mother brings the cup to my lips. Again I swallow, and then slumber.

My mother was not a typical Athenian woman, cloistered inside her home, allowed out only for funerals or festivals and then only when accompanied by a slave. Even more so than today, at that time women gained respect through being modest, managing their houses well and raising children. A few women always flaunted convention, but malicious things were said behind their backs and their husbands were ridiculed. But there were exceptions. Midwives and some priestesses could walk about unaccompanied. My mother, as I mentioned, was one of the former.

As a midwife she was free to move through the city, so when the pain in my arms and face lessened somewhat, she and I began daily pilgrimages to the Eileithyia shrine. When I could move only my fingers and toes, my mother would bundle me up and carry me like an infant the short distance to the sanctuary.

Today, of course, we have the large wooden statue of the Goddess of Childbirth lodged inside a handsome marble temple down by the Ilissos River. But when I was young, Athens was still recovering from destruction at the hands of the Persians and the Patron Goddess of Midwives was not the most important goddess in the city. Housed in a small structure made of mud and bricks, the Eileithyia statue was a small clay figure about the size and shape of a seated child. Her hair was piled above her forehead. She held a bird in her right hand and rested her left hand on her knee.

People customarily left onions, eggs, nuts, loaves of bread, small clay figurines and clothing along the walls of Eileithyia's sanctuary. Your grandmother would leave a honey cake, believing it to be the best gift she could offer Eileithyia, to thank her for guiding me back into the light. On the way home, she would sing softly to Asclepius, asking the God of Healing to release me from my ills.

Although these small excursions to the sanctuary made me uneasy, my mother's singing soothed me and I would drift off to sleep — only to be tormented by a nightmare that was always the same. A horse-drawn wagon rushes toward me. The clip-clop of hooves grows louder and louder. A dark shape looms over me, crushes me like a dry eggshell and renders me unable to move or cry out.

My mother could not remain at home for long. With no extended family to rely on, none having survived the last Persian invasion, we depended on the food — bread, meat, fish and vegetables — with which she was paid. Unwilling to be parted from me, she carried me from one pregnant woman's house to the next, through the offal-filled streets of Athens to farms outside the city walls, on roads lined with rows of green fruit trees. Upon our arrival, she would find a comfortable spot to put me down. On a good day, that spot was under a tree in a shaded courtyard; in inclement weather, she would find me a place on a couch inside the house. My need for sleep was strong at that time, and I was grateful for the chance to doze — until suddenly the nightmare horse would appear to run me down, jerking me awake with a start. Terrified, I would call out for my mother. Always alert for my screams, she would leave her patient, stroke my face and lull me back to sleep.

I didn't give it a thought then, but today I wonder at her strength. I was a stout child, weighing as much as a boy years older than me. I loved to eat and was always ravenous. I ate whatever my mother or Diotima put before me and then asked for more. My mother used food as an incentive to get me to move my arms. If I could reach the food, I could have it.

When you boys were the age I was then, I could carry you for only so long before I had to put you down and rest my arms, yet I don't recall my mother taking breaks during our walks. She was like Milo of Croton. Are you surprised that I compare a short, stocky woman to a tall, muscular man renowned for winning five Olympic wrestling titles? You may well be, but it was said that Milo of Croton built his strength by carrying full-grown bulls on his shoulders. I was the bull my mother carried around.

As my need for sleep diminished, I watched my mother tend her many pregnant patients. Her dress — plain and white — made a swishing sound when she moved. I watched her check a woman's secretions to see if the colours were right, or mix medicines to ease extreme nausea or assess the position and size of unborn babies by palpating the huge bellies of their mothers. When she bent over, I expected her long dark hair — worn around her head like an Olympic champion's laurel wreath — to fall, but it never did.

Mostly, my mother spoke with the women. She would ask about their well-being. Were they comfortable? Were they eating? Could they keep food down? Were they able to sleep? The women would relate their fears and my mother would answer questions and concerns in the soft, tranquil voice so familiar to me. She was like a stream, her unfailing gentleness lulling her patients into serenity. But her outward calm was deceptive because, like a stream, she was always moving, never at rest.

Often a distraught slave would come for the midwife in the middle of the night. Wrapping me in a blanket, my mother carried me to the home where the woman, often a first-time mother, believed her water had broken. More often than not, the fluid was only a mucous discharge or the result of a leaky bladder, but my mother always treated the woman's concerns calmly and thoughtfully, explaining that things were proceeding as they should and that the patient should not be embarrassed by her inconvenient summons. My mother had inside her a great well of warmth, enough that she could give her patients unending comfort.

I observed her many a time during the deliveries, for I was usually close by. Always calm and unflustered, she made certain she had everything she needed: olive oil for lubrication, warm fomentations for pain, sea sponges for cleansing, wool to cover the woman and water to wash her, bandages for swaddling the infant and lemon to scent the air.

She carried her supplies in a basket. Sometimes she would leave the basket behind after a baby was born, lending it to poorer families until they could make their own arrangements. It was a surprise to all who knew her that the basket remained intact as long as it did, for your grandmother was not a skilled weaver. Years later, Diotima admitted to me that she would repair the basket at night while everyone was sleeping. Diotima cherished my mother and didn't want the neighbours making fun of her.

Occasionally, a partner midwife assisted my mother when deliveries, such as multiple births, were expected to be unusually difficult. Sometimes a student midwife joined her. I liked those deliveries best, as I could listen to my mother's explanations and instructions.

"Let the mother choose the most comfortable position, unless you need her to move so you can get better access to the baby."

"Cut the umbilical cord once the pulsing has stopped."

"The afterbirth should be expelled spontaneously soon after the birth. If it does not come away on its own, pull it out gently."

"If the mother bleeds more than usual following passage of the after-birth, massage her lower abdomen and put the baby to the breast."

"Make certain the uterus is contracting and the bleeding is normal, then give the mother some time to get to know her new baby."

Most women breathed heavily and groaned and grunted during labour. More often than not, a woman would scream horribly. I was so frightened the first time I heard this that my hands numbed in fear and I called for my mother. "Screams are not necessarily bad," she explained later, when we were on our way home. "They are even necessary for some births. Screaming lets us release emotions before they get out of hand. They're also good for your lungs," she added with a smile.

As births often lasted a long time, especially in the case of first-time mothers, my attention would wander to the other people in a house. Understandably, given that birthing is usually painful and often dangerous, I saw mostly tension and fear; this was the case whether the family lived in a mud-brick house like ours or in a huge timber-and-stone dwelling. People were unable to relax until they knew that both infant and mother had survived. That was normal, my mother explained. However, when a woman was delivering her fourth or fifth child, her family was more at ease than were the relatives of a woman giving birth for the first time.

Of course, tragic things happened, too: stillbirths and women dying in childbirth. Each time I had questions. But in this respect I was fortunate. Most of the children I knew were expected to listen in silence to their elders, but my mother was different from other parents. We talked openly as we walked home, with my mother answering my questions as if I were an adult and her equal.

I especially remember the tension in one particular house. The family had two daughters already, and they cherished great hope for a boy. The parents had done everything they could to ensure a son. The wife had prayed at every shrine in Athens and had travelled, at great expense, to a healing sanctuary outside the city.

The baby was born: a girl. The infant was still covered in blood when the father snatched it from my mother's hands and placed it in a clay pot outside the front door. My mother ran from the house and into the night. As the new mother screamed for her baby, the other midwife in attendance tried to calm her. Weak from childbirth, the distraught woman staggered from her bed and stumbled, naked, through the courtyard to the front gate. In the torchlight, I saw blood trailing from the umbilical cord hanging between her legs. House slaves tried to cover the woman. Her husband stopped her and forced her back to her room. Just then, my mother returned. "I found someone. I found someone," she said, repeating it over and over again to the screaming woman until, finally, the anguished mother collapsed from exhaustion.

On the way home, my mother was silent and we walked for a while without speaking.

"Mama?" I asked, at length.

"Yes?"

"Why did they put the baby outside, into the clay pot?"

"Sometime babies are left outside if they are unhealthy or deformed or too great a burden on the family," she said, and then paused. "And sometimes," she continued slowly, "it happens because they are girls."

"Why?"

"Because, as in this case, the father did not want a girl."

"Why not?" I asked, disbelievingly.

My mother sighed. "I don't know. Some men believe boys are much stronger than girls and have a better chance of survival. Others think they will have a better connection with a son than with a daughter."

I stared at her, not comprehending.

"As is the case with most boys, Socrates, you were named after your grandfather. I think a man wants a boy to pass on his name to. It's a way for a man to fool himself into believing he is immortal — as if some part of him will never die." She sounded exasperated, as if she believed immortality to be an absurd and unrealistic goal.

"But everyone dies."

"Yes, at some point we all die."

"Will the baby girl die?"

"No. I found someone who will take care of her."

"So she will live?"

"Yes, she will live," my mother answered, and held me closer as she carried me home in the darkness.

Through the high, narrow window of the adjoining room, I can see the sky turning grey with the first light of morning. Our messenger has returned to take away the papyrus, ink and lamp. He promises to return tomorrow night with the same tools so I can continue writing. But if this proves to be my last communication, never forget that I love you all.

And please, do as I say and leave the city.

DAY 3

OUR MESSENGER WOKE me again in the night. This time he had to shake me, as I did not get much rest yesterday. After writing for so long last night, I spent the day sleeping, although only fitfully due to the noise. The cacophony in this awful place is constant. I cannot close my ears to the sobs, moans and wails of the other prisoners as they plead with the gods and the jailers to set them free.

It reminds me of my time as a 17-year-old at the military academy, where the boys in the barracks wept at their treatment by the old soldiers who trained us. The difference here is that the prisoners in the cells near me will not return home after completing their two years of military service. Instead, their crimes call for them to be strapped to wooden planks, with metal collars cinched around their necks. Slowly, the screws will be tightened, and the doomed souls will turn blue as they struggle to breathe until their necks snap. What a ghastly way to die! Hemlock poisoning, horrible though it will be, seems easy in comparison.

Along with the papyrus, ink and oil lamp, our messenger has brought me a plank and some straw to sleep on. Until now I have had nothing to sleep on but the bare floor, as the condemned are usually only held for a day before execution. I have also received the food you sent — but please, please, no more expensive meals!

It eases my mind to know that you are, indeed, planning to leave the city and go to Thebes after I die. But why wait until my end? You already know how serious my accusers are. Why risk your lives? However much I hope we will be allowed a farewell, I cannot be certain my accusers will allow it. So, please, I urge you once more to leave Athens as soon as possible. No matter what, I promise to keep writing until the end.

I believe I left off yesterday's letter with my mother carrying me around the streets of Athens. The day finally came when I could walk on my own and my mother felt comfortable being parted from me. It was unsettling not to have her around, for I had never known a moment without her. Although we may have been separated at some times before the accident, I don't recall them, the incident having obliterated all memory from my young life. Thankfully, I had Diotima.

Our Diotima was not always the stooped, toothless, grey-haired woman you boys know so well. When I was a child, she was dark-haired and strong-limbed, and she walked proudly upright. Her bronze skin was flawless and her teeth were straight and white. What I remember best were her eyebrows, thick and arched, giving her an expression of constant surprise.

Although I knew even at a young age that Diotima was our slave, I didn't understand what this meant. Eventually I asked Diotima how she came to be with us. Sitting down beside me, she told me her story. She was from a tiny village. Although she could not recall its name, she knew it was far away in the north, somewhere in Thrace. Her father fished, her mother sewed, and Diotima was the youngest of two sons and four daughters.

One day, when Diotima was a young girl, the Persians appeared and took the men of the village for warriors and the women and children for slaves. Diotima never saw any of her family again. She was taken to Sardis, at the edge of the Persian Empire, where a wealthy family purchased her as a slave. Once, she told me, she had actually visited the old palace of King Croesus. Amazed, I listened to the description of the palace: an unremarkable building of mud and brick, perhaps no more than twice the size of Crito's house. Surely not the kind of place you'd imagine to be the home of a king with the reputation of being the wealthiest man in the world — at least, until the Persians defeated him. Croesus was long dead by the time Diotima saw the palace, which had been taken over by the Persian governor of the area.

In time, the family that owned Diotima lost its standing — she never knew why — and she was sold to a kind but rather eccentric old man who lived on the island of Samos. A man of few words, when he spoke it was mostly in fables. Diotima loved his stories, learning them well in her years on Samos. The old man freed Diotima when he died; unfortunately, her freedom lasted only until the Persians arrived, beached their ships on the island and fought the Greeks. The victorious Greeks took Diotima with them for booty. She was brought first to Mantinea and then to Athens, where my father purchased her. Although Diotima's story was very sad, its element of adventure thrilled me, a boy trapped in constant monotony.

The first day my mother left me alone in Diotima's care, I was given bread warm from the oven, after which Diotima prevented me from brooding by putting me to work. Sitting beside me on a stool in a shaded part of the courtyard, she showed me how to comb the tangles out of wool. Her hands moved quickly and surely, making the job look easy. Although I knew wool combing to be woman's work, I adored Diotima and tried my best to do as she asked. Unfortunately, at that time, I had neither the hand strength nor the coordination to do the job properly, and quickly became frustrated. Tossing the wool and the comb onto the courtyard's hard-packed dirt floor I broke into tears.

Tears and tantrums were not uncommon for me at that time. Since I had awakened from my coma, everything I did required intense concentration and effort. Trying so hard to untangle the wool wore me out, and I wondered why things couldn't be as easy for me as they were for my older brother, Patrocles, whom I envied because he lacked my own weaknesses.

Seemingly unmoved by my distress, Diotima put her arms around me, held me tightly and sat with me quietly until my tears stopped. Then she comforted me, telling me I had been doing a fine job, and that combing wool was a skill that took time to master. I was too hard on myself, she insisted.

"But I can't even hold the comb!" I shouted in frustration, and began to weep again. Diotima waited until I was calm, then she told me a fable.

I would bet Diotima learned at least a hundred moral lessons from her former master on Samos, many of which she also told to you boys when you were children. That day in the courtyard, her tale concerned a thirsty crow that discovered a pitcher with water at the bottom. As the crow's beak was not long enough to reach the water, it tried, unsuccessfully, to push over the pitcher. Next, it dropped in a pebble — and, lo and behold, the water rose a little. The wise crow gathered more pebbles and began to drop them, one by one, until the water rose to the top of the pitcher. And so, at last, the crow was able to quench its thirst.

I was only six and a half then, and the moral of the story escaped me. To make it clearer, Diotima explained that cleverness was more important than strength, after which she suggested I try a different way of combing the wool. Still, the story and its lesson meant nothing to me. I continued to sit with my arms crossed, frowning to show my disgust.

Knowing me so well, Diotima decided to leave me alone while she worked in the kitchen. She realized she had planted the seed of an idea in my mind, and gave it time to germinate. Wise Diotima. After a while, I settled down and picked up the wool and the comb and dusted them off. This time I held the comb with a firmer grip. Doggedly, I worked away. When Diotima appeared in the courtyard again, I had made good progress with the pile of wool in the basket. Her smile of satisfaction was my reward, and I smiled back.

My hand strength and coordination improved with time. Soon, I was helping Diotima with other household chores: cutting vegetables, spinning wool and weaving. Often, at the beginning of something new, I would get frustrated at my inability to do a simple task well. As had happened the first time I tried to comb wool, I would get angry, and sometimes I wept. My beloved Diotima never lost patience with me. Instead, she would tell me another fable, explain its moral and then leave me to get over my temper. Usually, although not always, she would return to find me once more attempting to achieve what I'd failed at initially.

One day, Diotima took a few water jugs and asked me to go with her to the fountain house. I was delighted at the chance to walk with her around the Acropolis to the southern edge of the agora, where we took our places in the line-up of skinny slaves and poor women. Diotima seemed to know everyone. Most were friendly but, to my surprise, some appeared to recoil from me, almost as if I were diseased. After a few more trips to the fountain house, I finally asked Diotima why these people disliked me. I knew her so well that when I saw her lips tighten at the question, I realized she would wait to speak until we were alone.

Back home, she sat me down in the courtyard shade and brought me a cool drink. As I took a sip from my special Eros cup, I sensed she was ready to explain some things that had only been hinted at in my presence until then. She began by reminding me of the second day of the festival of Anthesteria. We — my father, mother, Patrocles, Diotima and I — had spent the morning at the agora, listening to the choirs of men and boys singing and dancing in honour of Dionysus. We chewed buckthorn to ward off the evil spirits that roamed the city, as the dead are said to walk with the living on the second day of this festival. Around our necks, Patrocles and I wore flower garlands that our mother had made for us. Although the flowers were starting to wilt, they still retained their sweet smell. In the afternoon we attended a number of parties given by our neighbours. Everyone drank in honour of the God of Wine and Ecstasy.

It was getting dark by the time we headed home and the streets were filled with intoxicated men of all ages, singing vulgar songs and swearing. Whenever a procession of recklessly driven carts passed us on the narrow streets, we had to hug the walls to avoid being trampled.

We arrived home to find a man waiting for my mother. His wife had gone into labour, he explained, and she wanted my mother to come to her as soon as possible. When my mother had gone, Diotima put my brother and me to bed. The sounds of drunken singing and laughter drifted over the walls of the house, keeping me awake. Eventually, unable to sleep and curious to see what was happening, I got up, grabbed my little cup with its picture of Eros, and crept out of the room, through the courtyard and out into the street. The sky was pitch black, the full moon obscured by clouds, but this did not deter the drunken revellers from riding their horses and wagons and chariots through the streets. It was probably too dark, Diotima said afterward, for them to notice a small boy.

The pregnant woman who had called for my mother was not as far along in her labour as her agitated husband had believed. Returning home to get some sleep before she was needed again, my mother found me in the street, unconscious, covered in blood, and still holding my little cup. The skin on the right side of my scalp had been torn away and my ear dangled from a flap of skin. Mother carried me into the house, laid me on my bed and stanched the bleeding. She tried to wake me, but I was unresponsive.

For days, my mother and Diotima did whatever they could to restore me back to consciousness. Alternately, they washed me down with soft sponges dipped in cool water and kept me wrapped in blankets by the oven. I was bled and covered with poultices. Nothing roused me. My distraught mother was even able to sew my ear back in place without me reacting. Ten days went by before I woke to see her bending over me.

According to Diotima, some people now feared me because I had been injured on the second day of the festival of Anthesteria. They believed evil spirits had invaded my body. "Do you think I am evil?" I asked her. Resolutely, she answered, "No."

Whether due to my injury or out of fear for my safety, I was not allowed out of the house by myself, even after I could walk again. The way some people looked at me, I wasn't sure I wanted to be out on my own. So when my mother, Diotima or my brother, were busy, I would pretend the house constituted the whole world, and go on little adventures. Of course, my world was really quite small. The courtyard altar, at which my parents prayed regularly, became the Acropolis, the kitchen was the agora and our bedroom was the fountain house. I would explore every nook and cranny of our home. Only one room was off limits: the andron.

An andron, as every child learns, is the man's room in the home: it is his private place where he can entertain his friends and isolate himself from the cacophony of family life. For me, our andron held a dual attraction. For one thing, I would learn that other boys were allowed inside their fathers' private rooms, yet neither my brother nor I had ever been allowed into our father's andron. For that reason alone, I wanted to see inside.

But our andron held an added mystery, a second reason for the room's attraction. In the many houses I had visited with my mother, a curtain normally separated the andron from the courtyard. Why, I wondered, did our andron require a wooden door and a leather lock? To me, the door seemed as thick as a city gate. Imposing. Impregnable. Solid enough to keep the Persians at bay, should they ever take the city again and we were forced to hide in our andron.

You boys never did see that door. I took it down and broke it up for firewood soon after Lamprocles was born.

I hated that door. In my young mind, it separated me from my father, and, as I understood later, it also separated my father from the rest of the world. I did not want a similar barrier to exist between you boys and me.

My father left home before the sun rose every morning. He had to walk a long way to reach the fortification walls where he worked as a stonemason. Before leaving, he'd check the lock of the andron — a narrow strip of leather tied in an intricate knot to secure the handle to the doorframe. On his return, he washed off the white dust of his trade, ate dinner alone, picked up the small oil lamp Diotima always kept filled, the flame flickering as he walked to the andron, then entered the windowless room and noiselessly closed the door.

Whatever unpleasant things I might say about my father, I must admit that the house was well maintained. Doors opened silently, shutters hung straight, and until the end of my father's life the roof never leaked.

Not long after my father retreated to the andron, I would begin to hear sounds from the mysterious chamber: the steady, sharp, "tink, tink, tink" of a chisel striking stone. I went to sleep with that sound in my ears every night until I entered the military academy. I knew my father was sculpting — *but what*? Whenever I asked my mother or Diotima what he was making, they always answered, "his own luck," and refused to elaborate.

My father was an ominous presence in our home. The impression he made on me as a child was that he was a man of enormous height. He was actually short, but stocky and strong. His forearms were muscular and covered with numerous tiny red scars caused by the stone shards that pricked him when he worked at the city walls during the day and in the andron in the evening. His hands were callused by the tools he held day and night.

I was frightened of my father. I kept my head down when he was about. His expression was permanently grim, almost as if he himself had been carved from the rock he spent his life working with. As a child, I would not have been surprised to see his face crack from mouth to ear if he were to attempt a smile.

Fear of my father did not keep me away from the andron entirely. Every day I glanced at the door, hoping he might have left the knot untied, but I was always disappointed. The knot would have been easy enough to cut, but not to loosen. Even if I had been able to undo the knot, it would have been difficult — although perhaps not impossible — to re-tie it exactly as Father had left it. I told myself that he never returned home until sunset, which should give me enough time to untie the knot, inspect the andron and put the knot back in place. Yet no sooner did I touch it, than my mother or Diotima would call out, "What are you doing?" and I would dash away, frightened.

As I've said, I was not allowed out alone. Although I had a fertile imagination and my mother and Diotima tried to keep me busy, there was not enough to keep me interested inside the house. Along the east wall of the courtyard, we had the kind of wooden lattice often used for creeping vines, but this one was bare. One afternoon, I decided to climb it. I was stronger by then, and made it to the top. It took great effort, but I managed to pull myself onto the gently sloping roof, from where I had a good view of our neighbours' houses and the stark Acropolis rock in the distance.

It is strange to look up at the Acropolis today with all its wonderful structures, and to imagine how barren it was long ago. No Parthenon. No Temple of Athena. No towering marble columns. Nothing but the scorched earth left by the Persians. On our rounds together, my mother told me that in the time before the Persians had come, when she was a girl, temples and statues had stood on that site. She remembered them as both beautiful and frightening. In my own youth, though, only broken pillars, charred timbers and rubble remained.

Feeling suddenly nervous about being so far from the ground, I took a few tentative steps to the middle of the roof and sat down. The clay tiles were warm beneath me, and I was quite comfortable sitting there, studying men and women going about their business on the street below. A delicious aroma wafted up from a kitchen fire somewhere nearby.

I had not been on the roof long when I heard Diotima calling me. Getting no response, she searched for me in every room. My mother, obviously alarmed, appeared in the courtyard and walked about, also calling me. Entertained by all this activity, I decided to remain silent. My mother and Diotima went on calling for me as they walked around the exterior of the house and then along the road. When they were far enough away not to see me, I climbed down the trellis and calmly waited for them to return.

"Where did you go?" Diotima asked, when she saw me.

"Nowhere," I said innocently.

Looking at me sideways, she asked suspiciously, "Did you leave the house?"

"No."

A glance in the direction of the andron. "Go in there?"

"No."

She stared at me. Since I hadn't left the house, not really, I didn't buckle under her gaze. I'm sure she knew I was lying, just as I was always aware when one of you boys was not honest with me. But as nothing serious had happened, Diotima must have guessed I had hidden somewhere as a prank or just to escape notice, and didn't press me further. A short time later, my mother returned. "Don't frighten us like that again," she warned.

Of course, a secret is not much fun unless you share it with someone, so when Patrocles got home from school I told him what I'd done. While Mother and Diotima were preparing dinner, I showed him how I had climbed the trellis. Tall for his age, and lithe, Patrocles followed me and was on the roof in an instant. My brother did not mind heights. He walked along the edge of the roof, his hands out to his sides for balance. Seeing my anxious expression and clenched hands, he pretended to lose his footing and fall. Fearfully, I closed my eyes and covered my face, which made Patrocles laugh. To my relief, he left the edge and sat down in the middle of the roof. I sat beside him. He turned his face to the sun to feel its warmth for a few minutes, before scanning our surroundings.

He looked at me. "Wouldn't it be great to see the city from the sky like a bird? Or like Icarus."

Perhaps Icarus was yet another god, I thought, and asked Patrocles about him. Patiently, he explained that Icarus was a man who'd had wings constructed from feathers and wax, so he could fly like a bird.

I was glad Icarus was not a god, for there were already so many to keep track of. It seemed to me that every few days we celebrated a festival honouring one god or another. I knew about Zeus, Poseidon, Hades, Hera, Dionysus, Eros, Apollo and his twin sister Artemis, the city's patron goddess Athena, and, of course, my mother's patron goddess, Eileithyia. As time went on I learned about Demeter, Ares, Hermes and a multitude of others. My mother had said it was important for me to know and honour all the gods and to keep my promises to them, for they were all-knowing and powerful, and sometimes vindictive and easy to anger.

"I wish I could fly," Patrocles said wistfully, as he fingered an amulet with a picture of Eileithyia, hanging from a leather strap around his neck. For some reason, I had never noticed it before. Just as I was about to ask Patrocles where he'd got it, he handed me a fig. Surprised, I stared at the fruit and then at my brother, wondering where the fig had come from, for Patrocles wore only a simple tunic. Did he have a bag hidden somewhere on his person? His melancholy vanishing, Patrocles grinned like a magician pulling off a particularly clever trick before a skeptical audience. I chewed the fig happily, my brother's mischievous grin making me forget about the amulet. We sat together on the warm roof, enjoying the view in quiet companionship.

This is my most pleasant memory of Patrocles. I only wish you boys could have met him. He was a fine lad and a great brother. I think, had he lived long enough, he might have turned out much like my dear friend Crito.

I was thinking it was time for us to leave the roof — I didn't want us to get into trouble with my mother or Diotima — when Patrocles spotted three boys whom we disliked, walking on the street below us.

The boys were brothers with swarthy complexions and heads of dark curly hair, who often stole our toys. How they managed this mystified us, for I was home much of the time and you'd think I would have seen them. I can't count how often Mother had to go over to their house to rescue our soldier figurines. The oldest brother was Lycon — yes, *that* Lycon. I bet you didn't know I grew up with one of my accusers. I have never spoken about him, for having suffered his torment as a schoolboy, I tried to banish him from my thoughts.

At any rate, Lycon and his brothers once snatched our turtle, Heracles — our beloved turtle, the only pet we were allowed to have because it made no noise and, therefore, didn't bother my father. When Mother retrieved it the next day, she found it close to death; apparently, Lycon and his brothers had tortured it in some way. Although we did our best to nurse our little turtle back to health, it died the next day of its injuries.

So now the three brothers were at the side of our house, looking around suspiciously. Stealthy as a cat, his green eyes gleaming in anticipation of the retribution he was about to visit on Lycon, Patrocles followed them silently as they rounded the corner and gathered at our courtyard door. They waited a few moments and then Lycon opened the door and peeked inside. It was obvious he was about to steal something of ours again.

Entering the courtyard, he skulked along the wall near the wooden lattice. Quietly, Patrocles crept to the edge of the roof until he was directly above Lycon. I thought he intended to pounce on Lycon, and was about to stop him. But I was too late, for at that moment my brother pulled out his penis and ejected a strong stream of urine. Helpless beneath the warm yellow rain, Lycon stood stunned for a moment then looked up, his heavy brow furrowed over deep-set eyes. Suddenly he saw Patrocles. Making a sputtering sound, he scrambled out of the courtyard. As fate would have it, he ran into my father, nearly knocking him to the ground.

My father seized hold of him. "Watch where you're going, boy!" he admonished. A second later, realizing he had nabbed the son of a wealthy neighbour, he released Lycon. Lycon ran off, although not before Father noticed that his hands were wet, caught the smell of urine and wrinkled his nose in disgust. My brother burst out laughing and Father's head jerked up. Seeing us on the roof, he immediately knew what had happened. His face turned as red as a clump of pomegranate seeds.

"Patrocles!" he yelled, and my hands began to tingle.

My brother's laughter stopped instantly. "They killed Heracles," he muttered, as he straightened his clothing.

It took my father a moment to realize that Patrocles meant our dead turtle, not the immortal son of Zeus. "Down!" he shouted.

Diotima came to the kitchen door and my mother paced nearby as Patrocles descended the trellis. I remained on the roof, so terrified that I was unable to move as my hands and feet went numb.

The picture of that terrible event is still fresh in my mind all these years later — my father's hand lifted and ready to strike, the red scars standing in angry relief on his muscled forearms, his teeth bared. A scene that was, for an interminable moment, devoid of movement. Then, suddenly, my father began to hit Patrocles: ferociously, again and again. My mother pleaded with him to stop, but in vain, for he seemed not to hear her. Finally, the beating ended, and my father stormed into the andron, ripping the leather knot apart as he flung open the door. My mother rushed to console Patrocles.

Later that night, as he always did whenever our father beat him, Patrocles spoke about running away. I hated to hear him talk this way, for I loved him dearly. I knew I was partly to blame for the incident, and apologized for tempting him onto the roof. "I'll tell Father it was my fault, then he won't be so angry," I said pleadingly.

"Don't bother. He will always hate me," Patrocles responded tersely. The word "he" had the sound of a curse. In the moonlight I saw him hold tightly to the amulet that hung from his necklace.

Morning has come and our messenger is here. I will continue my account tomorrow. Now I will sleep and dream of you all.

DAY 4

O UR MESSENGER WOKE me from a deep sleep. For a few moments I was quite disoriented, thinking myself back at home. Perhaps a rooster was crowing too early, for it was very still dark out. As I shook off the grogginess and my senses sharpened, I felt, as usual, great fear for your safety. I still wish you would reconsider my wish that you leave the city immediately, rather than wait until after my execution. In case you nurture the hope that I may "come to my senses" and try to escape, you should understand that this will not happen. I will not put you in harm's way. I will not leave this cell alive.

Your mother continues to send me my favourite foods. A month of this extravagance and we will be bankrupt. Plain food from now on, I insist! Otherwise I will give the food to the jailer and eat nothing myself. By the way, if food is a factor that keeps you in Athens, I'm sure arrangements can be made with Crito. I have spent much of my life trying to avoid accepting gifts from that generous man, but if you were to leave Athens, I would eat whatever he sent me.

And now back to Patrocles, whom I was writing about yesterday. My brother's stories about school entertained and excited me for years. How I yearned to join him there, to be free of the confines of the house. I would wait for the moment when he returned from school, when he would sit beside me in the courtyard, our legs stretched out in front of us — his, ever so much longer than mine — and he would tell me about his day.

Some of his stories made me laugh. There was the tale of the teacher who stood on his stool to see over the courtyard wall, swearing when the stool collapsed and he fell to the ground. Someone tossed a rotten egg onto the athletics field and the students had to hold their noses during javelin practice. And then there was the story about Lycon, our turtle torturer, who was in trouble for releasing a cat and a rat in class, and the teacher beat him with his sandal.

Patrocles told me what to expect when I started school.

My two main instructors would be the grammatiste and the paidotribe. The grammatiste taught reading, writing, arithmetic and literature. His students had to memorize poetry and plays, which sounded like fun to me. During my convalescence, Patrocles often recited one of the poems he'd had to memorize. My favourite was the *Iliad*. I loved the story of Achilles and his epic battle against Hector. Knowing how much I enjoyed it, my brother very often related the story, even though he must have become tired of it.

The paidotribe taught wrestling, discus throwing and other kinds of physical training. He concentrated on building strength and courage, thereby preparing the students for their entry into the military academy.

At last, the first day of school arrived. I remember Diotima singing as the sun rose. She sang frequently, but her singing sounded especially bright that day. My mother insisted on walking me to school. I longed to walk with my brother, like a big boy, but no matter what I said, Mother insisted on going with me. I was less embarrassed by her presence when I saw other boys accompanied by their fathers or slaves.

When the grammatiste called us into class, I was surprised to find the school similar to our house, only a little larger. Twenty of us sat on stools, crammed together in a courtyard without an altar. Patrocles sat on one side of me; on the other side sat a boy of my own age, named Crito.

The grammatiste asked for silence and scanned the class. His eyes fell on me. "So, you are Patrocles' little brother," he said. I sensed from his tone that much would be expected of me. Then he addressed the entire class. "One day all of you will be citizens of Athens. Here we will teach you how to behave. We strive for the ideals of strength, bravery and excellence. Of all the stories you will learn, the *Iliad* is the one that will guide and inspire you most." He spoke about the Greek ideal of victory at all costs, and stressed that we needed to model ourselves on Achilles, a man of action.

"Repeat after me," said the grammatiste. "Rage be now your song, Goddess, Rage of Achilles, doomed and ruinous, who caused the Greeks bitter loss and hurled brave souls into the House of Hades, leaving so many heroes as carrion for dogs and birds, and the will of Zeus was done. Begin, Goddess, when first there was conflict between the lord of men and brilliant Achilles."

Together, we recited the first verse of the *Iliad,* after which each student had to repeat the verse alone. The oldest students went first. Most had no trouble reciting, for they knew the poem already. Then it was the turn of the newest students. Four of us were starting school that day. The first two did fairly well. Next came Crito, the boy sitting beside me, and my lifelong friend to be. He recited the verse flawlessly.

The grammatiste turned to me. " Now, you," he said, and I stood.

"Rage…" I began, and stopped.

"Try again," the grammatiste said.

"Rage…" I repeated, only to stop once more, unable to recall the next word. "I can't," I said.

Something smacked the back of my head, and I turned to see the grammatiste putting on his sandal. I had not seen him come up behind me.

The grammatiste ordered me to sit, before he returned to the front of the class. "It is the sign of a man of standing to be able to recite the *Iliad* by heart," he told us. "From the great warrior Achilles, who fought to protect his honour and win eternal glory, we discover what is most important. Even the dullards must learn this." The last words were directed at me. I felt very stupid.

I had been looking forward to the afternoon, which was given over
to athletics with the paidotribe. At home, Patrocles and I would play
commonball with a ball fashioned from rags, and I knew this would be
the first game our instructor would have us play. "You'll be the best in
school," Patrocles would say encouragingly, when we practiced.

We lined up and walked some way to a well-grassed open field, where
the paidotribe lectured us: "Our duty here is to prepare you for the military academy, so that you can perform your obligations as citizens. The
physical training you acquire here will get you ready for the battlefield."

As expected, our first game was commonball. The whole student body
participated, with no separation of the older, stronger boys from the
younger, weaker ones. The paidotribe threw the ball into the air. Anxious
to show my agility, I raced to catch it, unprepared for the ensuing pushing and shoving. I fell, and another boy fell on top of me. Getting up, I
saw that my brother had the ball. He handed it to the paidotribe, a feat
for which he was proclaimed king. Patrocles joined the paidotribe on the
sidelines, and the ball was thrown for the next round. Once again, I was
pushed aside, landing on my back this time. The game was not turning
out at all as I had hoped.

From the sidelines, Patrocles cheered me on. One by one, the bigger,
stronger boys caught the ball and joined my brother where he stood.
Finally, only one other new boy and I remained on the field. Again, the
paidotribe threw the ball. I tried to jostle myself into position, but the
other boy easily pushed me to the ground and grabbed the ball. Using
a stick as his tool of discipline, the paidotribe struck me and named me
the ass.

We played three more times that afternoon. My brother won again,
and twice he was third. Lycon and his brothers mumbled resentfully
about slave tricks, but the truth was that Patrocles was quick and cunning. He would slither between the others at just the right moment and
snatch the ball in the air, the amulet swinging from his neck. If the jos-
tling got rough, he'd stay on the periphery, knowing the ball would likely

not be caught in the air. But after the first bounce, he'd dart away, catching it easily. The paidotribe congratulated Patrocles on his skill. I was the last one left on the field every time. I was the ass that day, and went home feeling defeated.

Back home, Patrocles tried to teach me how to do better at commonball. "Stay out of the scrum and watch where the ball will land," he advised, as we practiced together in the courtyard. "Remember, the ball is not always caught right away. Wait for it to bounce, then track it like a bird in the air and go to that spot."

At school, I tried to follow my brother's instructions, but I simply could not move fast enough, and I lost every time. Nor did I fail only at commonball, but I was also the slowest runner, the worst javelin thrower and the most uncoordinated wrestler. I tried very hard, I really did, but the paidotribe did not reward effort; he cared only about results. I felt the pain of the stick many, many times.

In the classroom I was even more inept than on the athletics field. Every few days we were called on to recite a verse, but my brain, like my limbs, did not cooperate. As my turn came to speak, I was afraid no sound would pass my lips. Fear made my hands and feet go numb. "Don't screw up, ass," Lycon would murmur behind me, reminding me of my failure on the athletics field. This made me even more unsure of myself.

"Ignore them," Patrocles would whisper, glaring at Lycon.

The grammatiste would call for quiet. "Begin, Socrates," he'd say, with a perceptible sigh.

The moment he said my name, my entire body, including my tongue, turned to stone. "Begin," he repeated.

But I remained mute. The slap of the grammatiste's sandal was followed by a gentle hand on my arm and my brother's soft whisper: "Sit down, Socrates." I knew I had to concentrate, to focus my attention. The problem was, I listened so intently to the grammatiste's lectures that I would forget where I was and find myself talking out of turn, asking questions as I did when my mother and I were walking home together after a birth.

"It is buzzing again. We must swat it," was the grammatiste's response to my interruptions, as if I were a fly in his ear, disturbing his sleep. The class laughed. Off came the sandal; I could almost feel it before it made impact. And then a great thwack, followed by a ringing in my ears. You would have thought, would you not, that I'd have learned my lesson and remained quiet? But, no, curiosity always overcame me, and soon enough I would be interrupting with another question. I guess I was of that age when I was nothing but questions. "Why has Zeus sent this horse-fly to torment me?" The grammatiste would groan and glance up-wards, as if appealing to the gods. "The insect will not speak again," he'd continue, before striking me viciously and repeatedly.

The harassing by other students began a month into school. It started with Lycon who, as you know, was already calling me an ass. At com-monball, he hit me purposely even when I wasn't in the scrum, and dur-ing foot races he tripped me. More than once, a discus or a javelin landed suspiciously close to me. Soon enough, some of the other boys began to follow his lead.

Although my brother was thinner and younger than Lycon, who was the biggest boy in the school, Patrocles came to my defence every time. Patrocles was quick with his fists, and fearless. Not the sort of adversary anyone likes to take on. But that didn't stop Lycon and his fellow tor-mentors. They simply took to waiting until my brother wasn't around before abusing me. Their strategy was to attack me from behind so I couldn't tell who had punched or kicked me. Usually I was able to guess the culprit's identity, but I avoided saying anything to Patrocles lest he be involved in fights 10 times a day.

I grew to dread school. Every night I had horrible nightmares, and ev-ery morning I woke feeling terrified. I would imagine being thrown into a hole, with my mother weeping over my beaten body as my father shov-elled dirt over me. I'd try to scream out to my mother to save me, but the words refused to emerge. Slowly the earth would cover me, pressing down on me, crushing my chest and smothering me. I'd fake illness so

I could stay home, and I stopped eating, too. The theme repeated itself. If I was content, I ate; if I was wretched, I lost my appetite. I guess this shows how you boys and your mother have changed me. By Zeus, you could have stuck a child's fist into my belly button, so large was it before I was imprisoned!

But I digress. My mother noticed my distress. When we were alone one afternoon, she asked what was troubling me.

"Why can't I be like Patrocles — tall and strong and fast?" I asked, and then burst into bitter tears. My mother waited patiently until I was calm enough to tell her about my problems in school. Briefly, I wondered whether she would be angry with me for being inadequate. I even imagined her leaving me to die in some desolate spot without food and water. Of course, she would never have done anything of the sort. Instead, recognizing my despair, she put me on her lap and held me tightly. "Have I ever told you about your birth?" she asked.

"No, Mama." I was still breathing unevenly.

"Well, then," she began, "the night before you were conceived, I dreamed of thunderbolts filling the sky above me. I realized the dream was a portent of happiness and that something momentous was about to occur. A few weeks passed before I learned I was pregnant. Overjoyed and excited, I began, right away, to prepare for your arrival. I sewed tiny clothes and wove a little reed basket for you to sleep in. Yes, *that* basket, Socrates, the one in which I now carry my midwifery equipment. My patients complimented me on my new beauty, for my skin glowed and my hair was thick and luxurious. While other prospective mothers were ill during pregnancy, I was healthy. Other mothers were tired, but I felt strong — because of you."

She paused a moment to kiss my cheek. "Your strength coursed through me, Socrates, making me stronger and healthier. I could smell a horse on the other side of the city and taste the least hint of spice in my food. I could work without rest from dawn until dusk. You were such an influence, that as I grew bigger even your father gained weight!" She laughed at the jest.

Then she cupped my face in her hands, and looked at me as if she were trying to read my thoughts.

"I often wondered about you, the precious child in my womb. Would you be a boy or a girl? I tried to guess your future attributes. Would you be strong like your father, smart like your grandfather, or wise like your grandmother? I wondered what your life would hold. Often, my thoughts focused on your appearance. Would your eyes be brown or green or blue? Would your hair be curly or straight? Would your face be round or oval?

"As my belly grew bigger and bigger, I became ever more excited. I sang lullabies to you, and at the sound of my voice you would move inside me. You were very active inside my belly, and kicked often. When you weren't moving, I often felt a foot right here." She smiled as she pointed to a spot on her right side, just below her ribs.

I touched myself in the same spot. "How it does it feel to be kicked, Mama?"

"Like this," she said, gently flicking my shoulder with her finger. "But in my belly."

"Did it hurt?"

"No. Actually, it was a great comfort to know you were growing bigger and stronger every day. And do you know, Socrates, the night before you were born, I dreamed I was a lion. I realized the dream was an omen, telling me you would be remarkable. The next morning I felt a pop and then a little gush of fluid ran down my legs. I had never been as happy in my life as in those first moments of my labour. I had spent the entire pregnancy wondering what your face would look like. I would soon find out.

"When I told your father your birth was imminent, he immediately shuttered the windows and locked the courtyard gate to keep out any malicious spirits. He also smeared pitch on the outside walls of the house, to drive away any evil beings that might cause you harm. Diotima made sure there were no knots in the room. I had forgotten about my hair, but she loosened it quickly. After a while, I began to feel contractions."

"How do contractions feel?" I asked. As the son of a midwife, I knew what contractions were, but not how they felt.

"Like when you have to poop really badly," my mother said.

A funny image appeared in my mind, and I quickly covered my mouth to hide a giggle.

"I felt my pelvic muscles contracting," said my mother. "For a day and a night the contractions continued. I started to get anxious."

"Because you wanted to see my face?"

"Well, that too." She held me more tightly. "Of course, I wanted to see your face and hold you in my arms. But the labour was long and I was getting very tired. Whenever I thought I couldn't hold out any longer, I would think about your face. That gave me strength — just to know I would see you soon. I had been on my hands and knees on the bed most of that second day, when the time finally came. An inner voice told me to move to the birthing stool. Diotima massaged my belly as I crouched over it. And then an odd thing happened — after I heard that inner voice, I began to feel like a wild animal."

At this point in the story, my mother growled like a bear. Having heard other birthing women growl, I laughed. My mother laughed, too.

"I knew what to do. I began to pant heavily, like a dog lying in the sun on a hot day." She drew a heavy breath and continued. "Just then, I looked up and saw a horse poking its nose through the bedroom window. This was really strange because there were no horses in the neighbourhood, and your father had secured everything tightly. Even stranger, the horse's breathing kept time with my own as I pushed. At last, Diotima looked between my legs and saw the top of your head. Then she reached out and caught the rest of your body. Finally, I was able to lie back. Diotima placed you on my stomach, and I closed my eyes in exhaustion." As if to demonstrate her fatigue, she let her tongue loll out dramatically.

"Suddenly, I realized I hadn't seen what you looked like, and I snapped open my eyes." Again, she paused.

Tensely, I waited for what came next.

"A baby without a face!" My mother laughed and shook her head. "I was so tired, it took me a moment to realize you had been born with part of the bag of water over your head. As if you weren't special enough before, now I was certain. I knew, at that moment, that you were destined for greatness. Gently, I pulled off the caul and stared in wonder at your beautiful little face. With your eyes still closed, you opened your mouth for your first breath and then let out a howl. You bellowed like a lion, loud and ferocious. Hearing your first cry, I wept with joy. Diotima let out a jubilant cry of her own.

"You were so beautiful, Socrates, and so strong. Your size amazed me. No wonder you had taken so long to come into the world! Once I had delivered the afterbirth, the horse seemed to sense that all was fine and left the window. To this day, I don't know who owned the animal or where it came from.

"There was very little blood on you, so there was almost nothing to clean off. Your father had brought home special water from the spring near the Ilissos River, and Diotima washed us with it. When I had made a sign over your forehead to protect you from the evil eye, Diotima hung an olive branch over the front door to let the neighbours know a boy had been born. I rested for six days after your birth, and you nursed or slept in the wicker basket. On the seventh day, your father walked around the hearth, carrying you in the basket and welcoming you into the household. He was so proud of his son, and very happy.

"Friends came to visit on the tenth day. We had a banquet to celebrate your arrival, complete with figs, raisins, chestnuts and honey cakes. Your father sacrificed a pig, and then we named you. That evening, Diotima and I walked to the Eileithyia sanctuary to give thanks for your birth. I dedicated a clay lamp to Eileithyia, to thank her for helping me bear the pain of childbirth and for your delivery into the light. I was very happy."

When my mother had finished her story, we sat silently for some time. I leaned against her chest and nuzzled my head into her neck. Wrapped

in her arms, I felt safe. Warm. Loved. Convinced that everything would
be well.

Whenever the grammatiste slapped me or beat me, after that, I reminded myself that I was special. And when the paidotribe struck me
with his stick, I told myself I was destined for greatness. When my classmates made fun of me — which they continued to do — I pictured myself victorious on the battlefield.

But being positive carried me only so far. No matter how hard I tried
to remember I was special, the constant failures and harassment at
school ate away at me like a gangrenous wound. When my mother saw
my unhappiness, she would sit me down, take me in her arms, and tell
me the story of my birth again. She always waited until we were alone.
Father would be at work, Diotima would be fetching water or shopping
at the market and Patrocles would be out with his friends. Listening to
the story was helpful, at least for a few days. A young boy's spirit, however, cannot stay buoyed for long on promises of the future.

Concerned for my well-being, my mother began to let me venture out
of the house on my own. I might well have been lonely but, thankfully,
one boy was friendly to me: my seatmate, Crito.

Crito was a handsome boy, with dark curly hair and piercing blue
eyes. Reserved and respectful, he excelled at academics and athletics.
Delighted as I was that he wanted to be my friend, I was surprised nonetheless, for I was an object of ridicule, while he was popular. I asked him
once why he befriended me. Crito has always spoken earnestly, as if he
is considering every word before speaking, and he took his time to respond. Finally, he said he liked the questions I posed in class. The simple
statement made me feel a little less stupid.

After school, the two of us would skirt the southern edge of the barren Acropolis and wander in the direction of the agora. We'd zigzag back
and forth along the narrow lanes to avoid stepping in human or animal
excrement, and dodge the carts pulled by donkeys or underfed slaves.

The agora, like the Acropolis, was altogether different then from the way it is today. The only building at that time that you boys would know was the round Tholos, and even that was just newly completed. Whereas I knew almost nothing of the world, Crito knew a lot, thanks to his father, who paid private tutors handsomely to educate him. It was from Crito I learned that the people who ran the city ate and sometimes even slept in the Tholos.

The building was also used to host foreign dignitaries and famous men. Crito said that if we were lucky we might catch sight of some war hero or famous athlete eating there at the city's expense. Once we actually managed to see Diagoras of Rhodes, a tall and imposing figure, with bulging muscles in his arms and legs. We were in awe of this man who had won his second Olympic boxing victory not long before. We waited for him to leave the Tholos and followed him to a gymnasium. I remember the gymnasium for its strong smell of olive oil. Unfortunately, we were stopped at the change rooms — we weren't old enough to be allowed in.

Next door to the Tholos was the newly started Strategeion, where a great hero of old, Strategos, was buried. According to Crito, generals would meet at the Strategeion, to discuss the management of Athens' land and sea forces. We often stood at the edge of the site, waiting to see whether the labourers, dirty and sweaty, had found the old hero and dug him up. I'm not sure what we expected to see: something magical, I'm sure.

Our next stop was often the Stoa Poikile. The Doric columns were up already, the roof was on and sculptors were working on the rear façade. Once that was completed, we were able to walk inside on the beautiful covered walkway.

Now and then we wandered back to the old Stoa of Zeus and looked at the war booty. The old structure was a far cry from the grand Stoa of Zeus we have now. It was, basically, a simple wooden structure crammed with armour and weapons. Shields, decorated with crabs, gorgons and scary faces, were affixed to the cornice, over the doors, on the doorposts and on the walls. Inside the old stoa, helmets with looming crests hung from roof timbers, and breastplates — some shaped like muscled chests, others unadorned — were nailed to posts in the ground.

After a visit to the Stoa of Zeus, we'd go in search of any new herms in the area. Representations of Hermes' head atop stone columns had always been used at road crossings and borders. Now, the head of the God of Roads, Borders and Luck, protector of merchants and travellers, was appearing at the entrances to gymnasiums, temples, stoas and even private homes. Although my family was poor, we too had a crude statue in front of our house. Our herm had a beard and male genitals at the ap-propriate heights. Beside the column, positioned on a wooden stand, sat a dish of water in which to rinse our hands.

Our explorations usually ended with an inspection of the market place, located in the centre of the agora. We never actually entered the marketplace, for Crito and I knew the rules; boys of school age were not allowed there. Had I been alone, I might have been tempted to flout the rules and sneak inside, but I didn't consider it because I did not want to disappoint my only friend.

Standing at the periphery of the market, we strained to see through the maze of tents and umbrellas and people. We saw men having their hair cut in the barbershops, harp-tuners working on broken instru-ments and shield makers busy at their craft. We smelled the fish that had been brought up from the sea, now spoiling in the hot summer sun. We watched poor men, women and house slaves buying honey, cheese, sheep and goat meat, eels, pepper, wine, lamps, flowers, perfume, rolls of papyrus and ink. And we listened to buyers and sellers engaged in what often sounded like arguments, voices raised, faces angry. Negotiations completed, buyers would spit out the silver obols they carried in their mouths and pay for their purchases. I was always amazed at how much people could carry in the space between cheeks and gums.

Once I found an obol on the ground. The obol bore the likeness of the goddess Athena in relief on one side, an owl on the other. Excited at my find, I immediately popped the obol into my mouth and began to run home, imagining the great things I would buy. Sadly, in my haste I tripped and accidentally swallowed the coin. I wept until I reached the house, where my mother enquired what had caused me such distress.

Hearing about the coin, she told me not to worry — it would reappear when I went to the toilet. For two long days I watched and waited and poked through my excrement. Finally, the coin emerged. I cleaned it off quickly and was about to pop it back into my mouth. Fortunately, I stopped in time when I remembered where it had been. I buried it under my straw mattress, instead. After that, I was never able to hold money in my mouth again. From the point of view that I was never forced to overcome my aversion, I guess my poverty can be seen as beneficial.

Once in a while, Crito and I would tag along behind the older boys, making certain to keep well behind them. They would saunter into the Kerameikos district, the potters' quarter of the city, past the men slowly turning wheels, past the rows of pots drying in the sun and the stacks of ornately painted vases, to the prostitutes standing in front of the brothels. No sandals and wool for these women. They wore platform shoes and diaphanous robes or saffron-dyed gauzy dresses. A few were quite naked. Outrageous makeup exaggerated their eyes and lips, and their cheeks were heavily rouged.

These women, the older boys said, were available for a 'mid-day marriage,' a phrase we didn't understand at the time. "One silver obol," they would call to the men walking by, spinning their parasols and coquettishly batting their eyes. "Come on in." Although our older classmates were too young to act on these invitations, they were old enough to be intrigued. Crito and I were too young to have any interest in the prostitutes, so we didn't follow the older boys there very often.

Now and then, during our explorations, we'd run into strange men who were rumoured to have been possessed by evil spirits. Some spoke noisy gibberish or mumbled quietly to themselves. Others walked with jerky steps, twitching, as if something inside them were broken. I recall a man who was almost always perched on a courtyard wall near the prison in which I now find myself. Crito and I called him Crow Man. His hair and beard were long and matted, and he was naked but for a skimpy strip of sackcloth around his waist. Squatting on his heels, he would clench his hands beneath his armpits, as if to simulate wings. Most of the time he was quiet, until the rare horse came by, when he'd flap and squawk as if he were a crow, making such a racket that city administrators would have to climb the wall and escort him away. He always went without a fuss. A few days later he would be back on his perch again, silent and stoic.

After class one day, a group of students gathered around the courtyard door. Crito was absent that day, and I stood by the door with my brother. I stared as Lycon pulled a pot from behind the herm. He held it carefully with the edge of his tunic, as if the pot would burn his bare skin. Looking challengingly around the group, he announced theatrically, "Today I will strike back for Prometheus." His brothers and a few of the older boys followed him as he strode away.

We had recently learned the story of Prometheus and Zeus. It had given me bad dreams in which I saw myself as Prometheus, tied to a rock, while an eagle sent by Zeus flew threateningly toward me. As in the story, the eagle fed on my liver. I knew that although it would grow back, the eagle would return again and again, tormenting me eternally for providing fire to mankind.

"What's Lycon up to?" I asked Patrocles.

"Getting himself into trouble, I hope," my brother said shortly, before running off in pursuit of Lycon and his gang. Feeling relatively safe with my brother in the lead, and wanting to see Lycon in trouble, I ran after them, too. We came to a spot behind the old Stoa of Zeus. Hidden from view by trees and bushes, Lycon was building a small pile of twigs and branches against one of the stoa's wooden beams.

"Embers," Patrocles said, guessing the contents of the pot. We looked at each other in horror — Lycon was about to burn down the Stoa of Zeus! Some of his brothers and friends looked frightened, and even Patrocles seemed nervous. Surely, the King of the Gods would take retribution for such a terrible act?

"Prometheus was punished because he gave us fire and taught us how to grow food and care for our wounds," Lycon announced. "By teaching us what we need to know for survival, he thwarted Zeus's plans to kill all men. Now, we will strike back in defence of the champion of humanity!"

With great solemnity, Lycon removed the lid from the pot, almost as if he were opening Pandora's jar and releasing the ills of the world. "We do this act in the name of Prometheus," he proclaimed grandly, whereupon he dropped the embers onto the pile of twigs and branches. Everyone stepped back hastily. I expected — such was the magnitude of the event that we *all* expected — that a great whoosh of fire would engulf the building in flames.

To our astonishment, the dramatic buildup turned to anticlimax as the twigs merely smoked a little, then died. The embers, which had been in the pot all day, had lost most of their heat. Visibly mortified, Lycon knelt and blew on them. The fire crackled to life and burned for a moment, only to die again. Lycon searched for more kindling, but there wasn't much dry stuff about. Finally, he found a flat piece of rock and scooped the embers back into the pot, almost as if they were holy, and replaced the lid.

Grateful that the King of the Gods had not been offended, the group of boys gave a collective sigh of relief. Lycon glared around him, embarrassed by his failure, as if daring someone to make a nasty comment. Wisely, his brothers and friends left the scene and went their separate ways. Only Patrocles and I remained. Clearly gratified by Lycon's failure, Patrocles smirked at him. I sensed my brother itching for a fight, and for a moment I thought they might come to blows. Lycon was a year older than my brother, and heavier, but Patrocles was quicker and usually bested Lycon in a tussle. When Patrocles finally walked away, I followed quickly behind.

As Patrocles and I passed the edge of the market, a beautiful bronze shield adorned with the painting of the Minotaur's head caught our eyes, and we stopped to admire it. When no adults appeared to take notice of us, we took a few tentative steps into the market for a better look. Suddenly, chaos erupted around us. I was pushed to the ground from behind, just as Lycon ran by. Had he shoved me? I had no chance to find out, for at that moment a straw basket of cotton caught fire beside me and in seconds the flames soared fiercely.

Patrocles rushed to the basket, overturning it with a kick. He tramped hard on the flames, attempting to extinguish them. I smelled burning hair and feared my brother was on fire. Panic-stricken, I lay on the ground, my hands and feet numb. Despite Patrocles' efforts, the fire began to spread to the fabric of the tent. Undeterred, he bravely went on attempting to put out the fire — although without much success.

I heard shouts for water. A flame licked at a carpet stall near where I lay and the stall caught fire. A fleeing man stopped and told me to run. He grabbed my arm and pulled it, slapping me when I didn't move. The slap stirred me, restoring life to my feet, so that at last I was able to stand. Frantically, I looked around for my brother, desperate to find him. Finally, understanding the danger, I began to run. Reaching the south wall of the city, I turned and saw smoke darkening the sky. I thought the whole agora was going up in flames.

I arrived at the gate of our courtyard, relieved to find my brother there before me. I was about to run to him when I saw two strangers clutching his arms. A weeping Diotima was telling them that my father was at work, but they refused to listen to her. Roughly, they pushed Patrocles into the courtyard, then left to look for our father, seeking compensation for their losses.

"A whole stall," Diotima moaned, when they had gone. "How will your father pay for it?"

"But I didn't start the fire!" Patrocles protested indignantly.

"Who did it then?"

My brother did not respond.

"Who did it?" Diotima asked again.

"I don't know," Patrocles said, and looked at me sternly. As Diotima went in search of our mother, Patrocles made me swear to Zeus that I would not speak of the incident to anyone, ever.

When Mother came home and asked Patrocles what had happened, he said he'd seen a burning basket and tried to put out the fire. A little later, the owners of the ruined stall returned, demanding to be allowed in and asserting their right to search the house. They didn't have to look far for evidence, as Patrocles was still wearing his singed tunic. The merchants insisted on taking the tunic with them as proof of the crime, and demanded 900 drachmas to make up their losses. Mother offered them all we had — one drachma and a few obols. The furious merchants left once more in search of my father.

I was in the courtyard when Father came home. Patrocles crouched in one corner, like a cornered animal, both hands clasping the amulet around his neck. Pouncing on him, Father struck him fiercely and repeatedly. "It would have been better if you'd been left to die in the pot!" he shouted.

The words struck me almost as hard as our father was striking my brother. At last, I understood why my father had always been so much harsher with Patrocles than he'd been with me — my brother had been adopted!

Had the news of Patrocles' adoption come at any other time, I would have asked my mother a thousand questions. When did he become part of our family? Where did you find him? Is his birth mother still alive? Was he really left in a pot to die? Why did you save him instead of some other baby? Why was I never told? But the fire and its aftermath pushed everything else from my mind.

Tension filled the house. My mother and Diotima spoke in whispers even when they were alone, as if Father could hear them from across the city. When my father was at home, no one spoke at all. My brother, until then bright and happy by nature, became quiet and sullen.

At school, Patrocles and I were unable to escape talk of the fire, which was now the topic of every conversation. None of our classmates had witnessed it, as most had gone home by the time it had started and none connected the fire with Lycon and his pot of embers. After all, why would they? Since the embers had been ineffective at the Stoa of Zeus, it did not occur to them that they might have set fire to anything else. But they did hear that two merchants had brought a singed Patrocles home. Not surprisingly, it became rumoured that Patrocles had started the fire. When he came to school with his face and arms bruised and swollen, our classmates believed his guilt. No innocent boy would have been beaten so badly.

To my shame, I didn't defend Patrocles at school or at home. What stopped me from telling the truth was not any sense of schoolyard honour. It was a combination of other facts. One was my promise to Zeus, for I feared the King of the Gods would smite me with a bolt of lightning if I said anything. The other was a deep rooted fear of being associated with Lycon and his sort.

The disaster brought the moral of one of Diotima's fables vividly to mind. I wonder — did she ever tell you boys the story of the farmer and the stork? I would think she must have done so, but in case she didn't, I'll tell you here. The story concerns a farmer who planted traps in his fields to catch the cranes that were stealing his seedlings. Later, upon checking the traps, he found a few cranes and a single stork. The stork pleaded innocence and asked to be released because it had not stolen the seedlings. Nonetheless, the farmer maintained that since the stork had been caught in the company of thieves, it must suffer the same punishment.

Diotima had warned me that association with dishonest companions led to bad consequences and she was right. I knew Lycon was rotten, and that he had drawn my brother into his net. Yet I remained silent because I feared that I, too, would be punished. I might be ostracized. I might go to jail. Worst of all, I might even be executed. My appetite decreased — I ate less and less — but with so much trouble in the house, no one noticed.

A month after the fire, my father attended a preliminary hearing in a wooden building beside the old Stoa of Zeus. I overheard Diotima telling my mother that the magistrate had asked questions of all parties. The prosecution's witnesses were merchants who had seen the incident and corroborated the plaintiff's allegations. My father, unaccustomed to speaking, let alone to opening his mouth in public, did not defend himself well. After hearing the evidence, the magistrate decided the case would proceed and a trial date was set. My mother suggested my father should hire a speechwriter, to which he responded, "And how do you suppose I would pay him?"

As the trial date approached, my stomach often clenched in pain. Patrocles regularly reminded me of my promise to keep my mouth shut. He needn't have worried, for I valued my life too much to risk it for his sake. At the same time, my thoughts troubled me, for I was well aware of how good Patrocles had always been to me: endlessly reciting the *Iliad* as I recuperated from the accident, encouraging me in school athletics and defending me from our older and bigger classmates.

A few days before the trial, Crito and I visited the construction sites at the agora. Stopping at the courthouse, we saw my father's name on the wall. Since Patrocles was too young to be sued, my father had been charged instead. I was not yet familiar with my letters, and it fell to Crito to read aloud the accusers' names, the charges and the date and location of the trial, as well as my father's name. I listened in despair, wondering what would happen to Patrocles, and what his fate would mean for me.

"Why did Patrocles start the fire?" Crito asked.

Without thinking, I blurted out, "He didn't! Lycon is to blame."

As Crito's eyes widened in surprise, I put my hand over my mouth, horrified at what I'd done. I could imagine Zeus tensing his arm to unleash his deadly attack. I waited — but nothing happened.

"Don't tell anyone," I begged my friend, wondering how I had managed to escape death, and anxious that if Crito repeated my words I would be ostracized or executed.

Crito promised to keep my secret. Apart from my brother, he was the smartest boy I knew. Perhaps he could explain why Zeus hadn't struck me down for divulging my secret. Perhaps he would know if I was in danger of being banished from the city or being put to death. Finally, reluctantly, I found myself telling Crito everything — that although I hadn't actually witnessed Lycon starting the fire, I knew he had fled the scene without the pot of embers and that Patrocles had only tried to help. I even told Crito about my brother's adoption.

Crito was unable to answer my question about Zeus. He could only recommend that I not tell anyone else. As far as the laws of the city were concerned, he said, anything could happen in court. About my brother he did have something to say.

"Maybe Patrocles will be sold into slavery," he mused thoughtfully. "Anyone finding an abandoned baby can take it home and adopt it. They can even raise it as a slave."

"My brother is not a slave!" I protested indignantly.

"It doesn't matter," said Crito. "It is up to your father to decide how to pay the fine."

I spent several sleepless nights, in fear that my father would lose the case and sell my brother into slavery. I didn't care that Patrocles was adopted. I loved him dearly and didn't want to lose him. Often, I thought about confessing the truth to my mother, but did not do so because I was still terrified of Zeus and feared the wrath of the courts if I were implicated and somehow found guilty!

Patrocles left home before sunrise on the day of the trial. When I got to school, he was nowhere to be seen. I knew right away where he had gone, so I headed for the law court. Patrocles stood near the entrance, scrutinizing the jurymen — mostly elderly — as they came in grumbling. I overheard a lame man say, "I don't like the looks of that stone-mason. I shall vote against him." The man walking beside him nodded in agreement. "I've seen him in the streets. He's an unfriendly fellow. I'll vote against him, too."

As the 200 jurors filed into court, I heard many similar comments. The jurors had made up their minds even before the trial began.

As my father entered the court, I felt a hand on my shoulder. "What are you doing here?" someone asked. The man was Crito's father, Thespis. Thespis was an older version of his son: tall, with dark curly hair and striking blue eyes. I was familiar with him because my mother had attended his wife when their children — Crito being the eldest — were born.

"I followed my brother," I told him.

Thespis gazed about him. Spotting Patrocles, he walked me over to him. Taking no notice of me, Patrocles looked doubtfully at Thespis. "You will not vote against my father, will you?" he asked. Evidently he, too, had heard the jurors' comments.

"I'll do my best to help, but you must go to school now," Thespis ordered firmly. "And take your brother with you."

Without argument, we turned and walked away. The rest of the day went by in a blur of anxiety.

Our relief was enormous when we discovered that our father had been acquitted and would not have to pay a penalty. Thespis had spoken for him, convincing the jury of Patrocles' innocence. I later learned from Diotima that my mother had asked Thespis to intervene. Crito had said nothing, as he had promised. I was overjoyed that my father did not have to pay a fine and my brother would not be sold into slavery.

What surprised me most was how things changed at home after the trial. My mother behaved coldly toward my father. My brother and my father no longer spoke to each other. Diotima tried to act normally, but I could tell her behaviour was forced. We no longer felt like a family.

From then on, I nurtured great hatred for Lycon. In time, I would see him as the cause of everything bad that happened to me over the next few years. Above all, I blamed him for the loss of my brother. As I saw it, the fire started by Lycon caused the avalanche that buried an admittedly romanticized version of my old, happy life.

Looking back now, I understand that my animosity toward Lycon was somewhat misplaced. Unfortunate though the events were surrounding the fire in the agora, Lycon's actions really revealed my own cowardliness. I could have saved my family much pain. The truth would not have caused me legal trouble. As for the god Zeus, well, he was no real threat, although I was too young and too naïve to know it then. If only I had been brave enough to tell the truth, I might even have avoided my present confinement in this small, dark, cramped cell.

DAY 5

I THINK I WILL name my messenger "the rooster," because his rough, gravelly voice has woken me from a dead sleep yet again. Diotima should make one of her mixtures to ease his throat. How much more pleasant for me if his voice were soothing and calm, like your mother's.

Having heard from my rooster that you are determined not to leave the city before the end, I will not request it again. I do caution you, though, to stay inside the house as much as possible. But if you must go out, stay in a group.

At least you have stopped sending me food fit for festival days. Thank you for that. I can now eat with the assurance that you are not starving on my account. And now, back to my story.

I took every chance I could to visit Crito's house. Apart from enjoying playing with my friend, I always hoped to see his father. I was very fond of Thespis, not only because of his help at court, but because of the way he treated me. Despite my recovery from the accident I had incurred during the festival of Anthesteria, there were those who still believed my body harboured evil spirits. Years later, some families still did not welcome my mother, even when I was not with her. I was happy that Thespis was not apprehensive in my presence, and so, when his wife was about to give birth to her fourth child, I went to their home with my mother.

Crito lived in a two-storey house quite a bit larger than ours. A beautifully carved herm — always with a fresh wreath on its head and a clean basin of salt water beside it — sat at the courtyard door. As I washed my hands in the salt water to prevent evil spirits from entering the house, I wished this were my home. Beautiful mosaic pictures decorated the walls, and dressers displayed expensive cups, vases and sculptures. There was even an inside bathroom.

A slave greeted my mother and me at the door before ushering us into a courtyard large enough to hold 50 people. My mother immediately went to Crito's mother, while I was directed to the andron.

Despite having made many previous visits to Crito's home, I had never been inside the andron. My heart beat with excitement as I passed beyond the curtain where Thespis and Crito were examining the hoplite armour that Crito would one day inherit. A shield bearing a painted scorpion hung on the wall. Beside it, I saw other military objects: a gleaming bronze helmet adorned with a white crest as tall as a hand, a bronze breastplate in the shape of a muscled chest, bronze greaves with padding meant to protect the shins, a short sword and spears as long as two men. I wondered whether my father kept similar objects in our andron.

In wonder, I took in the beauty of the armour, which looked for all the world like something Achilles might have worn in his epic battle against Hector.

Thespis was smiling as he took the helmet off the wall. I could hardly breathe for excitement as he placed it on my head. "What do you think?" he asked.

"It's wonderful," I answered, although the helmet was far too large and too heavy for me, and bumped against my forehead.

"Would you like to try on the rest of the armour, Socrates?"

Oh yes, I did want to try it on! Thespis took the armour into the courtyard, where he clad me in it. The greaves reached to mid-thigh. The breastplate weighed almost as much as I did. As for the shield, I was unable to lift it. The armour gave me the feeling of being crushed — but how glorious it was to wear it.

Possibly amused at my discomfort, Thespis laughed gently. "Is it heavy?" he asked.

"No," I gasped.

"Good," he said, suppressing a grin as he handed me the long spear with the leaf-shaped blade at the tip. "Try holding this in your right hand." I took a breath as I dug the end of the spear into the ground to steady it, but it wobbled in my grip. Thespis laughed again. "Careful with that lizard killer," he said, referring to the spiked point near my foot. Next, he hung a long sword from my waist. "If the spear snaps or you have to fight at close quarters, use the sword," he told me. The armour was so heavy that I accidentally let go of the spear just as one of Crito's aunts was crossing the courtyard on her way to the kitchen. She screamed in fright when the spear landed close to her.

Thespis smiled and apologized to his sister. "There's better equipment in the Stoa of Zeus," he said then. At the words, I looked up guiltily, wondering how much he knew of Lycon's attempt to burn down the stoa. But he went on speaking, taking no notice of my expression. "The women would probably prefer us to stay out of their way right now."

Thespis took the hoplite armour from me and rehung it in the andron. Then he, Crito and I headed for the agora, where the smell of cooking food and spices emanating from the merchants' stalls made my mouth water.

As we entered the Stoa of Zeus, I felt certain Thespis would recount some fable similar to Diotima's, except that he would focus its moral on character or bravery. Instead, he lamented the loss of the grand displays from the Battle of Marathon. "The best things were in the Temple of Athena before the Persians razed it to the ground," he said, before launching into the history of each piece of armour and weaponry in the stoa, including the battles they had come from.

I gestured toward a display of red-quilted linen armour and red wicker shields as tall as a man. "Did you bring these back from the battlefield?" I asked, naïvely.

Thespis shook his head. "No, they were brought here by the generals who gathered the greatest of the spoils as gifts to the gods."

"The helmets are the most prized," Crito put in.

"Right," said his father. "Can you tell us why that is?"

"Because a soldier will throw away his shield when he flees, but his helmet remains on his head unless someone takes it from him."

"Good." Thespis was satisfied with the response. "What happens if you throw away your shield in flight?"

"You disgrace yourself and your family."

"Correct. A soldier who does that is a coward. A trembler. Anything else?"

"A soldier's bravery in battle determines his worth. To avoid warfare is to demonstrate laziness and fear." Evidently, Crito had learned his father's lessons well.

"Very good." Thespis turned to me and pointed toward one of the suits of armour. "Socrates, do you know which battle that is from?"

I wanted Thespis to think I was clever. I valued his good opinion and was desperate to answer the question correctly. The problem was, I didn't know the right response. I waited a moment, hoping he would supply it, but he remained silent, waiting patiently for me to speak. Cringing inwardly, I said, "A big battle," and tried not to redden. Knowing Thespis would have received a better answer from a fig seed, I felt like a fool. I might as well have said, "I passed wind today."

"Yes, a big battle, and a good one, too," Thespis said, kindly. "The Battle of Plataea. Do you know about it?" Ruefully, I had to admit I didn't.

"Well, Socrates, Darius, the Persian king, was enraged when we conquered his people at the Battle of Marathon. Swearing to return and seize all of Greece, he spent years after that battle gathering together soldiers from all over his empire. After Darius's death, his son, Xerxes, continued his father's efforts, and created an army more massive than any in history: 2,000 ships of war, 50,000 cavalry and 300,000 soldiers, as well as labourers and slaves beyond count.

"Ten years after the Battle of Marathon, King Xerxes began his invasion. The Persian army faced little opposition as they marched through
Thrace, Macedon and Thessaly. Unable to stop their momentum, we
evacuated Athens. Still unopposed, the Persians marched into the city,
tore down the walls and burned Athens to the ground. Xerxes departed
for home, leaving his cousin, General Mardonius, to complete the con-
quest of Greece.

"The following year we assembled what remained of our forces. The
cities of Greece, so often at odds with one another, united to confront
the common enemy. Ninety thousand Greeks gathered for a last stand.
When Mardonius learned we were on the move, he retreated from
Athens into Boeotia, near the city of Plataea. General Aristides the
Just marched us to Plataea, where we took up positions along the high
ground. Mardonius initiated hit-and-run tactics in an attempt to lure us
down to the plain, where his cavalry would have had the advantage in a
fight, but his strategy was unsuccessful. Unable to entice General Aristides to the low ground, Mardonius finally brought his men to us and
readied them for battle.

"Satisfied with our superior position, General Aristides sacrificed a
goat, but the omens were not good, so he delayed engagement with the
enemy. For eight long days, we waited. Mardonius began a new tactic,
harrying our supply lines and blocking our access to the only freshwater
spring in the area. He knew that without water we could not stay on the
high ground much longer. In fact, we retreated to a position in front of
Plataea, where we would have access to water, but the retreat went badly,
and some of our forces were scattered. Seeing our disarray, the Persians
began their attack.

"Mardonius immediately set his infantry upon us. Guarding our rear,
the Spartans engaged the Persians first. The Spartan general sent a messenger to General Aristides, asking him to join the Spartan engagement
against the enemy. The general agreed to the request and my cohort
was sent off first, to assist the Spartans. Immediately after our departure

Aristides ordered the Athenians to stay their position, as the Persian phalanx was approaching.

"Alone among the Spartan soldiers, my cohort took up the right side of the formation. Numerically superior to us, the Persians sent their first line of soldiers to clash with our phalanx. You need to know, Socrates, that the Persian shields differ from our hoplite shields in that they are made of wicker: highly maneuverable and capable of halting arrows, but not strong enough to protect soldiers from spears, least of all, Athenian spears. The Persians tried to break our spears by grasping them, but we switched to swords in response. Although the fight was fierce and long, we pushed through the enemy lines at last, and scattered the Persians.

"From our position on the hill, I saw Mardonius on his white horse, surrounded by a bodyguard of 1,000 men. But the Spartans were closing in. Suddenly, I saw a Spartan hoplite throw his spear at the Persian general. It struck Mardonius squarely in the head, knocked him to the ground and killed him. With their general dead, the Persians lost faith and they fled. Finally, we routed them. We retrieved what was ours, and have pushed the Persians back every year since then."

Having ended his account on a note of grim satisfaction, Thespis led Crito and me to the wall of commemoration. Awestruck, my friend and I stared at the names of the many hundreds of citizens who had fought and died in battle. Thespis pointed out names of men he had known — men from his cohort or ones he had grown up with. He spoke with great reverence of the sacrifices they had made. "Respect, admiration, glory and immortality," he said, "these qualities are earned in battle."

At home that night, I thought about Thespis's story. Of course, I had heard almost the same words from my teachers in school and from my friends. Every boy grew up hearing these words, but listening to Thespis tell his story, they became more real, more important. Respect. Admiration. Glory. Immortality. The words became embedded in my skin and began to worm their way into my soul.

DAY 6

ANOTHER MORNING — a night, more accurately — woken by my "rooster." I am still not accustomed to the odd hours I keep now. Nor am I accustomed to doing so much writing. With the quill between my fingers, my hand cramps the way it did when I was first apprenticed to my father, and spent my days holding chisel and hammer. I manage to ignore the stiffness, however, once I get into my story.

Of all the events that shaped my life, I believe one of the most significant was the day my mother didn't know me. That day has remained like a raw wound in my mind since it happened. It was a festival day. Nine years old at the time, I was in the courtyard playing with my knucklebones when I heard, rather than saw, my mother sit down heavily on a chair. Turning, I was surprised to see her gazing at me as if I were a stranger. A few moments later she suddenly seemed to recognize me. "You're late for school," she said.

"There's no school today, Mama."

She looked down at her hands, her expression intent, and took a few breaths. "Yes, of course," she murmured, as if to herself. "No school today."

With some effort, she stood, went to the bedroom and lay down. Those few moments unsettled me, making me feel as though a river had stopped flowing, its ripples and eddies frozen. Concerned about my mother's well-being, I brought my knucklebones to her room and played quietly at her feet. She was still resting when Diotima summoned her for the evening meal. She tried to get up, only to lie back again. "Maybe later," she said. I brought her the meal and placed it beside her. She thanked me and then closed her eyes once more.

When I went to see her the next morning, I found her awake. Anxiously, I inquired how she was feeling. She was not sick, she told me, trying to reassure me with a smile. But that smile, so different from usual, did nothing to convince me; I could tell she was in pain. I wanted to stay home from school to take care of her, but she turned me down. "I have Diotima," she insisted.

When I came home later that day, I was relieved to find my mother preparing the evening meal. She had dinner with us and fell asleep at the usual time. In the middle of the night, however, the sound of her laboured breathing roused me. I lay awake awhile, listening, and wondered whether Patrocles or Diotima heard her breathing, too. I fell back to sleep, only to be woken again at dawn by her breathing — now a tormented-sounding rattle. Frightened, I got up quickly. In the dim morning light I saw that her skin had turned a sickly yellow-grey. I roused Diotima and she immediately sent Patrocles for the doctor.

The doctor finally arrived and examined my mother. She suffered from disequilibrium, he told us gravely. Her humours were out of balance; an over-abundance of blood had caused a fever and her situation was dire. In addition to recommending immediate sacrifices to Apollo and Asclepius, he took a small knife from his bag, pushed up my mother's sleeve and made a cut in her forearm.

I watched in terror as dark red blood spurted from the wound and dripped down my mother's arm and hand, gathering in puddles on the dirt floor. She was obviously in terrible pain. Her face had contorted horribly, her eyes were distended and she began to moan and groan loudly. Diotima and the physician had to hold her down on the bed.

Suddenly, the room was filled with a loud and inexplicable screaming, a noise that went on and on. The next thing I knew, my brother was dragging me from the room into the courtyard, where he forced me onto the ground. Only when Patrocles ordered me to stop screaming, did I realize that the shrieks I'd heard were mine. My hands went numb and all sound dimmed. I remained motionless as a stone on the ground, leaning against the courtyard altar, unable to rid myself of the image of my mother's pain-filled eyes.

Moments passed, and then I heard a great wailing cry, although not from my lips this time. Some time later, someone — I did not register who it was — told me my mother had died. A stomach-lurching nothingness overwhelmed me, as if I were falling down a bottomless hole. Needing to feel something solid, I pawed at the ground.

I remembered hearing that the soul leaves the body in a little puff of breath at the moment of death. Hoping that I could gulp in the air that had been my mother's last breath, and so keep her with me always, I arose and returned to the room. My mother lay on her back on the bed. I had not noticed Patrocles leaving the courtyard, but he was in the room before me, sobbing, with his face on Mother's belly. I sat down by her head and inhaled deeply. I stayed at her bedside a long time.

A group of women helped Diotima prepare my mother's body for burial. They washed her, anointed her with oil, dressed her in a clean white shroud that extended to her ankles and placed a laurel crown on her head. A thin linen chinstrap held her jaw shut. Inside her mouth they placed a coin, as payment to the ferryman for her ride across the River Styx to the Land of the Dead.

The mourners arrived the next day. Dressed in dark robes, they gathered around my mother's body, which had been placed on a tall bed in the courtyard. As my mother had no relatives in Athens, Diotima held her head while the women nearest to her touched her hands. Those who could not reach her body held their hands in the air and then beat their breasts, pulling at their hair and wailing. When their lament ended, more mourners came to pay their respects. I lost track of the women who passed through our courtyard, but there must have been hundreds. Each woman pounded her breast, tore at her hair and wept at sight of my mother. That night, Diotima cut off her own hair in my mother's honour.

Very early the next morning, before the sun was up, my father, Patrocles, Thespis and I, as well as two men I did not know, lifted the plank on which my mother lay and began the march to the cemetery. Patrocles walked unsteadily opposite me, absently fingering his amulet with his free hand. About 50 men walked ahead of us; their wives and children followed behind. We stopped at each street corner, where the women wept even more loudly than before, beat their chests and tore at their hair. Additional women, ones I did not know, joined the procession. All the while, I concentrated on not dropping my mother's body.

It took a long time to reach the cemetery, for it was situated well outside the city walls. When we finally got there, we laid my mother's body in a hole. The women in the procession paraded by, leaving offerings on the wooden plank in a trench beside the grave: honey cakes, wine, coins, laurel leaves, vases, shells and other objects.

When all the women had passed, my father set fire to the plank. All eyes turned to him as the plank burned. It was time for him to give the funeral oration. Patrocles had told me it was customary for the speaker to recount the history of the deceased. Many facts would be included: where the person was born and the names of their parents and their children, as well as their interests and the activities at which they'd excelled. Cherished memories of the deceased might be told and their good qualities would be listed. Sometimes a favourite poem would be recited. Funeral orations, Patrocles said, could last half the day.

I remember waiting for what seemed like a long time before my father was ready to speak. Finally, he cleared his throat and looked down at my mother. "Go to the gods," he said. Then he motioned to the men to cover her body with dirt.

Four words.

That was all my father had to say to the woman who'd married him, lived with him for so many years and put up with his difficult moods. The woman who had drawn stone splinters from his eyes and probably saved his sight. The woman who, as well as delivering hundreds of babies, had managed my father's house, kept him fed and raised their two sons. The woman who hugged us and cared for us, who nursed me back to health and carried me everywhere after my accident. My mother was a strong, loving wife and mother. She was the most wonderful person I had ever known. My mother was sunshine. And four words were all my father could come up with!

When we arrived back home, he pointed at the herm and the dish of water beside it and said, "Wash your hands. I don't want any more evil entering this house."

Tables laden with wonderful food had been set out in the courtyard, a meal of thanks to all who had helped with my mother's burial — more and tastier food than I had ever seen in my life. Bread, meat, olives, figs and my favourite: honey cakes. Diotima's doing, not my father's, I felt certain. Yet, tempting though the food was, I ate nothing.

After the funeral banquet our sombre guests departed and my father sacrificed a chicken at our courtyard altar as he addressed the greatness and wisdom of Zeus. Obligations discharged, he entered the andron and shut the door behind him. As I fell asleep that night, I heard the sharp tink, tink, tink of my father's chiseling. It was almost as though nothing of consequence had happened.

I had great trouble accepting the loss of my mother. Seeing a pretty flower, I might pluck it to bring to her. I would wait for her to sit next to me at supper. Diotima sympathized with my grief. Finding me at our courtyard door, as if I were waiting for my mother to return from a birth, she would lead me inside, feed me, tell me I was loved and then put me to bed.

At night I dreamed about my mother. In those dreams she was real for a time, but then she was gone again. In the morning, I would wake and weep at the emptiness in the room. It was as if the sun had stopped shining and the warmth of the world had been torn away.

I kept asking myself why the gods had taken my mother from me. Why had they robbed the world of such a wonderful person? She had done nothing but help others. Why not kill my father, instead? He was just a grumpy old man!

Finally, I came to the conclusion that I was the person the gods were punishing, and thought of several reasons why it could be so. Maybe Dionysus was still after me, for my childhood injury had taken place during a festival in his honour. Maybe it was Zeus. For one thing, I had done nothing to stop Lycon from trying to burn down the Stoa of Zeus. Even worse, I had broken my vow to keep silent about my brother's involvement in the agora fire.

And how many times had I accompanied my mother to the Eileithyia sanctuary without leaving a votive? How many funeral processions had I observed without washing my hands in the basin by the herm before entering our house to ward off evil, as is customary? How many other disrespectful things had I done? How many gods had I offended?

I prayed to all the gods I could think of. I promised to be a better person. I vowed to honour the deities every moment of my life, if only they would help me. I offered up my father, Diotima, even Patrocles, in exchange for my mother's return. When nothing came of my prayers and offers, I cursed all the gods angrily. Yet when I was calm again, dread would fill me at the thought of the terrible suffering the immortals might wreak in retaliation for my harsh words and thoughts.

A month after my mother's death, I woke one morning to find my brother gone. I thought he must have left for class early, but he was not at school when I arrived. That afternoon, I asked Diotima about him.

"He left," she said simply.

"Did he go somewhere with his friends?"

"No, he left Athens," she told me sadly.

"When will he come back?"

"I don't know, Socrates. Maybe never."

I was confused. "Why did he go?"

Diotima hesitated a moment before saying, "He didn't want to apprentice himself to your father."

"What do you mean?"

"Your brother would have finished his schooling soon. Then your father would have taught him to be a stonemason."

"I don't understand. Why didn't he say goodbye?"

Diotima sighed heavily and knelt down beside me. Taking my hands in hers, she held my gaze. "Patrocles thought it would be easier this way. He asked me to tell you that he'll send for you one day, when he is rich and has made his mark."

Stunned, I went to the bedroom and sat on the corner of my brother's bed. I thought of one particular deal I had offered the gods: my brother for my mother. My brother was gone and my mother had not been returned to me. Now I had no one. Crushed by loneliness, I sobbed bitterly and began to doubt the gods.

Shortly after my brother's departure, Diotima woke me very early one morning. "Get ready. You're going with your father," she said.

Certain I was about to be punished, I tried to think what I had done wrong. As we left the house, I waited nervously for my father to enlighten me, but he only motioned me to the door without speaking. Diotima gave me a little sack and said quietly, "Take this." Surreptitiously, I glanced inside and saw a small loaf of bread. *What is this for?* I wondered, apprehensively. Did Diotima know where we were headed? Did my father plan to leave me outside the walls of the city and order me never to return? Was I to be ostracized?

The night mist still hung in the air. My panic grew as we exited the city through the Piraeus gate and walked southwest beside a long wall in the direction of the port of Piraeus. The sun rose as we walked, burning away the mist. I had almost convinced myself that my father was about to put me on a ship and sell me to the Persians or the Spartans when, midway between the city and the port, I heard the sound of chisels on rock, similar to the sounds that came from my father's andron at night only much louder. As the noise intensified, I saw quarrymen offloading rough blocks of limestone from dozens of carts, and stonemasons working away with chisels and mallets, smoothing the jagged surfaces of the stone.

My father unwrapped a bundle he was carrying. Inside it were flat-faced hammers, double-pointed hammers and a variety of toothed and flat chisels.

"Observe what I do," he ordered, grasping a flat-faced hammer and a toothed chisel. I watched intently as he began to chip away at a block of rough limestone.

"Now you do it," he said, thrusting the tools at me.

I held the chisel and tapped it with the hammer.

"Wrong," said my father, taking the hammer from my hand and demonstrating the proper grip. "Hold it like this."

Obediently, I took back the hammer and gave the chisel another tap.

"Strike harder." My father sounded frustrated.

I lifted the hammer higher and swung once more, but I missed the chisel and struck my hand instead. Involuntarily, I dropped the chisel and held my hurt hand to my chest. My father only stared at me.

"Again," he said, without sympathy.

Picking up the hammer once more, I swung it, making good contact this time.

"And again."

I struck the chisel with the mallet.

My father nodded. "Keep going until I tell you to stop," he ordered, then began to chisel the block beside me. Why was he making me do this? *Is this some kind of punishment?* I wondered again. Out of the corner of my eye, I watched him doing what he had instructed me to do. Before long, he had created a smooth, flat surface on the stone. He turned back to me and watched as I struck the chisel over and over again. Before long, my hands were tense from gripping the tools. His eyes bored into me.

"It's not about whacking the stone until bits fall off!" he said eventually, clearly disgusted with my performance. "The line must be straight." He demonstrated the angle at which to hold the chisel. After watching me a while longer, he turned to his own stone and worked on the next uneven surface.

I kept tapping away. My palms hurt and my arm felt heavy, as if it were about to drop from my shoulder. Just when I didn't think I could hold the hammer a moment longer, my father told me to stop, and motioned toward the sack Diotima had given me. It was time to eat. My hand was so stiff from clenching the chisel, I could hardly grip the bread. Around us, men were laughing and joking, but my father and I ate alone and in silence. Tiny droplets of blood had dried on my forearms: cuts from shards of stone. I glanced at my father's heavily scarred forearms and thought about Patrocles.

In the course of the morning, my father finished turning his rough block of stone into a smooth cube ready for the wall. Quarrymen brought him another stone, and he began to work on it. I couldn't understand how he managed to work so fast, so easily, when the repetitive movements were taking their toll on me. My thumb hurt. My neck hurt. By the end of the day, there was not a part of my being that did not hurt. I was in agony. When we got home, Diotima asked about my first day of work. *First?* My eyes widened at the word. And then it dawned on me — I would not be returning to school.

The next day was much the same as the one before, as were the many that followed. Upon our arrival at the worksite my father would open his bundle and take out his equipment. Particular about his tools, he always kept them in good order: sharp, ready for work and laid out in the same way. He worked in silence, his rhythm steady, his pace so fast I doubted I could ever hope to match it. Now and then he might pause to admonish me or to give a grunt of disgust at my ineptitude, but that was the extent of our communication. He expected me to do a man's job.

The work was laborious and intensely physical and the pain did not lessen with the passing days. My back hurt, my hands ached, my fingers were raw. Night brought no relief. I would lie in bed, wishing I could find a way to ease the constant pain. Even when I slept at last, there was no escape. I dreamt of chisels and hammers and wedges and the endless tink, tink, tink of metal on metal. I had nightmares in which I lost my tools, my father yelled at me in front of everyone and the other masons made fun of me.

Diotima did what she could for me during this difficult time. She made sure I ate enough and had strength to face the day. Before bed, when my father was in the andron "making his own luck," whatever that meant, Diotima would tell me stories about her childhood and youth. As difficult as her life must have been, she kept the tales happy. She also told me fables she'd learned from the old man, her previous master on the Island of Samos. The lessons concerned subjects such as contentment and confidence and self-respect — concepts that were lost on me because I did not understand them.

Arriving home one evening after work, I found a visitor awaiting me at our courtyard door. It was Crito. He was clearly happy to see me.

"I thought you were sick," he exclaimed, "until my father told me you had become apprenticed to your father!"

I was so overjoyed at seeing him that I could not stop talking, blurting out everything I had learned during the long days at work. I told him of the wall we were building, extending from Athens all the way to the fortified port city of Piraeus in the southwest. The wall was so long that when it was complete it would take half a morning to walk from one end to the other. It would be as wide as a house and as high as 10 men standing one above another. What was more, an identical wall was being constructed parallel to the first one. Soon Athens would have two long walls, 220 strides apart, stretching from the city gates to the sea. Athens needed these long walls for access to the sea, so that if the city were ever under siege, we would still be able to get food and supplies. I told all this to my friend, ending proudly, "It is impossible for an enemy to take a walled city."

If Crito knew this fact already — after all, Thespis could have told him — he didn't let on. Instead, he acted as if I were a great source of information. So impressed did he seem that I showed him my blistered hands and my forearms marked with little red cuts from the stone splinters.

"Soon you will be like Milo of Croton," said my friend.

"But I'm only carving stone." I was puzzled that Crito would think of me in relation to the greatest Olympic wrestler in history.

"Milo was strong because he lifted a full-grown bull every day. The stone is your bull, Socrates. You will grow stronger and stronger as you work with the stone. My father says so."

How happy I was to know that I was in Thespis's thoughts!

Crito told me about things happening at school: who had earned the ire of the paidotribe and the grammatiste, and who was fighting with whom. I longed to go back there. I would gladly have traded my father's criticism for the slap of the grammatiste's sandal or the whack of the paidotribe's stick. Too soon, Crito had to return home, but first he invited me to his home to celebrate the next festival.

The morning of the festival of Dionysus was overcast, the light dim. Fearful something might happen to me, I walked nervously to Crito's home. I had not forgotten that other festival in honour of the God of Wine and Ecstasy, when I was so badly injured. I was suspicious that Dionysus might be holding a grudge against me, especially since I had cursed him and all the other gods and goddesses at the loss of my mother.

I made it to Crito's without incident, although I was still wary. My friend took me to the andron, where his father reclined on a sofa.

Thespis inquired about the progress of my apprenticeship. I told him that although I was not yet skilled, I was trying hard to do what I had to. I also showed him the blisters on my hands and the scabs on my arms. "It is the job of the son to surpass the father. I must carry his name forward in honour," I said, repeating my father's words.

"You should take pride in your work," Thespis said, "for what you are building will protect those who are less strong, less able to defend themselves. The walls will stand for hundreds of years and ensure continued prosperity for Athens."

His words made me feel good about myself, and I smiled at him happily.

"Do you remember me telling you about the Battle of Plataea?" he asked.

Naturally, I recalled that great afternoon at the Stoa of Zeus, and said as much.

"A play has been written about the Persian invasion." Thespis paused, as if awaiting some reaction from me. I remained silent, for I did not know what he expected.

"Would you like to see the play?" he asked after a few seconds.

"Oh, yes, please!" I exclaimed enthusiastically.

My response must have satisfied him, for he said, "Excellent. Let's go."

At the Theater of Dionysus we were met by a number of Crito's uncles and cousins. As I watched them joyfully greeting one another, I thought how wonderful it must be to be a member of such a big and happy family. If this were my family, I would never be lonely. And the thought came to me; perhaps Thespis could adopt me.

As we entered the theater and walked down the sloping hill, we passed hundreds of men and boys already settled. We found places for ourselves on wooden benches set into the hill near the stage. In front of us was an orchestra: 20 men with various drums, flutes, harps and all manner of wind and stringed instruments. The music started and the crowd grew excited. Then a group of men appeared on the stage behind the orchestra and began to sing. The music and singing continued for some time before others took the stage, rousing the spectators who cheered and moaned in unison.

I did not understand what was happening. To me, Thespis's story about the Battle of Plataea had been far more realistic and exciting than the drama unfolding on the stage. I watched Thespis to see how I should respond. I was actually concentrating more on him than on the stage.

A soft rain began to fall, chilling me and making me anxious for the play to finish. I listened with little patience as the actor playing King Xerxes — who had ruined his empire by trying to conquer the Greeks — made his final speech, in which he lamented his pride and overwhelming ambition.

The play ended at last. Relieved, I waited for Thespis to lead us out, but was surprised when the audience remained seated. I was even more surprised when a rousing cheer greeted a line of men and boys entering the theater. Without smiling, waving or in any way responding to the cheering, the group paraded around the theater.

I wondered if they were actors from the play, although there seemed far too many of them. Over the sound of the cheering, I asked Crito about them. Sons of citizens killed in battle, he told me. And for the first time I realized just how much respect was accorded to warriors: respect so deep that even their children were honoured. It was as Thespis had told me.

That night I lay sleepless, picturing myself parading before a theater of men, cheered not for being the son of a fallen citizen, but for my own bravery in battle. Vividly I remembered the words Thespis had spoken months before at the Stoa of Zeus. Respect. Admiration. Glory. Immortality. Staring into the darkness, I resolved to attain these qualities myself in a heroic battle. People would respect and admire me. I would be showered with glory, imbued with immortality. When history remembered champions like Heracles and Achilles, my name would be lauded along with theirs.

This was the future my mother had seen for me. I would fulfill her vision. I would be remembered forever.

What a great pity it is that I did not truly understand the theme of the play I saw that day. How arrogance and over-confidence — characteristics I would display myself one day in abundance — can be one's undoing. But then, what does a nine-year-old boy understand of hubris?

DAY 7

THUS FAR, I have written only about events I recall from my childhood: the events that I believe shaped me the most. Yet now I have started to wonder where the lesser details of my life fit into the general frame of my existence, and how they, too, may have influenced me. In those endless months and years I spent working with my father on the city's fortifications, I must have struck my thumb with the hammer a hundred times before I learned to hold the chisel correctly. How often did I trip on a stick or a stone in the street before I learned to watch for obstacles in my path? And how about our courtyard altar, against which I stubbed my toe at least once a month? In what way, I now ask myself, did these lesser things affect me? Did some of these events, unimportant though they may have been, teach me more vital lessons than my few precious days with Crito and his father Thespis? For Crito and Thespis always loom large in my mind.

From the day of the play about Xerxes onward, I celebrated every festival with Crito and his family. Whether the city was honouring Apollo and his twin sister Artemis, or Athena the Goddess of Wisdom or Heracles, Thespis always played host. I was treated like one of the family, almost like a son. My wish was coming true, I often thought happily.

Even more than my school lessons, it was Thespis who fully explained the expectations that would be placed on me when I turned 17. I had always known, of course, that I would have to attend the military academy, but because my father had taken me from school so early, I did not know much more than that.

From Thespis I learned the difference between the Athenian army's two kinds of troops — the hoplites and the peltasts — and the role each performed. It did not take me long to realize which warrior I wanted to be. A peltast's only armour was a small shield. He used a bow, a javelin and a sling, or sometimes even threw stones, depending on what was required in battle. Peltasts were skirmishers who protected the flanks of the hoplite phalanxes. They might be asked to harass enemy formations or to mask troop movements taking place behind them, but that was where their duties ended. A peltast was akin to a child in a man's army.

The hoplite phalanx was the unit that commanded respect. The hoplites had defeated the Persians at the Battle of Marathon and beaten them again at the Battle of Plataea.

As Crito and I grew older, we dressed in some of Thespis's hoplite armour and pretended to do battle. We'd heft the impossibly weighty bronze shields with both hands and clash them against each other — only once, because they were so heavy we'd have to put them down after that.

"Training at the academy will be very difficult," Thespis said once, as we were pulling the shields into the courtyard, watched by Crito's sisters from the shade of the courtyard wall. "You will be pushed to the edge of your strength and then be made to work even harder." He told us how he and the other young trainees of his day had been punched, kicked and yelled at by the old soldiers who had instructed them.

"As a hoplite, more will be expected of you than of the peltasts," he said gravely. "You will be the focus of the battle. You will face the greatest danger — but you will also gain the greater glory. On your shoulders will lie the future of Athens.

"You will be set up in formations that you must retain, no matter the terrain or the nature of the opposing enemy. Depending on how many trainees are at the academy, your instructors will arrange you in lines numbering between 20 and 25, creating formations eight rows deep.

Each line of the phalanx is like the finger of a massive hand. Together, you will act as a unit to defeat the enemy."

To show us how close together we would stand in the phalanx, Thespis put Crito by my right shoulder and his oldest daughter, Calliope, by my left. Then he put two shields on the ground in front of us.

"Lift your shields," he ordered Crito and me. When we were unable to lift the heavy shields with only one arm, he told us to support their weight against our shoulders. "Lock them together," he said, and showed us how to do it. "Now Crito's shield protects Socrates, Socrates' shield protects Calliope, and so on down the line."

"Who will protect me?" Crito asked.

"No one," said his father. "The far right is the most exposed position in the phalanx." Pausing, he stared intently at his firstborn and only son. "The position you are in now is the most coveted of the line. In the phalanx, it is called the first of the line. The man who demonstrates the most skill, strength and courage at the academy is honoured with this spot."

"Were you first of the line?" Crito asked.

"No, but I was part of the front line," Thespis said proudly. "All right, let's see you clash your shields again."

Calliope sat back against the wall with her sisters, watching Crito and me heave the heavy shields to our shoulders. Inspired by Thespis's lesson, I resolved that I, too, would be in the front line one day. No doubt Crito shared my thoughts as we picked up our shields, grunting with effort as we clashed them together, once, twice, three times, before dropping them to the ground. Thespis looked on, smiling in approval.

Soon, battle was all I thought about. On festival days, after the obligatory observances were completed, Crito and I talked about all the great things we would accomplish. As boys have a tendency to do, we dreamed grandly. We would vanquish the Persians permanently, and humble the Spartans. The world would come to know of our bravery and military genius. Together we would be a combination of the powerful Heracles and the clever Odysseus. The people would hail us kings of the land and emperors of the sea — and all this before we were 20!

How would it happen so quickly? The answer was easy. The academy would recognize our military genius as soon as we started there. We would be presented before the Assembly and the constitution would be changed to allow us generalships at such a young age. From there, it would be a simple matter of a few battles in which the enemy — Persian or Spartan — would be crushed without the loss of a single Athenian soldier. Word would spread to every city in the world that Crito and I were unbeatable. Our enemies would lay down their weapons at our feet and our allies would crown us with laurels. Oh, the glory! The respect! The admiration that would be ours!

At first, Crito and I shared these visions only with each other. Then, one day at work, I asked a stonemason, a one-eyed man named Acron, whether he had ever been in battle. Telling me he'd been a peltast bowman, he pointed out men who had thrown javelins or stones. None had been hoplites.

"I'm going to be a hoplite soldier and a general," I declared proudly.

"Sure you will, boy," said Acron, giving me what I took to be a wink — although he might have blinked. Tough to tell, with a one-eyed man.

Acron called over to some nearby men, "Socrates says he will be a general!"

"A general? You'll be a general when old Acron's eye grows back," joked one of the men, to a chorus of guffaws.

Hurt by the laughter, I said obstinately, "You'll see, I will win renown and eat in the Tholos for free, every day for the rest of my life."

"Okay, Achilles," Acron mocked. "Whatever you say."

"My name will live forever!" I insisted.

"Kid," said another man, "you'll be at the wall with us forever." Again, they all laughed.

My father pulled me aside a little later, when he could speak without being overheard. "Do not tell the men your thoughts," he muttered. "You make fools of us both."

He need not have worried. I didn't like having my ambitions laughed at, and I promised myself never again to share my plans with anyone else.

Little of consequence took place in the next few years. After the Persian army had been defeated at the Battle of Plataea and driven from Greece, Athens had built her walls as quickly as possible, in case another adversary, such as the Spartans, were to take advantage of her vulnerable situation.

Every tombstone and temple fragment had been used to create Athens' initial fortifications. Now that time, money and quality building materials were available, her defenses were to be strengthened. My father and I worked on the long walls until they were completed, after which we were transferred to the city wall where we laboured on improving the city's many gates.

I continued to spend festivals with Crito and Thespis, seeing my time with their family as a welcome reprieve from the company of my father, who grew testier with each passing day. Then, when I was 13, Thespis died. Like my mother's death, his was sudden and shocking, and hit me very hard.

Crito changed after the funeral, becoming simultaneously angry and unhappy. For some reason he was also distant, ignoring my efforts at friendship, and was always too busy to visit. As Thespis's only son, he was being groomed to take over the family business, which had been involved with agriculture for generations — buying and selling wheat, barley, olives, grapes and anything else that yielded a profit. It became Crito's duty to keep the business going.

I missed Crito's friendship. Without his company my working hours seemed endless, my leisure time dull. Other boys my age were also apprenticing to their fathers by then, but those who came to work at the wall did not accept me as one of them. I spent much of my time daydreaming, focusing on my grandiose plans for honour and glory as a hoplite soldier. There were times when my thoughts absorbed me utterly and my hands stilled. I would pick up my tools only when my father appeared and jerked me back to reality.

The other boys saw me as strange. They made fun of me, and avoided me whenever possible. They called me names, like Gorgon, after the hideous monster that lived at the edge of the world, or Cyclops, with its one eye bulging from its forehead. Silly names, yet hurtful, for I was self-conscious about my protruding eyes and unappealing features. I took to walking the old paths Crito and I had taken together, from the Strategeion, now nearing completion, to the Stoa Poikile, often called the Painted Porch for the beautiful scenes along its rear wall depicting the taking of Troy and the Battle of Marathon.

Invariably, I'd find myself in front of Crow Man. In my loneliness, I even said a few words to him. He'd preen himself in response — Crow Man being not much of a conversationalist.

Now and again I went to the gymnasium. I attempted nearly every athletic event: running, jumping, discus, javelin and boxing. I still lacked the coordination needed for most of these activities, but I had some success with wrestling; perhaps because I was low to the ground and thick limbed, with a strong grip. Over the years I improved so much that some began to say I might even take part in the Olympic games. That encouragement drove me to practice harder. I was becoming a good wrestler.

Once in a while, Lycon would also be at the gymnasium. Whenever I saw him arrive, I left quickly. In the years since our school days, he had turned into a brute. Big and tall, he possessed a cruel streak. He annoyed me every time I had the misfortune of running into him. He would greet me with, "Hello, ass," or ask if I'd played commonball recently, and then laugh uproariously at his own joke.

More than once I had seen Lycon deliberately trip up the little messengers who ran back and forth between politicians, merchants and the wealthy. Some little wisp of a boy, clutching a note tightly in his fist, or repeating a verbal message over and over to himself to make sure he re-layed it correctly, would suddenly find himself flat on his face, hands and knees bloody from the rocky ground, after Lycon had purposely extend-ed a well-timed foot. The cruel pranks were more than a youth's normal mischief, for I saw him doing it even as a grey-haired grandfather, pre-tending the mishap was accidental.

I recall a beautiful spring day when I was 16. I had just finished a wres-tling match by throwing my opponent and was feeling pleased with my-self — strong, capable, a winner — when I heard *his* voice: Lycon's. He had entered the gymnasium without my noticing, and now challenged me to a fight. I felt suddenly nauseous. Along one side of the gymna-sium, slaves were bathing athletes or rubbing their shoulders with olive oil. Sensing that all eyes were on me, I told Lycon I had just injured my-self and was, therefore, unable to wrestle again.

Standing there, covered in sand from the wrestling pit, I was sure that everyone, men and slaves, must have guessed the truth: I was afraid. Whenever I was around Lycon I felt like a schoolboy again, as if I were still the awkward, inept seven-year-old I had once been. In front of all of those eyes, Lycon taunted me and tried to provoke me. His high-pitched laughter followed me as I left the gymnasium.

Furious with myself for being afraid, I reproached myself all the way home. I arrived at an empty house; my father and Diotima were not about. Alone and angry, I found myself drawn to the timber door to my father's andron. Over the years, I had so often visited Thespis's andron, as well as those of Crito's relatives. Only my father's andron was forbid-den to me. That day, the exclusion added fuel to my anger.

Going to the andron, I fingered the leather lock my father used to keep the door sealed. Something about it taunted me, mocked me, tempted me. "I shouldn't do this," I told myself, knowing my father might return at any moment. But anger was stronger than dull reasoning. Kneeling, so that the lock was at eye level, I studied it carefully, memorizing the twists and turns of the leather strip. I held back until I could resist no longer.

Still covered in the sand of the wrestling pit, I wiped my hands on my tunic, grabbed one end of the leather strip and pushed it backward through the first loop. That done, I felt compelled to undo the lock completely.

My heart beat unbearably fast as I opened the door to the andron. My first impression was darkness, until my eyes grew used to the dim light and I was able to look around me. The room was tidy. Along a far wall were two couches with small tables nearby. A rectangular pillar of limestone, partly concealed by a large blanket and about the same height as me, stood by one of the couches. As my eyes grew even more accustomed to the dimness, I saw that a mosaic of a man on a galloping horse covered the floor. A lamp and a collection of small hammers, chisels and points used for detailed work were on a table by the pillar.

Feeling even braver now, I lifted the cloth from the pillar and saw a roughly cut head and torso topping it. Along the third wall of the room stood three more blanket-covered limestone pillars. Removing their blankets, I saw three more statues. The statues were identical in that all were exquisite carvings of Hermes, bearing my father's initials.

Awestruck, barely able to believe what I was seeing, I gazed at them. I knew that nowhere, not in front of any temple or gymnasium, not on any street corner or at any courtyard entrance, would I find herms made with more skill and care. For the first time, I realized what my mother had meant by saying my father was making his own luck, for Hermes is, among other things, the God of Luck.

As I stepped back to admire the herms, I noticed other objects hanging on the far wall. Walking over to look at them more closely, I saw a crescent-shaped wicker shield covered in goatskin and two javelins. Peltast equipment. Pathetic-looking gear, at that.

Of course! Realization set in suddenly, sickeningly. How could I not have known? I would be expected to provide my own equipment for battle. Hoplite armour has always been extremely expensive. Even prosperous families passed armour from father to son. One-eyed Acron and the other stonemasons were correct — I would never be a hoplite. Respect, admiration and glory were not in my future. My name would be forgotten. I would spend the rest of my life as a stonemason, covered in dust and coughing up black phlegm.

DAY 8

I WONDER, LAMPROCLES AND Sophroniscus, how much you two remember of your first day at the military academy? Not long ago — just a few years, really — I saw you put your names on the register before walking, seemingly bravely, into the barracks. Did you know that I saw the fear in your eyes as you left the safety of your home and entered that unknown world? I have been on the battlefield three times. I recognize the look of fear.

Although I attended the academy more than 50 years ago, I recall vividly each and every moment of my time there. Menexenus, have you heard many stories from your older brothers? If not, let me tell you mine — for your time, too, will soon come.

To my great relief, my father had never shown any sign that he knew of my earlier intrusion into his sacrosanct space. The morning I left for the academy, with the dew heavy on the grass, he finally permitted me to enter. When he called me to the andron, both his manner and his words were ceremonious, as if he were honouring me.

A year had passed since I had broken into the andron and seen what my future held. At the time, the room had held three blanket-covered herms, as well as one yet unfinished. On the day of my entrance into the academy, the number of herms had grown to four. Pointedly ignoring the covered sculptures, my father lifted the crescent-shaped wicker shield and the two javelins from the wall.

"Put it on," he said, handing me the shield.

I felt despondent as I fumbled with the pelte shield, trying to get my left arm through the strap and my hand onto the grip near the rim. My father watched me in silence for a few moments before cursing and wrenching the shield from me.

"Like this," he said irritably, shoving my forearm through the strap. "Now, clench the handgrip." He thrust one of the javelins into my right hand and forced open the fingers of my left hand, trying to get me to grasp both the shield's handgrip and the reserve javelin.

"Carry the javelin in your right hand," he instructed, "like this when in formation, like this when charging the enemy and like this to throw." He demonstrated the various moves as he spoke. "Understand?"

Unfortunately, my father's hand had moved so quickly from one position to another that I was unable to follow his instructions. I would have liked to have asked him to repeat them, but feared he would only get more exasperated. As we left the andron, he carefully retied the lock.

Given the momentous occasion, I had expected my father to accompany me to the barracks, but he refused, saying it would not look good. He and Diotima seemed content to bid me farewell at the courtyard door. I found myself blinking back tears as I said goodbye to my beloved Diotima, who had always taken such good care of me. I wondered when I would see her again. She must have sensed my unhappiness, for she took the opportunity to tell me one of her fables — her way of telling me things would be okay. Between my father and me, no emotion passed whatsoever.

I felt embarrassed as I walked away from the house. Even for a peltast, I was poorly equipped. No leather tunic, no cap or boots. How would others at the academy regard me? In no hurry to begin my training, I stopped at my mother's gravesite. A single honey cake lay by the grave, left by Diotima, I guessed. "I'm sorry, Mama," I said, lifting up the wicker shield, as if she could actually see it. In this way, I let her know that I would not, after all, achieve the greatness she had foretold for me.

Leaving the grave, I made my way to the barracks reluctantly. My heart beat faster as I drew nearer, and my hands grew slippery with sweat. From a distance, I saw hundreds of boys who had arrived before me, most of them accompanied by their fathers and their slaves. Clad as they were in a wide variety of armour, it was easy to tell the wealthy boys from the poor. The wealthy had their hoplon shields, long spears and bronze breastplates. Others, like me, had only shields and javelins. The poorest had no armour or weapons at all.

I joined a line forming near the doors. A man at the front asked my name. I said, "Socrates, son of Sophroniscus."

He referred to a roll of papyrus before him then looked up at me, motioned toward the barracks, and said, "Welcome to Hades, kid. Join the others and find yourself a cot."

The barracks were already crowded and I was relieved to find a vacant cot. Uncertain what to do, I placed my shield and javelin on the cot then stood there, looking around and waiting for directions. More boys entered the barracks and tried to get settled amidst much confusion and noise. Most did not know how to handle their weapons in close confines, resulting in much banging and crashing and calls to take care.

All at once, I spotted Crito at the far end of the barracks. More than two years had passed since our last contact. He had grown considerably since then. Tall and well muscled, with thick eyebrows, short hair and the start of a fine beard, he wore the hoplite armour we had played with as boys. It fit him well. Holding his helmet in one hand, and with his shield flung across his back, Crito resembled a hero as he spoke with a group of other boys, all dressed, like him, in full hoplite gear.

Feeling like a stranger, I averted my eyes when I sensed him looking my way. Crito wanted nothing to do with me, I thought. But I was wrong, for a short time later he left the group and approached me.

"Socrates, it's good to see you. How are you?" he asked. Somewhat reluctantly, I replied that I was well and eager to start training. I asked after Crito's mother and sisters and he inquired about my father's health. We spoke about the weather. The conversation was strained.

When we'd exhausted all small talk, Crito apologized for neglecting to see me for so long. As graciously as I could, I told him I understood; between grieving the loss of his father and taking up the duties of caring for the family business, life must have been difficult for him. Crito only nodded. A long silence ensued. I felt certain my friend was embarrassed to be seen with me, a lowly future peltast. I wondered why he had even deigned to greet me.

To fill the silence that was fast becoming awkward, I said, "You're going to be a hoplite. Just as we used to dream of."

"Yes," he said quietly, seeming ill at ease as he stood there, looking down at the ground. He glanced briefly in the direction of the boys he'd been speaking with, and I noticed they were looking in our direction and talking behind their hands. Were they making fun of me? I felt hurt, and angry with Crito.

"I'll let you get back to your friends," I said, making a show of rearranging my possessions.

"No, wait, Socrates. I have something for you," Crito said, and bade me accompany him across the barracks. Gathered around his cot, his companions were admiring a glorious set of armour consisting of a Corinthian helmet, a bronze breastplate in the shape of a muscled chest, greaves and a hoplon shield. All new and clearly expensive: 1,000 drachmas at least, I thought enviously.

"Very nice," I said lightly, wondering why Crito needed two sets of armour. In case one set became damaged, perhaps?

"This is for you," Crito said.

I stared at him. "What do you mean?"

"The armour. And weapons, too — they're outside."

"I don't understand," I said warily. Had my friend lost his mind?

"This is yours, Socrates." No sign of madness in the steady tone.

"I cannot… You… No…" I was stammering.

"Yes, Socrates — a gift from my father."

I could only shake my head in disbelief. "It's not possible," I protested when I could speak again. "Your father — "

"You really don't understand," Crito interrupted. "My father had the armour made for you before he died. It was his wish that you should have a set. I forgot about it until now. I apologize. I really should have told you, but as you said yourself, my life has been so busy with different obligations. Try it on, Socrates. If it needs adjusting, I'll have it done." He seemed to want to say more, but for some reason he was unable to.

I did not argue. I could not. I wanted the armour so badly. I hungered for it. I was greedy for it. As if they were my slaves, the other boys started to dress me. To my astonishment, the breastplate fit well around my chest and abdomen. The greaves were a little tight around my thick calves, but that did not matter for I was happy to have them.

"You look good," my friend said. "There's also a box for you to store it all in. I'll have it brought to you."

"Thank you, Crito. Thank you so much." I spoke jerkily, still in shock at my unbelievable good fortune.

"Thank my father," came his only response.

In a daze, I returned to my cot. Wanting to look properly at the armour, I took it off and arranged it on my bed. Crito's slaves appeared with an olive-wood chest — the one that sits in our andron now — which they placed at the foot of my bed. At my request, they agreed to return the pelte shield and the javelins to my father. For the rest of the morning, I did nothing but stare in wonder at the most beautiful things I had ever seen.

Once everyone had registered for training our cohort was called to the front of the barracks, where we were arranged in two long rows and ordered to march. Men, women and children stopped to watch us parade through the streets. Even without my hoplite armour, I was proud and held my head high. Now and then I glimpsed Crito ahead of me. For some reason, he appeared downhearted as he marched with his head bowed low and his back bent. *Is he thinking about his father?* I wondered. The father he had adored, and who had not lived to see his son become a citizen.

Below the eastern wall of the Acropolis, at the dark cave of Aglauros, we were ordered to halt. Silence fell as a man emerged from the cave, a handsome man with his hair and full beard closely trimmed. We recognized him immediately as Pericles, the most powerful and influential man in Athens. We barely breathed as we waited for him to address us.

"Thirty years ago, word reached Athens that the Persian Empire was preparing to invade Greece," he began, his voice clear and strong. "The brave citizens of Athens were not overly concerned, for we had bested the Persians at the Battle of Marathon, slaughtering them and pushing them back across the seas.

"Nevertheless, prudent as always, the assembly sent out scouts to confirm the information. And yes, it was true. King Xerxes of Persia was preparing to invade Athens. Only this time, the Persians were amassing the biggest army the world had ever seen. A contingent was sent in great haste to Delphi, to consult with the Oracle, the voice of Apollo, God of Truth, Prophecy and Light. The Oracle cried out ominously, 'Your statues shiver with dread. Black blood drips from the highest rooftops. Evil marches upon you. Miserable things are on the way. Get out! Get out of my sanctum and drown your spirits in woe!' These frightening words were brought back to Athens.

"The prophecy caused terror, and another contingent was sent back to the Oracle to learn whether anything could be done. This time the Oracle gave a solution. She said, 'A wall of wood alone shall be uncaptured.' She also repeated her first message. 'Await not the coming of the horses, the marching feet, the armed host upon the land. Slip away. Turn your backs. You will meet in battle anyway. Island of Salamis, you will be the death of many a woman's son between seed time and the harvest of the grain.'

"Back in Athens, General Themistocles argued that the wall of wood referred to the Athenian navy, and that the Island of Salamis would be the death of the Persians, not the Athenians. He asked the Assembly to vote on building up the fleet. He also recommended evacuating the city before it was too late. Although a decision was made to construct the fleet, the move of the citizens out of Athens was delayed.

"That summer, King Xerxes marched his army through Thrace and Macedon, past Mount Olympus, home of the gods themselves, and into Thessaly. The Persians burned everything in their path, including the temples. They raped every woman they encountered and hacked off the heads of every Greek man and child, even those who surrendered. Xerxes could not be stopped. The Persian army was soon at Athens' doorstep.

"The Athenian assembly finally came to see the wisdom of Themistocles' advice to evacuate the city, but, as the Oracle had warned, it was too late. Soon the Persians would reach the city; Athens could not be emptied quickly enough. Nonetheless, we tried our best in a race for our lives. Every ship was appropriated. Every available man was drafted to help in the evacuation. People were ordered to leave behind all they owned. No tableware, lamps, looms, glass bowls, pots, ladles, statues, toys or vases would be allowed on board the vessels. Only human cargo would sail.

"I was a lad of 14 at the time. I can still recall women, children and old men marching to Piraeus, there to be loaded onto the ships that would take them across the Saronic Gulf to the city of Troezen. People wept openly as they left behind their husbands, sons and fathers. I was shipped to Salamis on a warship. I recall vividly the crash of the oars in the water and the chanting of the rowers as they pulled in a steady rhythm. Looking back across the ship's deck, I was shaken to see loyal dogs swimming across the gulf after their masters, only to drown from exhaustion. Along the horizon, smoke was thick and dark against the blue sky. Xerxes was burning everything.

"Suddenly, I saw them — flowing like a stream of ants over every hill and valley. Endless numbers of Persians. A host so great, it took 14 days from the arrival of the first cavalry to the appearance of the final baggage cart. As the advance guard of the Persians came closer and closer, I realized the last of our soldiers would never make it.

Unbeknownst to me, however, a cohort of young men, most of them not much older than you, had volunteered to stay behind. Their aim was to buy enough time so that every citizen could be gotten to Salamis safely. That group, numbering just 500 strong, a number nearly equal to yours, bade the others farewell and marched from Piraeus back to Athens.

"They went directly to the Acropolis. The men barricaded the stone gateway with doors and beams. Once ensconced on the Acropolis, they drew the Persians' attention. The ruse worked; the Persians were lured to the citadel while the last of the Athenians boarded the ships. At first, Persian archers shot flaming arrows into the wooden enclosure. They had tied hemp dipped in pine resin to the tips of their arrows, and the wood burned. The smell of smoke cut through the salt air. In defence, our soldiers rolled stones onto the advancing Persians, managing to hold them off for two days. But finally, the Persians found a way up an unguarded slope that those on the hill had imagined was too steep to climb. There, the Persians scaled the Acropolis and broke through our last line of defence.

"Reaching the summit, they overwhelmed our men and destroyed the citadel. Every building was looted and burned, every temple razed to the ground, every sanctuary desecrated.

That battle does not immediately bring glory to mind, for it did not appear to be a victory. But, men, make no mistake, what a victory it was! Because those men inspired us on the narrow straits during the Battle of Salamis. They heartened us in the fields during the Battle of Plataea. They spurred us on at the Battle of Mycale. They knew the meaning of duty, responsibility and obligation. The duty to fight for those who fought before us and who are unable to do so now. To fight for our mothers and sisters, for our grandmothers and aunts. To fight for the many who are still to come. No monument was ever erected in their honour, for this cave is their tombstone as well as their shrine."

Pericles paused a few moments, allowing us to absorb the story he had told us. Then he said solemnly, "Now, on this momentous day, a day you will remember your entire lives, I call on you to take an oath. An oath to protect the laws and citizens of this city!

"Repeat after me," he called out. "We will never bring disgrace on our city by an act of dishonesty or cowardice. We will fight for the ideals and sacred things of the city, both alone and with the many. We will revere and obey the city's laws. We will strive to heighten the public's sense of civic duty. Thus, in all these ways, we will transform the city and make it even greater and more beautiful than it was before."

Pericles spoke with authority, and although we were only boys, we listened intently before repeating every word of the vow solemnly, as if the gods themselves were judging us. When we had finished, we continued to stand at attention while Pericles surveyed us. His eye fell on me as he spoke the next words, and it seemed as though they were meant just for me. My heart pounded.

"I can see," Pericles said, "as I look upon you, that you will make this greatest of cities proud. I see resolve in your eyes. I see strength in the clench of your jaws. I see, in the uprightness of your stance, men who will be true to the vow they have spoken. For you are now men of Athens!"

As if possessed of one voice, we all cheered, "Hurrah." And then a chill went down my spine. For the first time since my mother's death, I felt special. I looked over at Crito and saw him smile. Whatever had been bothering him earlier was, for the moment at least, forgotten.

DAY 9

T HIS AFTERNOON I had a horrible mishap — I knocked over my chamber pot. *Can you imagine the disaster?* Smelly waste everywhere. I asked the day guard for help, but he only advised me to get used to it. Thankfully, as I think I've mentioned before, my cell is cool during this unseasonably hot spring, and so the stench was not quite as bad as it might have been. Great thanks are due to our rooster — he took mercy on me tonight and cleaned up the disgusting mess. Strange, how often my stories involve similar incidents... like the time your mother... but that story can wait, I'll get to it soon enough. In the meanwhile, the chamber pot reminds me of another story.

On our second day at the academy, the day after our induction, our instructors kicked us awake early in the morning. Those who did not get out of bed quickly enough were doused with the contents of a full chamber pot — mercifully, only water. Following a cold breakfast, our cohort was separated into hoplites and peltasts. The sun was just rising when we were ordered to bring out our armour and were taught how to put it on without help. Wearing it, I felt proud as a king. Our instructors, mostly old soldiers, allowed us to clash our shields, one against another. By then, Crito and I had picked up our former friendship as if the years apart had never occurred, and we laughed cheerfully as we tried to knock each other down. Thespis had told us the academy would be hard work — but this was fun. *Little did we know!*

With everyone fitted out properly, we were assembled in rows and ordered to walk up and down the training field. I found myself tiring quickly. The bronze breastplate was so heavy that I felt like Atlas, burdened with the weight of the heavens on my shoulders. Carrying the shield was like holding a sack of corn at arm's length, and it was hard to breathe in the fully enclosed Corinthian helmet. Around me, the other boys were also breathing heavily and with effort. Some were even unable to carry the heavy shields more than a few steps, before lowering them onto the ground.

"Pick up your shields! Up!" yelled the old soldiers fiercely.

For the first time, I noticed scars on the arms and thighs of our instructors — battle wounds from where they were not protected by armour. They would show us no mercy, I realized. I willed myself to keep a steady pace, just as if I were back at the wall, shaping stone. I struggled to grip my shield with hands that had grown slippery. The helmet was stifling in the heat; sweat dripped from my nose and trickled down my forehead and into my eyes.

"When can we stop?" one of the boys asked pleadingly.

The scarred old soldiers did not respond. If a trainee paused to rest, he was screamed at until he got going again. Anyone idle for too long was subjected to punches and kicks. I don't recall exactly how long the ordeal lasted, only that by the time we were allowed to rest, three quarters of the boys lay sprawled on the ground. There weren't enough soldiers to abuse them all. The rest period was short; after a meal, we were ordered to march once more. Only about 20 of us remained standing when a halt was called for the day.

Physically exhausted though I was, my racing mind kept me from sleep that night. For as long as I could remember, I had dreamed of being a hoplite soldier, yet now I did not know if I had the strength to survive the training. Glory — if it existed at all — seemed far in the future. Judging by the stifled weeping all around me in the barracks, many others shared my despair.

Next day our training continued. I soon realized that some of the boys were just that: boys. Arriving at the academy, I had been blinded by the shine of helmets and shields, but now I was able to see beyond the armour. Many of my fellow trainees were pale and scrawny. Few even had whiskers on their chins.

During one long training session, a tall, thin, uncoordinated boy stumbled and fell near me, but was able to get to his feet without being yelled at. Not long afterward he stumbled again, and once more he managed to stand. Over and over, he fell from exhaustion, only to struggle up each time. Finally, he could not get to his feet after stumbling.

Admiring the effort he had displayed, and desirous of preventing the old soldiers from striking him, I ran over to him quickly and helped him to his feet. He looked at me gratefully. Concerned lest he collapse again, I put my spear arm under his shield arm, and walked in step with him. I noticed the old soldiers staring at me and was nervous when one of them advanced on me. He called for the cohort to halt and be silent, and then addressed us all.

"Stand by one another and fewer will die," he admonished. "Get to know your fellow hoplites, so they won't fail you."

The advice brought startled looks, but the lesson sank in. We were all in this situation together.

When not in physical training we sat through civics lessons, which I liked. I was easily the least educated of the future hoplites — all of the others had completed their public schooling. Many had even been privileged to have private tuition before attending the academy. Among these boys I felt very stupid. Although their conversation was not that of grown men discussing the nuances of a bill or a law, the words that slipped so easily from their lips were far beyond my understanding. For one thing, they already knew about the Assembly, the Council of Five Hundred and the Fathers of Athenian democracy. At work on the wall, my fellow stonemasons had talked only of things like the weather and the winners of the Olympic Games, or had entertained one another with bawdy stories about the prostitutes in the Kerameikos.

"Athens is like nowhere else in the world," our instructor told us. "Neither kings nor the wealthy control our city. Thanks to far-seeing men, the people organize our rule. Power is retained in the hands of Athenian-born men and we are sovereigns of our own affairs. After your time at the academy and your two years of military service, you will all be citizens of Athens. Regardless of your status, whether your fathers are generals or artisans, you will be expected to take part in the Assembly."

I learned that the Assembly met about 40 times a year. A quorum of 5,000 citizens was required before decisions could be made. The Assembly voted on issues such as laws, ostracisms and whether the city would go to war. It was also responsible for the yearly election of the 10 generals who managed the army and the navy.

"On reaching the age of 30, you will take part in the Council of Five Hundred," the lecture continued. "This council of 500 citizens is responsible for the day-to-day administration of the city. Its members serve for a year, putting into effect the decisions made by the Assembly."

All this information was new and interesting to me, but those who knew it already were clearly bored. Suddenly, someone passed wind loudly. Everyone laughed and looked in the direction of the offending noise. The culprit was Chaerephon, the boy I had helped on the field. The instructor called for silence and we quieted down immediately. Upon induction, we had been warned that bad behaviour would not be tolerated and we knew the penalties for misdeeds. But before the instructor could continue, Chaerephon broke wind again. His punishment was to spend the rest of the day marching around the grounds in full gear.

I had come to know Chaerephon since helping him. His family was even wealthier than Crito's. They owned many slaves whom they rented out to mine the silver at Laurium, south of Athens. Although gangly, with wild, dark hair, deep-set brown eyes, an untidy way of dressing and a generally slovenly image, Chaerephon was well liked at the academy. Generous with his obols, he was always ready to treat a person to a drink or a meal, which made him popular. He had no ulterior motive for doing these things; he was just naturally giving and had a great love of fun.

Chaerephon was the epitome of spontaneity. He liked a good joke at someone else's expense, but was no prankster. In many ways, his antics were like those of an irrepressible 10-year-old rather than an adult. His behaviour, so often preposterous and irresponsible — like relieving himself on your leg, or grabbing a handful of animal excrement from the field and hurling it at the person closest to him — made him the centre of attention, which he thoroughly enjoyed. It was said that his school grammatiste had a habit of placing a rock on his lap to keep him from moving about in his seat. I could well understand why a teacher would need to resort to such action, for he was always full of energy. He eventually grew out of these youthful shenanigans, but the impulsiveness remained his entire life.

Not only was Chaerephon rash, but he appeared fearless as well. If a volunteer was asked for, Chaerephon stepped forward without hesitation. He did so despite knowing that, more often than not, the old soldiers would clobber him when they demonstrated a new weapons move. Looking back now, after a lifetime's friendship, I realize that his most outstanding attribute was his extreme optimism.

Chaerephon's enthusiasms were contagious. One night, not long after his smelly offence in the classroom, a few of us joined him on a late-night kitchen raid. Crito came with us, which was surprising, because he was a person of rigid control, hardly ever behaving improperly or inappropriately. That he joined us this time shows Chaerephon's effect on us all. We knew there would be trouble if we were caught outside the barracks at night, but we followed Chaerephon, anyway.

As we rummaged about for something to eat, Crito took a bag of salt and mixed it with a little water in a jug. He carried the container onto our practice field and poured the mixture onto the grass. He didn't respond when I asked what he was doing, just looked at me with an impish grin. As Crito dumped the last of the jug's contents onto the grass, Chaerephon began to yell, "What are you doing? Why are you out of your beds?"

His voice was loud, piercing the silence of the night. Fearfully, we all ran to the barracks, leaping hurriedly into our cots just as an old soldier appeared. In the light of the lamp he carried, his face was grim with the look of a man determined to get to the bottom of the antics. Ordering us to stand beside our beds, he questioned the entire barracks. "If nobody confesses," he shouted, "this whole group will run all night." I regretted my own part in the caper, but was frightened, and remained as silent as my fellow culprits — with the exception of Chaerephon. Without hesitation, he stepped forward and confessed.

"Who else was out there?" asked our interlocutor.

"Nobody, only me," Chaerephon replied quickly, before any of us could say a word. "I was the only one."

Chaerephon's punishment was to be tied to a column on the field stoa for the remainder of the night. Although he had brought the soldier's wrath down on us in the first place, we all appreciated the sacrifice of his confession. Within a few days, the grass on the training field began to turn brown. Soon the patch was completely dead, shaped like a phallus and as long as a four-horse chariot. Enraged at the sight of the giant organ, the soldiers had Chaerephon tied to a column again, this time for a whole day in the hot sun. To his credit, Chaerephon never betrayed Crito. The grass remained scorched in the same shape for years afterward. Some still call it Phallus Field.

A month into our training, the daily physical conditioning was reduced and we began weapon and shield drills.

"You are a slave to your spear," taught our instructor. "It is your master. Never throw your spear! Even if you are routed, you will keep it with you. It dies with you."

The instructors showed us how to employ underhand and overhand grips, depending on the situation, and the amount of leverage each required. They were surprisingly patient with us, far more so than my father had been when he'd shown me how to hold the javelin. Then they lined us up side by side in order to demonstrate the way in which the shields should overlap to form a shield wall. It was exactly as Thespis had shown Crito and me so many years earlier. It made me feel good to know something before it was taught.

Another lesson: "You wear a breastplate and helmet for yourself. You carry a shield for the benefit of the whole line. An unbroken shield wall is almost impenetrable."

Facing one another in rows of 24, we clashed without our spears. When we were successful at keeping our line together during a shield push, the soldiers gave us our weapons to practice fighting at spear length.

"Show the enemy no fear," they shouted. "A man with a front wound will receive honour, for he died facing his opponent. Never turn. The enemy must turn first; it's easy to pierce the back of a fleeing man."

As Thespis had warned, my time at the academy was difficult. I had been pushed to the very limits of my strength, and then been punched, kicked and bullied to continue. Without Crito and Chaerephon, I don't know if I'd have survived. Chaerephon's antics brought sorely needed humour to alleviate the seriousness, while Crito delivered leadership.

Crito was strong and swift, a model to all. I never saw him fall in exhaustion, drop his spear or lose his footing during a shield push. He was easily the most skilled person at the academy. Every time I felt like giving up, I would look for him. The sight of Crito's grim determination to push through would inspire me. Thespis would have been proud of his son.

Not only did Crito lead us during battle exercises, he led us off the field, too. Many of the hoplite students were unfriendly, even hostile, to our peltast classmates. Not Crito. He had taken to heart the old soldier's advice for us to stand by one another. He got to know nearly all the 498 students personally and treated them with courtesy, particularly those who were unaccustomed to civil treatment. Single-handedly, he changed the attitude of the entire cohort. Before long, boys whose families were as wealthy and powerful as Crito's, perhaps even more so, tried all the harder to conduct themselves well to impress him.

I believe, my sons, that Crito could have been a great leader, the kind of man who would have made life better for citizens and non-citizens alike. Unfortunately for Athens, Crito never chose to put himself forward in the Assembly.

After 60 days of training, by which time I felt broken both physically and mentally, the day finally came to present ourselves to the Assembly. Our cohort was called out in front of the barracks one fine summer morning. Clad in full equipment, hoplites and peltasts stood and listened to a speech by an old soldier. His lecture ended, he began to announce our positions in the phalanx.

I thought I had a fairly good chance of making the front line, for thanks to years of working with stone I had built up more strength than many of the others and was usually one of the last standing during fitness drills. At weapons drills I had held my own. But I wasn't confident that I was the very best. I could only hope that effort counted as much as skill.

Due to our numbers, our hoplite phalanx would be 24 men wide and eight deep. The front line was announced first. I held my breath as names were called out, counting as each boy went to the front and took his position. Not one smiled. This was not a time for joy; rather, it was time to show one's sternness as a soldier.

By the time the old soldier had called out 19 names, and with only five positions left open, my hope of making the front line had faded. I could not compete with the tallest, the strongest, the most skilled, who would probably take up the remaining spots. In my disappointment, I had almost stopped listening, when I heard Crito's name called. Crito was our leader, so, of course he would be first of the line. I was consoling myself with the idea of being in the second line, when the old soldier said, "And the first of the line, the most honoured position in the phalanx, goes to Socrates."

It took an age for his words to register. I thought it must be a joke, or perhaps a dream. I couldn't possibly be first of the line. Glancing around, I saw that all eyes were on me. Hesitantly, I stepped forward. When no one reproached me I took another step, and then another, until I found myself beside Crito as the first of the line.

When the rest of the ranks had been ordered, we were led from the barracks. Men, women and children applauded as we marched through the city. We paraded around the Acropolis, past the agora and up the slope toward the Pnyx hill, where the Assembly gathered. Along the way, I spotted Diotima, smiling and waving. I longed to smile back at her, but I kept my eyes forward and my demeanour stern. Not that it mattered; she could not have seen my expression through my shielded helmet.

Ahead of us, we heard the murmur of thousands of men. As we crested the rocky hill and passed through the trees to the top of the Pnyx hill, the murmurs died and the citizens attending the Assembly parted to allow us entry. Through the silent crowd I led my cohort, past the ring of archers and up the speaker's platform, where I stopped, as I'd been instructed. I wondered briefly about the role of the archers — were they purely ceremonial or were they needed to quell an unruly assembly?

As I waited for my cohort to take their places behind me, Pericles mounted the platform and stood at my left, almost as if I were holding my shield to protect him. My heart beat very fast as he bent toward me and put his hand on my shoulder.

"I'm proud of you," he whispered into my ear.

Proud of me! How I had longed to hear these words. The first citizen of Athens, the most powerful and respected man in the city, was proud of me! In my elation, I felt as though I could float away on the breeze.

Once my cohort had been arranged, two pigs were sacrificed. The animals were still bleeding as they were carried around, their blood sprinkling and purifying the Assembly grounds. When the last of the blood had drained from the pigs, a herald stepped onto the speaker's platform. In a loud voice he prayed for Zeus's justice, Athena's wisdom and Apollo's foresight. He then called down curses on anyone who would mislead the Assembly. Finally, he asked, "Who wishes to speak?" Beside me, Pericles said, "I do," and took a step forward.

He addressed the gathering: "Men of the Assembly! Citizens of Athens! I present to you the next generation of Athenian defenders!"

The Assembly broke into a deafening cheer, the likes of which I had never heard before and would not hear again until years later, when Alcibiades reached his heights. Pericles waited for the cheering to end before he continued. He related the history of Athens and referred to our future responsibilities.

As he spoke, I stared across the Assembly. From the speaker's platform I had an unobstructed view. I saw family members — fathers, grandfathers and uncles — lifting their hands to attract the attention of their newly graduated kin. In a kind of despair, I searched the crowd for the one man I wanted so badly to see. I willed myself to find him. When I failed to see him, I told myself that one person would be easy to miss among so many.

Finally, having finished his oration, Pericles raised his voice. "Do you declare these men ready for military duty?" Every arm stretched up high. More than 5,000 of our fellow citizens cheered loudly again, as they voted their assent.

I should have enjoyed the moment, should have taken pride in the fact that not only was I now a trained soldier, but through hard work and determination I had earned the coveted position of first of the line. I should have looked forward to all that lay ahead. I was a hoplite. I would win renown in battle and make my name known throughout Greece, thereby fulfilling my mother's vision. But the moment of triumph was marred — because the one person whose respect I most desired, whose presence I most needed to witness my accomplishment, was absent. That person was my father.

Our first posting was with the Athenian garrison. To my delight, the friendship between Crito, Chaerephon and me continued. We spent all our off-duty time together, eating and exercising, visiting the Kerameikos, wandering through the market in the agora and also gambling.

During our second year of military service, our friendship grew even stronger. We were posted to the fort at Oenoe, a long day's march from the walls of Athens. There was much less to do at the fort than in the city — no cockfighting or sporting events to watch — so we went hiking in the hills, tramping as far as Plataea.

I was somewhat hesitant about having Chaerephon accompany us on these outings, as I doubted he would appreciate the seriousness of a visit to such an important spot in Athenian history, especially one to which Crito was connected through his father. Crito still missed his father very much and I was anxious lest Chaerephon upset him by making light of the Battle of Plataea.

But I need not have worried, for Chaerephon knew nearly as much about the battle as I had learned from Thespis. He spoke with astonishing veneration and solemnity about the gods and the role they had played in delivering the victory to Athens. Chaerephon had always given the impression of being a buffoon, a kind-hearted buffoon, but a buffoon, nonetheless. Slowly, I discovered that there was far more to him than his entertaining impulses.

Apart from hiking, we also experimented with other activities to ease our boredom. We tried to hunt, going in search of deer and boar. Occasionally, we saw potential targets, but were never close enough to strike.

During one such unsuccessful attempt, I saw a true predator perform. We were at the top of a hill one day, looking down onto a treeless valley, when Crito spotted a long-legged golden jackal. We heard the jackals constantly, their plaintive wailing waking us almost every morning and announcing the end of the day at dusk. This particular jackal was trotting along, seemingly aimless, stopping now and then to listen, pointing its muzzle to sniff. All at once, it caught sight of something in the deep grass. Staying out of sight, it crouched low before moving again, slowly, cautiously, toward its prey. Awed, I observed its stealth, the way in which it barely disturbed the grass while closing in on its victim. Suddenly, it darted forward and pounced, emerging from the tall grass moments later with a grouse in its jaws.

I kept watch for these sly predators after that. Jackals are essentially solitary creatures that defend their territory from others of their kind. When they feel threatened, they flatten their ears against their skulls, bare their teeth and snap viciously at any intruder. Only once, did I see two jackals working together, running in parallel to a small deer, as if corralling it. After a long chase, the deer was exhausted and the pair jumped on it simultaneously.

With little to do at the fort, the men often indulged in conversation. I enjoyed listening to them. My education at the academy had stimulated my appetite for knowledge and I was hungry to learn more. Not wanting to reveal my ignorance, I kept my mouth shut and listened intently whenever Crito, Chaerephon or one of the others spoke of their lessons in subjects such as mathematics, rhetoric and animal husbandry. There was much idle talk, too, for young men have a tendency to babble about anything — especially women, sports and drink. Yet there were also times when nobody spoke, creating a comfortable silence that made for friendly companionship.

After our two years of uneventful military service, we were free to return to Athens and our work. I was not as sad as I might have been when my service ended, for although I loved being around my friends, I looked forward to seeing Diotima and my father. I was now a man and a citizen. I would be allowed to eat with my father at mealtimes, instead of waiting until he was done.

You boys might not understand how important this was to me, for when you were young I always dined with you and your mother and Diotima. But my father was a traditional man who would not have dreamed of sharing his meal with a child. I pictured him taking me by the shoulders, looking into my eyes, and telling me he had missed me and that he loved and respected me. And I imagined him suggesting I display my armour in the andron.

Reality, as always, differed from my dreams. "A hoplite, huh?" said my father, when he saw me. His hair was fully grey now and his skin sagged at the jowls. I saw that the last two years had aged him.

"A hoplite, yes," I answered proudly. "First of the line, at that." I looked him in the eye, waiting for him to congratulate me.

But all he said was, "Well, there's work to be done on the Dipylon Gate. Speak to One-eyed Acron. He's in charge now."

And that was it. No "Well done" or "Good to see you, my son." No friendly conversation or expressions of pride. Just, "Get to work." I had been naïve to expect anything else.

I made the storage closet my room. I threw some straw on the floor for a bed, put away the olive wood chest containing my armour, then went to work at the gate. The andron still remained off limits to me.

My father had not changed, nor had I. I was as eager as always for battle and the glory that came with it. Slowly I came to realize that the chance to attain the greatness my mother had foreseen for me would have to wait. Athens had recently brokered a peace treaty with the Persians and arranged a truce with the Spartans. Of course, men being men, there were always discussions of war in the Assembly. Someone would claim that one city or another had insulted the honour of Athens, and that she must defend her interests.

How well I recall the first time I attended the Assembly after returning from the fort at Oenoe. I had expected order and courtesy, because the Assembly, with its ability to make decisions for the common good, was the pride of Athens, What I saw instead was chaos. Men ascended the speaker's platform to state their opinions but, too often, the clamour of the rabble, with their curses and accusations, drowned out the speakers' voices. They were like children in a school courtyard, constantly bickering with one another. It seemed to me that hardly anything worthwhile was accomplished.

One day, news came that the Spartans had blocked access to Delphi. Upon hearing this, the Assembly was stirred to action; the discussion was brisk and intense. Athens would return independence to Delphi. Although my cohort was not chosen for the fight, I watched as Pericles himself led a contingent out of the city.

Less than a month later, I arrived home from work to find a man leaning against a wall by the house. He was well dressed but dirty, as if he had been invited to a dinner party, only to find himself put to work digging a ditch instead. When he had introduced himself, he enquired whether I was Socrates, son of Sophroniscus. I confirmed that this was my name. His expression grew sad, and he sighed heavily.

Warily, I stared at him. I sensed something was amiss and felt a tightening inside me.

"Is Patrocles your brother?" he asked.

Since the day my brother had left, I had never stopped looking for him. I was forever expecting to see him on every street, around every corner. I lived in constant hope, even then, of being joyfully reunited with Patrocles.

"Yes! Where is he? Is he here?"

The man closed his eyes and rubbed his grimy forehead. "No," came the one-word response.

My tension grew.

It was a while before he continued. "Patrocles has been killed."

Instantly, I felt that too-familiar numbness descend upon me.

"When?" I demanded. "How?"

"A few days ago. An arrow wound."

"Where? Who killed him?"

"We were at Delphi," said the man. "A Spartan mercenary shot him."

"My brother was at Delphi?"

"He is… was… a peltast with my cohort."

"A peltast? For whom?"

The man looked at me in surprise. "Athens," he said, as if this were something I should have known. But it was taking some time for me to make sense of what I was hearing.

"He went to the academy?" I asked.

"Yes."

"You fought with Patrocles?"

"Yes, although I didn't know him by that name. To us, he was Ecphantus."

"*Ecphantus?*" I stared at him. "Why Ecphantus?"

Again, that look of surprise. "That is the name he gave when he signed up at the academy."

"I don't understand," I said.

The man explained that my brother had given himself a new name after leaving home so he would not be associated with my father. First he had gone to Thebes, in search of our mother's family, but he found no one related to her there. Returning to Athens, he found work at the port of Piraeus, building ship sheds. When he came of age, he joined the academy.

"He came with nothing. No armour, no weapons," continued the man. "He quickly showed himself to be the best, whether hurling a stone or firing a bow. The old soldiers were so impressed with him that they used their own funds to procure a new pelte shield and javelins for him. After his time at the academy, he returned to the shipyards until our cohort was chosen to defend Athenian interests at Delphi.

"The Spartans had already gone when we arrived at Delphi, but they had left behind a small force of mercenaries. When the mercenaries refused to engage us on the small plain in the valley, we dispatched our peltasts to engage them in the hills. Your brother led the group. An arrow pieced his stomach. Realizing he would not survive, he told me his story and requested that I find you."

Although I listened to everything the man said, I believed him mistaken. The person he spoke of could not have been Patrocles, for it was impossible for me to imagine him killed. "How can you be sure he was my brother?" I asked. "I find it impossible to believe he was living in Athens this whole time!"

The man passed a hand over his eyes. When he spoke again, his voice was low, a little rough. "I do not like to think of Ecphantus... I mean Patrocles... as gone, either. He was the finest man I knew. He volunteered for every assignment. He showed himself to be a man of daring. Be assured, if he had been a hoplite, he would have been first of the line — like you."

It took me a few seconds to absorb the last words. "He knew I made first of the line?" I asked in wonder.

The man nodded. "He saw you lead your cohort to the Pnyx hill and watched the Assembly cheer you. He was very proud of you."

"Why did he not seek me out?"

"He was ashamed of running away and abandoning you. He didn't have the courage to face you. He told me he loved you very much and he asked me to give you something."

He held out an object to me. Taking it, I saw it was the amulet my brother had always worn. The picture had deteriorated somewhat at the edges, perhaps the result of much handling, but the face was still visible — Eileithyia, the Goddess of Childbirth, my mother's patron goddess. On the other side of the amulet was an inscription I could not read. I began to weep.

"To punish the mercenaries for their sacrilege against Apollo, we threw them from the cliffs at Delphi. They all died," the man told me.

Did he imagine that this violent retribution could compensate for the loss of my brother? I composed myself before thanking him for bringing me the news.

When he had gone, I went inside, told Diotima the sad tidings and showed her the amulet. "I remember when your mother gave it to him," she said softly. Taking the amulet from my hand, she brushed it gently, as if touching the petals of a flower. Then she turned it over and touched the inscription.

"Do you know what it says?" I asked.

"It says, 'I love you,'" she answered sadly.

"Why did Mother not give me one, too?" I asked, thinking only about myself.

"You knew you were loved. Your brother did not," Diotima said, without taking her eyes from the amulet.

Her words made no sense to me. Of course, my brother was loved. My mother loved him, Diotima loved him, and I loved him. Even those who knew him only slightly were fond of Patrocles. He was kind and clever and fast. It was clear to anyone who had ever met him, that he would make something of himself.

I looked at Diotima. "What do you mean?"

"Patrocles did not love himself and so he threw his life away," Diotima said. Then she put the amulet back into my hand, curled my fingers around it, and walked very slowly into the kitchen. I saw that she was brokenhearted.

Later that evening, I told my father about Patrocles' death. He listened in silence. Afterwards, he went to his andron and carved away at his blocks of stone.

DAY 10

D O YOU BOYS recall our hikes up Mount Penteli? When it was time for you to apprentice yourselves to me, I took each of you up there in turn. For some reason, I thought it important that you see the spot where the Pentelic marble, used in so many statues and buildings, originated.

It may have been a drudge for you boys to spend time with your father instead of your friends, but I have fond memories of our hikes. On the day before our departure, I would have my hair and beard trimmed by a barber in the agora. On the morning of the hike, I dressed as formally as if I were planning to attend a dinner party. My normal custom was to go about the city barefoot, mostly to prove that I was as tough as a Spartan. For our hikes, though, I'd put on my best tunic, as well as the sandals that my old friend Simon made for me. I haven't mentioned Simon yet in this account, but I will.

Back to the hike: north through the city lanes we'd go, past the Acropolis rock with its magnificent buildings and then out through the Acharnian Gate. Once out of the city, we took a steady course northeastward, up the steep, rocky hill and through a forest of spruce, fir and pine trees. Along the way, I'd explain the uses of the marble from each quarry we passed. The best marble, naturally, was reserved for the great sculptures, like those created by Phidias for the Parthenon. That particular marble is white and flawless, with a hint of yellow that makes it look almost golden in the sunlight.

After you had listened attentively to all I told you, we would pause for something to eat and drink. As we rested we would look down at the city below us. I'd tell you boys what it would be like for us to work together, because I didn't want you to be surprised the way I was when I started to work with my own father. You had questions, but mostly you just listened and nodded. Sometimes I almost felt you were patronizing me, not uncaringly, but in a good way — as if you were thinking, *Here he goes again.* When I noticed your eyes begin to glaze over, I knew it was time to end the day.

Whenever I look up at Mount Penteli, I think mostly of those hikes. However, I also have less pleasant memories of the mountain. I recall a cool, cloudy day when I saw my brother's name, Ecphantus, the name he had used at the academy, inscribed on the wall of commemoration near the agora. I had expected to feel proud when I saw it, for Patrocles had answered the city's call and now his name would live forever. Yet there was nothing glorious for me about it.

After seeing that inscription, I was so overcome by emotion that I decided to climb Mount Penteli instead of going to work that morning. Reaching the peak, I found a rock and sat down. Below me, hundreds of slaves worked away with hammers, chisels and wedges, separating blocks of stone from the mountainside for transportation to the city.

Sitting there, I thought about my brother. In the 11 years that had gone by since I'd seen him last, I had clung to the hope that Patrocles would return to me, rich and famous as he had promised, and that we would be happy together. Instead, he had been in Piraeus all that time, only a short walk from where I had been slaving away on the long walls with my father. I could understand that Patrocles did not want to see my father, but why did he not want to see me? Had my brother been ashamed of me for some reason? And how about Diotima? Surely, he would have liked to have seen her again.

As the day wore on, the clouds grew thick and I lost sight of the city below. The sun went down; slaves finished work for the day. No city light penetrated the gloom. The air grew chilly and it began to rain. Alone in the darkness, wearing only my tunic, my wet hair was plastered to my face and I started to feel cold.

I told myself I would remain there on the mountain until I died of exposure. Not that I was actually serious about committing suicide, but I was filled with self-pity. As the temperature dropped and my body started to tremble from the cold, I stood up and trudged back down the dark mountainside. To this day, I associate loneliness with rain.

My reflections on the mountain did nothing to resolve my questions and grief. Needing to make sense of my pain, I decided to make a pilgrimage to Delphi to see where my brother had been killed. Chaerephon insisted on going with me. In no mood for his buffoonery, I didn't want him to join me, but as I didn't have the strength to refuse him, we travelled together.

Over steep hills and through deep valleys we walked. I hardly recall sleeping or eating. I took in so little, that I could not have said whether it was sunny or rainy, warm or cool. Perhaps Chaerephon regretted his decision to accompany me; indeed, he may have been bored and lonely, for I was sunk in a miasma of woe and, for a long time, literally did not speak a word.

It was awhile before I noticed other travellers on the road, from well-dressed men astride beautiful horses to slaves wearing only loincloths, from Spartan soldiers with long hair and red capes to Persians with dark skin and fine jewelry. Servants held umbrellas for the fair-skinned rich, and large families travelled together, dressed in simple white robes. I saw every colour of skin and hair, and all manner of footwear and clothing.

"So many people." I spoke for the first time since leaving Athens.

"Kings, merchants, farmers and slaves go to Delphi," Chaerephon said. "They come from Greece, Egypt, Persia and Sicily."

Although my schooling had been cut short, I had learned about Delphi from Diotima. The story goes that Zeus, whilst searching for the centre of his Grandmother Earth, released eagles from each end of the universe. The eagles met at Delphi, the navel of the world. Mother Earth sent her serpent son to protect the spot. As a young boy, Apollo shot his first arrow, accidentally killing the serpent son. To atone for the murder, he was sentenced to eight years of manual service.

Upon completion of his sentence, Apollo, the God of Truth, Prophecy and Light, created an Oracle, and promised to provide counsel to all who needed it. But Apollo is too powerful to look upon or to speak with directly — or so it is commonly believed — so he communicates through a priestess, a woman of blameless life. The priestess enters a trance, making herself a conduit through which Apollo can communicate with mere mortals. Suppliants bring their questions to the priestess — the Oracle of Delphi — and, through her, the great god Apollo dispenses his knowledge and wisdom.

As we continued on my pilgrimage, the procession moved further into a valley. In the distance, within the angle formed by twin cliffs, I was able to see Delphi. Sunlight fell on the sanctuary buildings, making them glow. As we drew closer, tall trees blocked my view. Our path grew steeper; traffic increased and moved more slowly. People camped along the road. Peering into the forest, I saw even more people.

Eventually we arrived at a crowded area consisting of a few stone buildings. The place resembled the agora in Athens, with its many merchant stalls and the lively sound of bartering filling the air. Was this Delphi? I wondered, confused. Where were the glittering buildings I had glimpsed from lower down in the valley? My questions were answered when Chaerephon drew me through the crowd, and we followed a busy path further up the mountainside.

Before long, we came to the sacred waters of the Castalian Spring, where men and women were washing their hair in a long, narrow cistern cut into the rock; for the sake of purification, some even submerged themselves completely. Finding a vacant spot, I dipped my hand in the water and brought it to my lips. The water was cold and pleasant tasting.

We continued walking along a wide, well-worn dirt path traversing the edge of the cliff. As we rounded the cliff, through the trees I caught glimpses of sunlight glinting off the golden buildings and bronze statues of the sanctuary which I had glimpsed from across the valley. Shortly thereafter, the path changed from dirt to flagstones, eroded through time by the trampling of thousands upon thousands of feet. Around us the crowds walked on and we were drawn along with them, up the hill on the winding path. People around us behaved reverently, as if they felt the growing power of Apollo.

Suddenly, the serpentine path ended and we entered the walled city itself. To either side, we saw altars stacked with votives of food, vases, clothing and flowers. Beyond the altars, packed closely together, stood beautiful marble monuments and treasuries that would have been the pride of a city. Athens had no buildings as beautiful as these. Despite my morose mood, I was stirred by the grandeur.

"This is the most important place in the world," Chaerephon said, in amazement.

We were transfixed. Every key moment of Greek history was here, recorded in bronze, gold and marble. Every building and statue had been erected to commemorate victories and to thank the Oracle for her advice.

Yet magnificent as these building were, they paled in comparison with the sights ahead of us, including a colossal Sphinx on top of the tallest Ionic column I had ever seen. Beyond that was a massive stoa, within which were thousands of inscriptions carved by slaves who had been freed by their owners. The inscriptions were short biographies that explained why the slaves had deserved their freedom.

Further along the path we discovered a wall carved with scenes of the war between the gods and the Titans. The figures, brightly painted and inlaid with precious metals, seemed to leap at us from the walls. Surrounded by such an abundance of treasure, all of it untouched, what amazed me most was that Xerxes and his massive army had not plundered the shrine. Then I remembered a story I'd heard years earlier about a Persian general who had wanted to pillage the sanctuary. A bolt of lightning had struck him, killing him instantly. No wonder Xerxes had decided to spare Delphi.

Up the stairs and to our right we came upon a huge bronze column made of three coiled golden serpents, supporting a bowl at its highest point. "This was dedicated to Apollo after the Greeks defeated the Persians at Plataea," Chaerephon said softly, as if speaking to himself, recalling lessons he had learned as a boy. Behind the column stood a stunning, life-sized statue, also made of bronze, depicting four horses pulling a chariot. The charioteer was unusually finely detailed, with lips, eyelashes, inlaid glass eyes and a silver headband studded with precious stones.

To our left was a statue of Apollo, four men high — the Big Man, as he was popularly called. In one hand he held the sternpost of a captured Persian warship. The inscription at the base read: "Dedicated by all the Greeks for the victory at Salamis."

Passing the Big Man, we finally came upon the Temple of Apollo, the ultimate destination of all the pilgrims. Walking around the blue and gold temple, we were awed by its sheer beauty. Six Doric columns adorned the front of the temple, with another 15 columns rising on each side. It was the largest, most magnificent building I had ever seen.

In front of the temple, attendants stood guard beside a huge, closed, double door. Words, now indelibly etched in my mind, were inscribed above that door.

Dear boys, I wish I could tell you that the words struck me with the force of lightning — that they were like a lighthouse flame guiding a sailor lost at sea, a beacon guiding me to my own port. I would like to tell you that I understood the words intuitively and absolutely. Had that been the case, I might not be writing to you now from this cell.

In fact, the words merely struck me as odd. I would have expected to see "Temple of Apollo" or "The Oracle." Instead, the engraving read: "Know thyself."

Know thyself.

"What does it mean?" I wondered aloud.

"That you must know your place when you stand before the gods," said Chaerephon, "It is a command that those who seek the gods' wisdom are to be respectful."

His explanation made sense — at the time.

We climbed further, beyond the temple and up the hill, to other porticos and monuments, past the stadium where the foot races of the local games took place. I looked down from above, watching people milling about the sanctuary like a colony of ants.

I was here. I had made it. *But what now?* I wondered. What had I thought I would find?

"Do you have an offering?" Chaerephon asked.

I looked at him. "For whom?"

"For Apollo, of course!" He was surprised.

It was my turn to be surprised, for I had not thought of gaining an audience with the Oracle. I wished only to see the place where my brother had died.

"I have nothing," I admitted.

Chaerephon made a clucking sound. "You must offer something if you want to see the Oracle. Gold, or a valuable carving, perhaps. Something."

"Without an offering, would the Oracle not answer a person with a crucial question?" I asked skeptically.

Chaerephon shook his head. "Impossible. You must understand, Socrates, that ambassadors, military commanders, famous athletes and those with the most valuable offerings, get priority. The priests won't tell you this, but it's the way of things. My father has been here twice. The first time he came with nothing but an honest man's need for help. The second time, he came with a silver ingot. He didn't get in either time."

"Will you see the Oracle today?" I asked thoughtfully.

Chaerephon laughed, not in malice, but in reaction to something he thought every man should have known. "No, the Oracle only sees people nine days each year. It will be another 14 days before she sees supplicants."

"Did you bring an offering?"

"Two silver ingots. I will share them with you," said my friend.

Generous Chaerephon's silver ingots must have been worth a small fortune: each brick of silver represented at least a hundred drachmas. His lavish offer kindled in me the first warmth I had felt since the news of my brother's death, and I loved him for it. But I would not accept his kindness, for I knew the Oracle's advice would be lost on me.

"Thank you," I said gratefully, "but I will find something. What will you ask the Oracle?"

"I want to know if I will be happy with the girl my father has chosen to be my wife."

"Will the Oracle tell you?"

"Yes, but Apollo does not dispense his knowledge easily." Chaerephon's expression turned grave. "The supplicant must have the wisdom to interpret the words that come from the Oracle's mouth. They are easy to misinterpret, for they will likely be cryptic."

"What do you mean?"

"My father often related the story of Croesus, King of Lydia. Many years ago, Croesus struggled with the question of what to do about the growing power of neighbouring Persia. Should he seek an alliance with Greece? Should he challenge the power of Persia, alone? Should he fortify his situation and wait before going to battle? Unsure of his decision, he ventured from Lydia across the Aegean Sea to Delphi, and sought the wisdom of Apollo. Granted access to the Oracle, he was allowed to ask his question: 'Should I attack the Persians?' In her trance, the priestess replied, 'If you go to war, you will destroy a mighty empire.' The king was buoyed by the Oracle's response. He saw himself as the man who would free his people from their Persian aggressors, thus raising his own name above the names of past kings.

"Upon his return home, he launched his campaign against the Persians, but the ensuing battle was inconclusive. Disbanding his army for the winter, he returned home. What he did not anticipate was that the Persian king would keep his army intact, march on Croesus and capture him. Too late, the Oracle's meaning became apparent: Croesus would see his own empire destroyed if he attacked the Persians — not the other way around.

"Do you understand, Socrates? The prophecy was fulfilled, but not in the way Croesus had interpreted it. Such is the wisdom that is required when a man parleys with the gods." Chaerephon paused and then said, "We should put our names on the list. Shall we line up to speak to the priests?"

Not wanting to share my thoughts with him, I merely said, "I will do it later."

Ever trusting, my friend did not think to question me. We agreed to meet again by the Big Man at sunset.

As Chaerephon headed down the hill, I sat and listened to the sounds around me: water trickling over rocks, a bird calling to its mate, bees buzzing amongst the wild flowers. Trance-like, I thought about my brother. When I came out of my reverie, the sun was dipping below the western mountaintop and the sanctuary's brightness had dimmed. Campfires crackled and flamed in the valley, creating thick smoke from one end to the other. As I made my way back down the hill to meet my friend, my senses were unusually alert to the aromas of cooking food and the cadences of songs and music.

Chaerephon and I waited those 14 days until the Oracle was ready to see supplicants. During that time, I slowly went from grief to a deep sadness that would stay with me for the rest of the journey.

I credit the perpetually optimistic Chaerephon for helping me come to terms, at least to some extent, with what had happened. His enthusiasm for life and his outgoing manner quickly attracted some of the people camped around us. Before long, I found myself surrounded by men, women and children from every corner of Greece, all happy to talk about their journeys to Delphi. Most were open about their reasons for coming. Their questions covered a wide variety of topics, from money to voyages, crops to inheritances, herd sizes to children. Some just wanted to know if they were destined to be happy. The people at Delphi came in search of answers related to their daily living.

The doors to the Temple of Apollo were finally opened. The names of the supplicants allowed to pose questions were announced, but Chaerephon was not among them. He was disappointed, but resolved to return, bringing more silver next time. I tried to reassure him that he would see the Oracle one day, if only through sheer force of will.

Joining a long line of men, women, children, horses and carts, we began our way home. As we crested the hill, leaving behind us the glow of Delphi, Chaerephon turned to me. "What would have been your question for the Oracle?" he asked.

I hesitated a moment before answering, "I want to know how my mother and brother are faring."

Chaerephon thought this an excellent question for the God of Truth, Prophecy and Light.

I felt guilty as we continued home, for I had lied to my friend. The fact was, I had not even put my name on the list to see the Oracle, because I did not believe she could answer my questions. Although I'd had reservations about the gods since losing my mother, and my brother's death had only increased my misgivings, I was not confident enough to stand alone as a skeptic. Chaerephon was a good and honest man, and I was afraid that my doubts about the gods in which he believed would cause him to think badly of me.

Suddenly, I understood why Patrocles had not sought me out — why he had stayed away from home all those years. Patrocles had cared about my opinion! Had he failed to return the conquering hero, as he had vowed to do, he might have thought I would respect him less or love him less. Perhaps he believed it preferable for me to cherish my memories of him, rather than to face the reality of what he was. I could be wrong, but I came to believe my brother didn't want to lose his standing in my eyes, just as I didn't want Chaerephon to think less of me because I was not the man he imagined me to be.

Returning home days later, I opened my olive wood chest. Inside it were my hoplite armour and Patrocles' amulet. Taking the amulet from the bottom of the chest, I cleaned off the dust with the corner of my tunic before placing it around my neck. Aside from replacing the leather strip on which it hangs, I have never removed the amulet from that day to this, but have worn it all my life to remind me of the brother I loved.

The rooster has arrived to pick up this latest roll of papyrus, I will ask him to deliver the amulet to Lamprocles, with the understanding that it belongs to all three of you. I hope you will think well of me — and of my brother — whenever you look at it.

DAY 11

SEVERAL UNUSUAL SOUNDS disturbed me while I was writing last night. The creaking of a nearby cell door, light footsteps in the dirt, hurried whispers. Suddenly my cell door squeaked open and an unfamiliar man appeared. My first thought was that perhaps Lycon and Anytus had finally decided to have me killed.

It turned out that I was not in danger, but was, in fact, being offered my freedom. Did I tell you that I have been sharing my food with a prison mate whom I had never seen? My unexpected visitor was the prisoner himself. Thinking he had no one to provide him with sustenance, I had asked the jailer to give him some of my food. What I did not know was that his friends had been waiting for the right moment to break him out of prison. In gratitude for my generosity, he insisted on helping me make my escape, too.

I thanked him for the offer, but declined it and told him why. He did not linger, but left quickly. When he had gone, I put down my quill for a few minutes, utterly taken aback by what had just happened. Mostly, I was surprised at the response my small act of kindness had evoked. Reciprocation is a powerful human urge. I wish I had more time to study it.

I insist that you do not allow this incident to give you ideas of planning an escape for me. You know how I feel about it. Even if it were possible, I would not agree to it. If Crito is cooking up a plot even now, tell him not to bother.

❧

On a cool and cloudless day in the spring of my 22nd year, I found an unusually excited Crito at my courtyard door. "Hurry, or we'll miss them!" he blurted out.

"Miss whom?" I asked, rubbing my eyes. I had a terrible hangover headache and only wanted to return to bed to sleep it off.

"You'll see," he said, and walked off quickly.

I had never seen my calm friend quite so excited, so I decided to find out what all the fuss was about. Moving as fast as my heavy head would allow, I followed him down the road. He made his way through the winding streets, dodging around people, moving very fast for a citizen whose pace was normally so sedate and measured.

Unable to keep up with him, I got further and further behind until I lost him in a crowd heading toward the Acropolis for the final day of the festival honouring Athena. For a while, thinking I knew where Crito was going, I walked in the same direction. But with my head feeling heavier with each step, and being too short to spot him over the hundreds of heads in the agora, I decided to return home to sleep off the wine. Just then Crito — who'd doubled back without me seeing him — grabbed my arm.

"By, Zeus, you're slow!" he exclaimed. "Don't drink so much next time, if you can't tolerate it."

I began to defend myself, but Crito cut me off and pulled me through the throngs until we arrived at the steps of the Painted Porch. There, between the middle columns, stood an old man. "Old," I say, and smile as I write the word. Were I to see him today, I would not call him old, for he was younger than I am now, and I do not think of myself as old. But he seemed old to me then: grey-bearded, pale, bent and fragile.

His eyes, though, were not old, but sparkled with life as he addressed the crowd. "… and I came before a massive gate barred by mighty doors. The maidens who brought me there bid the doors be opened. As the doors were thrown wide, I saw an enormous opening. The maidens guided the chariot and horses through the opening, where the Goddess of Avenging Justice greeted me. Taking my hand in hers, she said, 'Welcome to my abode, young man. You are here, far from the places of men, so that you may learn to know how the opinion of man differs from absolute truth. I shall teach you such things, that you may bring back my words to the house of men and teach them what is and what is not.'"

Was the old man a soothsayer? I wondered. Unlike Chaerephon, Crito was not the type to get excited about a fortune-teller.

"Why are we here?" I asked.

"Listen," Crito said, his tone hushed.

The old man continued his tale. "... for mortals wander about stupefied, like men who are deaf and blind. But I will take you down the one path to show you that which is indestructible, alone, complete, immoveable and without end ..."

The audience grew as he spoke, and the sounds of the agora — hawkers calling out their wares and arguing over prices — faded into the background. Slowly, I began to understand the reason for Crito's excitement and realized why he had brought me here. The speaker was a "thinker," as people called such a person: a seeker of wisdom and a lover of truth.

The crowd cheered when he finally finished his speech, and he bowed his head in thanks. In reply to a question I did not hear, he began to speak again. "Movement and change are merely appearances of an unchanging reality. Our everyday perception of reality is mistaken, for the world is beyond our comprehension. It is only by thought that we can bypass false appearances and arrive at knowledge."

"Then movement is impossible?" someone asked.

"Correct," replied the old man.

So fascinated was I, that I was unaware my head had cleared. Without thinking, I posed my own question. "Why is it impossible?"

Crito nudged me with his shoulder, as if we were in school again and he was warning me to be quiet lest the grammatiste smack me with his sandal. At my question, someone — a handsome man in his thirties, sturdy as an athlete — stepped from the crowd and stood beside the old man.

"Perhaps I can give you an example," he said, in a friendly voice.

I nodded.

"Imagine an arrow ready to be shot from a bow. When the warrior lets loose the string, the arrow is released with great speed and it proceeds to its target. How can it be denied that the arrow has no movement?"

"Exactly," came a voice from the crowd.

The old man regarded the young one with pride and joy, the way a father might look at a favoured son.

"How can I deny the movement of the arrow?" The younger man's manner was enthusiastic "Let me answer that question by asking you one." He looked directly at me. "Nothing can be in two places at the same time. Can we agree on that?"

"Yes," I responded.

"So an arrow is only in one location during any given instant of flight. Can we agree on that, too?"

"Yes."

"But if it is in only one place, it must be at rest momentarily."

I nodded.

"Thus the arrow is present, somewhere, at some specific location, at every moment of its trajectory?"

I nodded again, although I was having some difficulty understanding his argument.

"It follows, then, that motion is not really occurring; rather, it is a series of separate events. In other words, motion is not a feature of the external world, but rather it is a projection of something within us as our eyes tie together what we are observing. By means of this reasoning, motion is not an absolute reality, but a feature of our minds."

I gave him a baffled look.

"Let us examine this another way," he said, correctly interpreting my confused expression. "Can we agree that time is composed of instants, and that there is no shorter period of time than an instant?"

I had a sudden memory of the day my brother had urinated on Lycon. My father had come home, nearly catching Patrocles in the act. I remember watching from the roof of the house as my father lifted his hand, ready to strike my brother. The scene had seemed devoid of movement for an interminable moment. Time had stood still for me, then.

"Yes," I said.

"Can you see that at any given instant the arrow will not be moving? It will be frozen in time, like an object in a painting."

"Yes," I said, finally able to visualize what he said.

"Therefore, at any instant in time, the arrow is not moving."

"Why does it appear to move?" I asked.

"You only think it moves because your senses deceive you, unlike your intellect."

"In other words," I responded thoughtfully, "what I see is not real?"

"*Correct*! We cannot trust our eyes and ears. We can trust only logic."

I pondered his words, and tried to make sense of their meaning. *We can trust only logic.* Someone punched my shoulder. I rubbed my arm.

"Head in the clouds?" Crito smiled, punching me again.

Looking around, I saw that the crowd had gone, as had the speakers. Could I have been daydreaming? "Where is everyone?"

Crito burst out laughing. "A passing magician turned everyone to stone, so be careful where you step, Socrates — we don't want to crush our fellow Athenians."

Suddenly I felt foolish. "How long has everyone been gone?"

Crito couldn't answer, for he had fallen to the ground, laughing uncontrollably.

"Who were those men," I asked, when he sobered up at last.

"The old man is Parmenides of Elea. The young man is his student, Zeno."

Parmenides and Zeno. I was strangely drawn to them. There was more to it than their undeniable charisma, although exactly what it was, I could not have said. Fortunately for me, they remained in Athens for many months, giving me frequent opportunities to observe them. Their intellect was far superior to mine and most of what they said confused me. Beyond their claims about the universe, however, I was fascinated by their method of questioning.

Never once did I see them lose an argument, no matter the topic of discussion. If some member of the crowd disagreed with one of their ideas, either Parmenides or Zeno would ask the citizen for *his* opinion, upon which, through skillful cross-examination, one of them would demonstrate the contradiction in that man's thinking.

Discussions often became heated, but only on the side of the audience. Unlike their listeners, Parmenides and Zeno never raised their voices or made threats. Afterward, when the crowd had long gone, I often found myself alone, deep in thought, attempting to analyze how they had handled the discussion.

For some reason, they reminded me of my mother. So often, a woman in childbirth would be tempted to give up, her strength exhausted by hours of pain and effort. When this happened, your grandmother would persuade the labouring mother to continue pushing. At times, she might even threaten a woman by raising a fear for the baby's safety, but usually it was enough merely to remind the woman of her own natural ability.

Parmenides and Zeno did much the same thing. Although most of the men they conversed with were angry at having their ignorance exposed, their goal was much the same as my mother's. Where she had helped women give birth to babies, they helped people give birth to other ways of thinking. The biggest difference was that a woman had to let go of her baby, whereas some men would not let go of their flawed ideas, no matter how much Parmenides and Zeno coaxed them to try.

As my reverence for the two men grew, I tried to become just like them. I dressed the way they did and tried to adopt their manner of speech. I even tried to engage those I knew in argument, to see if I could uncover contradictions in their thinking. My efforts failed miserably, for I only succeeded in annoying my friends, acquaintances, and fellow stonemasons.

When Zeno and Parmenides left Athens, I searched out other men from whom I might learn. Plane trees had been planted along the edge of the agora when I was a boy. These trees were tall and strong now, and provided shade for astronomers, physicians, orators and all manner of men selling their knowledge. Much as I longed to learn from these people, I could not afford their fees. Frustrated that my poverty once again limited my education, I grew despondent — but I needn't have. Things were changing in Athens.

The threat of war with Persia was by now almost a memory and our truce with Sparta was holding. In this time of peace, our allies continued to pay tribute for our friendship and our protection. The city's wealth increased. With money came grand ambitions. The Acropolis had lain bare for over 30 years, the scorched ground a reminder of our humbling by the Persians. My generation no longer wanted to be reminded of their grandfathers' failures. That was the past.

Announcing the rebirth of the Acropolis, Pericles declared that the sacred ground had remained fallow long enough. New buildings were commissioned, among them the grand entrance to the Acropolis, the Temple of Athena Nike and the Parthenon.

The Parthenon was to be the largest temple in all of Greece, larger even than the Temple of Apollo at Delphi. The best masons, sculptors and artists were called upon. Athens, Pericles claimed, would become the centre of the Greek world. Athens would be glorious.

After Pericles' announcement, the city hummed with good will. Ship building continued, at an even more rapid pace. Athens did not forget the origins of her power and new-found wealth. With more ships came more sail-makers, blacksmiths, rope weavers and oar-makers. With more tradesmen came more merchants. Every kind of ware was for sale. A hundred different languages were spoken in the agora. More marble was transported to the city for sculptures, façades and tombstones. Grand new houses built of stone took the place of mud and brick dwellings.

The city erupted from its fortified walls and covered the hills as far as the eye could see. As a boy, I might have seen a messenger on his horse once a month. Now, daily I saw the dust rise as riders made their way back and forth between Athens and Piraeus and parts unknown.

During this prosperous time I stumbled upon a shop in the southwest corner of the agora near the Tholos, where Parmenides and Zeno had purchased their sandals. A man named Simon owned the shop. Simon was in his late 40s, about the same age as my father. Slight in build, he walked with the shuffle of a lame man, the result of a leg broken in a fall as a boy and never set properly. He was a gentle sort, always busy with hammers, nails and leather. He was a quiet fellow, too, unlike the talkative men who loitered in his shop.

Simon's shop, as neat and tidy as the little man himself, was the meeting place for a diverse and eclectic group of men. None of them were Athenian born and, therefore, they were not citizens, but a collection of craftsman and merchants who had come from the Ionian coast: from Clazomenae, Miletus and the Island of Samos. Perhaps they were drawn together because they came from the same area.

Like Parmenides and Zeno, the men at Simon's shop claimed to search for truth, using reason to guide them. They deliberated on topics ranging from mathematical principles and the composition of the universe to the way humans might have come into being. I remember the first thing I heard them discuss: the belief that the heart was not the instrument of thought, but that thinking occurred in the brain — the soft, squishy matter I would eventually see spilled on the battlefield. Although some of their theories shocked me, they also filled me with great intellectual energy. And to think I was receiving all this education at no cost!

Instead of discussing only their own ideas, these men were devotees of various thinkers. The thinker whose ideas I found the most interesting was a man named Anaxagoras, originally from Clazomenae.

All my life, I had been taught that gods and spirits were responsible for everything there was. The moon was the silver boat of Artemis; the sun was Helios's fiery chariot. Anaxagoras had other explanations. He had a theory that the moon shone due to light reflected on it by the sun, and that the sun was a hot rock. He even predicted a day when a piece of the sun would break off and fall to earth. He was proven correct when the world witnessed a fragment of the sun falling through the sky and landing in Thrace. The prophecy brought Anaxagoras to the attention of many powerful people, including Pericles, who'd asked him to be his counsellor, a position Anaxagoras still held at the time I listened to the craftsmen's discussions.

Although Anaxagoras's ideas were highly respected by those who frequented Simon's store, the man most highly regarded was Thales of Miletus. Thales was to these men what an Olympic athlete was to the stonemasons with whom I worked.

The most important of Thales' claims was that water is the origin of all things. According to Thales, moist substances turned into air and dirt, hence the ground on which we walk became solidified on the water on which it floated. Since the earth floated on water, Thales did not see earthquakes as resulting from supernatural whims; rather, he deduced that they occurred when the earth was rocked by waves.

For me, the ideas of Anaxagoras and Thales were important because they made me realize I was not the only one who doubted the existence of the gods. Natural phenomena could have other explanations. Such ideas were, of course, controversial. In fact, not long before this time the Assembly had enacted a law that made lack of respect for the gods a crime. To say that the gods did not create and control everything was, as it is now, blasphemy.

But a group of people can be bold together, when individually they might be silent. Perhaps more importantly, skeptical discussion is tolerated when everyone is well fed and no threats exist, as was the case in Athens at that time. Nevertheless, many of the discussions in Simon's shop still took place in hushed voices and with shoulder checks to see who might be listening.

During this thought-provoking time I became very ill. Heeding Diotima's counsel, I did nothing but sleep for days. When I was awake, I would lie still and listen to sounds outside the house. Through the walls I heard men and slaves arguing and children playing. In the evening I heard Diotima greet my father when he entered through the courtyard gate. She gave him his evening meal and then brought me mine.

After the sun had set, I would hear the deep, solitary whistle of a nearby owl. Night after night, I heard the bird's call, which struck me as lonely because it was never answered. As I drifted off to sleep, I sensed something amiss, although what it was I did not know. I attributed my feelings to my illness.

Early one morning, on the fifth day of my illness, I noticed water stains on the white wall of the room. The stains were old and this struck me as odd, for it was not like my father to neglect household repairs. Finally, I realized what had been bothering me. It was the silence from the andron, the absence of the sound of metal on metal.

Waiting until my father had left for work, I got up slowly, my body aching, and sought out Diotima in the kitchen.

"When did he stop sculpting?" I whispered, as if my father could hear me from the city wall. Diotima's shoulders sagged, and she looked at me sadly. "This past spring," she said quietly.

"Did he finish his project?"

"Do you know what he was working on?" Diotima asked.

I thought back to the day when I had broken into the andron and found the shroud — covered herms, as well as my father's old pelte shield and javelin. "He was making his own luck," I said, derisively.

"That's right, his own luck. Come with me."

Diotima led me to the andron and untied the leather knot, so quickly and expertly that I suspected she had done this often. She opened the door, and even in the gloom I noticed the absence of the herms.

"He sold them!" I said, and Diotima did not contradict me.

Looking around the andron, I realized that the ornate mosaic of the horse and rider were gone from the floor. Benches and tables stood askew and empty wine jugs were everywhere. The disarray was uncharacteristic of my meticulous father.

"He sold the mosaic, too?"

Diotima hesitated, as if she couldn't decide whether to share a secret with me. Then she said, "Your father came home from work one day and told me to go away for the night. You were with Crito and Chaerephon, and since I had finished preparing the evening meal, I left. It occurred to me that, finally, your father might be bringing someone home. I was relieved." She paused a moment. "Although he would never say so, he misses your mother very much."

I stared at her. The thought of my father having normal human feelings was difficult for me to accept. I knew nothing of my parents' feelings for each other, and, in fact, was unable to recall even any contact between them.

"The next morning," Diotima went on, "I returned to find your father looking dishevelled. After he left for work, I came in here. I saw that the herms were gone and that the beautiful mosaic had been removed from the floor." She was silent a while, before saying, "He doesn't sculpt any longer."

I was aware that the hands of elderly men could lose their strength. I knew several old masons who could no longer hold a hammer and chisel. But I had never seen my father rub his hands in pain like those old men. Then again, by that time I was no longer paying him much attention.

"Maybe his hands hurt?" I suggested.

"No, Socrates, that's not it."

Something odd in her tone caught my attention. Glancing at her in the dimness, I asked, "Do you know why he stopped sculpting? What was it, Diotima?"

As if struggling with herself, she remained silent.

"Diotima?"

"All right, Socrates." I heard resignation in her voice. "Your father hasn't sculpted since Pericles called on the best masons to rebuild the Acropolis — but he was not asked. Since then, he has been sitting in the dark and drinking."

"He expected to be called?" I asked in some surprise.

"Yes. He waited a long time."

"He thought he would help to construct the Parthenon?"

"That — or something else. Something special. Before you were born, your father was working on the city walls. The people in charge saw how quick and precise he was, and were impressed with his skill. He was asked to assist with the Painted Porch. He was even asked to carve figures and animals, not just to shape blocks. It was what he had always hoped for: to become a sculptor. His future looked so promising that your mother and I wondered if he might become famous."

"What happened?" My interested was piqued now.

"He disagreed with someone in power, and was told to report to the long wall. He thought — we all thought — he would eventually return to work either on the Painted Porch or on some other worthy project. But he was never called back. For 25 years he waited. Then Pericles announced Athens would no longer be a city of mud and brick, and that the Acropolis would be rebuilt. When your father learned that men less skilled than he was were being called to work on the Parthenon, he finally lost all hope."

How curious. I had never imagined that my father might have had his own dreams. It was like catching sight of one of the old soldiers from the academy, strolling down the streets of Athens. A man transformed from one persona to another. It was not easy to think of my father differently from the way I'd always known him.

"I am worried," Diotima said. "You must talk with him."

"He doesn't speak to me," I protested. "He speaks to no one."

"You must try. I see you all the time in the agora with strangers. You talk with them as if you have known them for years. Surely, you can do the same with your father?"

I had never heard Diotima voice worry or concern. She always appeared stoically content. I suppose hers was the face any slave puts on to please their master.

I agreed to try. It was the least I could do for Diotima, who had done so much for me.

Once my health improved, I joined my father on his morning walk to work. I noticed that he had grown stiff and slow and had acquired a faraway gaze, almost as if he were trying to look backward into a murky past. I commented on the weather, and he grunted a reply. His voice had an old man's quaver; he was probably in his early 50s. When had his voice begun to change? I asked about the upcoming games, and he only grunted again.

At work, he appeared lost. He no longer worked as quickly as he used to, and his lines had become sloppy. On the way home that evening, I sought to waken something inside him by inquiring about his sculpting, but even then he did not react. Over the next few days, I tried other ways of approaching him. And all the while I wondered: what could I say to a man about whom I knew so little?

That winter, my father died. In the end, he simply appeared to lose the will to live. We found him in the andron one day, as cold as the stone he had carved.

We buried him beside my mother. Crito and Chaerephon attended the funeral. Diotima's old friends, such as they were, also came. But no crowds of women beat their chests or rent their clothing in despair, and no stonemasons were even present. The funeral was a sombre affair.

Afterward, I wanted to give Diotima her freedom. She told me that my father had freed her years ago. She could have left at any time, but she had stayed because she loved us. I was surprised and wondered, briefly, what else I had never been told. I imagine that by now, you boys must also wonder what you have never known about me.

DAY 12

I SOMETIMES WONDER, my boys: what life expectations do you have? Do you crave respect and glory, as I did? Do you long for immortality? Do you want your names to live forever? What are your ambitions? I think of the grand plans Crito and I had as boys. Maybe your plans were once similar. It is one of my greatest regrets that I never thought to ask any of you about this.

By the time I was in my late 20s — an age at which I had hoped to be a man of standing and honour, adored by the citizens of Athens and feared by our enemies — none of my expectations had been met; I hadn't even fought in battle yet. I wished to speak to Crito about our boyhood dreams of becoming generals and conquerors. I wondered if he, too, was disillusioned with his life. But Crito had married and started a family, and seemed content with running his family's business.

Crito, as well as Chaerephon, who was also married and a father by then, invited me to spend festival days with their families. I accepted their gracious invitations less and less frequently. Their happiness made me feel even more of a failure. It pains me to confess this, but I actually hoped sometimes that something bad would happen to them. A real friend would have rejoiced at the happiness of those closest to him.

I was also losing interest in the topics discussed at Simon's. I was no longer intrigued by discussions about the manner in which the sun gave off light, or the cause of earthquakes. The daily problems of life stamped-ed through my mind now. I thought back to the supplicants Chaerephon and I had met at Delphi. Rather than questioning acts of nature, they had wanted answers with regard to work, children and marriage. They had been concerned about the quest for happiness.

Thinking about the people I'd talked with at Delphi made me ponder my own chances of happiness. I, too, would have liked a wife and family, but I was not as lucky as my friends, for I was not favoured as a prospective son-in-law.

Unsurprisingly, I was still reputed to be a person who had once been — and still was, perhaps — possessed by evil spirits. Additionally, there was my strange behaviour. For it was my habit to spend long periods of time absorbed in contemplation, even in public places. This was my way, and I couldn't seem to change. I suspected fathers of prospective brides may have wondered how the offspring of such an eccentric person might turn out.

Furthermore, I was known as someone who argued about the substance of the universe. This was also held against me. The law making lack of respect for the gods a crime had been used a few times to exile citizens. No father wanted his daughter married to a man who might endanger his family.

As for fatherless women, who were free to choose their own husbands, they, too, had no reason to want me. With my bulbous nose and bulging eyes, I was no woman's dream. A glance in a bronze mirror reinforced that inescapable fact. So did I have a chance to be happy, or was I doomed to spend life alone?

This question brought Crow Man to my mind. As boys, we had thought him crazy; now, so many years later, I wondered whether sheer loneliness had driven him to sit on his perch day after day, regarding the world with indifference.

I went for long walks, often visiting construction sites. Pericles' vision for Athens was taking shape. Thousands of slaves moved marble into place for the grand steps leading up to the Acropolis. The theater of Dionysus, on the south slope of the Acropolis, was being enlarged. The costly Pentelic marble columns of the Parthenon reached into the blue sky above the Acropolis rock. Male and female sculptures, idealized forms of Grecian beauty, were being chiselled, one hammer stroke at a time. I was not alone at the Parthenon, for crowds of people watched enthralled as artists and craftsmen busied themselves with their magnificent creations. Beauty and joy were everywhere — except in my soul.

Inevitably, my father would come to mind, and I wondered whether he would have been happy working up here, lifting his eyes now and then to look down on the city below. Somehow, I had trouble believing anything could have improved his bleak disposition.

Thoughts about my father led me to wonder what he had thought of me — what he had really, truly, thought about me. He must have understood that Patrocles was in every way my superior: physically, mentally and spiritually. Had it bothered him that the flesh of his flesh was not equal to that of a boy left out to die?

Frequently, I dwelt on my accident with the horse. Would my life have been different had the accident not occurred? Had it been the cause of my oddness? My destiny? My fate? Above all, I wondered when I would attain the success my mother had foretold.

These questions and a hundred others constantly occupied my mind. I remember a day during one of the festivals, when I went to Simon's shop looking for comradeship, and found the usual men there, debating the stars and quoting Thales. I listened in silence.

Suddenly, a voice we rarely heard asked a question. "Do you know the story of the man who walked into the well?" Astonished, everyone turned to look at the speaker; it was none other than the owner of the shop, Simon.

"An astronomer used to go out at night to observe the stars," he told us. "One evening, he wandered through the outskirts of Miletus, his attention fixed on the sky. Not looking where he was going, he fell into a deep well. Lamenting his cuts and bruises, he cried loudly for help. Hearing the cries, a neighbour ran to the well. After rescuing the astronomer, the neighbour observed, "It's all very well to probe the mysteries of heaven, but in doing so you overlook the common objects under your feet."

Someone laughed, and the others joined in. Simon smiled, almost like a simpleton. Moments later, the men returned to their earlier conversation, and Simon resumed his work on a sandal.

In the days that followed, I wondered whether Simon would tell another story, whether he would utter anything more than his normal, pleasant greeting. I watched him, as much as I listened to discussions that were beginning to mean less and less to me. I kept waiting for Simon to say something again, but he never did.

One evening, I stayed behind purposely when the others left the shop. As Simon cleaned and sharpened his tools, I asked him why he had told the story of the astronomer.

He looked up at me. "To see the reaction."

"Was it what you expected?"

"Perhaps," he said.

"Or perhaps not?"

He smiled. "Perhaps not."

"Your story reminded me of the tales our slave Diotima used to tell my brother Patrocles and me when we were young," I told him, as I fingered the talisman around my neck. How I wished my brother were here with me.

"Actually, it's a special kind of story. A fable." Simon continued to sharpen his tools. "A man named Aesop, also a slave, became known for his fables. Interesting that you heard them from this woman, Diotima."

"She said fables had lessons."

"Did you agree with her? Do *you* think fables have lessons?" Simon asked.

"Perhaps," I said.

"And perhaps not."

We exchanged a smile.

"What was the lesson of your story?" I asked.

"What do *you* think it was?"

I sensed he was testing me, but I did not mind. Thoughtfully, I observed, "The astronomer should have looked to himself rather than to the sky."

"It's how I interpret it, too," said Simon.

"Diotima said fables contained great truths," I mused.

"I believe they do."

"And yet the stories are not true."

Simon looked up from his work once more. "Perhaps they hold more truth than untruth. If they are not true, does it mean the lessons are less valuable?"

I gave the question some thought, before answering. "I would think so."

"Why?"

"Because the events they relate were made up."

"Let me put your mind at ease," Simon said. "The story about the astronomer is true."

"He was an actual person?"

"He was."

"And he fell into a well?"

"Yes."

"Who was he?" I asked.

"Thales of Miletus," Simon told me with a wry smile.

The next time I went to Simon's shop, I kept staring at him, wishing he would speak. Finally, I managed to catch his eye, and he winked at me. I was elated. Never had a wink meant so much to me; it was as if we shared a secret. More than that, for the first time in my life I felt the equal of someone.

Crito and Chaerephon were my friends, and no greater friends did a man ever have, but I was not their equal. Both were wealthy, well educated, well liked and respected. I was none of those things and never would be. True, I was very proud of having been first of the line, but I attributed that achievement more to luck than to anything else. If I had dropped my weapon once too often in front of the old soldiers, or stumbled during shield push practice, any one of my cohort, Crito in particular, could just as easily have won the coveted position. A single misstep and I would have been relegated to the fourth or fifth row.

Simon's wink encouraged me to stay in the shop until he closed it for the day. When the other men had gone, Simon spoke freely. After falling into the well, he told me, Thales — a great mathematician and astronomer — had taken the words of his rescuer to heart, and had set out on a journey of self-discovery. His favourite piece of advice, Simon said, was: *know thyself.*

"Do you know what it means?" he asked.

I quoted Chaerephon's words on our long-ago trip to Delphi. "To know your place when you stand before the gods."

"That sounds like something from a play," Simon said. "No, Socrates, I don't believe the words mean that."

"What *do* they mean?"

"I don't know, although I ask myself the question every day."

His answer surprised me, for I had never heard a man confess ignorance to his own questions. Questions were usually rhetorical. Statements were defended. No man of my acquaintance seemed unsure of his own mind.

"Perhaps, for each person, to know himself is different," Simon suggested. "Then, again, perhaps there is only one answer."

"How are we supposed to find the answer?"

Simon's eyes held mine. "Perhaps by asking ourselves the hardest questions about our values, our beliefs and the principles that guide our lives."

Looking back now, I know that his words were among the most important I had ever heard. From that moment on, like Thales before me, I turned my attention from the heavens to the study of people.

For the next 10 years, Simon and I discussed the differences between right and wrong, good and bad. We deliberated concepts such as justice, courage and moderation. My intellect was constantly stretched. New ideas came to me: sometimes illusory, sometimes visionary; never staying long in my mind; flickering on and off like fireflies on a dark night; discovered and lost and found again. Simon discussed these ideas with me, and helped me bring some order to them.

Like me, Simon had no one else really close to him. His wife was dead and he had no children. Sometimes, after he'd closed his shop for the day, he and I would walk to the Acropolis together and sit on the steps of the newly finished Parthenon. Beneath the glittering silver and gold façade, Simon freely shared his thoughts and feelings with me. There was strength in his honesty, a power greater than physical might. Only now, as I sit here in this cell, do I see candour as an essential quality for a person who wishes to have a happy life.

We would remain there on the steps until the sun set and the owls swooped down on the mice and the lizards, carrying them back to their high perches among the columns of the Parthenon. Simon's modest manner was so disarming that I eventually shared with him some of my insecurities, one of which was my lack of education. I have never forgotten the warm summer evening when he presented me with a wax tablet and a stylus, like the ones I'd had as a child in school. During my two years of school, learning a few letters had been the extent of my formal education; most of our time had been spent memorizing Homer and Hesiod. So when Simon taught me to read and write, I was both delighted and extremely grateful.

Although Simon was not in the habit of flaunting himself in any way, other men also recognized his worth. One such was the great Anaxagoras, thinker and counsellor to Pericles. When Pericles was still the leading man of Athens, a general for 25 years straight, his opponents had come up with a plan to reduce his influence on the city. Pericles was too politically astute to be overthrown in the Assembly, so his foes attacked his friends instead.

The sculptor Phidias was charged with stealing gold intended for the statue of Athena in the Parthenon. Aspasia, Pericles' courtesan partner and the mother of his youngest son, was charged with corrupting the women of Athens to satisfy Pericles' perverse sexual desires. Anaxagoras, the man who claimed the gods were not responsible for natural events, was charged with impiety.

These charges all had their consequences. Phidias was found guilty and died in jail. Aspasia was found innocent, but only because Pericles broke down and wept in court. Anaxagoras, not wanting to cause his friend further problems, left the city.

Before he departed, Anaxagoras recommended that Simon become his replacement. Simon was called to Pericles' home, but was back at work the next day, busy with his hammer, tacks and leather. The usual group gathered in the shop, arguing the nature of rainbows, were unaware that he had been offered a life of ease and had turned it down. I wonder now whether Athens could have avoided the costly 28-year war with the Spartans if Simon had accepted Pericles' offer.

That Simon was unaffected by what would have been the crowning glory of a life well spent, made me respect him all the more. In time, he became more than a mentor: he became a father. He supported me, encouraged me and insisted I was clever. He gave me what I had never received from my real father: abundant love and respect. Yet despite the years I spent with him, no matter how much we debated and discussed, I never came any closer to understanding the meaning of those words: *know thyself.*

What I did realize was that the more I learned, the more certain I became that I knew nothing.

DAY 13

A THENS WAS NOT fully aware of the true situation the day the Assembly voted to subdue a revolt in Potidaea, far north in Macedon. Nobody knew then that Athens was at its zenith, the centre of wealth, power and learning, and that it would not reach those heights again — certainly not in my lifetime. None but the wisest could have guessed that the Battle of Potidaea would precipitate a 28-year conflict with Sparta and her allies.

It was Chaerephon who gave me the news that the Council of Five Hundred had chosen our cohort to travel to Potidaea — although both he and Crito had been asked to stay behind in Athens. There was great concern that the Spartans would support the rebelling Potidaeans, invading the countryside around Athens and destroying the newly planted crops, as well as attacking the silver mines at Laurium. Crito was to remain in Athens because, as an importer of food, he could help ensure adequate supplies for the city. Chaerephon's presence was required because his hundred slaves worked the mines, and they had to be kept from revolting.

In preparation for battle, I checked the condition of my armour. In the early years following my return from military duty, I had made a point of regularly polishing the bronze breastplate and greaves and oiling their leather straps. I must admit, though, that as time went on, I had become less diligent.

I was filled with a terrible sense of dread as I lifted the breastplate from the andron wall. My vision narrowed and my hands tingled. It was like being back in the classroom, asked to recite some passage or other.

Sitting down on the couch, it came to me suddenly that I did not want to go to war.

When the day came to leave Athens, I found Diotima waiting for me at the courtyard door with my 10 days' ration of barley groats and wheat cakes. "Take care of yourself," she advised gently, as she handed me the sack. Her voice was so calm that for a brief moment I felt as though there was nothing to fear; everything would turn out well. But terror seized me a moment later and I felt certain I would not return.

"If I don't come back …" I began, my voice ragged; only to stop in mid-sentence, as a new thought struck me. Although Diotima was a freed slave, because she was a woman, she had no property rights. I couldn't even leave her the house.

"Return home to Thrace," I finished, instead. "You will find a few drachmas buried under the courtyard altar."

"You will come back. I know it," she protested.

"If I don't …"

"You will." She gave me a confident smile.

I was unable to return the smile. Despite Diotima's reassurance, I was certain I would never see her again. I wanted to thank her for taking care of me for so many years, for protecting and nurturing me after my mother's death. Yet I was wary about revealing my fears, my weaknesses, my cowardly thoughts, and so I kept silent. Wordlessly, I put on my helmet, slung my shield over my shoulder, picked up my spear and walked away.

As on the day of my admission to the academy so long ago, I first went to the cemetery and stopped at my parents' graves. A honey cake lay on each grave, undoubtedly placed there by Diotima, and I felt remorseful for neglecting to bring something myself. As I stood by my mother's grave, I recalled her telling me the story of my birth — her dream of lions and thunderbolts, and that I was born with a caul over my head. Her premonitions of my future greatness weighed on me heavily, for I felt unable to fulfill either her expectations or my own. "I cannot do it," I told her quietly.

Reluctantly, I left the graves and set off toward the port of Piraeus. I was acutely aware of walking alone, for the other men I saw on the road marched in company: fathers with sons, friends in groups. They conversed as they went, sharing tales of their grandfathers' feats and of battlefield heroics, similar to the stories I had heard from Thespis so long ago. It was the first day of summer and far too hot to be wearing armour, so many men had their slaves follow behind them, carrying their breastplates, shields, weapons and an assortment of clothing suitable for different conditions. I saw pack animals loaded with the tools needed to repair arms and armour, carts with rations for men and beasts and flocks of sacrificial sheep and goats. All were destined for the distant city of Potidaea.

The waterfront of Piraeus was a picture of disorder. Commerce continued unabated, even as additional men and materials from Athens were being funnelled through the port. Fishermen still stood at their stalls, hawking the day's catch. Drunken sailors stumbled in and out of taverns, singing loudly. Merchants made deals in lanes so filled with offal that the streets of Athens seemed clean by comparison. Corn, grain and slaves were unloaded and moved to warehouses. The harbour was filled with ships of war, merchant vessels and all manner of support craft; it was the largest collection of vessels I had ever seen. The smell of pitch used for caulking emanated from sheds along the water's edge. I fingered my brother's amulet and wondered in which sheds he had worked.

After learning which ship was mine, I stood and gazed at it in trepidation. This was the ship that would take me across the sea to battle. I had been posted to a boat with soldiers I did not know. They looked more like boys than men to me.

When the ship was fully loaded it received the signal to depart, and the rowers dipped their oars into the water. As we left the safety of the shallows for deeper water, I wondered what creatures lived beneath the surface of the sea: sharks, rays, octopi and squid, all of which I had seen fishermen selling in the market in Athens.

There was no wind the first day out of port, so we relied on the rowers. That night, beacon fires guided us to shore, where we beached the ship and camped. By next morning, the wind had risen strongly and we pushed the ship back into a turbulent ocean. The pitching, tossing and shuddering of the boat whenever we struck a wave was stomach-turning, and I wondered how people could choose to work on a boat. I could not begin to imagine what it would be like in battle with the ramming, grappling, boarding and fighting taking place on rolling decks without any firm place on which to plant one's feet.

For a few days we made so little headway that we beached the ships at night within sight of our previous night's camp. Finally, the weather broke and we made better progress. At one point, dolphins, smooth as polished marble and silver as new obols, shot through the water ahead of us. A good omen, the sailors said. How free the dolphins seemed, leaping from the water. How I envied them, living without the burden of expectations.

Ten days after setting sail we arrived at Potidaea, a city located on a narrow isthmus open to the sea on the east and west, and with walls the full breadth of the isthmus to the north and south. Our ship beached north of the city with the rest of the fleet. We were busy unloading when we heard a rumour that the Potidaeans had sent ambassadors to Athens to negotiate peace terms; we could expect to hear by the next day whether or not there would be a battle. Meanwhile, we set up camp as quickly as possible and prepared ourselves.

I was taken aback when I heard a familiar voice. "Not looking very good, are they?" And there was Chaerephon, smiling as he gestured toward the mass of men. "Look at them, Socrates. They have neglected their physical fitness. Even men in good condition will be hard pressed to carry the weight of their armour. What will become of these men when they have to exert themselves in battle?"

"Chaerephon?" I said, surprised to see him.

Smiling at my reaction, he went on blithely. "However, I am not worried. I asked a soothsayer if you and I and Crito would survive Potidaea. After examining a sheep's liver, he predicted we would all be fine."

"What are you doing here?" I asked.

He laughed cheerfully. "I couldn't let you face the Potidaeans alone."

"But you were ordered to remain in Athens."

"*Requested* — not ordered."

"And Crito?"

"He made the trip here, as well. We boarded the last ship leaving Piraeus. Unfortunately, he's irritable, and not only because of the tossing seas. Hardly spoke the entire journey. Maybe you can get a laugh out of him. I couldn't."

Chaerephon told me where I could find Crito, then left to make sure his armour was ready for the morning. When I finally came upon Crito, he was staring out to sea. I asked him about the trip and about himself, but Chaerephon was right — Crito was uncharacteristically surly. I wondered whether he was upset at leaving his young family.

"Why are you here, Crito?"

"What do you mean?" he challenged me.

"Why did you come to Potidaea?"

His face darkened. "I am a citizen of Athens."

"You were requested to stay in the city."

"My cohort fights, and so will I," he responded indignantly.

"You are angry. Why?"

"You insult me, Socrates."

"I'm sorry, I don't mean to." It was my turn to feel irritation. "I merely asked a question."

"You want to know why I don't run and hide. Do you think me a coward?"

"No!" I snapped.

"I took an oath, as you did, to protect the city and its people. I am an honourable man, and I mean to fulfill my oath," he said.

Had I been more aware, I might have recognized Crito's brusqueness as a sign of distress rather than anger, but I could not see beyond my own internal conflict. Turning my back on him, I climbed to the summit of a nearby hill. From there, I was able to look down over the camp, and to see the glint of shields and armour flashing like a handful of gold coins in the sun.

I wondered whether any among the thousands of men gathered there shared the terrible fears that plagued me. So absorbed in thought was I, that I ceased to notice the sounds and smells below me, losing all track of time until I realized the sky had turned black and that a biting wind was blowing from the ocean. I shivered.

As had happened so often before in periods of confusion, I had spent half the night thinking, mostly contemplating the concept of courage. Although I well knew that going into battle could be my chance for glory, a powerful fear urged me to run away. *Run and hide.* From the moment Chaerephon had told me about the coming battle, I had been struggling with the desire to desert.

As the grey light of dawn appeared on the horizon, I made a decision. I walked back to camp, where I found Chaerephon purchasing a good luck charm from a camp follower.

"You won me a wager," he said, smiling.

I looked at him, mystified. "I don't understand."

"When the sun began to set last evening, rumours spread among the cohorts that you had been standing on the hill since midday. After dinner, some of the men brought their bedding outside so they could see how long you stayed on the hill. I said I'd seen you standing in one spot for days, working out your ideas, and I laid a bet that you would remain on the hill all night. They took me up on it. Sure enough, when daybreak came you were still there. Twenty drachmas! Can you believe it? I made 20 drachmas!" Chaerephon laughed as he spoke.

I could only stare at him, bewildered that a man could laugh at a time like this, just before battle, just before our probable doom.

At that moment we were called to arms. Through the confusion of soldiers, slaves and beasts, I walked to the edge of the camp. Not far away was a dense forest of trees and brush, and I picked out my escape route. All I had to do was go around the next hill and I would be lost from view. No more than a few hundred steps. Yet almost immediately, I knew I could not run. My courage had not returned miraculously, but the idea that my friends and cohort would think badly of me was intolerable, even if I never saw any of them again.

And so, I walked to the front of the phalanx and took my position. Beside me, Crito was silent. I turned as Chaerephon clapped me on the back. "I'm glad you are here, Socrates. You give me strength," he said. Glancing down the line and seeing others nodding in agreement, I felt intense shame at my earlier cowardice. How appallingly close I had come to deserting my friends and fellow soldiers!

I was about to respond to Chaerephon when the commanding general, wearing a garland on his head, walked to the front and addressed us. "Know that a sheep has been sacrificed. The prophets have confirmed the imminence of battle and have foretold a bloodless victory."

Although I had no faith in prophets or the gods, the words filled the other men with confidence. I told myself that with good men and good soldiers on all sides, I would survive whatever lay ahead. The men bowed their heads in prayer to the gods, asking for deliverance from battle.

"Silence, and attention to the word of command!" a general shouted. "Up shields! Slope spears!"

I lifted my shield and rested my spear against my shoulder, ready to move. The trumpet sounded and we began our forward march, our arms clashing and tangling. We had not been properly drilled in far too long, and it showed. I strained to hear orders, but could hear only Chaerephon. "Come on, brave men," he shouted. "Show what you are made of!"

Then, at last, came the dreaded signal: "Level spears!" Grabbing my spear from the slope of my shoulder, I held it underarm for optimal thrust. Behind me, to build up their ferocity and their courage, men shouted and crashed their spears against their shields. "Stand by one another and fewer will die," Chaerephon yelled.

A great terror came over me suddenly, and my hands and feet began to feel numb. *Not now*, I told myself. *Don't stumble now*. Although unable to feel either my hands or my feet, I willed myself to march. I tripped over a stone, almost falling, but caught myself in time. I tried with every part of my being to banish my fear.

As the first stones hit my shield, I forced myself to remember my training. *The enemy must turn first. Do not flee*. I was on the point of losing control of my body when the first enemy spear struck my shield with horrible force, pushing me backward. I heard a man cry out. From the corner of my eye, I saw Crito fall. He clutched his neck and blood spurted from beneath his fingers.

Anger filled every part of me as I took a step to fill the gap where Crito had stood, and stabbed wildly about me with my spear. Suddenly, through the clang of spears on shields, and above the cries of enraged and terrified men, I was sure I heard the order from the generals to push. I echoed the order, as loudly as possible, to make it heard above the ghastly noise. My shield struck the enemy line and I felt Chaerephon's shield behind me, pushing against my back. The line moved forward. Spears struck my armour. My helmet was knocked off my head. I pushed on.

Suddenly, there was nothing left to push against. We had broken the enemy line. Skirmishes went on everywhere. Two enemy soldiers had engaged with one of our men, but I could not tell who the man was. He was on his knees, his spear gone. I jabbed at the enemy soldiers with my spear, giving the fallen man time to get up and pull out his sword. He swung it wildly to ward off a blow from a spear, but could not reach his attacker; his sword was too short and the enemy's spear too long.

The second attacker lunged at me. As I smashed aside his spear with my shield, I let out a loud and piercing scream, sounding more like a frightened child than a ferocious warrior. The attacker turned and fled. I should have given chase, but hesitated when I saw that the man who had fallen was down again. His attacker, intent on killing him, didn't see me as I thrust my spear into his side. The blow was poorly aimed, only glancing harmlessly off his breastplate. As the man swung around to face me, I felt suddenly panic-stricken, certain he would run his spear through me. To my astonishment, he dropped his shield and spear, and fled. Concerned only for my own life, I did not chase down my foe.

The man I had helped managed to speak. "Thank you, sir." His breathing was uneven.

I ignored him, wondering whether I should flee, but I scanned the area and saw no enemy soldiers nearby.

"You saved me," he said.

I nodded. We appeared safe for the moment.

"I am Alcibiades," he added.

And that was my first meeting with the legendary and enigmatic Alcibiades.

When the Potidaeans and their Corinthian allies had retreated into the walled city, I could only gape, appalled at the devastation. The ground was covered in dark blood. The air was filled with the moans of wounded survivors and the stench of sweat, vomit and excrement. Corpses, pierced by arrows, slashed by swords and speared by javelins, stared unseeingly into eternity. Fathers knelt over sons and brother held brother, all crying for their losses. At the perimeters of the battlefield, jackals gathered expectantly; birds of prey circled, waiting for us to depart, so that they could feast.

Chaerephon and I searched for Crito, only to learn that his body had been carried away. Stumbling along, I happened to come across my helmet and shoved it back on my head. When we had helped remove what remained of our fallen men, we stripped the enemy of their armour. The generals dedicated the best of the captured armour and weaponry as a trophy to the gods, after which we left the enemy to fight off the scavengers and collect their own dead.

I remember that at some point I paused to look toward Mount Olympus — you could see the distant mountain from Potidaea on clear, sunny days — and I thought of the foolishness of the generals. Nobody of importance lived on that mountain. Certainly nobody that deserved our thanks.

Chaerephon went off in search of Crito's remains. Unable to bear the thought of seeing my dearest friend's mutilated body, I did not join him. Instead, I washed myself in the sea, the cuts on my arms and legs stinging from the salt water. Passing many campfires as I returned to camp, I observed the different ways in which men reacted to battle. Some were silent and introspective, staring at their hands and rubbing their foreheads. Some wept soundlessly. Others talked very rapidly, proud of what they had achieved. Still others seemed relieved, happy that they had survived. They patted one another's backs, as if to say, "We did it. We're still alive."

Hoping companionship might dispel my morose thoughts, I sat down with the most upbeat men of my cohort and accepted a plate of lamb and a cup of wine. Apparently, having foolishly allowed his sheep to graze too close to the battle, a local farmer had been left with slaughtered animals. The smell of burning wood and roasting meat made my mouth water. Yet when I tried to partake of the meal, the food was like dust in my mouth and the wine like vinegar.

"Hello, fellows. May I join you?"

Turning, I saw the flames flicker over a perfectly formed face, now washed of blood and grime. It was Alcibiades, the young man I had helped on the battlefield.

"I brought something for you," he said, handing me a kingly gift: a quail egg. Then he passed around a jug of wine and congratulated the men on their victory. Young as he was, Alcibiades already radiated confidence.

"What did you collect?" he asked the others around the fire.

The men began to talk about the possessions they had removed from the dead. They discussed the beautiful trophy erected by the generals, and speculated about the men from whom the armour had been taken.

"Justice was done this day," Alcibiades declared jovially.

"You call it justice?" I challenged him.

"Yes," said he. "We vanquished our foe."

"But what is justice? Perhaps you can define it?"

A few groans sounded around the fire. "Don't get Socrates started," someone said.

"Particularly when he has been so quiet," added Chaerephon, emerging from the darkness. Cheerfully, he slapped me on the back and sat down beside me. His good mood angered me, for our best friend was dead. I would deal with the irrepressible Chaerephon soon enough, I resolved.

I turned my attention back to Alcibiades, who said thoughtfully, "I cannot, at this moment, define the concept of justice."

"And yet it is your opinion that it was achieved today?"

"Most assuredly, so."

"How do you know it?" I asked, getting to my feet. "Did your grammatiste teach you to discern the just from the unjust? If so, who is this teacher? Tell me, so I may go and learn from him."

Chaerephon grinned. "Be careful how you answer. Socrates likes to argue."

I glared at my friend.

"I didn't learn it at school," said Alcibiades.

"No instructor taught you about justice?"

"No, I learned it on my own."

"When was that?" I asked. "Did you know the meaning of justice a year ago?"

"Yes."

"Two years ago? Three, four years ago, you knew then, too?"

"I did."

"Ten years ago you were a child — were you not?"

"Yes."

"And ten years ago, I am certain, you thought you knew just from unjust?" I taunted.

"I did."

Alcibiades was answering as I had expected him to. "Are you sure?" I asked.

"I am."

"When you were a child playing at knucklebones, and lost, did you ever accuse the winner of being a cheat?"

"If someone cheated me, I did." Alcibiades said.

"So, even as a child you knew the difference between just and unjust?"

"Certainly."

"When exactly did you discover the difference?" I asked, waving a finger in his face.

"I cannot say." Alcibiades was more hesitant now.

I had the young man where I wanted him. "Then tell me, if you didn't learn it from a master, and didn't discover it on your own, how do you claim to know it?"

"I suppose… I do not know justice as I thought I did." His confidence was shaken, at last.

"So you don't really know the difference," I gloated.

"No, I suppose I don't." Alcibiades was clearly embarrassed.

I sat down to the sound of laughter, but it was not malicious laughter.

"Don't take it hard," Chaerephon comforted Alcibiades. "It is Socrates' habit to make people doubt themselves. He has cast his spell over me more than once. He is like the stingray that paralyzes you if you come too near."

More laughter.

"Rest assured," continued Chaerephon, "that many others before you have been unable to answer Socrates, and have been overwhelmed. You should know, too, that although I have heard many speeches about justice in the courts — good ones, at that — I still cannot say what it is."

Chaerephon's words must have made an impression on Alcibiades, for he looked less downhearted. As the men passed around the wineskin, Chaerephon elbowed me in the ribs, making me aware that the discomfort of strained muscles and bruised bones had begun to take hold. "I have news," he said, so softly that only I could hear him. "The dead walk."

I looked at him uncomprehendingly. "What do you mean?"

"Crito is not a corpse. He survived his wounds," Chaerephon said happily.

"*How*?"

"By the grace of the gods. A peltast carried him off when he went down. He is in his tent now."

Immensely relieved, and my pain instantly forgotten, I hurried off in search of Crito. I found him by a fire outside his tent, his face still smudged with dirt; his forehead, neck and one ear bandaged. Even in the dimness of the fire's dying flames, I saw that he was pale.

"I thought you had been killed!" I burst out, elated.

"I was not so lucky," he responded.

"Don't say such things!"

Crito's eyelids were heavy, his mouth turned down at the corners, his hair dishevelled. He appeared dejected.

"Are your wounds properly dressed?" I asked, concerned.

"A healer swabbed them with wine," he murmured, somewhat absently. Glancing up then, he looked at me sadly. "You saved me, Socrates."

I shook my head. "I did nothing."

"Yes, you did." He was suddenly ill-tempered. "Chaerephon told me so, as did the peltast who pulled me free. When I went down, you stepped in to cover me. Then you called for the line to push."

His anger puzzled me. "I only repeated the command that had been given already."

"Nobody gave the order. It came from you."

How I wished I had really been my friend's saviour, but I could not take credit for what was not true. "I heard the command," I insisted.

"Stop being so humble!" he shouted, and winced at the pain of his wound. "You called out an order and the phalanx obeyed."

I was even more confused. "I followed orders, Crito."

Crito was silent a while and then he said, "My father predicted you would make a formidable defender of Athens. He knew you were destined for greatness, and he wanted to be part of it. It's the reason he had the hoplite armour made for you."

"I was very fond of your father," I said, thinking how close I had come to deserting.

"And he respected you."

I looked at my friend in surprise. "Are you certain?" Although Thespis had treated me well, I had always felt stupid in his company. I did not recall being able to answer even one of the simple questions he posed.

"My father respected your determination and your ability to overcome your injuries," Crito said. "He saw in you a noble spirit."

Noble spirit, indeed, I thought. I, who had come so very close to abandoning my friends. "Your father was mistaken," I said slowly. "I am not the man he thought I was."

"Oh, but you are, Socrates. And so much more than that." Crito gazed toward the sea, almost as if looking at me would cause him pain. When he spoke again, his voice was quiet. "I wanted him to respect me, too."

The words astounded me. "He loved you!" I exclaimed.

"That is true, but he didn't admire me," Crito said sadly. He shook his head, as if uncertain whether to continue. After a while he said, "After my father died, you and I didn't see each other for three years, I'm sure you remember." Another pause. "It wasn't because I was busy, Socrates. I didn't want to see you because I was jealous. I knew I should tell you about the gift of the hoplite armour — and yet I almost didn't give it to you."

We were both silent for a while. I did not know how to respond to Crito's unexpected confession. In the end, I waited for him to speak first.

"I wish I were as brave as you," he said, at last. "I was frightened of battle and wanted to stay in Athens. When you came upon me yesterday, you knew my heart, and that angered me. Your insight made me feel exposed. I wondered how you could possibly know my uneasy state of mind. Did it show on my face? In the way I stood or held my hands? I asked myself how you could tell. I felt as if my soul were unprotected."

Still, I remained silent. "What would my father have thought of me?" he asked sadly, his eyes as tormented as if Thespis had been watching him at that moment.

I should have been honest. I should have told Crito that I had not guessed his state of mind. I should have admitted that his fears were the same as mine. Had I shown real courage at that moment — the courage to expose myself for what I was — I believe I might have prevented the journey I embarked on: the journey that has led me to this jail cell. But I was a coward, and I walked away.

DAY 14

I DID NOT SEE much of Crito while he was at Potidaea. When we were together, we were both cautious, not wanting to start on a topic neither of us wanted to discuss again. Our reasons for this were similar in some ways. Crito may have thought I was judging him although, in truth, his confession did not cause me to think any less of him. If anything, I felt great sympathy for my friend. For the first time I realized that, despite his wealth and position, he needed the same protection as other people; this made me regard him as more human than I used to. At the same time, I was reluctant to have Crito think less of me, so I did not admit my own fears. Indeed, I felt very much alone, unable to share my own human frailties with even my best friend.

Apart from my sense of isolation, I was also angry that I had failed to achieve the respect and glory I had longed for all my life. True, I had stayed to fight — but unwillingly. I had not fled battle only because I was worried what others would think of me if I deserted my cohort. I had survived by blind luck, and when the time came to chase down the enemy and finish them off, I thought only about retreat. Not the actions of a hero, or so I believed.

After the battle, the Potidaeans and their Corinthian allies had hidden behind their huge city walls. Why would they not? For one thing we could never scale such substantial fortifications; for another, the Potidaeans and Corinthians correctly feared beatings, torture, slavery and brandings, were they to come out of hiding.

We needed to ensure that no supplies entered Potidaea. To that end, we constructed our own walls to the north and south of the city, and had our ships block it to the east and west. I offered my skills as a stone-mason. I worked from dawn until dusk, but when I finally lay down, ex-hausted, my mind still plagued me. I could no more escape my thoughts than I could escape my shadow.

Unaware of my desire for solitude, young Alcibiades had himself as-signed to work with me. He reminded me of a friendly dog, bouncing with energy and anxious to please. I did not speak much with him, and was curt when I did. But he did not seem to mind my brusqueness. On the contrary, rather than listening to me talk, he preferred to speak about himself. I learned that Alcibiades was wealthy and of noble birth, able to trace his family history back to the last king of Athens. His father had died in battle when Alcibiades was only three, and Pericles had become one of his guardians. With his background, he was born to be a ruler, a fact he believed was his aristocratic right. He was very young when we met, only 19, yet already quite sure of himself. His self-confidence seemed impreg-nable. He saw himself as a future legend, destined to become a myth, to be mentioned in the same breath as Achilles and Heracles.

Not surprisingly, Alcibiades was conceited, much taken with his own cleverness. Once, he recounted a wrestling match in which he had taken part as a youth. Overmatched, desperate and about to be thrown, he had bitten his opponent's arm. His adversary had released him, crying out, "You bit me like a woman!" To which Alcibiades replied, "No, I bit you like a lion." The story was an early indication of his ability to turn a dis-tasteful action into victory.

I was astonished when Alcibiades brought men of his cohort to meet me, introducing me in the most complimentary way. Not only was I the hero who had saved him, but also, I possessed the wisdom of the seven sages. Following his lead, his friends also treated me with undeserved deference.

Despite my inner turmoil, I found myself warming to Alcibiades. He had undeniable charisma and showed great interest in my past, pester-ing me with questions while plying me with the drink he so obviously enjoyed. The more he learned about me, the more his admiration seemed to grow, and that, too, surprised me, for I saw my life as quite ordinary, even dull.

Apart from those in his cohort, men of all ages and types were drawn to the handsome Alcibiades, and they often appeared at the wall in search of him. Among his many admirers were a couple of men you will be familiar with, Critias and Anytus.

You know Critias, of course. What Greek has not heard of him? You likely know that he was a member of an aristocratic family. You may not know that as a younger man he fancied himself an intellectual, and loved to brag about a book he had read or had managed to procure for his library at home. Plain-looking though he was, Critias possessed a measure of charisma and political astuteness that made him appear clever. He spent his time at Potidaea composing poems, which, I must admit, weren't too bad. I recall he also aspired to being a playwright. An astounding choice for a man who would one day become a mass murderer!

And then there was Anytus, the other man responsible for confining me to this cell. Anytus' grandfather had started a leather tanning business and his father, Anthemion, expanded it into a significant enterprise. Chaerephon had done some business with them, and maintained that Anytus' father was a decent fellow — which was more than could be said for the son.

Although indifferent toward Critias, I took an instant dislike to Anytus. Headstrong and haughty, he was given to insults such as, "With looks like yours, Socrates, the gods must hate you," and "Everyone has a right to be ugly, Socrates, but you abuse the privilege."

These insults were peculiar, because Anytus himself is far from handsome — and I'm not saying this only because he has threatened your lives. He has a weak jaw, a low hairline and small, deep-set, dark eyes. This rather unpleasant face sits atop a long body and short legs. As a result his strides are impossibly long, making him look a bit comical.

Anytus fawned over the striking Alcibiades and resented the fact that the object of his ardour preferred my company to his, even though my friendship with Alcibiades was platonic. In revenge for Anytus' taunts, I would throw my arm affectionately over Alcibiades' shoulder, taking satisfaction in the sudden throbbing of the vein in Anytus' right temple.

Although Anytus was 10 years older than Alcibiades, he tried his best to emulate the younger man. He attempted to copy Alcibiades' charm and came across as insincere. He took up the same athletic pursuits as did Alcibiades and frequented the same women. He even took to drinking as vigorously as the younger man.

Summer gave way to fall and fall to winter. That first winter in Potidaea was the coldest, wettest, most miserable one I had ever experienced. Icicles hung from the trees, my breath was visible in the air and the whiteness of the snow was blinding on those rare occasions when the sun shone. The only winter that was worse was the year Critias and The Thirty ruled Athens. That was a terrible time, about which I will write another day.

Our camp had grown into a massive tent city by then. Districts had formed. An agora had sprung up where you could buy food or get your hair cut; it included a gymnasium and roughly erected temples. We even had access to a Kerameikos of sorts, where painted women and oiled men displayed themselves for midday dalliances. Most of us suffered from boredom. Worst of all was the stink of the latrines, not moved regularly enough, which could put a man off his food for life. How bad must it have been, then, for the men, women and children behind the walls of Potidaea?

The following summer, when we had been at Potidaea for more than a year, Chaerephon appeared with news. As feared, the Spartans had invaded the Athenian countryside and burned the fields for a second year in a row. Instead of leaving immediately after setting fire to the crops, they had stayed on for another 30 days, emboldening the local slaves to revolt.

More than 200 prominent men — Crito, Chaerephon and Alcibiades among them — were recalled to Athens to help remedy the situation. At the same time, thousands more soldiers were brought to Potidaea to help maintain the siege. The new arrivals brought reports from Athens that the war with Potidaea was costing an enormous amount of money. Eighteen hundred talents of silver — one third of the saved wealth of Athens — had been spent thus far, with no guarantee that the siege would be successful.

More infuriating than the money wasted was Pericles' refusal to engage the Spartans on land. The Athenian fleet harried Sparta's coastal allies, ramming war vessels and fishing boats alike. But, believing it prudent not to confront the extremely well-trained Spartan army on the battlefield, Pericles had allowed them to destroy the farmland surrounding Athens and the country homes of the rich, while forcing the local citizens to remain inside the walls of Athens. Enraged, the Athenians stripped Pericles of his generalship. For the first time in 28 years, he was not re-elected as one of the 10 generals.

Athens had other problems, too. A disease, which began to be called "the plague," had broken out shortly before the reinforcement soldiers sailed for Potidaea. The soldiers claimed that Apollo had caused the plague, for according to the Oracle, the God of Truth and Light had sided with the Spartans when Athens had broken the peace treaty signed 13 years earlier. The plague, as they saw it, was Athens' punishment.

Newly arriving soldiers brought with them the disease that was causing havoc in Athens. The illness began with red eyes and pains in the joints, back and head, accompanied by a dry hacking cough and vomiting. As the disease progressed, victims complained of great internal heat, and desperate cries for water were heard everywhere in the camp. Men raved, seeming not to know who they were any longer. Death generally came within seven or eight days of the onset of the disease. Those who managed to survive often lost the use of their arms and legs; some went blind.

The disease caused such terror that only physicians would aid the dying men, and then they sickened, too. Men pleaded for permission to abandon the siege. Some hid. Others ran away. Amulet makers, potion mixers and holy men did great business with the sale of protective spells. A thousand men died and another thousand were incapacitated. Even scavengers kept away from the corpses. Although the disease had largely abated by the end of the summer, the men continued to fear for their lives and avoided large gatherings as much as possible.

After a few months, the people of Potidaea could no longer withstand the siege. Our generals conferred with the Potidaean generals. Terms were set and the besieged citizens were permitted to leave the town. They emerged from the gates looking like walking skeletons. Most had only loincloths or scraps of fabric with which to cover themselves. Their faces bore masses of sores, their eyes were sunken and bones protruded through their skin. Rumours had been heard of cannibalism during the siege. We had not known whether to believe these tales, but seeing the way people averted their gazes from us, we took the rumours to be true.

With victory came our freedom to return home. Although it was winter by then and travel by ship was not safe, after nearly two years away most were worried about their families and many were willing to undertake the risky journey. As the latest communications from Athens had contained troubling stories about the plague, we were filled with foreboding as we wondered what we would find upon our return home.

The docks were unusually quiet when we arrived at Piraeus. Absent were all the normal activities. No boats were being repaired, no sheds being built. No fishermen hawked their catches. No slaves were sold. The only sound was the cry of the seagulls. Fear gripped the men as they left the ships. Even those with families were hesitant to enter the city.

I disembarked nervously and walked through the abandoned streets of Piraeus. Almost immediately, I was hit by an odour that was both sickly sweet and musty. Then I saw dead men, women and children piled in the dusty passages between houses, their corpses horrible shades of green and purple. Eyes bulged out of sockets and tongues protruded from dry mouths. Never had I seen anything like it, not even on the battlefield. As at Potidaea, even the scavengers knew better than to disturb the corpses.

Retching at the repugnant stench, I passed unmolested through Piraeus and hurried along the north long wall back to Athens. There, the deceased were piled in plain sight, heaped together along with the carcasses of dead livestock. The buzz of flies was incessant. My skin felt as if it were crawling with ants. I'd had no word from Diotima while I was at Potidaea, and I braced myself to find the bloated black corpse of the only family member I had left.

Arriving home at last, I hesitantly opened the courtyard door. "Diotima?" I called out.

No response.

Closing the door behind me, I entered the courtyard. "Diotima?" I called again, more loudly this time.

A woman I did not know emerged from the kitchen, holding one of my father's javelins.

With visions of Diotima having been forced from the house and chased away or even killed, I gripped my spear. "Who are you?" I demanded harshly.

"Xanthippe," the woman said, as indignantly as if I were the stranger in the house, not she. "Who are you? What do you want?" She spoke aggressively as she shook the javelin in her hand.

"I am Socrates. This is my home. Where is Diotima? What have you done with her?"

"Socrates?" Her voice dropped to a whisper.

"Yes. Now answer the question, woman!" I yelled. "Who are you?"

"Oh, Socrates," she said on a new note. "Diotima will be so happy that you have returned!"

The words gave me hope. "She is alive?"

"Yes! She has gone to draw water."

I ran to the public fountain, still holding my spear and pack. I found Diotima on her way home.

"Socrates!" she cried out, her voice thick with emotion. Dropping the jugs of water, she reached up and embraced me. Although she was very thin, she hugged me with the kind of strength a hoplite would be proud of.

After asking Diotima if she was well, I wanted to know about the strange woman in our home.

"She's there for her protection," Diotima explained.

"From the plague?"

"And from thugs."

It was late as we walked back to the house together. Our shadows lengthened behind us as we strode westward, toward the setting sun. Diotima filled me in on what had happened while I was away. The first summer, Pericles had advised people living in the countryside to enter the long walls and to bring with them everything they could. Caravans of families had arrived with their livestock and household furnishings. Some had even brought the main beams from their homes.

After ravaging the land and destroying the crops, the Spartans left. It was when they reappeared the following year and did similar damage that the sickness had begun.

As at the camp in Potidaea, the plague had driven people so crazy with thirst that they had jumped into wells and reservoirs. Those newly arrived from the countryside had suffered the most. It was the hot season and no houses were available for them. They lived in poorly ventilated huts and died in agony. The dead were dumped in mass graves, where they were burned and covered up with earth. When still more died, their bodies were abandoned in temples and in the streets. Funeral pyres were lit wherever bodies were piled.

"In the midst of horror, men became beasts," Diotima said, clearly revolted as she described the situation.

Because people believed they lacked a future, they became indifferent to the law. No one expected to live long enough to be brought to trial and punished. People thieved and killed. Diotima had heard stories of men breaking through the walls of homes to get at the women barricaded inside.

"Xanthippe's father and brothers died of the plague. Her mother and sisters were raped and killed. She was the only one left in her house. I met Xanthippe at the fountain, took her in and kept her inside." Diotima looked at me in sudden fear. "Did you catch the plague, Socrates?"

"No."

"We must get you home. You must stay inside. Only those who caught the plague and survived are safe."

"What about you? Did you catch it?"

"No, but I am old. You are the one who matters."

"Do you know anything of Crito or Chaerephon?" I asked, ignoring her concern.

"Nothing."

"I must find them."

"Come home, Socrates," Diotima pleaded. "Stay inside with Xanthippe. I'll inquire about your friends."

"No," I said and, changing course, I set off to find them.

Let me make something quite clear to you boys. It was not bravery that led me to expose myself to the plague. Nor did I sacrifice myself to help Crito and Chaerephon. I still reproached myself for my cowardice at Potidaea. I suppose I was also somewhat suicidal.

I went first to Crito's house and found him there. He was very thin and weak, as were his wife and sons. They had all caught the plague, but something — luck, or inner strength — had helped them recover. When I asked for news of Chaerephon, Crito said he had learned that Chaerephon's wife, a delicate woman, had died. That was all he knew, for he had not left his home in some time. I said I would make enquiries and promised to return later with water.

Approaching Chaerephon's house, I heard someone raving inside. "They've abandoned me! They've abandoned me!" I found Chaerephon on the floor of his andron, thrashing about and shouting, his eyes wide and wild. Around him, couches and tables had been overturned; pottery had been smashed. "They've abandoned me! They've abandoned me!" he continued to shout. I had witnessed this kind of crazed raging at Potidaea. Sadly, I suspected my friend did not have long to live.

I tried lifting him onto one of the couches, but his thrashing made that impossible. All I could do to make him comfortable was surround him with blankets and pillows. Then I searched the house. Seeing no sign of servants, I assumed they had deserted. In one of the bedrooms I found the oldest and youngest children, bloated and covered with flies. The stench of death made me vomit. I covered the children to protect them from the flies then went to the fountain for water. Returning to the house, I found Chaerephon passed out. I bathed him and sat beside him, not knowing what more I could do.

At some point, I became aware of sniffling noises. Following the sound to the storage area, I found Chaerephon's two middle children, five and seven years old at the time, huddling behind sacks of corn. Their eyes were wide with fear and swollen with weeping. They had been hiding for days but, fortunately, had not caught the plague.

I took the children back home with me, where they stayed with Diotima and Xanthippe in the safety of the house. After taking jugs of water to Crito, I went once more to Chaerephon. By then, he had recovered his senses enough to recognize me. I told him I would take care of his children and comforted him as best I could.

DAY 15

THE PLAGUE EVENTUALLY disappeared, as had happened at Potidaea. All told, 30,000 citizens and 50,000 women, children, foreigners and slaves died. Countless others were left physically disabled, unable to walk or use their arms. I did not keep a tally, but by my reckoning I would say that hundreds of people I knew personally perished. They included many from my cohort, co-workers from the wall, neighbours, acquaintances, friends and even old Crow Man. For me, the greatest loss was Simon.

I have wondered so often since the trial whether I might have chosen a different path had Simon remained a part of my life a little longer. Could he have saved me from my fate? Simon was wisdom personified; he helped me focus on what was truly important. Without him, I lost my way. Of course, it's also possible that I am so inflexible that no one could have changed me. Whatever the case, I miss him terribly. Thankfully, he was the only person really close to me who died of the plague.

Much to my surprise, Chaerephon and his two remaining children were spared. I can't imagine what it would have done to the man if his entire family had been taken. I expected Chaerephon to feel bitterness toward the gods, even to doubt them as I did after losing my mother and brother. Instead, his belief became more extreme than ever. He donated more of his wealth to public projects and observed the holidays more strictly. He even maintained that his faith had not been strong enough, and that the gods had abandoned him for that reason.

Crito changed, too. In a sense, he became more the person he had been all his life. Always courteous, he lavished affection not only on his family, but also on the slaves he treated as family. His brush with death seemed to have instilled in him a greater appreciation for life and those around him. Constant good cheer replaced the moroseness he had displayed after the Battle of Potidaea. Indeed, he seemed to possess a certain lightness, a kind of internal peace. It was as if the experiences of the past and his expectations for the future no longer weighed on him. I envied him that.

It is telling that both you boys, at different times and different ages, have asked me the same question about Crito: "Why is he always smiling, Father?" You will recall that my response was always the same, too: "Because he is Crito."

As your mother had no family left in the city, not even distant relatives, she remained in the house with Diotima and me. You will be happy to know — if you didn't know it already — that she made a favourable impression on me from the start. Her eyes were dark and lively, her lips full and sensual and as deeply red as pomegranate juice, her form lithe yet voluptuous.

I was intoxicated by your mother; at the same time, I felt nervous when she was nearby. In the evenings, she would sit in the courtyard, combing out her long hair. Although I was often there, too, my presence did not seem to disturb her. I would pretend to concentrate on sharpening my chisels, when all the while I was actually thinking of the lovely girl sitting so near me. How soft and delicious her lips looked; I wondered if I would ever get close enough to discover their taste. I found every excuse to dally in the courtyard. Since I could spend only so much time on my tools, I would chop firewood, repair imaginary cracks in the courtyard wall or offer to help Diotima comb the tangles out of wool, as I had done as a youth recovering from my accident. Anything to be around your mother!

I couldn't stop thinking about her. At one time, the ideas Simon and I had discussed had kept my mind occupied, especially the question of what it meant to *know thyself*. But now I could think only of Xanthippe.

She was beautiful and gentle, yet practical, too. Besides being an excellent cook, she was a wonderful seamstress, able to make even finer clothes than Diotima, which was saying something.

Eventually, Athens regained its sense of balance and control. People walked about the streets more calmly and behaved more appropriately. Merchants and customers slowly returned to the agora. Thievery and anarchy diminished as law was restored. When society returned to normal, your mother insisted on going to the fountain house alone. I followed her without her knowledge, to make sure she was safe. She walked with her chin up, as if daring anyone to taunt her for being out in public, especially unaccompanied. She seemed fearless. She refused to be confined like a typical Athenian woman, although later — selfishly — I would admonish her for her unseemly behaviour.

One day, she greeted me at the door and asked how I was.

"Quite content," I replied.

She asked me questions about stone carving and about my work on the city wall. Shyly, I described what I did. She wanted to try her hand at carving. We had no stone in the courtyard, but I showed her my tools and explained how to hold them.

She took the chisel from me. "Like this?" she asked. She held the chisel incorrectly, so I had to help her with the grip. Later, she told me she had always known how to hold a chisel, for her father had been a carpenter, but she had wanted me to touch her hand, which I did. Holding my gaze, she stroked my forearm tenderly, her touch as gentle as that of a harp player. Daringly, I put my hand on her waist and was amazed when she did not pull away. Instead, she embraced me, and I felt warmth flooding through me. I will say no more than that, for children are not interested in the private matters of their parents.

From that day in the courtyard, our courtship progressed quickly. I greeted her every morning with a comment on her beauty. I composed poems and delighted in reciting them to her. I brought her flowers nearly every day. The day of our wedding was the happiest of my life. My guilt at surviving the battle eased after our marriage, and the loneliness I had felt all my life vanished completely. I experienced a joy in simply being. Entering our courtyard at the end of each workday was like being caressed by a fresh ocean breeze.

Not long after our wedding, Alcibiades, the young man I had saved at Potidaea, sent me a message inviting me to a dinner party. Clad in a long purple cloak and a white linen tunic trimmed with gold, he stopped by the house to pick me up. I was a little dazed by his finery, for I still fashioned myself after Parmenides and Zeno, and wore only the simplest clothing, with no trimmings or adornment of any kind. On my feet I wore the sandals Simon had made for me years earlier.

Alcibiades was courteous to Diotima and gallant to your mother. I was concerned my beautiful bride would fall for the good-looking man, as he was nearer her age than mine and radiated an aura of infinite confidence and charisma. I need not have worried, though, for she didn't seem at all taken with him. I couldn't help feeling relieved.

The dinner party was at the home of a friend of Alcibiades. He led me to an immaculately kept house, somewhat, although not overly, larger than those owned by Crito and Chaerephon. When I asked who else would be attending the dinner, he said, "Just a few old acquaintances." Expecting to see his youthful cohort from Potidaea, I looked forward to a night of dancing girls, jugglers, joviality, and, above all, good food. My mouth watered at the thought of roasted hare, peacock eggs and iris bulbs in vinegar.

We were ushered into the courtyard. One wall displayed a mural of Achilles: the tiled floor presented a mosaic of Heracles. The mosaic reminded me of the one that had been in my father's andron. Not for the last time, I wondered which rich person's house it now adorned.

Instead of the youths I had expected to see reclining on couches in the tastefully decorated andron, the room contained eight men, among

them General Laches and the host, General Nicias. Although I had never met General Nicias, I knew of him. He was a distinguished-looking
man of great wealth, having inherited a large fortune from his father. It
was said he had a thousand slaves at the silver mines of Laurium, and
received, in return for their services, a share of the mines' proceeds.

Upon our arrival we found the men in the midst of a heated discussion.
They greeted me politely, but without warmth. Indeed, they seemed to
look me over in the manner of men accustomed to judging the painted
ladies of the Kerameikos, or slaves they might be interested in purchasing. I sensed their judgment of me was not favourable.

Alcibiades and I took our seats on a luxurious couch and were handed
cups of wine. As I took my first sip, I sensed how the evening would proceed. The wine was heavily watered, which meant conversation would
be of a serious nature. This was not the cheerful gathering I had hoped
for. The conversation was obviously an extension of discourse at the Assembly. The topic of discussion was Cleon, a beady-eyed man accused of
being a warmonger, who preyed on the fears and prejudices of the lower
classes as a means of gaining power in the Assembly.

Since I was not, by nature, very political, I merely listened while the
generals argued for joint opposition to Cleon. According to General
Nicias, the time had come to negotiate peace with Sparta, for we had
lost too many hoplites to the plague and had depleted our emergency
reserve of silver during the siege at Potidaea. In addition, a disturbing
rumour had been heard that the Spartans had sent ambassadors to the
Persian King. It would be impossible for Athens to take on both Sparta
and Persia.

As the conversation continued, I observed that Alcibiades drank a
great deal, with a boy servant refilling his cup a number of times before
anyone else needed more. General Nicias motioned to one of his slaves,
whereupon a beautiful woman appeared and began to play a harp in the
centre of the room. She was a skilled musician, I noticed, but the men
went on conversing and paid her no attention.

After a time, Alcibiades turned to me, said he was expected at another dinner party, and told me he would return. I was surprised he would leave me alone in a stranger's house, but said nothing, as I was unsure whether this was common practice for the very wealthy. In my insecurity, I also wondered whether I had done something to embarrass him.

I sat alone on the couch, excluded from the conversation. It was like being back in school, where I was tolerated only because my brother and Crito were popular. Now, here I was at a dinner party only because I was associated with Alcibiades. Although the other guests were not as blatantly hostile as school children — they would not call me names or throw rocks at me — they made me feel the same as I'd felt years earlier. The unspoken message was: *you do not belong*. By Zeus, I thought, I hope the food, at least, is good.

I must admit that the wealth and power of the other men intimidated me. All my life I had been taught to regard the rich as the elite — a difficult lesson to unlearn. I could not help thinking that the other men in the room slept on soft fleece beds, while I slept on straw.

As I waited for Alcibiades to return, I drank more wine to calm my nerves. Suddenly, Anytus, Alcibiades' sharp-tongued admirer from Potidaea, entered the room with a few men I did not know. He came inside, his short, stubby legs taking those impossibly long and purposeful strides I had noticed before, and reclined on a couch close to me. I caught his eye, and was aware that he saw me, too, although he quickly averted his gaze. The men he was with fell about on other couches and whispered among themselves.

"As I was saying," said Anytus, loudly enough for his words to carry over the sound of the harp, "Alcibiades is too good to be fooled by some poor rube claiming to be a wise and clever man."

It was obvious he was talking about me.

"Alcibiades is quick to discover those of no value," he continued. With a fake laugh, he turned to me. "Oh, Socrates. It *is* Socrates, isn't it? What a happy occurrence. I have been looking for you."

I was in no mood for his games. "And you are …?" I asked.

His face twisted unpleasantly. "Anytus, son of Anthemion."

"Anytus… Anytus…" I glanced upward, as if searching my memory. "Ah, yes," I said then, snapping my fingers, "I do recall the name. Your father is a good man. Some say a great man. I have heard he is modest and humble and an upstanding member of the community. You must be very proud to have such an admirable father."

"I am," he said.

"And you were looking for me? What can I do for you?"

"We were discussing who should lead Athens, now that we have lost Pericles."

"A good question. No doubt, you have an answer?"

I knew from Alcibiades that Anytus had political ambitions, and fancied himself the future of Athens.

"On the contrary, Socrates. We have all heard of your lofty thinking. We know that you discuss all manner of topics in the agora, and walk about with your head in the clouds. So we would like to hear *your* opinion." He chuckled, as did his friends, at what he evidently thought his cleverness. "Please, do tell us." He cocked his head and smiled, feigning sincerity.

Aware that he wanted to belittle me, I said calmly. "I do not know."

"The wise and learned Socrates doesn't know?" Now he pretended astonishment.

"No, I don't."

"How disappointing. My friends and I came here to find you, and you have nothing to offer?"

I heard some snickers. The other men in the andron had halted their conversations and were listening to us.

"Not only that, my dear boy," — I emphasized the word "boy," although he was over 30 — "but I don't know anyone who does."

Anytus regarded me, his expression unreadable. "How very strange, because I know of someone who knows the answer. You know him, too."

"My memory is bad. Of whom do you speak?"

"Alcibiades, of course."

"What does Alcibiades say?" I asked.

"That the men chosen to lead Athens are those whom the gods have endowed with the finest of characteristics. They are born for it."

"Born for it? Do you mean they have the right parentage?"

"Yes," he responded.

"Are you saying that great men, great leaders, are born to great parents? Just as the best chariot horses are born to the best mares and stallions?"

"Correct," said Anytus.

"What about those who do not have the right breeding, who are not born to the right parents?"

"They are simply not our equals." Anytus made a gesture that embraced the wealthy and powerful men in the andron. "They cannot do what comes so naturally to us." He emphasized the word "us."

"I understand," I said, and wondered how well Anytus knew his history. "When we speak of great men, we speak of such as Pericles?"

He bowed his head dutifully. "Of course. Pericles was a man without equal. He rebuilt our city. He gave us back our pride. He made Athens the centre of Greece."

"Yes," I agreed, "a great man, indeed. His father commanded at Mycale. What better pedigree could a man have? And Pericles brings to mind another man: Aristides. Was he not great?"

"You mean Aristides the Just," Anytus said, as if giving me a history lesson.

"What do you know of Aristides the Just?" I asked.

"He was a general at the Battles of Salamis and Plataea, and a man of noble family."

"Ah yes, very noble. And, of course, there is Themistocles." I was prodding him to continue, luring him into a trap.

"Another great man," Anytus agreed, without hesitation. I glanced around. Everyone was watching us. General Nicias lifted a hand to silence the harp player. The room fell silent.

"Do you recall Themistocles?" I asked.

"He was a hero at the Battle of Salamis. A leader who recommended the building of our navy, which allowed us to defeat the Persians, and..." Anytus paused.

I wondered if he had realized his error. Pericles himself had spoken of Themistocles as a hero whose naval vision and tactical genius at the Battle of Salamis had saved all of Greece from the Persians. But Themistocles had been an immigrant child with parents of no significant lineage and he had grown up in the Kerameikos district. Themistocles' second wife was from my neighbourhood, so I knew a fair bit about the man. One story I'd heard was that, as a boy, he would persuade well-born children to exercise with him so he would appear to be one of them.

"That is right." I spoke before Anytus had time to correct his statement, as I assumed he had recognized his error. "A great man, Themistocles. If not for him, we'd all be slaves, speaking Persian!" I pressed on. "It must follow, naturally, that in your opinion the children of great men must also be born to greatness. As you say, the best chariot horses come from the best mares or stallions. I take it you still maintain that?"

"Most assuredly."

"Then let us speak of Pericles. No doubt he was a great man."

"No doubt at all!" Anytus said loudly, aware that all eyes were on him.

"He had two sons from his first wife. Both died of the plague a year before their father succumbed. You knew them, did you not?"

"I did," he said, pretending sadness.

"What did you know of them?" I asked.

It so happened that Pericles' sons had been nicknamed "the cabbage-sucking twins." Although not actually twins, they were equally dim-witted, despite Pericles' efforts to have them educated by the best instructors, including the great thinker, Anaxagoras.

"Unfortunately, we will never see what level of greatness they could have reached," Anytus said sharply.

"Correct. And then there is Pericles' remaining son, Pericles the Younger. He is not yet of an age for us to know what he might become. Unfortunately, therefore, we cannot use Pericles as the perfect example of your learned opinion."

"I agree."

"But going back to Themistocles — most of his sons survived to full manhood. Who are they, again?"

Anytus hesitated, so I mentioned the names of the children, most of whom had done nothing much of note. Only when I mentioned the name of Themistocles' youngest son, did Anytus' eyes brighten.

"A famous horseman," he declared, triumphantly. "It is said he could hurl a javelin while standing upright on horseback."

"True," I agreed, "A fine cavalry man, indeed. But he gambled away his inheritance on horse races. A massive sum, too! He didn't turn out wise and good like his father, did he?"

Anytus looked stunned, as did the others in the room.

"But I must be in error," I said, openly sarcastic now. "You must have meant another Themistocles — one with whom I am not familiar. Aristides, on the other hand — you did mean to include him as a great man? I speak of Aristides the Just, general at the Battle of Plataea, just so there is no confusion."

"Absolutely," said Anytus.

"And the son of Aristides the Just — what became of him?"

Anytus would know this, I felt certain. Everyone in Athens knew it. Aristides' son was still living in Athens, an indigent old man wearing threadbare clothes and living off the generosity of the city. He ate at no cost at the Tholos, by virtue of his father's reputation. Aristides had also had two daughters, both unmarried and also supported by the city.

Anytus remained silent, so I spoke for him.

"That's right — the son of Aristides the Just did not prove himself better than any other man, did he?"

Silence was thick and heavy on the air. Everyone was looking at Anytus, waiting for him to respond. I also waited, but, as before, my opponent did not speak.

When Anytus didn't respond, I said, "None of these men amounted to much, despite their grand parentage. Do you not agree?"

Anytus remained silent, his expression awkward.

"I want to thank you," I said. "You have been very helpful. You have allowed us to determine that men bred and educated for greatness often turn out to be grave disappointments. As a matter of fact, distinguished lineage would seem to be a recipe for mediocrity, if not outright failure!"

Anytus sneered at me.

I looked at him. "Oh, yes, I forgot! We began our conversation by praising your father. A good man, we agreed. A great man, even." Briefly, I wondered whether he was clever enough to understand the insinuation.

I watched his eyes fill with a fiery rage. He got to his feet, came over to where I lounged on a couch, and stabbed his finger into my chest. "Be careful with your slander, Socrates. It will get you into trouble."

I feigned shock. "Anytus thinks I defame him," I said, speaking to that gathering of powerful men. "He considers himself a future leader of Athens because of his natural gifts. But do not fear," I called to him, as he was leaving the andron, "Perhaps you will be fortunate and escape the affliction of failure."

Shortly after Anytus left the party, I departed as well. There seemed no reason to stay. I was nearly home before I realized I'd left without eating. Stupid move. Who was the cabbage sucker now?

DAY 16

I T WAS VERY hot today. The kind of day on which Athenians stay inside to escape the unbearable heat. I have mentioned that my cell stays cool even on hot days; however, the guards have been complaining endlessly today, even more so than the poor souls awaiting their end as I do, so I know it must really be bad. This is the first time I've felt somewhat fortunate for my confinement in this cell. Don't tell anyone — they'll think I've lost my wits.

I have also heard rumours from the guards that the ocean winds have been weaker and less consistent than usual for this time of year. Not significant for the ordinary Athenian, perhaps. For me, though, it may mean an additional few days before the sacred ship returns from Delos. A slight reprieve until my sentence — all our sentences — will be carried out. I figure I have 12 to 14 days left.

I wonder, have you boys packed your belongings? I continue to hope you will go to Thebes, as I've advised. You should remember that some of my students are from there — young men of great wealth, who will know the right people to help you get situated. Take advantage of their kindness, I beg you. Don't be stubborn, like me.

Today's heat puts me in mind of a similar day long ago. I was sitting alone in our andron, brooding over events that had happened recently. I had not heard from Alcibiades since the dinner party, nor did I expect to. He would have learned about my acrimonious discussion with Anytus, and known I had offended his friends. These men, with their high opinions of themselves, would probably think I had insulted their sons. Those who held their fathers in great regard would believe I had insinuated they were all failures. Alcibiades had revered his long-dead father, so he would no doubt be insulted, too.

Although I had intended the insults at the time, I was disappointed to lose the attentions of Alcibiades. The fawning of the handsome, well-connected young man had bolstered my self-esteem, and its absence reminded me of what I still did not possess, and perhaps never would. At the age of 40 I still did not have the things I had desired since I was a boy. Convinced that my life was a failure, I was depressed. I was disagreeable at work and curt with my friends. Worst of all, I no longer treated your mother with the love and attention she deserved. In short, I had started to behave very much like my father.

On the particular hot afternoon I'm recalling, Chaerephon and Crito paid me a surprise visit.

"I saw her! I saw her!" Chaerephon exclaimed, before I could get out a word of greeting. His voice throbbed with excitement.

It was months since I had seen him. Fearing the air of Athens still carried the plague, he had taken his two surviving children to his home outside the city. His appearance shocked me, for he was dirty and seemed not to have bathed in some time. I led my friends to the andron and Diotima brought us something to drink.

"I spoke with the Oracle of Delphi!" Chaerephon burst out.

My eyes widened with astonishment. I knew of only one other person who had actually spoken with the Oracle.

"When? What happened?" I asked, my despondency immediately forgotten.

"I went to Delphi after leaving Athens. I travelled the same road you and I walked years ago. When I arrived, I put my name on the list and handed the priest my offering."

I was intrigued. "What did you give this time?"

"A talent," he said.

My jaw dropped. One silver talent. Six thousand drachmas. More than I could earn in 10 years of work, possibly half of Chaerephon's wealth. I glanced at Crito, whose raised eyebrows told me that he, too, found it difficult to believe. Oh, impetuous Chaerephon!

"For seven days I sat and prayed to Apollo," Chaerephon went on. "I begged the God of Truth and Light, 'Let me know your wisdom!' Eight days went by. Then a priest stood beside the statue of Apollo and revealed the names of those who would be allowed to pose their questions. I cannot begin to express my joy upon hearing I was one of them!

"The Oracle emerged from the temple. She was young and wore a plain, white, ankle-length dress. I followed her along the path to the sacred Castalian spring, where she purified herself in a cleft of rock surrounded by trees. After she had finished, the other successful supplicants and I followed suit. The Oracle led us back up the hillside, through the sanctuary, past the statues and stoas and temples. She paused to inhale smoke from burning laurel branches held by a priest and then entered the temple.

"I lined up with the others outside the temple door. The man in front of me had brought a goat to be sacrificed. The priest poured water onto the bleating animal, but when it failed to tremble correctly, its owner's session was cancelled. I worried that I would suffer the same fate and be barred from the temple, for I, too, had purchased a goat.

Hardly breathing, I watched as the priest poured water over my animal. To my relief, it trembled correctly, from the hooves upwards, whereupon the priest sacrificed it and examined its entrails. Telling me the signs were favourable, he asked the nature of my question for the Oracle. He then wrote the question on a piece of papyrus, sealed it, and handed it to me. Then at last — *at last!* — the door was opened to me." Chaerephon's eyes shone with wonder, as if he were about to enter the Temple of Apollo again.

"As the door swung open, I caught a whiff of some fragrant aroma. I stepped inside the temple, and the door closed behind me. I found myself in a dark chamber, lit only by torches on the walls. It may have been a trick of the eye, I can't be sure, but that first chamber appeared to be made of black marble. As a priest led me from this chamber into another, we passed a statue; the light was faint, and I could just make out the image of Zeus. On we went, toward a hearth in which a small fire burned. From the flames emanated the smell of roasting goat, laurel leaves and burning barley. Beside the hearth were a huge altar and a spring.

"Now we entered the inner sanctum. I stepped down into a sunken space below the level of the temple floor. Against the far wall stood a golden statue of Apollo, as well as the Omphalos stone that marks the centre of the world. The Oracle sat in a recess on the opposite side of the sanctum, slumped over on a three-legged stool placed above a chasm. On either side of the Oracle stood two priests; all were silent.

A sweet, unearthly scent rose from the chasm, so heady it made me feel woozy. The Oracle was motionless, in a trance. In one hand she held a dish, in the other a sprig of laurel. The priest with whom I had entered the temple bade me place my question in the dish. As I did so, the torches flickered, as if blown by a breeze. The Oracle's breast heaved and she threw back her head. Suddenly, her face came to life. As it glowed with the power flowing through her, she took on the look of an old woman. She began to moan and wail, and I grew frightened.

"The priest who had shown me where to place my question interpreted the Oracle's unfamiliar language for me. 'Who are you? Whom do you represent? What will you do with the information you receive?' he asked me. I responded, and he gave the Oracle my answers. She spoke again, in a wail of pain. The priest confirmed my question could be asked. Breaking the seal on the papyrus, he read the question to the Oracle. Once more she spoke in the unfamiliar language and the priest interpreted. When he had finished, I thanked Apollo, the Oracle and the priests, and was guided out of the dark temple and back into the sunlight."

"What was your question?" asked Crito.

Chaerephon turned to him. "I asked if there was any man wiser than Socrates."

"*What*?" I exclaimed, stunned.

"I asked if any man is wiser than you," Chaerephon told me.

The statement was so far beyond anything I could have imagined, I could only stare at him wordlessly.

"What did the Oracle say?" Crito asked.

"I expected the answer to be cryptic and rambling. Instead, it was simple," Chaerephon replied.

"What was it?" I found it difficult to speak calmly.

"No one is wiser," came Chaerephon's shocking response.

"No one is wiser?" I repeated disbelievingly.

I was dumbfounded as my friends stared at me. I had only one thought: *I wish my father could have heard this.*

The following day was as hot as the one before. I went to visit Crito. His children had recovered from their illness and played around him in the relative coolness of his andron.

"Do you think Chaerephon fabricated his trip to Delphi?" I asked. "Do you think it's true he spoke to the Oracle?"

"You think he lied?" my friend asked.

"I don't know. After all, Chaerephon is Chaerephon."

Crito smiled. "Yes, he is."

"I think what he told us may be his way of thanking me for protecting his children during the plague," I said thoughtfully.

"He is grateful, yes, and for a lot more than what you did during the plague. But Chaerephon is a believer, Socrates. He may be impulsive, but he is also very pious."

"Do you think he is honest?"

"I do."

I looked him in the eye. "Are you an honest man, Crito?"

"Don't start with me," he responded firmly. "Just tell me what's on your mind."

Looking at the children playing at his feet, I asked, "Have you ever lied to protect someone's feelings? Perhaps you've told your wife she looked beautiful when she appeared tired?"

"Yes."

"So it is fine, sometimes, to speak untruths, if it benefits a person you care about. In other words, some lies are acceptable?"

Crito glanced at his children, then back at me. "Possibly. But I wouldn't be concerned in this case, Socrates. As you know, three priests witnessed the event."

"So you say. I have not met them."

"Don't you understand? Chaerephon would suffer dire consequences if he were found to have lied. No, my friend, I believe he consulted the Oracle of Delphi, and heard the words he reported to us."

Crito had given me much to think about. I was quiet for a long moment before asking, "How would the Oracle have heard about me? And don't tell me it was from Apollo."

Knowing how I felt about the gods, Crito laughed. "You are a skeptic, Socrates, I know that. But remember, Delphi is the centre of the earth. All kinds of people gather there. The rich and powerful, as well as the poor from all over the world, all make their way to Delphi. As they wait in line or sit around their campfires, they share stories about their lives and homes. You must have experienced this yourself when you went there with Chaerephon."

I nodded.

"The priests are there every day, listening to people talking and hearing a lot. They constitute the greatest repository of facts anywhere. They know things no one else can know, and have accurate information about events in the most distant places."

"Maybe so — but it doesn't explain how I would have come to their attention," I said doubtfully.

"Imagine you are a priest at Delphi," said Crito. "Every day you speak with hundreds of people who want to see the Oracle. You write down the names of the supplicants and accept their offerings. You ask about their questions for the Oracle, the reasons for the questions, and what they intend to do with their new knowledge. You also ask them about themselves: from where they hail and their occupations; about their families, their athletic interests, their political beliefs and what they have seen of interest during their travels. And once in a while, you hear about a man who seems to be known by people from as far away as Egypt, Thrace and Persia. A supplicant may say, 'I met a man who walks about the agora of Athens, and speaks with anyone who will listen. He goes on about the importance of knowing thyself.'

"So now you are intrigued, because you are a priest of Apollo and these words — *know thyself* — are inscribed on the building where you work. You want to know more. What does the Athenian say? Does he have an explanation for the words, and if so, what is it? He says he knows nothing, yet he wishes to find an answer, the supplicant tells you. You, the priest, ask, 'And did you provide him with an answer?' 'I tried,' says the supplicant, who is honest with you, for he is in the presence of Apollo, and fears a lie will hurt his chances of speaking with the Oracle. 'But each time I did so, the man showed me that I didn't have an answer, and that I was as ignorant as he was.' Curious, you ask, 'What is this man's name?' And the supplicant responds, 'Socrates, son of Sophroniscus, of Athens.'"

Crito paused, but I was impatient to hear more, and urged him to continue.

"Imagine the fascination of the priests when they hear the same story again and again. A man from Athens, the most prosperous city in Greece, promotes the most important words in Delphi. Don't you think it appeals to them, Socrates? Isn't it akin to your praising the merits of Simon's sandals to everyone you know? What excellent publicity for Delphi. Why do you wonder at it?"

Troubled, I looked at him. "Because I don't believe that *know thyself* means to know your place before the gods, as Chaerephon and the priests believe. And because — "

Crito held up his hand, interrupting me. "I know your interpretation," he said. "You believe you know nothing. And that's all very well. But what would the priests of Delphi make of that? If you, Socrates, don't know the answers, and if you prove to those you converse with that they don't know the answers, either, who does that leave?"

"The gods," I said slowly.

"Correct! And which god is known to converse with mortals, if only through a mortal woman?"

I drew a deep breath, then exhaled. "Apollo."

"Exactly." Crito smiled at me, satisfied.

DAY 17

RUMOURS OF CHAEREPHON's encounter with the Oracle spread quickly through the city, but the result was not what I expected. Men spoke in whispers when they saw me, and boys pointed when they thought themselves unobserved. When I mentioned this to Crito, he teased me, saying I should be used to the attention by now.

I was annoyed. "Be serious."

He reminded me of the old story of Croesus, king of Lydia, who asked the Oracle of Delphi whether he should go to war with the Persian Empire. "When the Oracle responded that if he did so, he would destroy a great empire, Croesus thought she meant the Persian Empire, not his own. Maybe now the Athenians interpret the Oracle's answer to mean you are not a wise man but a cabbage sucker," Crito said, laughing.

I didn't think he was funny, but he was probably correct.

Nonetheless, a few people did seek me out. They expected rites and ceremonies, as if I were a priest possessed of some secret knowledge. They touched me in hopes of receiving visions. They wanted succour from their afflictions or asked me to grant them eternal life.

Once, a disturbed man even tore the amulet from my neck and ran off with it. Furious at the theft of my brother's talisman, my only tangible reminder of him, I ran through the crowd, pushing aside citizens, foreigners and slaves until I found the thief at the newly started Stoa of Zeus. I tackled him and wrestled the amulet away from him. Not very becoming behaviour for a wise man.

I insisted to the people I met that I was not a prophet or a soothsayer, but a man who searched for answers, as they did. When I tried to engage them in discussion, they turned away. They didn't want to analyze their existence. They wanted quick and easy answers.

No one of importance sought my counsel. I don't know what I would have said if they had. Not only had I not discovered any great truth, I could not offer wisdom along with witty sayings. However, my reputation did allow me one benefit; I met several interesting people, one of whom was Diagoras of Melos. People called him "Diagoras the Atheist."

I wonder whether you boys remember Diagoras? Years ago, he visited the house regularly. Then again, you may have forgotten him, for you were quite young the last time he came. He was as tall as Crito, although less thickly built. Brown-eyed and brown-haired, he had a ready smile. His face was heavily scarred from all the fights he had been involved in. With no children of his own, he was quite taken with you boys, enjoying what he called your "untainted enthusiasm for life."

Diagoras was a well-known non-believer. A story about him concerned a ship during a bad storm. When the captain and crew questioned whether the presence of a godless man on board had caused the storm, Diagoras asked if they thought other boats suffering the same storm also carried non-believers as passengers. Whenever I heard Diagoras' clever responses, as this one certainly was, I envied his intelligence.

I had my own experiences with his impiety. Diagoras once asked me to meet him in the agora during the festival honouring Heracles, greatest of the Greek heroes. The festival took place on a perfect summer day, when the temperature was ideal for the athletic events. Crito had been invited and Chaerephon insisted on joining us, as well. I believe Chaerephon saw himself as my moral guardian, with a duty to shield me from evil influences. His piety had not weakened since he regained his health after the plague, and I think he felt a responsibility to guide me back to the light.

We found Diagoras concentrating intently on making a fire in front of the old wooden Stoa of Zeus; construction had just begun on the new one. The occasion brought back the memory of my neighbour and former classmate, Lycon, who had tried to burn it down so many years earlier. I wondered what folly Diagoras was up to. A crowd had gathered to watch him build the fire. When it was burning, he placed on it a pot filled with water, then squatted on his heels and surveyed his audience. I greeted him, and introduced Chaerephon. Diagoras and Crito knew each other already.

"What are you doing?" Crito asked.

"I'm about to cook some turnips," Diagoras responded.

"Why here?" asked Chaerephon. "Why don't you cook them at home?" Aware of Diagoras' reputation, Chaerephon was suspicious.

"This is where I need to cook them." Diagoras' tone was a little too innocent.

"But why here?" Chaerephon persisted.

"I wish to share my meal with as many friends as possible."

Diagoras fed more wood to the fire and we talked about the beautiful weather. The crowd around us grew larger. Although athletic events were normally held outside the city because of space limitations, the people watching Diagoras began to wonder if part of the festival had been moved inside the city walls.

"Have you heard of Heracles?" Diagoras asked, straight-faced.

Enjoying his dry humour, I burst out laughing at the ridiculous question.

"Of course," Chaerephon responded stiffly, as if his intellect and integrity were being challenged. Crito's usual grin widened.

"You do know, then, that when Heracles was driven mad by Hera, the Queen of the Gods, he slew his wife and six sons?"

"Of course." Chaerephon sounded irritable.

"When he recovered his sanity, Heracles was filled with regret." Turning from Chaerephon, Diagoras addressed the whole crowd, his voice loud enough now to be heard all the way to the Tholos. "To atone for his heinous action, Heracles travelled to Delphi to ask Apollo's advice. The Oracle instructed him to serve the king of Argos for 12 years, after which he would be rewarded with immortality. As we all know, Heracles performed 12 feats of incredible strength, courage and cunning during his years of service, thus becoming the famous hero revered in all of Greece."

Diagoras pulled a fine wood carving of Heracles out of a sack and showed it to the listening people, who exclaimed respectfully at its quality. The fire was burning well by now, the water in the pot bubbling vigorously. With all eyes on him, Diagoras made a big spectacle of dropping a few turnips into the pot.

"Personally," he went on loudly, "I don't think Heracles did enough penance to atone for killing his family!" And to the shock of his audience, he threw the carving of the god into the fire. "Perform your 13th labor and cook my turnips!" he yelled.

I burst out laughing, while Crito covered his mouth to stifle his mirth. But we were the only two amused by the scene. After the shock of seeing Heracles' likeness thrown into the fire by a mere mortal, the crowd broke up quickly, fearing association with an immoral madman.

"You take great risks," I said to Diagoras, when everyone had dispersed.

"Not really," he said.

"Anaxagoras was exiled from the city for writing that the sun was a hot rock in the sky," Crito said.

"I can barely write." Diagoras looked at him, his expression deadpan.

"You know what I mean," Crito said.

"I do, but Anaxagoras had the ear of Pericles. He was exiled because he had influence, not because he promoted impious ideas. I can't think that anyone would take the trouble of going to court to have me exiled."

What Diagoras said made sense to me, yet after that things became a bit difficult for him, all the same. His atheism was blamed when the plague returned the following summer. Still, although a few hostile men attacked him, he didn't seem bothered. The disease ran its course fairly quickly and without much loss of life this time, and Diagoras resumed his irreverent talk and demonstrations.

But there was more to that fateful afternoon at the stoa. Soon after leaving Diagoras, we came across Lycon giving a speech under the plane trees of the agora. Bigger than ever now, and sporting a second chin, he had made himself a public speaker and speechwriter. The insults he had tossed at me during my brief time in school proved to have been training for the slander he now threw around in court. As paid speaker for many prosecutors, his speeches before juries had taken down more than a few good, honourable, hard-working men. Many lost their farms and homes after being falsely accused of crimes such as theft or failure to pay for livestock.

I never saw Lycon take the side of an honest man. Only the wealthy — many of whom happened to be corrupt — could afford his fees. One victim of his brutal dealings was a man I happened to know — a mason, decent and hardworking — driven to such despair that he took his own life. After his death, his wife was forced to marry a hard-hearted fellow who became a taskmaster to the children left behind. Lycon had a knack for attacking men who had no experience in the courts.

When I spotted him beneath the plane trees, he was flaunting his speechmaking abilities, trying to drum up more business for himself. As if to lend weight to his oratory skills, he held a scroll of papyrus in his hand. In the past, I would have ignored him as I walked by. The rational thing to do when you come across a poisonous snake is to give it wide birth, and I had always feared this particular snake. But that was not what I wanted to do in this instance. Inspired by Diagoras' brave demonstration, and feeling more cantankerous than usual, I had an irresistible urge to strike the snake with a stick.

"You speak well," I called loudly from the rear of the crowd. "What are you teaching?"

Crito and Chaerephon stopped walking, looking first at me and then at each other.

"Socrates," Lycon said, recognizing me, and clicking his tongue in disgust. "I teach the noblest of arts."

"And what is that?"

"Speaking," he responded.

I pretended to think about this. "Am I, then, to call you a rhetorician?"

"Yes, Socrates. A good one, too."

"Do you claim you can make other men rhetoricians?"

"I can."

"What is the prime concern of rhetoric?" I asked.

"The art of speaking well," he replied, without hesitation.

I feigned ignorance. "And what is the goal of a man who learns to speak well?"

In the audience were a number of men with whom I had argued at times. Recognizing my method of questioning, they chuckled.

Lycon laughed, too, as if I were joking. "The goal is to persuade and motivate."

"What do you mean by persuade, Lycon?"

"To cause someone to do something."

"That sounds wonderful. What do you mean by motivate?"

"To inspire action!" he responded enthusiastically.

"Ah, action. That sounds excellent, too. And where might the art of persuasion be used?"

"Why, in the courts of law and the Assembly."

"What do you do there?"

"Persuade the judges in the courts or the citizens in the Assembly. If you have the ability to speak well, the physician will become your slave and the moneymaker will gather treasures for you." Lycon spoke grandly, as much to the onlookers as to me.

"In other words," I said, "speaking well gives you the power to rule over others."

"Correct."

"You must have a lot of power yourself," I observed, "if you can teach people to make slaves of others."

"Yes."

"I see people in the audience who desire to be your pupils. A good many, judging by the size of the crowd." I allowed a moment to go by before I continued. "Can you teach *anyone* the art of rhetoric?"

"Indeed, I can," he replied confidently.

"You must be a very good teacher."

"I am."

"And you must charge a lot?"

"I charge a fair price for the knowledge I impart."

"That is good to hear," I said. "However, you must take care whom you teach."

"Why?" he asked.

"Well, Lycon, you say you can create slaves of others. What if you taught a man the art of rhetoric, and he used it to convince a jury to condemn an innocent man? Would that be a good thing?"

When Lycon remained silent, I said, "What you teach is wrong, because people can use it for wicked purposes, such as turning a jury against a good man."

The crowd murmured restlessly; a few made rude comments.

Lycon looked concerned, but only for a moment. Grinning smugly, he said pityingly, "Oh, Socrates, your lack of education has made you dull. Or was it the horse that stepped on your head that did that?" He laughed. "As I said, I teach the noblest of arts. Let me offer you an example — if you can follow it, of course.

"I have frequently gone with my brother, an excellent physician, to see his patients. Although sick and needing help, some were afraid to follow his advice and agree to the necessary remedies. They would not let him give them medicine, or apply knives or hot irons. But because I was there, I was able to persuade them to heed my brother's advice. In each case, the patient regained his health. Had I not been there, they would surely have died.

"So you see, Socrates, what I teach is good. And as for your concern that my good teaching could be used for evil purposes, let me say that rhetoric should be used like any other art. The student rhetorician ought not to abuse his power any more than a pugilist should abuse his. He ought not to harm others.

"Further to your concerns, suppose a man trained in the gymnasium becomes a skillful boxer. What would happen if he struck his father or mother or one of his friends? That would not be a reason to detest his instructors or to banish them from the city. After all, they taught their art for a good purpose, to be used against enemies in self-defence, not in aggression. You will understand, therefore, that the instructors are not at fault. Rather, those who make bad use of the art are to blame.

"The same argument holds for rhetoric. The rhetorician needs to use his art fairly, as an athlete would use his athletic powers. If, after becoming a rhetorician, he makes bad use of his skill, surely his instructor ought not to be held responsible. For the teacher intended the student to make good use of what he learned. So, it must be the student, not the instructor, who should be detested, banished or put to death."

A masterful speech, I had to admit. The crowd applauded and Lycon gave them an oily, confident smile. Seeing this, my eagerness to hit the snake was even greater.

"A good answer," I said, with mock humility. "You truly have a gift. Do you mind if I ask another question?"

Lycon sighed. "I think we should consider the audience, Socrates. They must be getting weary."

"Oh no, they are enjoying this. I think they would like to hear more."

Again, the crowd applauded. Lycon smiled. "Still the horsefly buzzing about. Go ahead, then. Ask your question."

"You say you can make any man a rhetorician?" I asked.

"Undoubtedly."

"You can teach him to persuade the multitude on any subject?"

"That is correct."

"The rhetorician will have greater powers of persuasion than the physician, even in a matter of health?"

"Certainly."

"If he is to have more power of persuasion than the physician, he will have greater power than even the healer who has mastered his subject?"

"Yes."

"Although the rhetorician is not himself a physician?"

"Correct."

"And this person who is not a physician must, obviously, be ignorant of what the physician knows."

"Clearly."

"And does the same hold of the relationship of rhetoric to all the other arts, be they carpentry, music or blacksmithing? In other words, the rhetorician need not know the truth about things; he has only to discover some way of persuading the ignorant that he has more knowledge than those who do know?"

I saw that Lycon did not like my tone, but he tried to hide his feelings. "Yes, Socrates. And is this not a great comfort — not to have learned the other arts, only the art of rhetoric, and yet to be in no way inferior to the practitioners of those arts?"

"So if the physician or the shipbuilder speaks of facts, the rhetorician can persuade the multitude of things contrary to those facts?"

"That's right. I teach people to speak convincingly on any topic, regardless of their experience in the field," Lycon said.

"In effect, your goal is to influence people?"

"Yes."

"Regardless of the facts?"

"Yes."

"So, what you teach is purposeful manipulation?"

Finally, Lycon protested. "I help to correct wrongs and deliver justice."

"By teaching deceit," I observed.

When he did not immediately respond, I went on. "You teach men to undermine the truth. You instruct them to do injustice. Do you not think it is bad to inflict evil on people, like a tyrant who has his people killed? How bad is it to banish an innocent person or to confiscate his property? Don't you think that orators actually bring unhappiness?"

"I teach men to do good!" Lycon fumed.

"It would be fine if you taught truth and your pupils turned out evil despite your good intentions," I said, trying to keep my voice even, "but that is not what you do. You teach evil in the form of lies, so that your students can get up to anything they want: killing, banishing, raping."

People were getting visibly angry with Lycon, but I wasn't through yet. I spoke fast now, as if the words would burn my mouth if I didn't spit them out quickly enough. The words had been living in my head for years.

"Picture a young boy, perhaps a boy like yours, or yours, or yours." I pointed to different men in the crowd. "Imagine the boy is blamed for burning down a business in the agora. He is innocent, yet his prosecutors — men trained by Lycon — convince the jury of his guilt. To avoid destitution and to protect the rest of your family, you sell your son into slavery. How would you feel about that? How would you feel if your son's new master ill-treated him? How would you feel if he were beaten and kicked and starved? And how would you feel about a man like Lycon, who caused you this pain? A man who teaches others to lie and to manipulate? What would you do to a man like that?"

Lycon looked as shocked as if I had stabbed him with a knife. At first, he seemed merely stunned. Then a dark flush crept up his thick neck, his face twisted and his expression turned to one of unmitigated hatred. There would be no new students for him today. As he passed through the crowd, he was cursed at and shoved. Although my speech had not been my most elegant, it had been effective, for many an Athenian had been the victim of smooth talkers in court.

I can tell you that after Lycon stormed off, I felt good. Really, really good. I had hit the snake hard, and I had done so publicly. I felt avenged for the way he'd treated me as a boy in school, although I still owed him for what he had done to my family.

My triumph over my old tormentor emboldened me. No longer did I seek out the average man to debate with. Instead, I set my sights on the affluent and influential. I argued with them on any topic. I used the methods of questioning I had learned first by watching Parmenides and Zeno, and had then honed in my long discussions with Simon. I had become skilled at uncovering inconsistencies in people's beliefs. It became easy for me to show that the self-important and the arrogant knew nothing, and I took pleasure in humiliating them.

My brashness attracted a small following. The young, in particular, liked me for making fun of the pompous people who ruled the city, thereby encouraging me to be even harsher with those with whom I quarrelled. Crito and Chaerephon warned me I was taking too many risks. Poking fun at the powerful was dangerous, they said.

"They can go to the crows," I responded, not realizing that I was becoming as arrogant as the men I was targeting.

I allowed my own self-image to inflate even further. I began to resent your mother. Independent woman that she was, she had always walked about Athens with the freedom of a citizen, unaccompanied. She had done so since our first meeting. Now that I was becoming someone important, I didn't want people to think I was henpecked and I told your mother to stop traipsing about the city.

I didn't stop to consider your mother's perspective. She had a husband who would stand motionless in the middle of a crowd for half a day, like some possessed half-wit; who asked impious and dangerous questions about the gods; who associated with non-believers; who attacked the morality of the rich and powerful; whose own impropriety put everyone he knew at risk. And he was worried about looking foolish because of someone else's actions? Your mother would have been better

off being married to the Crow Man of my youth. At least his behaviour
didn't put his family in danger. Although I eventually apologized for my
hypocrisy, my behaviour caused a rift between us that lasted for years. I
now regret the time we lost being angry with each other.

Round about this time, Cleon was gaining influence in the Assembly. Claiming that moderation was a sign of unmanliness, he managed
to convince the Assembly to abandon Pericles' defensive strategy, and
to make war with Sparta. Our navy raided Spartan allies along the coast.
We achieved some minor successes, including our triumph at the Battle
of Pylos.

But Pylos was not a complete victory. Although the Athenian general
in charge of the navy achieved mastery at sea, control on land was another matter. The general in charge of the landing was unsuccessful, for
he had failed to provide a sound strategy to fight the stranded Spartan
hoplites and his command suffered heavy casualties. To my delight, that
general was Anytus, the conceited snob I had once demeaned at General
Nicias's dinner party.

When Anytus returned to Athens he was charged with treason, but
was acquitted. Rumour had it that he had bribed the jury, which did
nothing for his already tarnished reputation. At this low point in Anytus' life, his son approached me in search of guidance. He gave me the
impression of being a decent man, not a mean-spirited person like his
father. I found it odd that the son of a man I disliked would ask me what
he should do with his life. He told me his father wanted him to run the
family tanning business, and had planned out his life for him. I advised
him to focus his energies on the search for truth rather than on any ideas
his father wanted for him. My advice may have been good, but it was
given out of spite toward Anytus and increased that man's antagonism
toward me.

Then Athens achieved a major victory. To everyone's surprise Cleon — *General* Cleon — who had never led a force of any kind, won at the Battle of Sphacteria. He captured over 400 Spartan hoplites, 120 of whom were aristocrats. Now that Athens held such important hostages, the Assembly was able to threaten Sparta that if ever they invaded the farmland around Athens again, these prisoners would be executed. With that, the invasion that had occurred every year since I had gone off to Potidaea ended. The Assembly was so grateful to Cleon that he was granted free meals in the Tholos for life, just as if he had been an Olympic champion.

This rare defeat of their army only spurred on Sparta to greater effort. One of their generals marched the length of Greece and captured the Athenian colony of Amphipolis. The Spartans now had control of a huge silver mine, which, together with the mines at Laurium, south of Athens, had allowed Athens to create a substantial navy. In retaliation for the Spartan capture of Amphipolis, the Athenian Assembly decided to invade Sparta's ally, Boeotia. Once again, my cohort was called to war.

My dread, as we marched to the city of Delium where we would attack the Boeotians, was only slightly less than I had experienced before the Battle of Potidaea. I was somewhat reassured by the fact that our army would be immense, comprising 7,000 hoplites, 8,000 peltasts, 20,000 slaves, merchants and camp followers, and a long train of beasts of burden to haul food and provisions. The sheer sight of our army, I told myself, would surely make the enemy give up instantly.

Although I dreaded the battle, desertion was no longer an option, for I had your mother to think of now and I could not bear the idea that Xanthippe might judge me a coward. As a matter of fact, I acted so self-possessed, that when I saw tears in her eyes as we bade each other farewell, I acted as if I were just going to the agora for a haircut. I didn't even hug her goodbye.

We marched for a while through the northeastern plains, then straight north through a low mountain pass. I hiked alongside my good friends.

Chaerephon was as calm and easy-going as he had been at Potidaea. He said he had consulted a soothsayer, as he had done before sailing for Potidaea, and had been told all three of us would survive. Crito, too, seemed at ease. Perhaps he had got over the fear he'd admitted to feeling at Potidaea. We had never discussed the topic and I didn't raise it now. I didn't want my own fear to display itself unintentionally.

Delium was only a distance of two days on foot, yet the trek was arduous for many. Although the men of my cohort were now in their midforties, they were not even close to being the oldest of the soldiers. The plague had drastically reduced the number of men available for war. In order to create such a massive army, men much older than those in my cohort had been called up. Among our number were more than a few great-grandfathers, some nearing the age of 60.

General Laches led us across the border into Boeotia. We met no opposition on the way — perhaps, I thought, because the sight of us was too much for the Boeotians. Near Delium, we came upon a dilapidated temple of Apollo. We were ordered to dig a ditch around the sanctuary, pull down nearby stone houses, fortify the dirt walls, build wooden towers and erect battlements above the temple. Some of the men grumbled loudly as we worked, maintaining that Apollo would be angered by our treatment of his sanctuary. Nothing good would come of this sacrilege.

By the end of the fifth day we had completed the fortifications. As we saw no sign of the Boeotian army, it seemed pointless for us to remain there. We left a small garrison of hoplites at the temple and the rest of the army headed homeward. Late in the afternoon, we hoplites stopped to rest near Oropos while the less encumbered peltasts continued on their way. As the last of our peltasts vanished in the distance, we heard the horrifying news — the entire Boeotian army was on its way!

General Laches ordered us to prepare for battle. My determination to see the fight through was strong, but so were my nerves. I made sure no one saw me go behind a bush and vomit. With the enemy in sight, I was aware of nervous talk and false bravado in our ranks, and caught the stink of frightened, sweaty men.

To my surprise, my cohort was ordered to the rear of the phalanx, my line at the very back, with Crito to my left and Chaerephon in front of me. It was up to us to make sure those in the middle and front of the phalanx did not shirk their responsibilities. The irony that I must push on men who might otherwise desert was not lost on me. Although I felt safer at the rear of the phalanx, I eyed Crito's scar and wondered if it was my turn for a spear point to the neck.

Over the crest of the hill, the enemy appeared. Their hoplites were equal in number to ours, but they had the advantage of at least 10,000 peltasts. Although the evening was cool, my enclosed Corinthian helmet suddenly stifled me and I struggled to breathe. General Laches took his position to my right.

The sacrifice was made, after which one of the other generals addressed the army. He said that although we were in a country of foreigners, we were fighting for our own country. If we defeated the Boeotians, the Spartans would lose a powerful ally. The general had not finished his speech when thousands of screaming voices rent the air and the enemy rushed toward us. My hands and feet began to tingle. General Laches ordered us to engage. I stumbled and fell, knocking my helmeted head against a rock. Oddly, the resulting jolt of pain broke my numbness. Leaping to my feet, I chased after the men of my cohort. As I rejoined the rear of our phalanx, our first row of men clashed, shield to shield, with the Boeotians.

From the safety of the back row, I saw that we had the better of the enemy. Our right wing surrounded the enemy's left wing, and our left wing pushed the enemy's right wing backward. The day would be ours and I would survive.

Unexpectedly, a great cheer rose all at once from the enemy. The Boeotian cavalry, which had been hiding behind the hill, emerged. A thousand enemy horsemen, their horses snorting loudly, engaged our right wing, massacring our soldiers, thrusting spears into the backs of fleeing Athenians or simply riding them down. Then our left wing began to fall to the enemy, as well. As the men at the front lost their nerve, our ranks broke and skirmishes erupted everywhere.

Suddenly, the enemy's cavalry were right behind us, and we were surrounded. I lost track of Crito and Chaerephon. General Laches shouted to us to retreat, but we did not hear him; his commands were drowned out by the shouts of the enemy.

Our men ran in every direction. There was no escape. *This is the end,* I thought, *I will never see Xanthippe again.* Looking up, I saw a soldier racing toward me on a white stallion; the man carried a golden shield emblazoned with Eros, the God of Love, who was armed with a thunderbolt. I could only stand there, motionless as a statue. Suddenly, the horseman reined in his mount and a familiar voice called, "General Laches, Socrates, safety is this way." Taking in the eyes behind the helmet, I recognized Alcibiades. "Hurry, before you are completely enclosed," he shouted, and we followed him out of the frenzy.

DAY 18

HARD TO IMAGINE, dear boys, that 18 days have gone by since I began writing my story for you. At least I am getting used to sleeping during the day and writing at night, for I was up before our rooster came into my cell this evening. I spent the time before he arrived gazing at the few stars I can just barely see through the high window of the next room. How long it has been since I really looked at the stars! There is something wonderful about them, something magical. I cannot tell you which stars I see now, for even at the best of times I was never very good at identifying the constellations. Orion, the hunter, is the only one I have ever been able to pick out with any certainty.

The last thing I mentioned yesterday was the retreat from the Battle of Delium. There was such confusion in the flight from the battlefield that Athenians ended up killing their fellow Athenians as they struggled to get away from the massacre. The army scattered in all directions, with some men fleeing to Oropos, others to the sea, and still more of us up Mount Parnitha. The Boeotian cavalry gave chase, cutting us down like summer wheat. Thankfully, the engagement occurred late in the day, when it was nearly dark; otherwise it would have been much worse. Night shielded our escape.

Next day, we sent a herald to the Boeotians, asking their permission to recover our fallen. It was refused. Not until we relinquished the Temple of Apollo at Delium would they allow us back onto their territory. General Laches refused to surrender the temple, and the bodies were left to decompose. Seventeen days later, when the Boeotians managed to recapture the temple, we were finally allowed to collect our dead. We were

horrified to discover more than a thousand dead Athenian hoplites pu-
trefying in the heat. Scattered amongst the corpses of the decaying soldiers were the bodies of at least a thousand butchered slaves and camp
followers. Their mouths were wide open, as if they had screamed in fear
and pain before dying. This was the biggest loss Athens had sustained in
the eight years since hostilities had broken out with Sparta and her allies.
Our march back to Athens was sombre.

Arriving home to a relieved Xanthippe and Diotima, I was happy to
learn that both Crito and Chaerephon had survived. They had escaped
via the sea, having found a ship to take them to the port of Piraeus. Later,
when I reunited with them over a meal, we confined ourselves to speaking of fairly trivial topics — the weather and the recent games. As if by
tacit agreement, we did not talk about the horror of the battle. I believe
that, like me, my friends could not bear to relive the slaughter.

Despite my desire to forget the massacre, I thought often about the
battle. Mostly, I thought about Alcibiades and his golden shield emblazoned with Eros. The shield reminded me of the little cup I'd owned as
a child, with the picture of the dancing Eros. Although I had stopped
being superstitious years before, I couldn't help wondering about the
connection between Alcibiades and myself. Even a man who considers
himself rational and logical can be forgiven occasional fantasies of other-
worldly connections.

The link with Alcibiades became even stronger when I ran into Euripides, a man I had known in my days at Simon's shop. Happy to meet
again, we sat down and spent a while reliving that time.

Euripides told me an interesting story about his youth. When his father had made a visit to Delphi, the Oracle had told him that glory was
in store for his son. Thinking Euripides was destined for greatness as an
athlete, his father had had him trained from an early age in all the Olympic sports. "But I was no athlete," Euripides told me. "True, I have won
contests, but not the kind my father expected." Euripides, as you know,
won many prizes for the plays he wrote.

His story made me wonder whether, perhaps, the greatness my mother had foreseen for me, the glory I so badly desired, would not be gained in battle, after all. Possibly, my success would be attained in some other field. Was I more inclined to intellectual pursuits than to soldiering and athletics? Could I become a great thinker, like Thales or one of the other seven sages? Maybe I would achieve glory as a counsellor to the rich and powerful, as Anaxagoras had been to Pericles.

Euripides' story made me recognize the chance I might have had with Alcibiades had I behaved differently. I would not let such an opportunity pass me by again, I vowed. Thereafter, I would cultivate relationships with young men who showed promise — men such as Alcibiades.

One day, when we had been home from battle less than a year, Crito and Chaerephon arrived at my door. They both looked extremely distressed.

"Has something happened?" I asked anxiously.

They hesitated. Then Crito said, "We thought we should tell you — someone has written a play about you."

I thought immediately of Euripides, who was known to make heroes out of ordinary people. But I could see from my friends' faces that this particular piece of writing would not please me.

"Have you seen it?" I asked.

"No," replied Chaerephon.

Perhaps it wouldn't be quite as bad as their expressions implied. Or so I hoped. "We should see it together," I suggested.

The play was called *The Clouds*. We arrived to find a few thousand men already seated for the performance. The bright afternoon sun reflected off the polished marble seats of the recently refurbished Theatre of Dionysus. Crito directed me to the front of the theatre and Chaerephon handed me a folded blanket to sit on. We had been there only a short time when the audience became quiet and the actors took their positions.

On a bed in the centre of the stage, a middle-aged man tossed and turned, clearly distressed about something. Sitting up, he lamented upon his life. His main woe was his son, sleeping soundly beside him, who had taken to raising and racing horses, an expensive pastime that had caused the father to go deep into debt. His soliloquy ended, the father woke the son and asked him to give up the horses. The boy declined, whereupon the father invited him to enter a new school called The Thinkery. There, he would learn to argue his father out of debt. The son knew of the school. He said it was only for losers and failures, and that the instructor was that pale-faced quack, Socrates.

Although Crito and Chaerephon had warned me, the sound of my name took me by surprise. I turned to look at my friends, but they were staring intently at the stage and refused to meet my eyes. Before I could speak, the next scene began.

A man suspended in a basket appeared on the stage. He was hideous. Bald and fat, he wore a mask sporting large, bulging eyes, an enormous nose and a beard. Perhaps I should have guessed the identity of this abhorrent creature immediately, but the fact is, I did not. The audience cheered as the father addressed the man in the basket, calling him Socrates.

I watched incredulously as the repugnant Socrates character explained the reason he was in the air — he was studying rain and the reason for thunder. Furthermore, he taught his students not to believe in the gods. As my character descended from the clouds and waddled across the stage, his big, hairy hands gesticulating wildly, the audience hissed, whistled and made a tremendous racket.

Is this how people see me? I wondered. More and more of my self-esteem was ripped away with each scene; it was like being flayed. Then someone behind me, a foreigner to Athens, no doubt, asked, "Who is this idiot, Socrates?"

At that I stood up, turned, and bowed grandly to the audience, pretending not to care how I was being portrayed. What else could I do? The audience delivered more cat-calls and whistles as I was recognized.

Next, my character tried to teach the father how to baffle others by turning an inferior argument into a winning one. After much effort at instruction, the Socrates character ridiculed the father for being a stupid learner. Further on in the play, the son finally yielded to his father's threats and enrolled in The Thinkery, where he became a loser. An argument ensued when the son refused to help his father deal with his racing debts. The father lamented the fact that he had followed Socrates' teaching and had turned his back on the gods. In obedience to them, he agreed to burn down The Thinkery. The play ended with my character lumbering across the stage to escape the burning building.

As the audience laughed, my head swam with exhaustion and my stomach lurched violently. It had been strange and confusing — above all, most unpleasant — to see myself portrayed on the stage. Chaerephon and Diagoras the Atheist were mentioned as being friends of Socrates, but neither had made an actual appearance in the play.

How many people would see the play? I wondered. Years ago, as a boy accompanying Crito and Thespis to the theatre, I had taken as fact the plays we had seen. What would those who did not know me think of this play? What effect would it have on my reputation?

Afterwards, Crito hesitantly asked me my opinion of the play. Still in a daze, I said it was clever. Back home, however, I thought about how foolish my character had appeared, and how the audience had snickered when they saw me leaving the theatre. It was like being in school again, with Lycon and his brothers making fun of me. The laughter of the audience had been wounding — hurtful in a way I had not imagined I could be hurt as an adult. I wondered whether it was possible to outgrow painful childhood experiences, to leave behind things we want to forget? If so, it wasn't true for me.

As if all of this was not bad enough, the playwright rewrote and reentered the play in competitions again and again for some time to come. What a nightmare it was!

The summer after the play, my cohort was called to battle once more. Cleon, who now dominated Athenian politics, wished to humble Sparta. He promised unprecedented wealth for the city if its ancestral enemies were put down, once and for all. Sparta, Cleon claimed, was now weak, and it was time to act. He would lead the attack himself.

Although many citizens were tired of the conflict that had gone on for nearly 10 years, Cleon's charisma and his ability to manipulate the emotions of the Athenians won out over more rational opinions. Accompanied by 300 cavalry and 1,200 hoplites, we boarded ships and set sail to retake the city of Amphipolis.

Saying farewell to your mother and Diotima was more difficult this time than when I had departed for Delium. I think the long distance to Amphipolis made the impending conflict seem more dangerous. Once again, though, I acted as if I were merely going on a routine trip to the agora rather than sailing to battle. When your mother expressed her fears, Diotima comforted her, insisting it wasn't my time to die, almost as if she were an oracle with knowledge of the future. Her words were successful, for they made the parting bearable.

Crito, Chaerephon and I sailed on the same vessel this time. Chaerephon was as calm and unaffected as he had been before the battles of Potidaea and Delium. Once again, he had consulted a soothsayer before leaving Athens, and been told that we — Chaerephon, Crito and I — would survive. Crito and I exchanged glances, the meaning of which Chaerephon understood.

"It doesn't matter whether you believe it or not," Chaerephon said, grinning, "I know it to be true."

Crito and I did not press the matter. This was not a time to argue faith. Instead, we talked about our stomach-churning trip to Potidaea so long ago and speculated about what we could expect at Amphipolis, and about where Cleon might put us in the phalanx.

This trip across the Aegean was better than the first one, with good winds and a tranquil sea. Eight days after leaving, we arrived at the mouth of the Strymon River. Together with our allies, who provided ships, troops and cavalry in equal numbers to our own, we beached our ships and set up camp.

For many, many days we did nothing. No reconnaissance of the city took place, even though Amphipolis was less than a morning's hike into the hills from our encampment. We constructed no siege engines, although the city walls and ramparts of the enemy were significant. Most days were grey, rainy and cool, with wet grass, puddles and mud everywhere.

Not surprisingly, the men were in poor spirits. "Why are we here if we are not fighting?" one man would ask another. "What is Cleon waiting for?" Popular though he was in the Assembly, clearly the men here did not care for Cleon or think much of his skill as a commander.

Unlike the others, I was happy to wait. We were told that the Thracians were holding some Athenians hostage in Amphipolis, and there were rumours of Spartans, as well. I had seen Spartan soldiers at Delphi, with their red tunics and long hair, going about barefoot to show how tough they were. They did not paint frightening images of gorgons on their shields. They had no need to. Just two painted lines connected at the top, like two sticks leaning against each other: the lambda, the symbol of Sparta.

On average, the Spartans were no bigger or stronger than the Athenians, but they were very well trained. Above all, the Spartans had what is probably the biggest asset in battle: confidence. Despite their rare loss at the Battle of Sphacteria, when Cleon had captured 120 of their hoplite aristocracy, the Spartans believed they were better than anyone else.

Aware of their reputation, they cherished it and committed themselves to maintaining it. They did not believe any opponent stood a chance against them. They knew what they had to do and they were able to do it. That, alone, made them nearly invincible.

More than anything, I feared the Spartans' swords, for they were shorter than ours. In a crush between two phalanxes, there was little room for our longer swords. Theirs could be thrust through gaps in our shield walls, piercing unprotected groins, armpits and throats. As a member of the front line, I was in greater peril than the other hoplites — even more than the others in my line, because I knew from experience that fear caused numbness in my extremities, as well as an inability to control my body. I had been lucky to survive the battles at Potidaea and Delium.

A month after our arrival at the Strymon River, Cleon called on us to form the line on a hill opposite the main gate of Amphipolis. It was yet another grey day. I could taste and smell the impending rain. From our position, I could not see anyone at the walls, and nobody came through the gate to meet us. Perhaps no Spartans were there, after all, and what we faced was actually a revolt of the populace against Athenian rule. This was the sort of information Cleon would keep to himself, not letting us know that we would be fighting our own people.

The call to march and level spears was given. The order was not carried out well. Both Crito and I observed this, and we exchanged unhappy glances. In a sloppy line, we marched down the hill toward the front gate. At that moment, rain began to fall in great heavy drops. We splashed through the mud and our clothes grew heavy. Lightning flashed. "Zeus is angry," someone muttered, and then thunder boomed and the men trembled in fright.

We got so close to the city that I was able to see men's feet and horses' hooves beneath the gate. Still, nobody emerged. Cleon ordered us to turn 90 degrees and march by the walls, intending to taunt whoever was there. We passed the city gate: first the left wing, then the centre, and finally the right wing. *What an idiot,* I thought angrily. Cleon was going to get us killed. When they did not take our bait, Cleon ordered us to turn another 90 degrees, to expose our flank and march away from the city: an insult to those inside — and suicidal for us.

Suddenly, a group of 200 armed men rushed out through the gate. Painted on their shields were lambdas. The men were Spartans. Everyone panicked, as did I. As usual, in times of great fear, my hands and feet went numb, and I tripped and fell, lying motionless on the wet ground, as though dead. Men ran about madly, desperate to get away. The Spartans chasing my fellow hoplites almost trampled me, apparently taking me for a corpse. As skirmishes developed around me, I regained control of my extremities and stood up so fast that I nearly fainted. I caught sight of Cleon, tossing aside his shield and spear as he ran. He didn't get far before a javelin struck his back, and he crumpled to the ground. I had no need to see more. I retreated up the hill as fast as I could.

As had happened at the Battle of Delium, the enemy pursued us into the mountains and down to the seashore, stopping only with the darkness. The following day, we sent out an emissary to ask for a truce so we could recover the bodies of our fallen. Nearly half of our contingent had been killed, 600 hoplites. The Spartans had lost only eight men.

DAY 19

I WONDER HOW MUCH you boys know about Alcibiades — apart from what I've written so far, that is. I don't believe you ever met him in person, although I know you saw him from afar. Many things have been said about the man who was once considered the brightest light of Athens, and much has been made of my association with him. Despite the rumours and the theories of the court, my influence over him was not great, although for a long time I convinced myself otherwise.

Shortly after returning from Amphipolis, I was sitting outside the house one afternoon, my back against the wall below the kitchen window. It was the end of summer and I was enjoying the pleasant weather, grateful for my good fortune in surviving the slaughter and hoping I would never have to go to war again. Inside the house, Diotima and your mother moved around, preparing the evening meal. I was enjoying the sound of your mother's soft humming, when I heard a greeting from the street.

Two expensively dressed men strode toward me. One was Alcibiades. The other, I learned, was Hermogenes, his new brother-in-law. Alcibiades waved; I smiled and waved back. I stood up when they stopped beside me.

"I am surprised to see you here, Alcibiades. Are you lost?" I asked wryly.

Alcibiades laughed with his familiar practiced charm, as if I had just made the best joke he'd heard in a month. "No, dear Socrates, we are not lost. We are here to see you. How are you?"

"Very well," I said, a deliberate calmness hiding my eagerness to know the purpose of the visit.

"Good. You look well. Whenever and wherever I see you, you look well. Why is that? How do you manage to remain as calm on the battle-field as you do sitting outside your own home?"

Alcibiades glanced at his brother-in-law. "Hermogenes," he said to him, "you are aware, naturally, of the fame of General Laches, the supreme commander of the fleet that forced the cities of Mylae and Messana to yield to Athens? So you will be surprised to learn that I have seen the great general act like a frightened child in comparison with the man before you."

Turning to me, he said, "How do you do it, Socrates? At Delium, the battle was lost. All hope was lost. The army was in disarray. Soldiers scattered and screamed for their lives. Pandemonium was everywhere. By chance, I came across you and General Laches. In the general's face I saw panic, but you showed no fear. In fact, you looked just as you do now. Calm and at ease, but with a look in your eyes that said, 'Come at me if you dare.'"

Alcibiades looked back at his brother-in-law. "I was on horseback. I told General Laches to take heart, for I would lead him out of the fray. Throwing down his shield, the general chased after me. Not so, Socrates. He did not fling away his weapons. He did not turn and run. Instead, he stepped backward, slowly, warily, bravely facing the enemy the entire time, as a well-trained soldier should. His heroism allowed General Laches and many others to escape safely."

I snorted at Alcibiades' account of Delium, for it was far from the truth. Nonetheless, it was extraordinarily gratifying to be spoken about in this fashion. Alcibiades had a way of making me feel good about myself. What he didn't know — and I was not about to tell him — was that on that day at Delium, I walked backward slowly for a reason: my hands and feet were so numb with fear, I could not have moved them more quickly had I wanted to.

Remembering my duties as a host, I led the two men to the andron and bade them be seated. I asked what I could get for them. A drink?

Something to eat? As you know, your mother is an expert baker, and just that morning I had caught a whiff of a delicious aroma coming from the oven. I spoke courteously, trying not to show how very curious I was about the visit. Thankfully, they waved away my offers of refreshment.

"What can I do for you, Alcibiades?" I asked.

"I wish to speak with you," he responded.

"I always appreciate the chance to chat with someone as perceptive as you," I said. "What do you wish to talk about, Alcibiades?"

For once, he did not smile. "I wish to appear before the Assembly."

Questions rushed instantly to my mind. Was he approaching me for help? What exactly did he want of me?

"You wish to be an adviser to Athens?" I asked, calm as ever.

"Yes," he said.

"About what do you wish to advise the Assembly?"

"War or peace, or any other concerns of the city."

"May I ask why?"

For the first time, he hesitated. "It is my wish to unite all Greeks," he said, then.

"So that you can obtain absolute power?"

"No, Socrates. Not 'absolute' power, but 'just' power."

My eyes met his. "'Just' power, Alcibiades? Have you now determined what is 'just' or 'unjust'? At Potidaea you did not know."

"Perhaps I still do not know the answer to your satisfaction. But it is not power I am after."

I knew what he wanted. Alcibiades had made his desires clear when I first got to know him in Potidaea. For him, it would never be enough to have his name inscribed on the wall of commemoration for his sacrifice in battle. To Alcibiades, such achievements were as meagre as if he were to find himself etching his name on the prison wall I now stare at day and night — a pathetic attempt to shout, *"I was here! I mattered! Remember me!"* No, Alcibiades wanted to be like Heracles or Achilles. He wished people to speak his name with reverence, to be regarded with awe. He wanted his name to live forever. I understood his cravings, for they were the same as my own.

No longer able to contain my curiosity, and anxious to discover his reason for seeking me out, I asked, "Why, then, are you here? Do you need something from me?" I willed him to ask me to assist him.

Thoughtfully, he said, "Perhaps I can give you something."

"And what is that?"

"I want to make you the wisdom and conscience of Athens."

Unwilling to let him know he had just put my own desire into words, I tried not to smile. Keeping my tone grave, I asked, " How do you propose to accomplish that?"

"I need your instruction."

Inwardly, I cried out with joy, but I could not let him glimpse my interest. I knew only too well that anyone, man or woman, who had ever pursued Alcibiades, had been tossed aside when he was through with them. He had been married less than a year and already the gossip about him included rumours of liaisons with half a dozen married women.

"Did you not see the play, *The Clouds*?" I asked. "I am known as a fool."

He waved a dismissive hand. "That play was nonsense. Anyone who has ever had contact with you knows you are anything but a fool. The Oracle herself named you the wisest man in Greece."

"The Oracle speaks in riddles. I have always assumed I was being ridiculed."

"Not so," Alcibiades protested.

"Well, we won't argue the point. Rather, tell me what you want of me." I said.

"I want you to instruct me regarding the needs of the people of Athens."

I feigned laughter. "Remind me — have I ever told you about my friend, Simon?"

He shook his head.

"Simon was a cobbler who owned a small shop near the Tholos. He made the best sandals in Athens, if not in all of Greece. I have a pair in the house; they have survived three battles and many long walks on the rocky slopes around Athens. Yet, despite some scratches and scuffs, they are still as good as the day I purchased them. Simon was a true craftsman, but he was far more than that. He was a clever man whose wisdom was as deep as the open seas. He introduced me to many important concepts and forced me to analyze my ideas with greater reasoning than I had ever attempted before. He tore apart my world and showed me the folly of my own beliefs. He was my mentor and a great friend."

Both men listened intently as I went on. "You will, however, know the next part of my story, Alcibiades, as Pericles was your surrogate father. In the last years of his life, Pericles was besieged by men who lusted for power. He had led Athens for a long time, and now younger men wished to assume his mantle.

But Pericles still held great sway in the Assembly. The reverence with which most Athenians regarded him had never been stronger. At the same time, there were those who resented him and were jealous of him. In order to sully Pericles' reputation, and to drag him down to the level of ordinary mortals, his intimates were charged with various crimes. Of course, you are aware of the outcomes. Phidias died in jail, Anaxagoras went into exile and Aspasia escaped with her life only after Pericles broke down in court and wept."

"I do remember those things," Alcibiades said.

"What you don't know is that Simon came to the attention of Pericles through Anaxagoras. When Pericles met Simon, he immediately recognized the cobbler's unique strength of character. In the absence of Anaxagoras, and needing another counsellor, Pericles offered to pay Simon to leave his shop and come to live with him. Simon refused. Do you know why?"

Alcibiades shook his head.

"Well, I asked Simon about it," I said. "His response was: 'I am a cobbler. What do I know of being a counsellor to the most powerful man in Greece?' And so now I say to you, Alcibiades: I am a stonemason. What do I know of war and peace and the affairs of the city?"

"A man is a good adviser because he has knowledge. Those are your own words Socrates," said Alcibiades.

"As well, I am a poor man."

"It will make no difference to Athenians whether their counsellor is rich or poor."

"Your friend Anytus would not agree with you."

Alcibiades did not hesitate. "Anytus is a cabbage sucker. My plans cannot be accomplished without your help, Socrates. Pericles told me he was not born wise; he acquired wisdom through his association with Anaxagoras. In the same way, I need you. You claim to know nothing. I also know nothing. Is that not what is meant by *know thyself*? I want to bring that wisdom to the people, and you can help me do it. I need you. Will you not assist me? We can study together so that I can improve myself. I will be your disciple, Socrates," he ended humbly.

What more could he have said? He had pleaded with me in front of his brother-in-law. Naturally, I agreed to help him. In that moment, I saw my future as surely one sees the sun on a clear blue morning. At the thought that I would be advisor to the next Pericles, I wallowed in the false happiness that comes from pride.

DAY 20

ALCIBIADES AND I began to spend a lot of time together, sometimes in the company of his brother-in-law, Hermogenes, and sometimes with Critias, Alcibiades' admirer from Potidaea. We'd go for long walks around the agora, as well as in other places throughout the city. I made sure people saw us together. Before long, strangers greeted me warmly in the streets, young people sought my instruction and I was invited to dinner parties. Endless good food and drink — and all because of my association with Alcibiades!

Cleon's death had brought about a power vacancy in the city. Both Alcibiades and I recognized the opportunity. I was unable to teach ways of seizing power or creating revolution, for I was, and still am, politically naïve. Rather, our discussions focused on the art of discovering the truth. I taught Alcibiades what I had learned from Parmenides and Zeno and, above all, from Simon. I demonstrated that if you asked enough questions, you could eventually uncover discrepancies in people's arguments.

Alcibiades was anxious to learn my methods. We practiced by discussing prudence and temperance, amongst other topics. I noticed how easily he became frustrated, and reminded him that he was only 25 years of age. He had lots of time to mature and to learn. Most men were 30 or older before they put their names forward for generalship. But Alcibiades was impatient; he wanted his life of greatness to begin as soon as possible — understandably, when you think about it, for which of us feels any differently about our plans for the future? Certainly not I.

During a walk in the agora one bright warm day, we came upon Diagoras the Atheist. He and another man were standing in front of the new Stoa of Zeus. Although not yet fully built, it displayed an expensive array of votive gifts, cups, plates and huge jars, all painted with scenes of men on their knees aboard ships.

The two men were arguing about the existence of the gods. Their discourse was like the back and forth between boxers exchanging jabs. Diagoras was the quicker of the two, questioning and prodding and questioning again. I motioned to Alcibiades to listen, for Diagoras was very clever at uncovering an illogical argument.

"How can you say the gods do not care for the suffering of men?" the stranger asked. "Look at these votive pictures! They all show people who escaped the fury of the sea by praying to the gods, who then brought them to safe harbour."

Diagoras appeared to consider his words carefully, before he responded. "Yes, indeed, but where are the pictures of all those who were shipwrecked, and perished in the waves?"

The argument continued in this vein, with the stranger growing angrier and more frustrated as Diagoras cleverly refuted each of his claims about the gods. After a while, we walked away, leaving them to continue their discussion.

I noticed that Alcibiades looked disturbed, but he waited until we had gone a short distance, before he spoke. "The things your friend says are dangerous. Men have been exiled for saying less."

"That is true, it is dangerous to express what is unpopular," I agreed. "But it's necessary, all the same, if you are set on revealing incorrect thinking."

Alcibiades was quiet. Although he did not respond to my statement, he appeared to give it thought.

Only months after he had first approached me, Alcibiades had started making speeches in the Assembly. He was well received there. In a natural extension of his charisma, he knew how to express his ideas clearly and was able to defend himself against the chaotic bickering that often ensued. Many began to regard him as the future of Athens. He had both the looks and the cleverness of a god — a man of limitless potential. At the time I really believed his success was a product of my tutelage. Now, sitting alone in my cell, I realize how arrogant this belief was.

With Cleon dead, and the tremendous losses at Delium and Amphipolis still raw in people's memories, the Assembly was open to discussion of peace with Sparta. That winter, ambassadors travelled back and forth between the cities. The Assembly had embraced Alcibiades so quickly that he was asked to accompany Generals Nicias and Laches on these peace talks. In the spring, after 10 years of war, a 50-year truce was negotiated, with each side obliged to return what the other had owned before the outbreak of hostilities. Everyone in Athens was happy with the announcement. Everyone, that is, except Alcibiades.

"They paid no attention to me," he said of the Spartans. "They talked only with Nicias and Laches, treating me as if I were just an errand boy."

I counselled patience, but my advice did not please the young Alcibiades.

It fell by lot that the Spartans would be the first to return what they held. They released all their Athenian prisoners of war. In response, Athens released the Spartan elite whom Cleon had captured during the Battle of Sphacteria. Both exchanges went smoothly.

The next step was to return occupied territories. This was where the problems began. The Spartans did not return Amphipolis to Athens. The Assembly accused Sparta of acting in bad faith. Sparta contended that they had removed all their troops from Amphipolis, but that they did not have sufficient control over the local population to return the city to Athens. The regional government was in control, they argued. Upon hearing this news delivered to the Assembly by a herald, Athens refused to return the peninsula of Pylos to the Spartans. The peace treaty, not yet a month old, began to unravel.

To my dismay, Alcibiades publicly advocated for aggressive moves against Sparta. "Sparta cannot be relied upon," he told the Assembly. "They only want a treaty with Athens in order to gain time to take care of domestic problems with their slaves, and to build up their strength so they can attack Athens again."

The Spartans sent ambassadors to speak at the Assembly. After having a secret conference with Alcibiades, the ambassadors told the Assembly they did not have the power to negotiate, but had come only as observers. Alcibiades allowed the Athenians to think that Sparta had sent the ambassadors as a delaying tactic and repeated his belief that Sparta was planning an assault. Incited by Alcibiades, the Assembly was enraged and came close to lynching the Spartan envoys.

The next day, as I was working at the Piraean Gate, an errand boy approached me with a dinner invitation from General Nicias. The boy waited patiently for an answer. *Why does General Nicias want to see me?* I wondered. After all, I'd had no contact with the man since the dinner party at his house eight years earlier, when I had insulted Anytus and the group of Athens elite. But the wealthy and powerful no longer intimidated me as they had in the past. So, mostly out of curiosity, I accepted the invitation.

After telling your mother and Diotima where I was going, I washed off the white stone dust and donned my usual tunic, plain but clean, and my sandals. Arriving at Nicias' home, I observed that the house was unchanged. I thought of my father when I saw the mural of Achilles on the wall and the mosaic of Heracles on the courtyard floor. Again, I wondered what had happened to the mosaic that had once adorned our andron floor, and to the herms I had looked for but had never seen in the course of my travels.

General Nicias was waiting for me in his andron. Since we last met, he had begun to show his age somewhat — his brown hair had receded from his temples and his once dark beard was now flecked with grey. I reminded myself that he was only a year older than me, and that my hair was turning grey, too.

"Is it just us?" I asked, as our opening pleasantries were exchanged.

"Yes," said the general. "Can I offer you something?"

I said I would have whatever he was having, and watched him pour heavily watered wine. Another serious discussion, I thought wryly. Had I really expected anything else?

General Nicias handed me a cup, bade me sit on a couch, and then settled himself on the couch next to mine. He began to speak about the weather and the upcoming games. He was trying to be gracious, I realized, and wondered what was on his mind.

"You have some influence over Alcibiades, I think?" he asked, at last.

"Only Alcibiades has influence over Alcibiades," I replied, diplomatically.

"You guide him, though." His tone made the words a statement rather than a question.

"We discuss many things," I said quietly, deciding not to commit to anything before I knew what he was after. I hadn't forgotten my feelings the last time I'd been in this andron, and the unspoken words: *You are not wanted. You do not belong.*

"The gods have blessed Alcibiades with many fine qualities," Nicias said. "Looks and intelligence. Cleverness." He said the last word deliberately, letting it hang in the air a moment. "He is also hungry for success."

I nodded. "That's true. Like any Athenian, Alcibiades desires glory."

"Can a man want glory for the wrong reasons?" Nicias asked.

"What are the right reasons?" I countered.

His lips lifted in a resigned smile. "You have not changed since we first met, I see. You still use words as weapons. Very well, let me be blunt. I have some disturbing news, and I am counting on you to keep to yourself what I tell you."

I kept my face blank. "What is your news?"

His eyes met mine. "You must understand that what I am about to tell you is..." Nicias hesitated a moment, as if he were trying to find the right words. "It is sensitive, Socrates. Confidential, if you will."

I nodded at him to continue.

"Alcibiades has gone behind the Assembly's back," he said

I stared at him in surprise. "How?"

"The Spartan ambassadors came to the Council of Five Hundred a few days before they spoke to the Assembly. They told the Council they had absolute power to negotiate any and all outstanding issues, including the return of Amphipolis. Sparta wants peace and they will do whatever is necessary to achieve it. This includes helping Athens to reclaim Amphipolis."

I responded, "But this is not what the ambassadors told the Assembly."

"Correct — but they should have. Indeed, the Council of Five Hundred recommended that the ambassadors speak to the Assembly, that they explain the Spartan position and their intentions for peace."

"Why didn't they?" I asked.

"Alcibiades," said Nicias, frowning in disgust.

I waited, saying nothing.

"Alcibiades met secretly with the ambassadors before they were due to speak to the Assembly. In that meeting, he advised them not to disclose their power to make peace."

"For what reason?"

"Alcibiades promised to withdraw his desire for war and to support the treaty — on condition that the ambassadors told the Assembly they did not have full powers."

"He didn't keep his word," I said thoughtfully.

"He did not." Either General Nicias was really troubled, or he was a supreme actor. Taking a deep breath, he went on. "Alcibiades is too young to lead. We cannot have war, Socrates. I ask you, for the sake of every citizen of Athens, to speak with him. I beg of you, show him his folly."

Thoughts whirled in my mind. I did not know whether I could trust Nicias. Was he was telling me the truth about Alcibiades, or were his words a political ploy to discredit the young man? Was there any way for me to confirm his allegations? It was impossible for me to gain access to the ambassadors in order to find out the truth. Even if it had been possible, I doubted they would tell me the actual facts. Were I to ask Alcibiades directly, would he be forthright? Would I alienate him if I questioned his intentions? These machinations made my head hurt. Once again, I realized I was not cut out for politics.

When I left General Nicias's home that evening, I told him I would consider his request but that I needed to think about it.

Eventually, without any mention of Nicias's accusations, I asked Alcibiades if he would renounce his call for war. He refused. To the contrary, he continued his hawkish ways in the Assembly, blaming Nicias for negotiating a bad treaty. Days later, at the annual vote for the 10 generals, Alcibiades got himself appointed a general. Immediately, he stopped seeking my counsel and did not speak to me again for several years. This did not come as a big surprise to me, as it was typical of the way Alcibiades used people.

I remember then pondering what it meant to *know thyself*. After my discussions with Simon so long ago, I had concluded that the words meant I knew nothing.

Could I have been so terribly wrong? I had changed my definition once before. Why not change it again? Perhaps, despite all my years of deep thinking, Alcibiades understood the aphorism more intuitively than I did. Was it possible that to *know thyself* meant to *embrace* what you are, and to charge ahead with fulfilling your desires? My time with Simon had led me to reason that we must restrain our desires, examine our every action and make conscious choices. But Alcibiades seemed to be that rare man who managed to go through life without doubt. I could not say the same for myself. *Do I need to reevaluate my beliefs?* I wondered.

Alcibiades' desertion left me in a terrible mood. I saw his abandonment as destroying my last chance to achieve glory, or even respect. Had it not been for your mother, I might well have remained short-tempered and brooding for a long time.

But just at this dismal time, your mother gave me magnificent news. She was pregnant!

What a wonderful time it was. Your mother was excited, and she grew more beautiful with each passing month. I became more attentive and spent more time in her company. Diotima, who was getting old and slowing down, would dance unexpectedly in the courtyard for no apparent reason. The house was full of joy and the baby had not even arrived yet!

At last, the big day came. The sun shone and the sky was a brilliant blue with just a few white clouds, puffy as newly combed wool. We didn't bother to cover the house with pitch to ward off evil spirits, or to untie all the knots in the room in which your mother gave birth. Your mother is no more superstitious than I am. Diotima and I were her midwives. Your mother was calm and made hardly any noise. The labour was extremely short, not at all like a typical first-time birth. To my great delight, I caught the baby in my hands — a perfectly formed little boy. As I handed him to your mother, the infant gave a strong cry then took the breast.

We called him Lamprocles, after your mother's father. She offered to name him after my father, but I insisted we honour hers. What I didn't tell her was that it was my intent to insult my father by not naming our firstborn after him, as if he could have felt the affront from beyond the river Styx and the Land of the Dead. Let it be known that your father is a mean-spirited man, although only I knew quite how low I could go.

After Lamprocles had finished feeding, Diotima and I washed him. When he was clean and swaddled, I cradled his tiny head in my hand, his back resting along my scarred forearm. He closed his eyes to sleep. He was so innocent, so helpless and perfect, that I found myself weeping silently.

It was the same with all three of you boys. Each time I held you in my arms after your births, I felt the same awe. A new life. A new beginning — for you, for your mother and for me. I promised you that I would never be like my own father. I would protect you and love you always. Your mother would not have to give her sons amulets to remind them they were valued.

A short time after he was born, Lamprocles cried for more food. Your mother fed him again, and then I put him to sleep in the very basket my mother had made for me. With your mother resting comfortably in bed, Diotima and I sat in the courtyard and drank some wine.

At that very moment I decided to remove the timber door from our andron. I would allow no structure to come between my newborn son and me. And while I was at it, I would remove the trellis my brother and I had climbed all those years ago, the day Patrocles urinated on Lycon. I didn't want any child to climb onto the roof and then fall off. Funny how, once you are a parent, you want to shield your children from doing the things you did yourself. This is, after all, the reason that I am writing my story — because I want you boys to avoid my mistakes.

Happy about my plans for becoming a great father, I said to Diotima. "This was certainly nothing like my birth."

"What do you mean?" she asked.

"No horse poking its head through the window. No caul on Lamprocles' head."

Diotima was bewildered. "What horse? Who had a caul?"

"Have you forgotten my birth?" I asked, chuckling. "Mother said a horse poked its head into the room when she was in labour. That it breathed in time with her breathing."

Diotima looked at me as if I had just joined the ranks of the cabbage suckers.

"And the caul," I went on. " I was born with one."

"You must be confused," Diotima said firmly. "There was no horse at your birth, and you were not born with a caul. I was there, I should know."

It was my turn for bewilderment. "But I don't understand. My mother told me the story a hundred times."

"There was no horse and no caul at your birth," Diotima said quietly. "Before you were born, your mother delivered a little girl with a caul. She died of the plague. And we chased goats out of houses, but never a horse."

I listened as she related the real story of my birth: it was as ordinary as any birth could be.

"I'm sorry," she said, when she saw that I was devastated. She added something more, but I can't tell you what it was, for I had stopped listening. I could only wonder why my beloved mother had fabricated such a strange story, and whether it had somehow affected the glorious future she had once seen for me.

DAY 21

THE SUMMER AFTER Alcibiades was elected one of the 10 generals of Athens, he led a small group of hoplites and peltast archers in the direction of Sparta. Along the way, he gathered soldiers from former Spartan allies and they all marched into Spartan territory. Over the next few years, many such raids took place. Alcibiades claimed them as major victories, although no pitched battles ever took place. I couldn't help thinking that the attacks were his way of getting back at the Spartans for their lack of respect when he accompanied General Nicias and General Laches to the peace talks.

One day a delegation arrived in Athens from the Sicilian city of Segesta. The delegates told the Assembly that old disputes had arisen with their neighbour, Selinus. Selinus was receiving aid from the powerful city of Syracuse, and was even now blockading Segesta by land and sea. The Segestan ambassadors pleaded for support from the Athenian Assembly.

Claiming it was the duty of Athens to support her allies on the island of Sicily, Alcibiades immediately called for an expeditionary force. He recommended an attack on Syracuse, a city about the size of Athens. If the army successfully took over Syracuse, he insisted, Athens would acquire the island of Sicily, as well as nearly unlimited resources with which to continue the war against Sparta.

General Nicias, ever the dove, argued against the attack. He thought war with Syracuse was a mistake. Athens had not dealt with Sparta properly in the past and was only just recovering from the plague in terms of both money and manpower, and now Alcibiades wanted war with a distant power, thereby creating new enemies. This was madness, he told the Assembly.

At this time, Hermogenes brought me interesting news. According to him, not only did Alcibiades have a taste for other men's wives, but his enthusiasm for horse racing and other luxuries was also causing him problems. He had recently entered seven chariots in the Olympics, an unheard of extravagance and well beyond what even he could afford. Alcibiades, Hermogenes claimed, was waging war for plunder. He was endangering Athens for his own profit. The expedition to Sicily was an excuse for him to acquire money.

One evening soon after, I had the experience of life repeating itself, or so it seemed. I was sitting outside the house after work one evening. Sophroniscus and Menexenus had both been born by then and Diotima was playing in the courtyard with the three of you. Your mother was in the kitchen, humming contentedly as she prepared dinner.

In an almost identical replay of a scene that had taken place years earlier, I saw two men striding toward me. The taller one waved; I smiled and waved back. As before, the man was Alcibiades, in his long purple cloak. Where this scene differed from the first was that now his companion was Autolycus, the son of Lycon. Listening to the introduction, I told myself I could not blame the young man for his choice of father, and thus greeted him as warmly as I could. Thankfully, Autolycus had not come for advice — I would not have the opportunity to err, as I'd done with the son of Anytus.

"I am surprised to see you here, Alcibiades. Are you lost?" I asked, as if I were reciting by rote from that long-ago script.

As before, Alcibiades laughed as if at a joke. "No, Socrates. We are not lost. We are here to see you. How are you?"

"Well," I told him.

"That's good. You look well. You always do. Why is that? How do you maintain the same calm on the battlefield as you do sitting outside your own home?"

And then, to my utter disbelief and amazement, he told Autolycus the story of how he and I had saved General Laches and others around us on the battlefield. I swear, he did not deviate by a word from the last time he had told it.

What game is he playing? I wondered. Did he not recall the past?

"Have a seat, Autolycus," Alcibiades said, finally breaking the pattern of that previous encounter, and giving the young man a wink. "Wait here, I must a have a quick word with Socrates."

"Shall we walk?" I asked.

"No," he said, and asked if we could go to my andron. When we were alone, Alcibiades' bravado dropped from him like a cape. "Socrates," he whispered, his tone earnest, the smell of wine strong on his breath, "I am in trouble."

I heard fear in his voice for the first time since our meeting in the battlefield at Potidaea.

"Socrates, you know of the Sicilian expedition?"

I told him I had heard that delegates from Segesta were pleading for support in their war against Selinus and Syracuse.

Alcibiades nodded. "Correct. My advice to the Assembly was that we should assist our ally. Victory would bring riches to Athens, thereby expanding our area of influence. I argued that it would be easy for us to recruit allies on the island of Sicily, and that we would not have to use many of our own forces. Nicias, as you can imagine, opposed intervention before attacking me. He claimed I wanted the expedition for my personal benefit. Imagine the nerve of the man! The Assembly ignored his remarks and agreed that we should help our ally. I proposed sending 60 ships, a few thousand hoplites and some peltast archers."

He paused to rub his temples, as if he were in some pain. "Nicias, sneaky dog that he is, suddenly capitulated. In his view, he said, we needed to send a significant force to ensure the success of the expedition. He recommended sending 140 war ships, 5,100 hoplites and 1,300 peltasts, as well as archers and slingers. Not even Pericles dispatched such a large force by sea! I've been given supreme command, as the invasion was my idea in the first place."

I was puzzled. "But you have led armies before now," I observed, not understanding his anxiety. Was this not what Alcibiades had always wanted — to command and gain glory?

"Until now, I have led only a few hundred hoplites and peltasts."

"You have fought battles before," I protested.

"Skirmishes," he corrected me sadly, before continuing his rant. "We are speaking of foreign territory, Socrates. There is so much none of us knows. The area itself. Which cities will receive us in their harbours. Where we will drop anchor. Where we will obtain water and food. Where we will cook. You have been to battle yourself. You know how many slaves and attendants are needed to support each soldier. Besides, Socrates, the war ships and the soldiers are the least of it. We'll need at least 300 merchant vessels to transport bakers, masons, amulet hawkers, priests, whores and so forth. This will go badly, I know it! And when it fails, I will be ostracized or worse! What am I to do?"

I must admit, his concerns were well founded. Should Alcibiades fail to fulfill his promises, he would be held responsible. Huge fines, ostracism, possibly even execution might result. A general could profit mightily from success; however, he could suffer just as greatly from failure.

I thought about my own reluctance to fight again. "There must be a way to stop the expedition," I said.

"No! If I stop it now, people will take me for a coward."

"You are not a coward if you vote against war, Alcibiades. Don't you know that foresight is a sign of wisdom?"

"The Assembly is not interested in wisdom! They want results! Victory! Glory!" he cried. Then he was silent.

"We'll think of a way," I said.

He looked at me with hope in his eyes. "Together?"

"Yes, together," I replied, as convincingly as I could.

"I knew you could help me. You are the only person I can count on. There is something about you, Socrates; I don't know what it is. Other men are like shallow puddles while you are the ocean. I was never able to see to your depths. I wish I could be like you."

After a little more discussion, I led Alcibiades out of the andron and back to young Autolycus, who was waiting in my usual seat below the kitchen window. When they had gone, I resumed my previous seat and thought about what I had just heard.

Alcibiades wished he were me.

Except for the day when Chaerephon told me of the Oracle's claim, that no man was wiser than me, I had never felt quite so pleased with myself. Happily, I took a deep breath. The air had never smelled so sweet. I inhaled again, deeply, but this time I smelled sewage. The next thing I knew, a warm liquid that reeked of ammonia was pouring over my head and between my lips. Jerking up my head in astonishment, I saw your mother leaning out of the window, holding the now empty chamber pot above my head. Spitting the vile stuff from my mouth, I asked what in the name of Hades she thought she was doing.

"You're easier than a Kerameikos whore!" she yelled back at me through the kitchen window. "Only you're worse, because you don't get paid! All it takes is a few compliments, and you're his. Alcibiades is a fraud and a scoundrel, and you are too blind to see where you are headed. He casts you off, and you mope around as if one of your children had died, and then you spread your legs like a prostitute when he returns."

She had been listening at the andron door, and I had not realized it. So stunned was I by her outburst that, uncharacteristically for me, I was speechless.

Covered in urine, I stormed off to the river. As I washed myself in the tepid water of the Ilissos River, I thought about the stories I had heard from Hermogenes about Alcibiades. True, Alcibiades was not perfect, but then neither had Pericles been perfect as a young man. Indeed, as a youth he had been given to rashness and sexual proclivities.

Had it not been for the calm counsel of Anaxagoras, his baser nature could well have subverted his brilliant future. I saw the similarities between Pericles and Anaxagoras, and between Alcibiades and myself. I was not blind. I understood the clay I was trying to shape. But I knew I could help Alcibiades. I could guide him. I could be his midwife and bring forth his better nature.

It occurred to me then, as I rinsed off the urine, that I had once seen a man similarly soiled, a man I hated above all others — Lycon, who trained people to speak well in public, and who made the weak argument a better one for the benefit of his clients. A liar, a bringer of unhappiness, I had called him.

For the first time, I wondered whether I was any different from Lycon. I had trained Alcibiades in the art of speech using my own methods. Although I called that art "truth," I understood it could be used for the purpose of manipulation. Did that mean that there was little difference between the path Lycon had taken and the one I was now following? I disliked thinking of myself in the same light as Lycon, and so I did my best to banish the thought. But even then, I knew I was being hypocritical.

Alcibiades did not heed my advice, after all. He said nothing to the Assembly and preparations for the campaign to Sicily continued. Fortunately for me, my cohort was not called upon to take part.

A few nights before the expedition was due to leave, someone went around and mutilated the herm statues that stood everywhere in Athens. Heads were broken, genitals were lopped off and some were painted Spartan red. Athenians did not take kindly to the sacrilege. It was understood that the God Hermes was there to protect the city, and if Hermes were offended he could withdraw his protection. Had not Apollo brought plague to the city when Athens had broken the peace treaty with Sparta? Athenians called for swift and violent retribution against the guilty, before the gods could react.

Somehow, rumours began and then suspicion took root that Alcibiades and his friends were exactly the kind of men who might have committed this vandalism. Although I had no proof, it was not hard to imagine what could have happened. Seeing it as the only way out of his predicament, Alcibiades might have thought up the bright idea of desecrating the herm statues. Easier for him — if, in fact, he really was the culprit — to manipulate a court through clever speech than to lead an expedition doomed to failure. It was entirely possible that he could have rounded up a group of his sycophantic followers, got them drunk and encouraged them to have a little fun. Perhaps he had not done any damage himself, thus making his defence in court even simpler. Maybe he had even started the rumours.

In the Assembly, Alcibiades indignantly demanded to stand trial for the crime of which he was accused. But with all the preparations for the mammoth expedition already having been made, it was ruled that he should lead it, and the trial was postponed until his return.

Most Athenians gathered at the port of Piraeus to watch the departure of the largest fleet ever put to sea by a single city. You boys may not remember this, but I took you to watch the ships depart. What a spectacle it was! Hundreds of sails, oars churning water, the pounding of drums in rhythm with the oars, the stomping and neighing of horses. When I mentioned knowing the man in the lead ship, you, Lamprocles, asked if the man I knew was Achilles and if he was sailing to Troy. I laughed and told you that the ships were headed for Sicily, and that the man leading them was a mortal named Alcibiades. But your question was significant, for Athens had set itself a goal worthy of an epic poem, and Alcibiades certainly saw himself as a modern day Achilles.

DAY 22

E VERYONE IN ATHENS seemed to be discussing the Sicily
campaign. It would have been difficult to find anyone without a
relative of some sort involved in the expedition. So it didn't take long
for the news to spread that one of Alcibiades' associates had decided
not to travel with the fleet. Although this person was never identified, he
claimed to have private knowledge that led him to inform on Alcibiades,
accusing him of being the primary perpetrator of the herm desecrations.

A warrant was executed for Alcibiades' arrest and a ship dispatched
to bring him back to stand trial. He was apprehended in Sicily but managed to jump ship, a sure sign of his guilt, most thought. Alcibiades was
condemned to death in his absence; and I, his teacher, was condemned
widely to scorn. Fortunately, you boys were too young to be affected by
these events, but I know that your mother — and probably Diotima, too,
although she never remarked on it — was badgered in the streets and in
the agora.

With the defection of Alcibiades, General Nicias and General Lamachus were placed in charge of the campaign. At first, the news was good.
In the first battle with Syracuse, the more experienced Athenians won
the day, losing only 50 soldiers to the enemies' losses of 260. The following spring saw some skirmishes around Syracuse, in the course of which
General Lamachus was killed. The ever-cautious Nicias was now in sole
command.

Meanwhile, Syracuse pled for Spartan assistance. Sparta responded, sending a force of 700 armed sailors, 1,000 hoplites and 100 cavalry. The arrival of the fierce Spartans boosted the confidence of the

Syracuse troops, and the combined armies took the fight to the Athenian contingent.

Nicias, exhausted by now, and ill after leading such a massive undertaking, sent the Assembly a request: supply more men and materiel or cancel the campaign. The Assembly voted to send reinforcements. Once again, my luck held, and my cohort was not one of those sent to join the expedition. The following spring, 73 war ships and 5,000 more hoplites set sail for Sicily. But the new arrivals provided little relief.

As these events were transpiring, I received secret news from Hermogenes regarding Alcibiades. Despite his numerous infidelities and reckless spending, not to mention his death sentence for desecrating the herms, Alcibiades' wife had remained loyal to him. She had accompanied him to Sicily and had jumped ship with him. So strong was his charisma that a few others decided to stick with him, too. I learned that after his escape, Alcibiades had fled to Sparta. To my horror, it appeared that he had turned traitor!

Did Alcibiades prostrate himself before the Spartan king and request sanctuary? I doubt it. That would have been out of keeping with his personality. Indeed, I can imagine him strutting into the king's presence and promising to deliver Athens, with the reminder that as both his father and grandfather had been ambassadors to Sparta, he himself was a Spartan at heart.

Alcibiades' defection upset me badly. While it was one thing to knock the heads and penises off a few herms — that didn't bother me, at all — it was quite another to join the enemy and actively help to destroy his friends and fellow citizens. If Alcibiades had had an ethical reason for leaving Athens, I might have understood. But this action was motivated by spite!

What have I done wrong? I wondered. *What could I have done differently? What have I not taught him?*

If there was one thing for which I was grateful, it was that only Hermogenes and a few of his intimates knew of Alcibiades' desertion — at first, at least. But secrets do not remain secret for long. Eventually, the desertion became common knowledge and an important topic of conversation. People walking the streets of Athens wondered how it was possible for a man of such promise to have come to such an end. Alcibiades had been our best and brightest, they said. He could have been the next Pericles. I was not surprised when their ire turned to me. I was accosted in the streets. People set their dogs on me. I was punched and kicked. In short, I was blamed for all the ills that now befell Athens.

While the defeats were occurring in Sicily, Sparta took the battle against Athens closer to the city and entered Athenian territory. The Spartans captured and fortified a nearby village, turning it into a military post. This meant they did not have to return home during the winter months. Instead, they maintained the village year round, preventing the farmers from using what little land Athens had available for cultivation, and thwarting attempts to receive supplies over-land. The Spartans also attacked the silver mines at Laurium, where they freed 20,000 slaves and halted production of the silver that had been the main source of Athens' wealth. The sudden loss of income from the mines put a grinding halt to all Athenian military and civil projects.

Athens was being worn down by war on two fronts, and people were growing disconsolate. Food was becoming scarce and safety was a concern. The Assembly spoke of withdrawing from Sicily, but discussion did not move quickly enough and the situation worsened. The Assembly had been receiving regular updates about the conflict, but now the reports stopped coming.

Eventually, a sailor — the only man known to have returned alive from Sicily! — arrived in the city. Crito, Chaerephon and I, along with what seemed like every citizen remaining in Athens, went to the Pnyx hill to hear him relate his experiences to the Assembly. Wedged so tightly against one another that we had little space to breathe, we listened, aghast, to his story.

Apparently, after much loss in Sicily, the newly arrived support force had wanted to retreat. At first, General Nicias refused their request. Far from Athens, and without direct knowledge of the sentiment in the Assembly, he feared being put to death for not taking over the island. But after more setbacks, Nicias finally agreed to retreat.

It was at this time that a lunar eclipse occurred. Nicias, whom I knew to be much influenced by divination, consulted soothsayers who instructed him to wait 21 days before leaving Sicily. The delay allowed Athens' enemies to mount a great sea attack that utterly destroyed the Athenian navy. Deprived of ocean craft, General Nicias marched his remaining troops inland in search of friendly allies. He found none. Instead, troops from Syracuse and Sparta attacked the fatigued Athenians. Nicias surrendered and was put to death. Those who survived were branded, put to work in the quarries near Syracuse and slowly starved to death.

The entire expedition had been destroyed.

The appalled Assembly listened in silence to the sailor's tale. As the citizens absorbed the full meaning of what had taken place, people became enraged with all who had supported the expedition. Fear followed fury when they realized the terrible situation in which we found ourselves. The city had no money, few ships and fewer soldiers. Athens was ripe for invasion.

As so often happens in uncertain times, rumours abounded. People were convinced Syracuse would take advantage of our loss and send an assault fleet against Athens. They also feared that Sparta would invade, taking advantage of our weakness and inability to defend our port at Piraeus. Additional rumours had it that the Persians were entering into an alliance with the Spartans, and would provide Sparta with money and ships.

Athens needed ships quickly. All carpenters, even those without shipbuilding experience, were put to work in the shipyards — to no avail, as it turned out, for we were even short of men to wield the oars.

With the people of Athens in a state of shock, a wave of piousness swept the city. "We are losing because the gods are against us," many cried. Charges of impiety were brought against numerous people, including my old friend Diagoras the Atheist. But he knew he was in danger, so by the time officials showed up at his house to arrest him, he had already fled the city. A sign was posted on the wall of the Tholos promising a reward of ten drachmas for his head. Not much money, certainly not enough to tempt anyone to pursue him, but a highly symbolic gesture from a bankrupt city, nevertheless.

Crito and Chaerephon suggested more than once that I leave Athens, asserting that the city was no longer safe for a man who was a known skeptic as well as an associate of Alcibiades. They were right, of course, and I did give thought as to where I might take you boys, your mother and Diotima. Still, I continued to hold off, hoping things would improve. In any event, I did not know where we would be accepted. Athens had been behaving aggressively for a long while, disdaining even our allies and extorting money for their "protection" from Sparta and the Persians. Providentially, whether through luck or because of the fact that I had fought in three campaigns and was known to have acquitted myself bravely, no charges were brought against me.

With Athens in panic at its sudden reversal of fortune, the Assembly recommended that the city take emergency action and set up a body of 10 experienced men to advise the Assembly. The newly appointed body learned that Alcibiades was living not in Sparta, as had been thought, but in Persia, and that he wished to return to Athens. During his exile he had been working to advance Athenian interests, and had won the trust of a powerful Persian governor who could guarantee Persian money and a fleet of 150 war ships. On hearing this, it suddenly became expedient for the Assembly to remember that Alcibiades had wanted to be tried for desecrating the herms *before* he had left for Sicily. Only an innocent man, they reasoned, would have made such a request.

Once again, Hermogenes told me the truth. Alcibiades had worn out his welcome with the Spartans. He had slept with the wife of the Spartan king, got her with child and defected to Persia before he could be killed. Upon reaching that realm, he had advised the Persians to hold off hostilities in Greece, and to let Sparta and Athens exhaust each other in battle. This course of action would allow the Persians to conquer Greece more easily. Hermogenes' information, although valuable, did not reach the ears of as many people as it should have. His intimates had become more tight-lipped after being attacked as punishment for Alcibiades' defection to Sparta.

The problem, the body of 10 maintained, was that for Alcibiades to secure support from the Persian king, Athens needed to be controlled by a smaller group than the 5,000 who regularly attended the Assembly. It was proposed that another 390 men join the 10 already advising the Assembly. The intent was to make governance less unwieldy while ensuring power was not in the hands of too few. Although many Athenians opposed such a change, it was argued that Athens' desperate situation made it crucial to do whatever was necessary to ensure the city's survival. The proposal was agreed to, the constitution was rewritten and the city came under control of The Four Hundred.

Utterly disregarding their promise to improve the running of the city, The Four Hundred became dictators. Heavily armed men patrolled the streets, imposing their will wherever they went. Executions took place. Fear and hostility swept the city. Mercifully, a few months into the rule of The Four Hundred, thousands of Athenians gathered spontaneously at the Pnyx hill, where they decided to depose The Four Hundred, drive them out of the city and reinstate democracy. One of the exiled men was Critias, Alcibiades' admirer from Potidaea.

In a strange twist of developments, the new assembly decided to recall Alcibiades anyway. Athens wanted her once-brilliant and adored man-god back. But he refused to return. I learned from Hermogenes that Alcibiades wanted to come back with glory. Still fearing prosecution for the incident with the herms, not to mention the rumours that he had assisted the Spartans, he felt he needed some victories with which to sway public opinion.

To this end, he contacted what was left of the Athenian fleet stationed at the Island of Samos. Athens' navy had been so badly crushed that those who remained wanted someone to bring back security and, above all, pride. Alcibiades, with his charisma and honeyed tongue, understood the desires of the fleet and promised to get them what they wanted, what so many of us want: respect and admiration. Although I don't know exactly what he said, he convinced the soldiers and oarsmen to submit to his command. He must have loved that: his own private navy! Naturally, he never delivered the promised Persian help; however, in the years that followed he did provide some much-needed naval victories over the Spartans.

It is perplexing how fast one's standing in a community can change, and how short are people's memories. With Alcibiades' reputation restored thanks to his naval victories, my life quickly improved. People stopped accusing and accosting me in the streets. Young men approached me, asking if I could make them "the next Alcibiades."

However, not all who sought me out were desirous of wealth and fame. Some wanted to discuss and to learn. One young man, I was gratified to discover, risked his life to chat with me. He was from the city of Megara, a Spartan ally, whose citizens were not allowed to enter Athens. In order to speak with me, he dressed up in a woman's clothes and veil and entered the city at night!

I should have been quite pleased with my situation. I had admirers, your mother continued to care for me, although she had ample reason not to, and you boys were growing into perceptive, handsome young men. Yet my thoughts often strayed to the things I did not have.

About that time, we acquired a puppy. I hoped he would grow into a guard dog, for I sometimes felt unsafe in the house; I also wanted protection for all of you when I was at work. The rascally little thing was all ears and paws and slobber. There wasn't a thing in the house it didn't try to chew. We gave bones to the little menace, to deter it from chewing on the furniture. The tactic didn't work; the puppy buried the bones instead of gnawing them. You boys named it Zeus.

One day, upon returning home from work, I was upset to find that Zeus had got into the andron and had dug up the floor. Since it had subsequently been decided that the dog was "yours," I ordered you boys to fix the floor. Somewhat unsettled, I went outside and sat in my usual place beneath the kitchen window. A short time later, Menexenus, then just five years old, appeared and held out what looked like a tiny, elongated stone. "Father, what is this?" he asked.

I took the stone from him and examined it. No more than the size of a thumb, I turned it over in my fingers. "It's a penis!" I finally said. "Where did you find this?"

"In the andron," Menexenus replied simply, and walked away, as if no further explanation were necessary.

Curious, I got up and went into the andron. Zeus was running around barking, Lamprocles and Sophroniscus were on their knees, digging up the floor, while Menexenus stood by and watched.

"What are you doing?" I shouted, looking in dismay at the mess you boys were making.

"There's stuff down here, Father," Sophroniscus said calmly, unmoved by my anger and my raised voice.

"What kind of stuff?" I demanded.

Sophroniscus pointed to a pile of stones. "Look."

I strode over, picked up one of the stones and brushed off the dirt. The piece was limestone, and it had the shape of a nose.

"Exactly where did you find this?" I asked.

"Here." Sophroniscus pointed to the hole.

"There's so much!" said Lamprocles. He glanced up at me a moment then went back to digging.

I picked up another stone and brushed it off. It, too, was limestone, but had no distinguishable shape.

"Another penis!" Lamprocles yelled. He held it up for us to see, as thrilled as if he had discovered a nugget of gold.

By now, you were all excited. Your mother and Diotima appeared in the andron, drawn by your raised voices.

"What is going on?" Xanthippe asked.

"We were trying to fix the floor," said Sophroniscus. "Lamprocles found a stone penis sticking out of the ground, and we wondered what it was attached to. So we went on digging."

"Did you find anything else?" your mother asked.

Lamprocles nodded, his eyes shining. "We found lots of smooth rocks, some shaped like noses and ears."

Diotima limped over and picked up one of the stones. Her eyes widened and she put her hand to her mouth in shock. She said nothing as she bent to pick up a smaller piece of stone. Carefully, she brushed it off; we saw that it was a blue ceramic tile

"What is it?" Xanthippe asked.

"The herms," Diotima said quietly.

My thoughts went instantly to the desecration Alcibiades had left in his wake before going to Sicily. "How did Alcibiades sneak these into our andron?" I asked.

Diotima's eyes met mine. "These are not from the herms Alcibiades mutilated."

"Then where did they come from? I asked.

"Your father," Diotima said.

My father? He had died years ago. Diotima must be losing her mind. I did not want to offend her, but I needed to explain to her that she was mistaken. I was about to speak when it hit me!

How many herms had I examined in Athens, Delphi, Potidaea, Delium and Amphipolis, when I was searching for work bearing my father's name? How many times had I wondered why I did not come across a single thing? Why did not even one herm in front of our house bear his name? What had happened to the herms your grandfather laboured so long to create? Where were they?

At last, I knew the answer. The herms were all here, buried below the floor of our very own andron. With that realization, came another. When my father understood that he would never again be called on to work on a prominent project, he smashed his herms, dug up the tiled floor, and buried more than 25 years of painstaking toil beneath it. A lifetime of effort and isolation amounted to nothing. Suddenly, my father's life seemed to me sad, lonely and pathetic.

DAY 23

I COULD GO ON writing about Alcibiades for days. But as time is running out far more quickly than I would like, I realize the need to end his story.

If I recall the passage of time correctly, eight years after sailing to Sicily and four years after his recall from exile, Alcibiades finally returned to Athens. He returned a hero, although he chose the unluckiest day of the year to arrive — the day when, traditionally, the statue of Athena is cleaned and Athens must survive without the protection of the goddess.

Actually, I believe he chose the day deliberately, to show the Athenians that chance could not touch him. That he was, in essence, himself a god.

As would be expected of a god's return, most of the citizens, including me, went to the port of Piraeus to see him arrive. As he stepped onto the docks, his purple cloak blowing in the breeze, the waiting crowd cheered and chanted his name enthusiastically. He waved, before striding briskly toward the city.

I would have liked to have taken you boys with me to the docks, but your mother forbade it. Angrily, I called her a few choice names — thoughtless words I now regret. So I stood alone to meet Alcibiades. He may have walked like a god, and even been hailed as one but, in my eyes at least, he had lost his godlike appearance. His face had become puffy, as happens with men who have drunk too much and for too long. His arms were soft and he had developed a belly. No longer was he the dashing youth he had once been, endowed with good looks and strong muscles. Alcibiades had become a greying, middle-aged man.

I hailed him through the ruckus as he came closer. People moved aside, expecting him to greet me. Indeed, he glanced in my direction, and we locked eyes for a few moments. But he pretended not to recognize me and continued up the hill without greeting me. This glorious return was his to enjoy, and he would share it with nobody. Men and women close by witnessed the deliberate snub, and whispered amongst themselves. I felt as if I had been stabbed in the stomach.

When I got back to the house, your mother looked at me questioningly, as if to ask, "Well?" When I was unable speak or hold her gaze, she realized the meeting hadn't gone the way I had hoped. She had every right to say, "I told you so," and to call me a fool. But as you know, your mother has a forgiving nature and does not hold grudges. She said nothing, just embraced me and kissed me on the cheek. I held her tight and told her I loved her.

I never saw Alcibiades again.

Shortly after his return to Athens, the charge of sacrilege against him was officially withdrawn and his property was returned to him. The Assembly voted Alcibiades supreme commander of land and sea. In addition, it granted him 1,500 hoplites and 100 ships. The following spring he left again, to great fanfare.

But this was the beginning of a great change. Alcibiades was defeated in battle again and again. The Assembly, always capricious, stripped him of his command. Fearing for his life, he fled and tried to ingratiate himself once more with the Persians, unsuccessfully this time.

Hermogenes' sister, tired of sharing her husband with his many lovers, had left him by then, so I lacked her brother's usually reliable information. I did hear, however, that Alcibiades had taken up residence somewhere near Sardis, and had been about to go and plead his case with the Persian court when soldiers surrounded his house. Frightened, he stayed inside, hoping they would leave. Instead, they set fire to the dwelling. When Alcibiades tried to escape, an arrow pierced and killed him.

Learning of Alcibiades' death, I thought of Anaxagoras, the great thinker and counsellor to Pericles. Early in his life, Anaxagoras had studied the heavens, as Thales before him had done. Anaxagoras had predicted that sooner or later a piece of the sun would break off and fall to earth. Years later, he was thought to have been proven correct when all of Greece saw an arc of fire in the sky, followed by a fiery fragment that landed in Thrace. When the fragment cooled, it was found to be nothing but a chunk of brown rock.

I saw Alcibiades as that chunk of rock. In his youth, he had been like the sun, luminous and beautiful, with people observing him in wonder and awe as he blazed his way across Greece. But as he grew older and his glory faded, he revealed himself to be human after all. Perhaps he glowed more brightly than most, but only for a short time.

With Alcibiades' aura extinguished, Athens was cast into darkness as the Spartans went directly for the Athenian jugular. They sailed for the Hellespont, the narrow waterway through which the city imported much of its grain. The Athenian navy pursued in haste to defend the critical supply line, but the Spartans utterly defeated our fleet.

The losses were enormous. One hundred and fifty-nine ships were captured or destroyed. Thirty-eight hundred sailors were killed or enslaved. Only nine ships escaped. The news spread quickly to Athens, where it was received with immense sorrow and humiliation. When the few survivors reached the port of Piraeus, each man went to his house and waited for the end.

The Spartan fleet did, indeed, arrive in Piraeus. While their ships blocked the harbours there, the Spartan king laid siege to Athens on land. The Spartans were unable to breach the city's high walls, but they did not need to, for they hemmed us in on land and sea. All they had to do was wait. I would soon understand what the poor besieged souls in Potidaea had experienced.

All too quickly, warehouses were emptied of corn and barley. Before long, everything people had stored in their homes was gone. By the time winter set in, horses and donkeys were killed and eaten. Household pets went missing. Diotima and your mother boiled any plants they could find to make soup. Most people lost their dignity. Slaves and dogs scavenged while great numbers of unaccompanied married women went begging in the streets. Theft was rife. Even the wealthy had hollow eyes and sick coughs.

I was getting old by this time — I *am* old! — and the deprivation took its toll on me. I was no longer as tough as a Spartan, as the saying goes. I felt the cold more than I used to. I wore my sandals all the time. I lost eight teeth.

You boys did not go hungry, for your mother and Diotima always managed to scrape together just enough to keep us going. Somehow they even kept our dog alive.

But you boys were affected in other ways, simply because you are the sons of Socrates. Bad enough to have a skeptic and a lunatic for a father, but when I was blamed, at least partially, for the fall of the city, that was too much for any child to bear. I only saw one fight — between Menexenus and some boy from school — but I believe you were all tested, and for that I am profoundly sorry.

As you doubtless know, no politician exists who speaks more loudly than an empty belly crying for food. So dire was the situation that the starving city had no option but to surrender. As a condition of that surrender, Athens had to agree to tear down her walls.

I was among the many drafted for this job. Pushing the big square blocks of stone off the top of the wall was arduous work. The stones came down, one by one, thudding heavily as they struck the ground. Labourers and slaves hauled them to Piraeus, to be made into homes and piers. When the top row of stones had been removed, we went on to the next ones. Because they were lower, these stones landed less heavily, but no less painfully to my ears.

Pulling the stones from the wall — so many of which I had carved myself — was much like stripping a corpse of its clothing on the battlefield.

Only this was no enemy I was undressing, but something I had carefully and thoughtfully helped to create. I remember Crito's father, Thespis, proudly stating that the wall would stand for hundreds of years. It did not even survive my own lifetime.

We made it to the base of the wall in some places, where the stones had been pressed deeply into the ground by the massive weight resting above them. Some of these stones had been laid more than 75 years earlier; they were the first ones placed after the Persians had been driven from Greece. Those initial fortifications had been built as quickly as possible, as Athenians hurried to create some form of protection against another invasion, be it from Persia, Sparta or some other enemy. They used every stone they could find, even ones removed from burnt-out temples and grave markers.

One hot summer day, as I paused to mop my face with a corner of my tunic, I happened to notice a particular block of stone. A closer look revealed it to be smoothly polished marble. The block was quite large: long and wide, and as deep as a tall man. It was slightly pink in hue, with a few pink-orange veins running through it. It bore no carvings or inscriptions, although something may have been written on the underside.

A single shoot, about a finger high and bearing three green leaves, grew from the middle of the marble block. It seemed to pop right out of the cold marble, rooted in no discernible soil. *How did this bit of life originate?* I wondered. *How could it have grown?*

I marvelled at its delicate strength. Around the new growth the marble was cracked, fissures extending in all directions. Although men spend days breaking stone with chisels, hammers and wedges, this sprout, soft and supple, was slowly, inexorably, splitting the marble. I wondered how long it would take for the marble to crack completely. Were I to leave it undisturbed, I could imagine the sapling's roots growing through, over and around the stone, crushing and obliterating it.

Leaving the young growth undisturbed, I moved on to dismantle another section of the wall. For the rest of the day I caught myself smiling as my thoughts went again and again to the little green shoot. Life from lifelessness, I thought. That night, instead of going home feeling defeated and sad, I whistled as I walked. I was uncharacteristically happy as I reached the house and was greeted by the simple sounds and sights of home: your mother's usual singing as she prepared the evening meal; Zeus, yapping cheerfully, his tail wagging in greeting; Diotima's voice in the bedroom as she entertained you boys with a fable. Entering the kitchen to kiss your mother's cheek, I felt that good things were still possible.

As the wall was being dismantled, the Spartans appointed a group of 30 Athenian aristocrats to control the city. This group, The Thirty, was made up of men who had been members of The Four Hundred seven years earlier. Exiled for their participation in the anti-democratic uprising, now they had been reinstated as citizens and been given authority to run the city. Critias, Alcibiades' old admirer from Potidaea, became the leader of the group, which was now tasked with setting laws under Spartan rule and turning Athens back into an oligarchy.

The new regime was, in many ways, a continuation of the rule of The Four Hundred, only worse. Sparta assisted The Thirty by giving them troops to impose their will. The Thirty's first targets comprised the men who'd had them exiled when they were members of The Four Hundred. The Thirty fabricated various reasons for arresting their previous accusers and executed them without trial, confiscating their wealth. Thousands left Athens in fear, including Chaerephon, who fled with his family to Thebes.

To pay for the support of the Spartan garrison, Critias ordered each member of The Thirty to arrest and execute a resident alien and confiscate his property. One member of The Thirty refused to comply. Seeing this as a threat to his authority, Critias denounced him as a traitor, on the excuse that the man was trying to reinstate a democratic government.

The wretched man managed to escape to a nearby altar where he asked for sanctuary, but the keepers of the prison found him, dragged him away and then forced him to drink hemlock. His screams were heard all over the agora. No one was safe.

Critias was not a fool. Well did he understand that the more people he implicated in his horrific schemes, the more power he would gain over them. He forced every man he knew to obey the rules he had enacted for The Thirty. Fifteen hundred people were killed without trial. Anybody who opposed the new regime was brought to trial on charges of treason. One of the victims was Autolycus, son of Lycon.

The following winter, a group of citizens who had fled Athens in search of safety gathered in Thebes to form their own pro-democracy army. On the coldest day I have ever experienced, the kind of day when you can see your breath and icicles form on your eyelashes, the pro-democracy army returned to Athens, staging a daring attack from the port of Piraeus. Although outnumbered five-to-one by the combined Spartan garrison and the forces of The Thirty, the citizens' army was victorious. Critias and a number of his cronies were killed. Sparta, distracted by an internal power struggle, was unable to send troops to retake the city. And so ended the rule of The Thirty.

To my great sorrow, my friend, Chaerephon, who at the age of 65 had joined the pro-democratic cause, was also killed during the uprising. I was not there when it happened. I was not even aware it had taken place until a student of mine told me that Chaerephon had fought until his spear was splintered and his shield was split.

The loss of Chaerephon was a great shock for me — as difficult and as painful as any I had suffered until then, including the loss of my mother, my brother and Simon. Despite our many years of friendship and mutual affection, until his death I hadn't realized quite how important Chaerephon was to me. I had taken for granted all the time we'd spent together at dinner parties, in the gymnasium or simply in one of our courtyards, enjoying pleasant conversation. His death created a vast chasm in my life that nothing has filled.

Daily, I am reminded of him. In particular, I think of him when someone touches my shoulder. I know why this is. My memories of Potidaea, where I so nearly abandoned my friends, have remained vivid. How can I possibly forget Chaerephon behind me in the phalanx, when he grasped my shoulder and said, "I'm glad you are with us, Socrates. You give me strength." I still remember turning around, about to make some comment, when the general walked up to the front line and addressed us.

I never managed to speak my words; I don't even recall what they would have been. Yet now that he is gone, every time someone touches my shoulder, I expect to see Chaerephon's silly, lopsided grin, and I want him to tell me that his death was a cruel hoax, a joke, a lie someone told me.

This makes no sense, of course, for Chaerephon really is dead. When I realize the person touching me is not my old friend, I find it a great trial to not show my disappointment. Each time I feel the loss of Chaerephon all over again. If only I could tell him what he meant to me! But it is too late for that now. I will never be able to thank him for his friendship. I will never have the chance to tell him I loved him. It is extraordinarily frustrating that there is simply nothing I can do about my loss.

Chaerephon's death was, for me at least, the worst event of that terrible year. But it was not the only bad thing that occurred. Anytus had never been able to rehabilitate his name after his failure at the Battle of Pylos. Indeed, he contrived for more than 20 years to find a way of restoring his former standing. But although his treason was not proven in court, a rumour persisted that he had bribed the jury to find him innocent.

None of his attempts to regain his reputation had succeeded — until, that is, The Thirty were ousted. At that time, Anytus embarked upon a new campaign, which he began with the claim that he had remained in the city to help prepare it for the return of pro-democratic forces. He had been the one, he asserted, who had opened the Piraeus gate so the pro-democratic forces, Chaerephon among them, could enter the city.

As further proof of his loyalty, he told the Assembly that he had tracked down the impious man who had brought the wrath of the gods upon the city. Finding the man in Corinth, he had had him killed. This infamous person turned out to be none other than my friend, Diagoras the Atheist. Although I wasn't there to witness it, I learned that the Assembly had cheered Anytus in a manner befitting a runner who had won an Olympic sprint. Anytus, finally, had been forgiven.

I, on the other hand, was vilified. Someone had started the rumour that I had instructed Critias, leader of The Thirty. As a result, many Athenians blamed me for their woes. The claim was ludicrous; it was nothing but a lie. True, Critias had joined Alcibiades and me a few times on our walks through Athens. And we had attended many of the same dinner parties over the years. Yet at no point had Critias ever been my student. Nonetheless, Athenians love their gossip, and that baseless gossip became their reality.

I know this was a difficult time for you boys because of the taunting and name-calling, as well as the fights you fought to defend my honour. Once again, you were victimized for being the sons of Socrates. Will you ever escape that misfortune? I wonder. I don't like to think about it.

It didn't take me long to learn who had started the rumours. I was at the Painted Porch with Crito when, from across the agora, someone began to scream at me. I should not have been surprised to see it was Lycon. He called me a murderer. He accused Critias' men of killing his son, and since — according to him — I was Critias' teacher, he blamed me for Autolycus' death as well.

What an ironic statement from a man who had once argued that the teacher was not responsible for the student! But Lycon was not interested in debating irony. I have sometimes called him a snake because of his treacherous behaviour, but at that moment he resembled an angry jackal: ears back, ready to bite. Although he was elderly, over 70, he came at me, fists swinging. Crito and a few bystanders restrained Lycon and helped me fend him off. This did nothing to deflect Lycon's vitriol, and he continued screaming and yelling at me. Only when his wrath was finally spent did he spit on the ground and walk away.

Just then I spotted Anytus, leaning casually against a nearby wall. Meeting my eyes, he grinned slyly. I understood immediately — Anytus had accused me of being Critias' teacher, and he wanted me to know it. He held my gaze a while, so enraging me with the smirk that never left his face, that I had a sudden urge to run him through with my spear. Then slowly, languidly, like a predator that had just eaten its fill, he strolled off after Lycon.

There go two jackals, I thought. *I wonder which will bite the other first.* I should have remembered that jackals don't fight each other when larger prey is there to bring down.

DAY 24

THE DAY I learned about the accusations against me was fittingly cloudy and grey. I was at the fountain house, filling jugs with water — a job beyond Diotima's strength now — when I heard angry shouts coming from the direction of the law courts. Turning, I saw a man rushing toward me, and realized I was the target of his anger. He was a stranger, a young man in his early 20s, with a large nose, long straight hair and a scraggly beard. Several other men in his vicinity were also looking at me menacingly.

The young man stopped in front of me. Without preamble, he said loudly, "Socrates, you are charged with refusing to recognize the gods acknowledged by the city, with introducing divinities of your own and with corrupting the youth of Athens. You will be judged for these crimes." With that, he walked away, followed by his tough-looking companions.

Initially, I attributed the outburst to some joke, a prank by one of my students. Yet for some reason, I decided to walk across the agora to see whether the accusations had truly been made. Sure enough, standing out vividly against the white paint of the courthouse wall, written in red letters, I saw the charges against me. Almost exactly, the words were the same as those uttered by the stranger.

Below the accusations were the names of my accusers: Anytus, Lycon and Meletus. I had no idea who Meletus was. Only later did I learn that he was the angry young man from the agora. My accusers demanded I be punished with death. *Those two jackals*, I thought. *I should have expected it.*

"You must leave Athens," Crito advised me, as soon as he heard about the charges. A look of frightened concern had replaced his usual smile.

His reaction both surprised and disappointed me, for I had hoped he would tell me to thrash the idiots in court — to make them regret their decision to prosecute me. Crito knew only too well how I felt about both Anytus and Lycon.

"So, too, says Xanthippe," I remarked, trying to hide my dismay as I rocked my newborn grandson, my tiny namesake, in my arms. "She thinks we should leave Athens."

"You should consider your wife's wisdom," he said.

"Do you think I will lose the case, Crito?"

"It does not matter what I think."

My arms stilled. "It matters a great deal to me. Answer the question, Crito. Do you believe I will lose?"

"Yes," he said, flatly.

I stared at him. "Have I corrupted the youth of Athens?"

"No."

"Have I created new divinities?"

"Not that I know of."

I gave him a look of annoyance, and he said quickly, "No, of course you haven't."

"Do I take part in the city festivals honouring the gods?"

"You do, Socrates." Crito was exasperated. "But you do not *believe* in the gods. Many Athenians have doubts; we both know that. Your problem is that you give voice to them."

"In other words, you believe me guilty of one of the charges."

"I do," Crito said. "The thing is, even if, by some miracle, you manage to convince the jury of your innocence, you will still suffer because of your past associations with Alcibiades and Critias. Athenians regard Alcibiades as having been your student. Critias, too. Those two did a lot of harm, Socrates, and the citizens want to blame someone for the depths we have sunk to."

"So you do not think I can win?" I persisted.

"No." Crito looked troubled.

"When have you known me to lose an argument?" I asked, continuing to rock my grandson.

"You won't be defending an idea in the agora, Socrates. This is different. You will be being judged in court."

I shrugged. "Of course. I know that. But the agora or the court, I have beaten Lycon before in debate and I can do it again — easily."

Crito shifted uneasily on his chair. "You are not a political person, Socrates. The jury will be swayed by emotion rather than by long-winded argument. Besides, my friend, I know you. You will be haughty, not humble. Even Pericles had to weep and plead in order to save Aspasia, and that was a different time. Athens was strong then, as strong as she has ever been. Now, people live in constant fear. They are frightened that the wrath of the gods will descend on them if an impious man does not show proper respect."

"I will not leave Athens," I objected, stubbornly.

"Your life is in peril!" Crito cried out, exasperated once more. His old wound, the one he had received so long ago at Potidaea, stood out against his neck, red and angry, as if the gash were fresh. I had never seen it like that before. Then I noticed the concern in his face, and realized how frightened Crito was for me. Oddly, the realization calmed me.

"My life is in peril every day," I said patiently. "I could be run over by a horse, be beaten up by angry neighbours, choke on a nut or be taken by disease."

Crito's brow furrowed. The scar seemed to pulsate.

"Or Xanthippe could pour urine over my head again," I added, hoping the joke would bring back his smile, even make him laugh a little, but in vain. "Hear me out," I went on more seriously. "I not will leave Athens unless I must. Let me go to the preliminary hearing, at least."

"And then you will leave?"

"I will consider it," I conceded.

On my way to court the next day, I walked past many herms. My thoughts went to my father, not only because of his carvings, but because he had been brought to court once, too. He had won his battle, as would I. But I would do better than he had. I would not rely on the assistance of friends or acquaintances for success. I would defend myself and I would win.

Conversation ceased as I walked up the stairs to the hearing. "Justice for Athens," someone yelled behind me. At that moment, perhaps for the first time, the situation became real in my mind. Momentarily, I was unnerved. Maybe your mother and Crito had been correct, after all. Was it stupid of me to believe I could hold my own? Was it possible that these were charges against which almost nobody, even if they were innocent, could defend themselves?

I touched the amulet that hung around my neck and thought of my brother, who had sacrificed himself for nothing. For 50 years he had been beyond joy and love. Briefly, I thought seriously about taking you all away to some distant city, where I would change my name and spend the rest of my life in hiding.

The notion was fleeting, because my thoughts then went to Lycon. I remembered the name-calling, the physical abuse and the manner in which my family had suffered because of the fire he'd started at the agora and the trial afterwards. It was time to be finished with this rabid dog, once and for all. Time to rid myself of the demons of my youth.

I thought angrily of Anytus — of his insults and of his guilt in the murder of my friend, Diagoras the Atheist. I remembered his lie that I had been Critias' teacher. It was time for me to put him in his place, too. The more irritated I became, the more my resolve strengthened. I refused to be bullied out of my home, especially by a couple of scavenging mongrels that needed to be put down.

At last, I came before the chief magistrate. He decided the charges against me were legitimate and of enough merit to warrant a trial. His ruling did not upset me. On the contrary, I was happy with his decision.

A trial date was set, and I looked forward to once more humiliating Lycon and Anytus publicly.

In the days that followed, I noticed men loitering near the house. They did not talk amongst themselves, nor did I see them smile. Day and night they just stood there, watching the house. Zeus barked wildly when he saw them. It was obvious these were Lycon and Anytus' men. I decided not to mention them to your mother as I didn't want to upset her. But I think she knew, anyway.

On the fateful sunny morning of my trial date, it did not occur to me that I would not return home. I did not dream that I would never again hear Diotima or your mother speaking in the kitchen; never again stub my toe on the unused courtyard altar or see you boys leap from it, feathers in your hands, as you tried to fly like Icarus. The morning of the trial, I was convinced I would win.

Crito showed up at the house with his son, Critobulus, as well as half a dozen of my young students. Again, Crito was not smiling.

"Are you still determined to go through with this?" he asked.

"I am."

"Then let's be sure you have a chance to defend yourself properly. We will accompany you."

"No one will stop me from going to court, Crito. They will harry me only if I try to leave Athens. My family needs you more than I do, so I beg you to stay with them here. I'll walk alone." I spoke confidently.

But Crito would not be rebuffed. He wanted people sympathetic to me to attend the trial, as many as possible. We talked at some length. We finally agreed that those of our friends who were not Athenian citizens, and who, therefore, could not be chosen for jury duty, should remain at the house with you boys, your mother and Diotima, for your protection.

I embraced you all before leaving for court. Your mother had tears in her eyes. Diotima was uncharacteristically downcast. They are perceptive women, and possibly they foresaw the outcome of the trial. You boys all appeared stoic. I wonder — did you sense what would happen? Preoccupied as I was with the trial, I didn't notice that Zeus was nowhere to be seen.

As we made our way to the court, the men loitering nearby followed us. Crito kept a wary eye on them. But I was not concerned about being attacked. My thoughts were on the trial and what awaited me there. Due to the critical shortage of money in the city coffers, jury members' pay had been dropped from three obols to one. If less than 200 jurors showed up, my case would be delayed. I was anxious to see Lycon and Anytus get their due, and then to be rid of the whole affair. So I hoped at least the required 200 jurors would appear.

When Crito was satisfied we were physically safe, he asked, "Should we debate your defense?"

"It's unnecessary," I told him. "I have been preparing all my life for this. I can handle the likes of Lycon."

Suddenly, Crito was angry. The scar on his neck became prominent. "Do you know how often Athenian juries put innocent people to death?"

"No one will put me to death," I replied calmly. "Lycon is not as clever as he thinks he is."

"Maybe not, but you are overconfident, Socrates. I wish now that we had brought your wife, the boys and your grandson to court. Maybe it's still possible. They might influence the jury."

I was indignant. "I will not expose my family to this. This is *my* fight."

Crito looked more troubled than ever. "You must play on the emotions of the court. They will be swayed by nothing less. Avoid long speeches, Socrates. Keep your sentences short. And remember, this is no time to confuse people with your logic. If you do, either you will bore them or they will think you are too high and mighty to speak simply."

"I will speak as I must."

"At least act humbly in court," he pleaded, to which I gave a derisive snort.

"Socrates, you must treat the jurors with respect!"

"Oh, Crito. Always the voice of reason," I said, putting my arm around his shoulder. "This will work out, I know it will. And just think, if by some chance I am found guilty and am put to death, you will not have to worry about me anymore."

Crito gave me a look that told me he did not appreciate the joke.

The agora was far busier at this hour than I had seen it for years. Perhaps not even since the days of Pericles, when Athens was in her prime and merchants, moneylenders, cobblers and all manner of other men and women flocked to the city. The sheer number of people made it difficult to walk; I wondered if I had forgotten some festival. Yet despite the size of the crowd, the usual clamour was oddly subdued. Fruit sellers were not yelling out their offerings, slaves were not haggling with fishmongers and the idle banter of men was strangely muted. Instead, a low hum filled the air, a sound somewhat like that made by a nest full of honeybees. I felt many eyes watching me.

Then the whispering began. "It's him. He's here," I heard, as people started to heckle me. Suddenly, it dawned on me: all these people had appeared to watch me.

My trial was to be held in the Green Court — the only court large enough to hold the number of jurors who had turned out to judge me. As we arrived, Crito and many others put their names in a large ceramic jug, hoping to be chosen for jury duty. In no time, the jug was filled with tokens. The court would be full today. The tokens were drawn, and I was happy to see that both Crito and his son Critobulus were to be on the jury. Two friendly faces, at least, would be among my judges.

Crito led me to the edge of the Green Court, lifting the rope to allow me entry. I ducked under the rope, followed by Crito and his son. Crito seized my arm as I was about to walk down the stairs to my seat.

Turning, I saw fear in his face. He did not speak, but gave my arm a small shake, as if to say, "Do your best."

I took my place at the front of the courtroom and scanned the jury. Staring down at me, I saw 500 men, all holding green wooden staffs to show they were in the right court. Then I searched the faces in the court itself, hoping to see more men I knew to be kindly disposed toward me. Apart from the friends who had accompanied me today, I saw only a few others on whose support I thought I could count — certainly not as many as I'd hoped for.

In response to some booing and hissing, a smattering of clapping broke out, but this was quickly drowned out when those members of the jury who opposed me knocked their staffs against the stone seats. The noise disturbed a flock of birds in a nearby plane tree, and they took wing. Watching them soar out of sight, I thought of other trials that had taken place here. My father's case had been heard in a different, smaller court, but both Phidias and Aspasia had been tried here. Thanks to Pericles' tears, Aspasia had been found innocent. Phidias had not been as fortunate. Come to think of it, he may well have died in the very cell in which I now languish.

All at once, I saw Lycon and Anytus. With them was Meletus, the youth from the agora who had shouted the charges against me. As they took their seats, Lycon threw me a menacing grin. *I hope you die alone and in pain*, I thought, cruelly.

The jury was sworn in. The lead juror, a man I knew to be a potter in the Kerameikos, rose to his feet, sacrificed a rooster, washed the blood off his hands in a basin of water and dried them with a towel. He then turned to address the jury. The tension in the court was like the moment before battle, when the call is given to march. I could see that the lead juror felt it, too; he looked nervous as he began to speak.

"The Green Court is in session today. Socrates, son of Sophroniscus, is accused of several crimes. They are as follows: he is a corrupter of the youth, he does not believe in the gods of the city and he worships other new divinities of his own. Meletus, son of Meletus, Anytus, son of Anthemion, and Lycon, son of Memnon, have brought these accusations against him. The prosecution will begin at once."

Clearly relieved that the first part of his duties was over, the lead juror sat down. He nodded to the man by the water clock, who removed a plug, and water began to flow from the jug. The prosecution's time had begun.

Meletus got to his feet. This surprised me, although not for long, for it made sense that he would do the speaking. For one thing, if Lycon were to lose, as I was confident he would, his reputation as an orator would be damaged. For another, since the men of the jury were generally young, it was a better strategy to have a younger man address them.

"Citizens of Athens," Meletus began, "you have heard the accusations against Socrates. I will deal with them as they were read out by the esteemed lead juror."

Except for the rustling of clothing and a man coughing somewhere in the audience, the courtroom was hushed.

Meletus took a step toward the jury and launched into his address. "Fellow citizens, I come before you today, not to speak as one man accusing another of things for which there are no excuses. Rather, I come before you as a citizen concerned for the well-being of our great city. Among us is one who is like a curse upon Athens. He is like a growth that has been allowed to infect our city for far too long. His mere presence is painful to our patroness, Athena."

Lycon and Anytus exchanged ugly smirks.

"I wish to pose a simple question," Meletus continued. "How did the structure of our society come about? From the animals we sacrifice? From the land upon which we walk? From the men we call our brothers? No! I say it came about from the foundation laid down by our betters. It came about from the gods! We all know these facts. Any man who denies them is a man with whom I do not wish to be associated. For such a man is a subverter of truth who threatens our beliefs, our values and our virtuous ways of life!"

Virtuous ways of life? I almost laughed out loud, but forced myself to stay impassive. I could count on my fingers and toes the virtuous men I knew in the city, and still have a few digits left.

"One among us, however, does not believe these truths. He is a poisoner and corrupter of the hearts of men. To the illustrious citizens on the jury, this evil person may not appear a threat, for they have the wisdom to understand the difference between right and wrong and are, therefore, able to ignore wicked instructions. The man before you today, however, has other methods of undermining our great city. He threatens our youth!"

Meletus paused for several moments. Considering his youth, he played his audience well. Although his tone was nasal and not impressive in itself, he was able to modulate his pitch and vary the pace of his speech. He spoke in a way that gained the jury's full attention. At another time I might have actually enjoyed his rhetoric, no matter how ridiculous it was.

"That's right," he went on, "he threatens our youth! He corrupts the hearts of those who are still impressionable. Once tainted, the heart of a man begins to rot. If the infection is not eradicated quickly, it will spread. Eventually, these affected young men cause damage, not just to themselves but to all of Athens. I do not speak theoretically, but factually. Here I name Alcibiades. Alcibiades was of the most noble birth, from a blood line that carried the highest ideals of "city before self." Furthermore, he had the protection of Pericles, the incomparable first citizen of Athens, whose hand and mind are seen everywhere in our great city.

"But even a young person with a noble lineage and the benefit of a wise patron can be led astray by evil-doers. Alcibiades had the misfortune to come into contact with the man who appears accused before you. They met on the battlefield: a young man growing into his own and a middle-aged man whose bite was like a viper's poison. Once his fangs had pierced the innocent boy, they did not let go. Socrates led poor Alcibiades astray, away from the path of righteousness."

Lycon's eyes gleamed with satisfaction, as if his prize student were taking part in a hard-fought wrestling match.

"Under the spell of his teacher and master, Alcibiades did unspeakable things. Things I do not have the heart to repeat here. He went away for a time. During this period of freedom from his evil master, he reverted back to his natural tendencies for goodness and excellence, bringing honour to Athens through his glorious victories. Athens forgave Alcibiades and accepted him back, as it would a favourite son.

Upon his return to Athens, however, the viper struck and poisoned Alcibiades once more. With his virtue and strength sapped by Socrates, Alcibiades lost his way again, this time to the detriment of our city. We lost our fathers, sons and brothers to Spartan swords. Our democracy was overthrown and Athens lost its soul."

I will not waste precious ink or what is left of my limited time by writing much more about what Meletus had to say. But I will tell you that he went on ranting about my impiety and my insolence, recounting the fateful day when he was walking through the agora and heard me speaking about the fallibility of the gods.

It was clear to me that Lycon had worked with young Meletus, for his speech was polished and eloquently delivered. More importantly, he spoke with such certainty that I am convinced he is a religious fanatic and truly believes I am evil.

The stream of the water clock slowed, and Meletus ended his speech.

"... and so, men of Athens, the gods watch and know and judge. They will not look kindly on a city that harbours an irreligious man. By the grace of the gods, we have recently escaped the shackles of our enemies and have reintroduced our democratic way of life. What will the gods do to us if we let such a man as Socrates go unpunished? It is my belief that they will abandon us, and we may never again recover our city."

A great murmuring passed through the crowd as Meletus grew silent. I heard snippets of distasteful conversation and jeering. I also noticed many waving their fists. The jury was clearly not well disposed toward me.

The water clock was refilled, and I was called on to stand. I felt the warm, mid-morning sun on my face as I stood still and waited for silence. The murmuring slowly ceased. The court was hushed as I prepared to speak.

DAY 25

"Citizens of athens," I began, raising my voice so the crowd gathered beyond the jury could hear me. "My accuser, Meletus, has spoken persuasively. In fact, so taken was I with his rhetoric, that I almost forgot who I was and came close to believing his words!"

Those friendly to me chuckled, but most of the jury remained stone-faced.

"But then, as I sat listening, I touched my bulbous nose, my bulging eyes, my bald head and my not inconsequential belly, and I realized that I am only Socrates, not the wicked man Meletus has made me out to be."

A few more chuckles this time.

"Now that I have recovered myself, I am at ease, for I am confident I can refute all the accusations brought against me. And I will do so in a manner consistent with the way I have conversed with your fathers and their fathers before them.

"What does me the greatest harm, perhaps, is my reputation. Many of you do not know me personally, but you will have heard stories about a man named Socrates. You heard these tales when you were young, and they settled in your minds as truths. 'Socrates is a strange man,' the stories went. 'He is a man who studies the reasons for rainbows and earthquakes, and who thinks the moon is a giant rock and the sun a ball of flame.' The truth is, these are not my studies, and many of you present can attest to that truth."

At this point, some discussion took place amongst the jury members. Several nodded as they conferred — approvingly, I believed — with those around them. I would have liked them to have continued their discussion. After all, it appeared to me that some of the jurors were defending me. But I was conscious of the water running, so at the first sign of a lull in their discussion, I continued.

"If you were to hear the answers of those who know me — people such as my distinguished friend, Crito — you would understand that these curious matters do not hold my attention. Why then, you ask, is Socrates so notorious? Why have plays been written about him? Why have we heard stories about him since our childhood? Surely he must have done something wicked to have earned such an evil name and to deserve the accusations of this court?"

Muttering began to sweep the court, which quickly increased to a level over which I could not be heard.

"Citizens, please do not interrupt me!" I yelled, losing my calm.

Some in the jury called for silence and the noise died down.

"Thank you," I said. "Now, as I mentioned, I will explain a few things. Let me call your attention to a man you would have deemed, I am certain, beyond reproach. A pious man, who fought and died to return democracy to Athens. Most of you will have been familiar with him. His name was Chaerephon. Many will know, too, that as an impetuous youth, he journeyed to Delphi, where he boldly asked the Oracle to tell him the name of the wisest of men."

Some hissing from the gallery interrupted me briefly. I waited until it stopped before I continued.

"The Oracle's answer was that no one was wiser than Socrates. Those of you here today, who knew Chaerephon, can no doubt confirm this."

Heads nodded slowly around the court.

"Why do I mention this? Not to boast, but only to explain the reason for the disparaging stories about me. Please understand, my fellow citizens, that upon hearing of the Oracle's words, I was baffled. Most of you will know the oft-told tale of King Croesus, who asked the Oracle whether he should go to war, and was told that if he did so a great empire would fall. Croesus believed the Oracle meant the Persian Empire would fall, when, in fact, his own empire was destroyed. Knowing this story, I asked myself—how do I interpret the riddle that Chaerephon brought back from Delphi? I knew only too well that I lacked wisdom, yet the words came from the Oracle, the mouthpiece of Apollo, the God of Truth. After much thought, I resolved to find someone who might provide me with a solution. I needed to find a wise man."

I paused a moment and scanned the court.

"The first man I came across was a craftsman, a tanner," I went on. "I will mention no names, although both his father and his son are called Anthemion."

The jury laughed. The vein in Anytus' right temple throbbed noticeably and his jaw muscles clenched in anger.

"I hasten to tell you that I do not disparage tradesmen, for my good friend, Simon the cobbler, was one of the finest men I have ever known. Now, this particular tanner knew a great many things about his own craft, for he had spent much time learning and perfecting it. Yet when I asked him his views on lofty ideas such as temperance and courage, he was as ignorant as I was, contradicting himself again and again during our conversations. As gently as I could, I pointed out his inconsistencies. Despite my soft manner and kind words, he resented my criticism and began to hate me. I understood this, for nobody likes to be told they are wrong, especially someone who has a strong self-image coupled with weak knowledge.

"Undeterred, I sought out another man who claimed to be wise. He is a well-known orator and is present here today—but I will not point out the son of Memnon to you."

This time only the jury chuckled, and I caught a sneer from Lycon.

"I asked this man the same question I had asked of his fellow citizen. 'Teach me prudence and justice,' I begged. We were in front of a large group at the time, and he lectured me on his astuteness. Confused by his speech, I asked many questions; but instead of enlightening me, he was unable to answer. It seemed to me that he felt humiliated. Once again, to my great disappointment, I did not find a man who could explain the Oracle's words to me. But because this man felt I had demeaned him publicly, he also developed a great animosity toward me.

"My fellow citizens, I was not dissuaded by my lack of success. On the contrary, I continued my search. I approached poets in the hope of finding a wise man. I quoted passages they had written — passages whose words were concise and powerful, words to move the soul. I asked these poets to explain the meaning of these compelling passages, hoping they could teach me what I needed to know. They were haughty and proud of their work, yet sadly, they could not explain the meaning of their own writing, and were thus unable to impart any wisdom.

"Please, believe me when I tell you that I approached many other men as well. I asked political leaders why they voted as they did. I asked the rich what had made them choose their way of life. I found that men with the greatest reputations were often the most foolish, and I swear to you by Zeus, none of them knew what they were talking about.

"My investigations stirred the ire of many, for people do not take kindly to having their ignorance revealed. But I proved the Oracle correct; I am called the wisest not because I have any great wisdom, or even any wisdom at all, *but because I know that I know nothing*, whereas others claim to have wisdom when really they do not.

"Furthermore, my discussions with these claimants of wisdom are invariably witnessed; often the witnesses are the youth of Athens, who find it amusing to see pretenders made to look foolish. By watching and listening, they learn to imitate my methods of examination, after which they find that they, too, can confront men who claim to be wise and make them appear foolish. Then, instead of being angry with the young questioners who have learned my methods, the older, foolish men turn their anger on me. For that, I have been called an evil influencer of youth.

"I ask you, what evil have I taught? I have never proclaimed a religious doctrine that is in any way contrary to Athenian practice, nor have

I declared insidious political policies. I am in trouble for one reason only — I have dared to ask questions."

This time silence greeted my words. I waited a few moments in order to let my next words make a proper impact.

"My three accusers have brought these spurious claims before you for precisely this reason. I am accused not because I have done anything wrong, but because they have been made to look foolish. This, my fellow citizens, is the truth. I ask you, therefore, to banish these old stories and prejudices from your minds and to focus, instead, on the issue at hand."

These words were greeted with some booing and hissing, which I tried to ignore.

"I have explained the reason for my reputation. Now I will move to my defence. What are these charges that are brought against me? They say I am a corrupter of youth, and that I do not believe in the established gods, but have created gods of my own.

"Let me address the first of these charges: that I do evil by corrupting the youth of our city. In fact, it is Meletus who does evil, by pretending interest in a matter about which he really cares nothing."

I looked at my accuser. "Let me ask you a question, Meletus. Do you think the improvement of the youth of our city is important?"

Meletus stood to answer. "Yes, I do."

"Of course you do — since you have so zealously unearthed the corruptor of our youth."

Laughter reached the jury from somewhere in the crowd.

"To ensure there is no doubt about what the *corruptor* has done, could you please tell our esteemed citizens and judges the name of the *improver*?"

Meletus continued to stand in silence. I waited. The jury waited. When I sensed the jury was getting restless, I prodded him.

"Have you nothing to say, Meletus? After all, it stands to reason, does it not, that if you cannot tell us who improves the youth of our city, how can you know who corrupts it?"

I glanced from the uncouth young man to the people who would be my judges. "Gentlemen of the jury, does this not prove what I said? If Meletus cannot identify the improver of the youth, then he has not given full thought to the matter. In that case, this trial is based on nothing more substantial than the desire of a few men to slander me for making them look like the fools they are!"

Red-faced, Meletus finally spoke. "The laws!" he said with some vehemence.

"That is not what I asked," I responded, with seeming patience. "I want to know who the improver is."

Meletus hesitated. Then, like a predator facing down its helpless prey, he said, "I have the answer. It is the judges. The men in court today."

"Ah, so the members of the jury sitting before us now are the ones who instruct and improve the youth of our city?"

"Correct."

"Every jury member here today, or only some of them?"

"All of them."

"By Zeus! That is good news!" I exclaimed in mock relief.

I heard some chuckling amongst the jury, as well as from the crowd outside the court.

"So, Meletus, what do you say of the audience beyond the rope? Do they improve the youth?"

"They do."

"And the Council of Five Hundred?"

"Yes, the Council of Five Hundred, too."

"What about the Assembly? Do they corrupt the youth, or improve them?"

"They improve them."

"Oh, this is excellent news, indeed. It appears that every Athenian citizen improves the youth of our city. Each one, that is, except me. What a good thing it is that you have brought me to the court's attention today!"

"It is," Meletus agreed, condescendingly.

"Happy, indeed, would be the condition of our youth if they had just one corrupter and all the rest of the world were their improvers. But your answer — that everyone in the city improves the youth, while only I harm them — is ludicrous. It shows, Meletus, that you are careless, and that you have *never* given proper thought to the education of the young. This is seen in the fact that you don't care about the matters spoken of in this very indictment.

"And since we are on the topic, how can it be that I corrupt the youth of our city? Is it my crime that I discuss matters of self-restraint and moderation? After all, Meletus, did not the Seven Sages of Greece, including Thales himself, espouse these same ideas? Do you group Thales the wise with Socrates the evil-doer? Would you have brought Thales to court?"

When Meletus remained silent, I continued scornfully. "I see that you are unwilling to respond, so let me do so on your behalf. Of course, you would not group me with Thales. Yet you accuse me of corrupting the youth."

Discussion ensued among the jury, as well as among those gathered beyond the ropes. It was difficult to be certain, but I thought I had won the point.

"Perhaps I have missed something?" I asked. "Have I shown the youth things that our city finds distasteful? Have I shown them how to rob temples? Break into houses? Sell citizens into slavery? May I remind you, Meletus, that I have fought in three battles? At Potidaea, I was in the front line of the phalanx. My own position in the line was at the far right. Does the Academy give corruptors of the youth the most honoured position in the line? Tell me, Meletus, does it"

He grunted, but said nothing.

"As you continue to remain silent, then let me answer for you. No, the Academy does not."

Finally, Meletus spoke. "I know of men whom you persuaded to obey you rather than their own fathers!"

"Thank you for mentioning that. You are, of course, correct. But I should point out that I have done so only in the matter of education, of which I have long made a study. Let me ask you, does a man concerned with his health obey his parents — who may be tanners or orators or poets — or his doctor, who has made health his life study?"

I was not surprised when he did not answer.

"Oh, Meletus, it appears your tongue has vanished again. So I will do the jury a favour and answer for you. The answer is 'no.' When seeking advice upon a particular topic, we listen to those who have made that specific subject the focus of their lifetime of study.

If I am really corrupting the youth, or have corrupted them in the past, I want them to come forward to report all the evil I have brought upon them, and tell us how terribly they have suffered. They have not all died of old age or of some tragic event, for I see them here, in this court. I see Crito and his son, Critobulus; I see Plato, son of Ariston. These and many more are here, in the jury and the crowd. Call upon any of them, and I will gladly yield the floor so they may testify against me. But that will not happen, because none of these men whom I am accused of corrupting — neither old nor young — will name me as the person who destroyed them.

"I cannot fathom what evil I teach. Nor can you explain it, Meletus."

I glanced over at Crito. To my disappointment, he looked nervous and shook his head, as though to deter me from my line of questioning. I decided to take his unspoken advice.

"Let me move on to the next issue. The indictment reads that I do not believe in the gods the city believes in. Is this a proper understanding of the charge, Meletus?"

"Yes," he confirmed.

"I wonder if you can answer another question. I know this will be difficult, as your tongue has legs of its own and runs from you when you need it most. However, please try to keep it in your mouth, and answer me this. Do you mean I do acknowledge some gods, but those gods are not the ones recognized by the city? Or do you mean I have created new gods? Or do you perhaps mean I am an atheist?"

"You are an atheist," Meletus said, with a tone of finality.

"Very good. Thank you for making that clear. Perhaps you can answer another question. Do I not take part in the festivals of the city?"

He was silent.

"Please answer me, Meletus, or I shall be forced to answer for you."

Several of my supporters spoke up.

"Answer Socrates," one of the jurors demanded of Meletus. Others joined in, saying, "Yes, answer him."

"He will not," I said. "So I will answer for him. I do take part in the festivals. Perhaps, then, Meletus did not mean that I am a complete atheist. Perhaps he is convinced I have sacrificed to new divinities in place of Zeus or Apollo or Athena?"

"You have," said Meletus.

"You are a liar!" I exclaimed. "No one has ever seen me do such a thing. Nor have I ever taken an oath to any other gods or named new ones!"

At this, the jury erupted. They were accustomed to statements and tears and pleading in the courtroom. A painfully slow examination of each accusation was wearying them. I was trying their patience and losing control of my defense. Sensing the jury's intolerance, the observers beyond the rope added their heckling to the pandemonium. Crito's head was in his hands — a sure sign that I had lost the jury.

"Please, bear with me," I shouted.

The jury and the crowd became slightly quieter.

"Meletus, another question. Do the gods know all?"

"They most certainly do."

"Do the gods make mistakes?"

He shook his head. "Most assuredly, they do not."

"In that case, why did the Oracle — the very voice of Apollo, the God of Truth and Light — name me the wisest of men if I do not believe in the gods?"

I didn't wait for a response.

"You cannot answer," I said, "because if you did, it would mean either you are wrong to accuse me of atheism, or the gods themselves are wrong — which, as you stated, cannot happen. You swore in the indictment that I teach and believe in divine or spiritual agencies that are not of the Athenians. But you provide no proof. You have included this charge only because you have nothing of substance of which to accuse me."

The water in the clock was close to dripping its last. I was out of time.

"Dear citizens," I concluded, "I believe I have said enough to answer the charges that Meletus, Anytus and Lycon have brought against me. As you can see, they have accused me of nothing real or factual. They brought up this spurious indictment and wasted your time simply to gain revenge, because I made them look like fools."

DAY 26

W HEN I HAD finished speaking, nothing was left but to wait to hear my fate. I tried very hard to keep up my spirits and stay hopeful, but it was not easy. I watched as the men filed down the stairs and received two small round bronze ballots each, one with a hole in the centre and one without. The lead juror gave instructions as the ballots were being distributed.

"The ballot that has the hole is a vote in favour of the prosecution. The solid ballot is a vote in favour of the defendant. Place your vote in the bronze urn and your discard in the wooden urn."

In full view of both my accusers and me, the jurors walked toward the two urns. To keep their votes secret, they clutched their ballots tightly until the moment they dropped them into the urns: first the vote, then the discard. Each metal clang sounded in my ears like a judgment — against me, I was sure, since most of the jurors looked at the ground as they passed me.

Thinking about my testimony, I knew very well that I could have conducted myself differently. I had belittled people and had raged at them and poked fun at them. I had been a fount of vindictiveness, filling my speech with an excess of emotion and disdain. Were I a juror listening to my words, what would be my conclusion? *The man is an arrogant ass who thinks too highly of himself.*

Glancing at Crito, I saw he did not look happy. Despite my efforts to remain optimistic, I could not push away my feelings of tension as the counters tallied the votes. When I was close to bursting with suspense, the chief counter handed a wax tablet to the lead juror. The juror studied it and then stood. The jury became silent.

"By a vote of 280 to 220, Socrates, son of Sophroniscus, is declared guilty of corrupting the young and not believing in the gods in whom the city believes."

I had anticipated the verdict. Nonetheless, I was stunned. A cheer erupted in the court. Amid much shouting, I was led the short distance to the jail and into this small, dark room.

I felt nauseous as I tried to focus on my options. After the noon recess, I would have to choose my sentence. I was sure that Anytus, Lycon and Meletus would ask for my death. It was up to me to counter their request.

If I asked for a lenient sentence, my request probably would not be granted and I would be put to death. The more realistic option was to ask for exile. I knew most juries were hesitant to put a man to death and much preferred banishment. My situation frightened me, but more than that, I was angry with myself. If I were exiled, I would have to leave behind my home, my friends and my city. Would Xanthippe come with me? You boys? Diotima? Surely, you should not have to leave behind everything you knew and loved just because your father had behaved like an arrogant ass!

Just before I was about to be led back to the courtroom, the door to my cell creaked open and the jailer informed me I had visitors. Naturally, I expected Crito and his son. Instead, to my great dismay, I saw Lycon and Anytus. Lycon came in carrying a heavy sack and looking pleased with himself. Anytus stood by the door, as if on guard. Meletus was nowhere to be seen. Perhaps he was keeping the prison guards occupied. I wondered if I were about to be knifed.

"Things did not go well for you, Socrates," said Lycon.

"It was less than I had hoped for and no more than I expected," I responded guardedly.

He smiled coldly at me. "We are going to ask for your death."

"I imagined you would, but you will have to wait," I said, with more confidence than I felt.

His expression was unpleasant. "I will not have to wait as long as you think."

"I will ask for exile and get it. We both know that."

He gazed at me with a sickening assuredness, as if he were in sole charge of what was happening. "True, there is a chance you could get exile. But you will not ask for it," he said, shaking the sack in my direction. Something dark dripped from it.

I was not sure why, but the small hairs rose on the back of my neck. I forced a scornful laugh. "I am not ready to die yet."

"Then you had better prepare yourself!" Lycon shouted, suddenly angry. "Because if you don't get death, your family will."

With that, he threw the sack at me, stormed out of the cell and slammed the door shut. Filled with foreboding, I opened the sack and looked inside — only to gasp with horror. The sack contained our dog Zeus, beheaded and eviscerated. It was all I could do to push back the bitter bile that rose in my throat.

So jittery was I after Lycon's threat that I had to do something to keep myself calm. I diverted myself by counting the steps from my cell to my seat at the front of the court: 112 steps. As I sat down, the atmosphere was hostile, filled with much talking, shouting and arguing. This became muted as the head juror stood and spoke.

"The Green Court is in session. Socrates, son of Sophroniscus, has been found guilty of being a corrupter of the youth, of not believing in the gods of the city and of creating new divinities of his own. These accusations have been brought forth by Meletus, son of Meletus, by Anytus, son of Anthemion and by Lycon, son of Memnon, who are demanding a penalty of death. Is this still the position of the prosecution?"

Meletus stood and addressed the court. "Yes, we still demand that Socrates be punished for his guilt with death."

The head juryman rose again. This time, he looked directly at me. "What have you to say in your defence, Socrates?"

My forehead and the palms of my hands were wet with perspiration. "Keep your knees steady beneath you. Do not faint," I told myself. I focused my thoughts on you boys and on your mother, and tried to breathe deeply. As I stood, the man at the water clock pulled out the plug. My time to speak had begun. I knew what I had to say. I had only to speak my mind.

"Citizens of Athens," I started, struggling to keep my voice calm over a mouth dry as dust. "I am not grieved by the vote of condemnation. I expected it, for I am the stinging horsefly and you are the lazy horse that I try to spur to action. No one likes to be stung, and so you swat at me, hoping to crush the life from me. Now that the fly has been caught, I am expected to counter the demand for the death penalty. For what shall I ask? What do you give a man who implored you to seek wisdom before wealth, happiness before notoriety? I can only ask for that which is my due…"

I paused and looked around. No idle conversation was heard in the court; no eyes were averted; nobody wondered how soon they could go home. Even the crowd outside the ropes, a thousand men and women, watched in silence. For the briefest of moments, I considered asking for exile. Even if Lycon's threat to kill you, my family, were really serious, I entertained the idea that with help from my friends I might be able to keep everyone alive long enough for us to escape to Macedon or Thrace, or perhaps somewhere else far away. But a voice inside me spoke loudly. "You cannot put your family at risk. Do what you must, to protect those you love." My eyes met Crito's. I had never seen him look quite so tense, not even on the battlefield.

"What is to be done with me?" I continued. "I believe there can be no more fitting reward than a lifetime of free meals at the Tholos."

My outrageous words evoked an audible gasp. I caught the look of astonishment on Crito's face. Myriad conversations began simultaneously. Men shouted and screamed at me for my impudence, for making a mockery of the proceedings, for my shameless disdain for all that Athens represented. Lycon, Anytus and Meletus sat quite still.

Again and again, the head juror called for silence. Finally, some sort of order was brought to the situation. The courtroom was not completely silent, but it was quiet enough that I could speak once more. Clearly, my proposal had been enough to sway even more of the jury toward honouring the request of Lycon, Anytus and Meletus. To ensure my death sentence, only one more thing remained for me to say. I raised my voice to make certain I could be heard.

"I make this proposal because I have wronged nobody. To propose a penalty of less severity would be to admit guilt of the charges. And when you have voted me a lifetime of meals at the Tholos, know that I shall spend all my free time — since I will no longer need to earn a living carving stone — conversing with you and your children about wisdom and other important issues. I will continue to examine my life as I do yours, for the unexamined life is not worth living."

Another uproar ensued. When the head juror regained control, I saw that some time remained on the clock, but indicated I had nothing more to say.

The members of the jury quickly made their way to the urns and dropped in their votes. Evidently, less deliberation was necessary this time. I watched Meletus, Anytus and Lycon, each looking smug and self-satisfied, their victory over me all but assured. The votes were tabulated and recorded, and then the tablet was handed to the lead juror.

He looked at it with a frown before taking a breath and turning his head toward me. "Socrates, son of Sophroniscus, you have been found guilty of being a corrupter of the youth, of not believing in the gods of the city and of creating new divinities of your own. The penalty of death has been demanded. In response, you have offered the penalty of ..."

Here he paused, as if he could not believe what he was reading, then continued, saying, "... a lifetime of free meals at the Tholos. By a vote of 360 to 140, you are sentenced to death. You will die by consuming hemlock."

It is one thing to expect an almost certain outcome, quite another to be faced with its reality. Although I saw the jury members stand and gesture at one another, as if arguing, I did not hear a sound. Everything was muted. My hands and feet were numb. Fear overwhelmed me as it had when I was a boy in school and later on the battlefield.

What just happened? What have I done? I wondered. *There is no shield to hide behind this time, no comrades to protect me, no luck to save me. This time I can do nothing to prevent my death.*

It seemed as though I had been sitting there a long time, finally the lead juror addressed me.

"The Delia festival began this morning. The sacred ship has just sailed to the island of Delos and the city must be kept pure until it returns. Your execution is deferred for approximately one month. Socrates, do you have anything to say?"

All at once, it was as if some other, calmer, wiser being took control of my body, for I was in shock and doubt that I could have composed the speech I did. "I do," I heard myself say. With the numbness leaving my extremities, I stood and addressed the jury and the crowd beyond. "To those who voted for my death, I wish you to know that I was not convicted for lack of words. I was convicted because I was not given enough time to defend myself. I could have wept and wailed like others who have come to this court before me. Perhaps, indeed, I could have secured my acquittal in this way, but such behaviour would have been beneath me.

"Even this sentence of death does not lead me to regret the manner of my defence. If a man is willing to say or do anything, he can avoid death. If he loses in battle, he can throw away his weapons and fall on his knees before his enemy, thus perhaps escaping death. I would rather die being true to myself. The only thing I have done wrong is to dare to ask questions.

"For those of you who voted for me, let me take a moment to ask you a favour. I am about to be taken to jail, the place where I will die. I may never see my sons again and will no longer be their companion and instructor. Since I will not be there to aid them in the trials that come to all men, I have this request of you: if my sons care more about wealth than the keeping of their own souls, if they pretend to be what they are not, or speak of things they do not truly understand, I desire that you reproach them as I have reproached so many others. If you do this for me, my death will be no great loss, as you will raise my sons to be good and solid men. That is all I ask of you."

The jury members were quiet when I had finished speaking. So, too, were the men and women assembled outside the court. In silence, I walked up the stairs to the edge of the court. Someone lifted the rope for me and I crept beneath it. I spoke to no one as I walked the 112 steps back to my prison cell. There I found, still waiting for me, the sack with Zeus's lifeless body on the floor.

DAY 27

THIS MORNING I opened my eyes to find Crito sitting across the cell from me. It was very early; the sun was not yet up and I had slept for only a short time. I saw him before he noticed I was awake.

"Hello, my friend," I said, shivering from the morning chill.

"Hello, Socrates." The smile to which I had been so accustomed was absent.

"How did you get in?" I asked curiously, for I had been told no visitors were permitted until my last day of life. When he did not speak immediately, my heart began a sudden racing. "The ship from Delos has arrived, hasn't it? Tomorrow I will be executed?"

Crito was silent. He looked as though he might weep. His silence, coupled with his expression, was answer enough.

I took a breath and collected myself. "How long have you been here?"

"I came some time ago." His voice was breaking.

"Why didn't you wake me?"

He cleared his throat. "Sleep is a cure for the troubles of life. I wanted you to be out of pain for as long as possible."

"I am not in pain, Crito."

"I don't know how you have managed until now. I cannot believe how easily you bear this."

"I have managed — although not easily," I told him. "My heart nearly gave in just now, when I realized the ship had arrived. Perhaps you can never be ready to die when you still desire to live. But at our age a man ought not to fret at the idea of his end. Even without this sentence, my death would have happened soon enough, anyway. After any exertion, my body hurts for a long time. The discomfort in my knees and hips is always there. Some of my teeth have rotted and fallen out, and the others are loose. Perhaps this early demise will relieve me of the woes that would have come to me. Sight weakened. Hearing diminished. The rest of my teeth gone and eating mush — the ultimate cruelty for someone who loves to eat. Constant misery. Not to mention the loss of my faculties. Age is an ailment that does not improve with time. Besides, Crito, my death sentence will be much harder for Xanthippe, Diotima and the boys to bear than for me. My life will end soon, but they will be burdened with sadness and loss."

"Your friends will be burdened, too, Socrates. That is why I am here."

His words troubled me. "Is all well? Is my family still safe?"

"Half a dozen of our friends are in your courtyard now. They will remain there as long as they are needed."

"Good! Thank you, Crito, for all you have done. I understand that you have put yourself and your family at risk by coming here. I'm afraid I haven't spent much time lately thinking about anyone but myself."

"I am not at risk, nor is my family."

"I hope you are correct." As I spoke, I thought about you, my dearest boys, and about your beloved mother and Diotima. Then I brought my mind back to what was happening. "I must apologize, Crito. You are here to talk about something."

Crito's expression was sombre. "You've just mentioned the difficulties your wife and your boys will endure when you are gone."

I nodded.

"Then don't abandon them."

His words astonished me.

"Crito," I began slowly, "you must believe me when I tell you I would like nothing more than to leave this cell and be with my family until the natural end of my life. If I could, I would postpone my death while my family is alive. But that is not possible."

"Are you afraid that if you escape, your friends might get into trouble and end up in this prison with you?"

"Yes ..."

"Don't worry about that, Socrates. Money will satisfy those who would inform against us. I have money, as do many others who are willing to help."

"Where would you take me, Crito?"

"To Thessaly. They would welcome you there."

I listened quietly as he outlined a plan that he and the others had come up with.

When he was finished, I raised my head and looked at him gravely. "I cannot do it. I will not attempt escape."

"Why not? You have an obligation as a father to nurture and educate your children!" Crito said heatedly. The scar on his neck bulged, red and raw.

"I know that," I answered him calmly. "But I have an even bigger responsibility to keep them alive."

"You cannot abandon your family! That is not the way of a father!"

"I am not abandoning them." I sounded more curt than I had intended to. But I did not want to have words with Crito, especially now. He could not know what was in my mind.

"Do you recall Diagoras the Atheist?" I asked.

"Of course."

"I spoke with him before he left Athens. He was aware that he had upset too many people for too long. He thought if he went far enough away and didn't bring attention to himself, he would be forgotten. And, indeed, he was. For 10 years, no one heard anything about him. After all, who would search him out for a measly 10 drachmas? Then Anytus found him in Corinth, and had him killed."

"I remember. It still makes me angry," said Crito.

"And me. Anytus did it only in order to rehabilitate his own name. Imagine — Anytus searched the length and breadth of Greece to track down Diagoras. I wonder how much effort he expended to find and kill him? He did not even dislike the man. I doubt he knew him personally." I paused and looked at Crito. "But if I were to escape, what do you think Anytus would do to my family? He would track us all down. He would find us. He has the resources. He is angry. And Lycon even more so."

"Yes, but — "

"If I escape and take my family with me, do you honestly think Anytus and Lycon would not search us out?"

Sunlight was beginning to enter the cell now, and I saw Crito more clearly. He looked very weary. His eyes drooped at the corners and his shoulders slumped forward like a rounded willow. Brown and purple spots dotted his hands. For the first time, I noticed how much my friend had aged. When had this happened? Was this how he saw me, too? Is it how you, my family, see me? Am I bent and worn? Does my voice have an old man's quaver, as did my father's before his death? I also wondered how much poor Crito had slept since I had been sentenced to death and put in this cell. It had been much harder for him than I'd realized.

"I do not fear for my life, Crito," I tried to reassure him. "I fear for the lives of the people I love. If I were to escape, Lycon and Anytus would spare nothing to have their blood. My family and my friends would be in danger. I would jeopardize everyone I know. Did you hear about Zeus, my dog?"

"Yes," Crito said.

"Do you not believe that Lycon and Anytus seriously desire my death?"

He nodded.

"Then you must see how this will end if I try to escape."

A look of exhaustion passed across his face, as if he were a parent of 12, worn out by childcare. "What does Lycon have against your pets?" he asked, finally.

I thought about my poor turtle, Heracles, tortured to death by Lycon a lifetime ago. Heartless though it may be to find humour in the death of innocent animals, I guffawed. Nerves, probably. It was the first time I'd laughed since my incarceration. Not only did it feel good, it broke the tension.

"I don't think you should name your pets after the gods anymore," Crito said, with mock seriousness.

"I promise," I told him, and we both laughed.

"You were right when you said my arrogance would catch up with me," I replied. "With all that animosity toward me, I was foolish to think I could talk my way out of the charges. I realize this is all my fault."

"How is it your fault?"

"I went about the agora interrogating anyone who had the temerity to disagree with me. I caused hundreds of people to detest me, especially after Chaerephon's return from Delphi and the news of the Oracle's proclamation. I was an arrogant ass. Had Lycon and Anytus not taken me to court, doubtless it would have been someone else whom I embarrassed publicly. Lycon and Anytus may be vile men, but I provoked them into making the charges."

"Into a death sentence?" Crito sounded unconvinced.

"Yes. I have been taunting them for a long time. As a young man, Anytus was in love with Alcibiades; he lusted after him. I was aware of it the first time I saw them together. Of course, I should have known he would try to make me look bad so that he could look good. It would have been easy enough to deflect his anger. Instead, I criticized him when I was able to, especially after his failure at the Battle of Pylos. I kicked him when he was down. To make matters worse, I gave his son advice that was not in the boy's best interest and set him against his father. Now that boy is a drunk and a wastrel. If I were Anytus, I would feel enmity toward me, too."

"And Lycon?"

"He was loathsome to me when I was growing up, but he was still a boy. As boys do, Lycon wanted to get even with my brother for peeing on him and beating him in schoolyard fights. When he set the merchant's tent on fire, he could not have known it would result in such damage to my family. Had I been the culprit, I wouldn't have owned up to the destruction of the shop, either."

"You wouldn't have started the fire in the first place," Crito observed.

"To get back at Lycon? I might have," I responded. "The day I saw him in the agora giving a speech, I should have passed him by as I usually did — but I let my baser feelings get the better of me. I was a grown man who should have known better. A man should be allowed to live down his past. Worst of all, Lycon blames me for the death of his son."

"You did not cause Autolycus' death. You were neither Critias' teacher, nor did you instruct any of The Thirty."

I gave my friend a thoughtful look. "Diotima has a favourite fable about a farmer and a stork. Its moral is that when you associate with dishonest companions, bad consequences follow. I am associated with Critias through Alcibiades. Therefore, this is my own fault."

"You are not accountable for Alcibiades, either!" Crito said vehemently.

It was nice to hear him defend me, even if no one else heard.

Sadly, I said, "I cultivated a friendship with Alcibiades. He was not forced on me."

"You tried to teach him prudence and temperance," Crito protested. "Necessary virtues for a good leader and human being."

"True," I agreed. "But I failed."

"You are not to blame, Socrates. Alcibiades was as rotten inside as a wormy apple. No one could have known it from his appearance."

"I should have known. I did know. His bruises showed through the shiny veneer. I noticed it at Potidaea, when he was still a young man. Yet later, when I saw what he could do for me, I ignored his obvious flaws. I understood I was making a mistake, but I ignored the voice whispering inside me, the voice I have counselled so many others to heed. I wanted so badly to..."

Here I hesitated, still desirous that Crito think well of me. *Don't stumble so close to the finish line*, I told myself. *Be honest. Admit your fear.* "I wanted so much to be respected," I went on, finally. "I never felt... good enough."

Crito snorted. "*Not good enough*? My father held you up as the ideal of perseverance and cleverness. When you were only seven years old, you asked questions in class that the grammatiste could not answer. You were too quick-witted for him."

"I never felt like an ideal person. I felt stupid and ugly and ... incompetent. I envied you, Crito — your poise, your athleticism, your education."

"I was given training. The best my father could afford. You were given nothing."

"You are far more than your training, " I said. "For one thing, you have courage."

"I do?"

"Yes. Do you remember the day before the battle at Potidaea?"

"Oh, Socrates, I was frightened at Potidaea," he said, his voice low.

"As was I."

Crito looked at me disbelievingly. "*You* were frightened, Socrates?"

"Terrified. I didn't want to fight. It's difficult to tell you this, but I was going to desert. I even had a plan. I sought you out before the battle, hoping for reassurance. I don't know now what you could have said, but I needed your courage."

"*My* courage? *You* led the phalanx! We all looked up to you."

"It was the only thing that kept me from running away — knowing I would be despised if I abandoned you all."

Crito was silent for a few moments and then said, "That is what makes you brave, Socrates. You fought like a hero, despite your fear. I can think of nothing braver."

"You are wrong. Pride urged me on. Pride is one of my defects, perhaps my worst flaw." I looked at Crito in the dim light of the early sun. "But about the battle — do you remember what you said to me, afterward?"

My friend did not seem interested in reliving a moment of supposed weakness all these years later, an incident we had never discussed. He was silent a while, but finally he said, "I do remember. I admitted my shameful behaviour. I was jealous of you, and did not want to give you the armour that was rightfully yours."

"That was not shameful, Crito. You were young and in pain. I understood that, even then. But that is the point. You admitted your torment to me, and *that* was the epitome of courage."

"Courage — because I admitted my shame?"

"Courage, because you exposed yourself despite fearing how I might judge you. I have always respected you for that, Crito.

"Did you know my father was a sculptor? He carved beautiful herms, but I doubt he showed them to anyone, not even to my mother. I would have liked to have asked him about his sculpting and to have watched him at work. I would have been overjoyed just to clean up after him. It would have been wonderful to be involved, somehow. But he hid himself away. Never shared his thoughts. He led a very lonely existence.

"When my boys discovered his buried herms, I wondered why he had destroyed them. Why he had spent so many years carving them, just to shatter them. I thought anger was the cause. Now I realize he acted out of fear. My father was afraid to expose his deep desire for recognition. He was afraid of how others would judge him. He lacked the courage that you showed at Potidaea. I don't have it, either. In the end, I am no better than my father."

Crito shook his head. "I disagree."

"You mean well, my friend, but there is no reason for disagreement. I know what I have done and how I have lived. I have made so many mistakes. I have failed myself over and over again, only because I lacked courage. When I was very young, my mother told me a story about the uniqueness of my birth: how it foretold my greatness. I believed her. I had no cause not to. Much later, Diotima told me what really happened. My birth was not exceptional, no different from any other. I wondered why my mother had lied to me. Perhaps she had intended to tell me the truth one day, but she died when I was still young. Only as my boys grew up did I begin to understand. My beloved mother wanted me to see myself as she saw me. Beautiful. Irreplaceable. Miraculous. Exactly the way I see my own sons. She must have hoped that in this way she could protect me, like a shield, from the ugliness of the world."

"That is what caring parents do," Crito said.

"It is important for children to feel good about themselves. If we think as well of ourselves as do those who love us, then yes, self-confidence is a good and splendid thing. But I took her story to mean I would find fame and glory, and that my name would live forever. I made the need for glory the main goal of my life. Like the foundation of a wall, it was laid early, and I added to it, block upon block.

"Please understand, Crito, I do not blame my mother for my situation. I only mention it now to explain that I have not thought as deeply about my own beliefs as I have advised others to do. I did not unearth the foundations of my own wall. I did not see how my desire for glory adversely affected my life."

"Everyone wants to leave their mark on the world." Crito gestured toward the names etched into the walls of the cell. "We all want to be remembered."

Following his eyes, I thought back to my first day here. "I should have known better," I observed, as I absent-mindedly traced some of the carved names with a finger. "After I die, I will not be around to hear what people say of me. Once my children, my grandchildren and my students all pass on, I will be forgotten entirely. Even those whose names live for a hundred years, maybe a thousand, will eventually vanish from living memory.

"So, my friend, where is the value in being remembered? It feeds the ego for a short time, but brings no lasting happiness. I have lived too long on the surface of things. I have been observing the ocean's waves, fooling myself into believing I understood its nature, when, in fact, below the surface the water teems with a greater abundance of life than I ever conceived of. I did not dive deeply enough below the surface. I did not question every decision I made. I did not dig and dig and dig into *why* I believed *what* I believed. I did not have that kind of courage. Looking into the lives of others, I was able to make judgments easily enough, but I did not examine my own life properly."

Crito frowned. "Of all the people I know, Socrates, you are the *only* one who questions himself so deeply. You claim you know nothing. How much deeper could you have looked?"

I regarded him sadly. "During my time with Simon, yes, I believed that I truly knew nothing. But then I went astray. After learning of the Oracle's proclamation that I was the wisest of all men, I grew arrogant and stopped my honest search."

"You are much too hard on yourself," Crito protested.

"Let me finish! I do not share these things with you because I want your pity. I do it so that I may face my end without regret. You say I am too hard on myself. Don't you understand? It has to be like this. Each time I made a decision, I should have asked myself, 'Why do I choose to do this? Is it because I question how others will perceive me? Or is it because I would make this choice even if I were on a deserted island, and there were no glances, glares or judgmental stares to sway my action and self-perception?'

"Do you recall the Crow Man we used to see perched on the courtyard wall near the agora? He behaved as he pleased. Not to create attention or to be different. Something was broken inside him, I know, but imagine being able to live as you choose, accepting that others perceive you as odd? To *not* conform, despite the fear of exclusion. To be true to yourself."

I was quiet a few moments. Then I said, "We Greeks are so concerned with our image. When the boys were young, they would walk around easily, unashamed, comfortable in their own skins. When do we lose that innocence, that ability to ignore the multitude? I admit it is nearly impossible to mute the voices of those around us, but I believe it is the only path to accepting ourselves for whom we really are. Some weakness in me needs the approval of others, and I fear I will pass on that weakness to my boys."

"They will be fine," Crito said confidently. "You will see that — "

I interrupted him. "No, Crito — "

"Let me finish," he said firmly. "I will not embarrass you too much, for I know how you hate to hear about yourself. But you need to hear this, Socrates. You have done what was necessary. You love your boys and your wife, and have told them so daily. Your sons have grown into exceptionally fine young men. Any father would be proud of them. You have guided them, and you have shown courage even by the impossible standards you set for yourself. Despite all you say, I have seen it numerous times.

"And you have ignored the multitudes. You have lived out the ideals you set for yourself. Most especially, you are doing so now, as you reach the end. You have exposed your fears and failures to me. You have shown through action and deed that you, of anyone I have ever heard of or known, do truly *know thyself.*"

"You are very kind, as always, Crito. But still, I do not agree."

My good friend sat down beside me. Putting his arm around me, he said, "You disagree only because you do not see yourself as others do. Put your mind at rest, Socrates, your sons are on the journey you would wish for them. They will find what you want them to find. On the lives of my own children and grandchildren, I swear this to be true."

"How can you be so sure?" I asked, in some despair.

"Because for many years I have observed the life of a good man. I have watched the path he has taken. I can gauge the future of your sons from your own history."

"Thank you, Crito," I said. And then I put my head into my hands and wept.

DAY 28

Execution day. I have only a short time left.

Whether because of the very short space of time remaining to me, or because I have been restricted to this cell for so long, I find my senses are extraordinarily alive and alert. I feel the smallest movement of air against my cheek as a nearby door opens. I perceive vibrations of the earth from even the lightest human footsteps. I hear the quivering of tiny feet as insects crawl up the wall. I taste the greasy smoke of goat meat in the air. And — call it fanciful if you wish — I smell the poppies that bloom around the Acropolis this time of year. I gather all I can with my eyes and ears and fingers, as if I need to carry these experiences on some long journey and must take the memories with me. I doubt I will need them, but I do it anyway. I only wish time would slow down. I want to savour everything.

As I think back over all I have written, I am surprised at the sheer volume of words I managed to put down. As you know, I always considered writing inferior to verbal communication; yet I doubt I could have shared the story of my life in any other manner. If I had sat down with you boys, and related my life face to face, it would have been impossible for me to be quite so honest. So I see value to writing, after all.

I have been wondering how I would have turned out if I'd had more insight into my own father and his thoughts. I like to think I might have avoided much of my heartache and distress, and so I hope you will learn from my mistakes and find that hidden treasure of happiness that is so elusive.

I continue to wonder what people will say of me when I am gone. My concern is that they may say kind things, thereby undoing the intent of my written words. How often have I known detestable people who were praised undeservedly after they died? The ones I fear the most now are those I call my good friends. What will Crito or Hermogenes or one of the others say about me? I beg you not to be swayed by them, for they mean well, and will offer unduly generous words. Please believe me when I say that I really am the person I have portrayed in these scrolls.

By exposing my fears, I have achieved something else — acceptance. Even as a youngster, I never liked myself. Whether it was my brother Patrocles or Thespis or Crito or Simon, I would always rather have been someone else.

At last, I am at ease in my own skin, and as a result I feel far less weary than before. With my end only moments away, my hands and feet are not numb. Fear will not turn me to stone this time. I feel light as a feather swaying in the wind. Believe me when I tell you I am not afraid to die. I am fine with being forgotten.

Now that I know you've been left alone by my enemies, I can selfishly say I'm glad you didn't take my advice to leave Athens as soon as I was convicted. It means the world to me that you will be there to say good-bye, and to see me off on my final journey. But I do urge you to leave this city as soon as possible and find a new life in Thebes.

Diotima, thank you for taking care of me, and for being my protector and surrogate mother. I am extremely grateful to you for all you have done for me, as well as for encouraging me to write my story. It is your subtle wisdom that has allowed me to find peace at the end.

Xanthippe, my wonderful wife, I apologize for causing you years of strife. For so long, I believed you had much to learn and thought that I would be your teacher. Now I understand that I was the one in need of instruction. I hope you will forgive my arrogance. You shaped three fine young men, while your foolish husband considered it more impor-tant to walk among the people of Athens, spouting opinions he took for wisdom. Thank you, Xanthippe, for ridding me of the loneliness I saw as my fate. You epitomize tenderness, compassion, intelligence and beauty. I should have worshipped you as you deserved: as a goddess.

My sons, you are good, bright, strong men. I am proud of each one of you. You have brought me joy all your lives. Trust your inner voices. Treat yourselves well. Never forget these things.

I have so much more to say, but my time has run out. They have come for me. I am ready. I love you all.

EPILOGUE

By Lamprocles, eldest son of Socrates

O N THE LAST day of Father's life we were allowed to enter the cell in which he had lived for 28 days. We found him seated on the ground, his ankles shackled. Although we should have been prepared, his appearance shocked us, for he seemed much thinner and older than he had the last time we had seen him.

He beamed when he saw us, as if we had been away on some extended journey and he was overjoyed at our return. The jailer released him from his chains and we noticed abrasions around his ankles. He stumbled at first, as he tried to stand, but when he managed to get to his feet, he quickly hugged my mother, my brothers, Diotima, and me. The jailer left the cell — for which we were grateful — and locked the door behind him.

After embracing us, my father bent and rubbed his legs where the shackles had made them raw. As circulation returned, he began to walk around the cell. So cheerful was he, that a stranger who did not know better would have been forgiven for thinking he had spent the last month in his own andron, thinking and writing, and that he was now about to attend a dinner party. How he was able to appear so untroubled, I don't know, for I was in pain just knowing he was going to die.

"How do you feel, Father?" I asked.

"Quite light," he replied. "Actually, I feel a bit like Atlas, letting go of his burden."

Playfully, he stretched up his arms and lowered them again, as if he were lifting an imaginary rock and then putting down it again. He must have sensed our discomfort, for after embracing us all again, he told us how much he loved us and then spoke about mundane things.

With sunset approaching, my father realized it would be time soon for him to drink the poison. First, though, he wanted to take a bath, so that nobody would have to wash his body when he was dead. As he went into the adjoining room with my mother, I followed them both with my eyes. That room, I knew, was the place where he would take the poison. Feeling quite ill at the thought, I turned away.

Despite the dimness in the cell, I noticed carvings on the wall, and went closer to examine them properly. To my astonishment, I saw that they were, in fact, names. An experienced stonemason by trade, I marvelled at the effort it must have taken people — previous prisoners — to etch their names so deeply into the walls without tools. Curiously, I looked to see whether Father had carved his name, but, as far as I could see, he had not.

After bathing and changing into clean clothes, Father returned looking much better. Just then, Crito entered the cell in the company of some of Father's students. Mother started to weep. Father whispered something in her ear — I did not hear the words — and Mother bit back her tears and caressed his cheek.

All talking ceased when the jailer reappeared. Approaching Father, he said, "I am sorry to do this, Socrates, for you are the noblest and finest of all who have ever come here. Sadly, it is time for you to drink the poison." I could tell his words came from the heart, for his voice was rough with emotion.

The hush in the cell was now absolute. A moment passed. Then Father looked at the jailer and said, "Thank you. I will do as you ask."

He looked at us, then. "I want you to know that this man, the jailer, has been good to me. Do not be angry with him when I am gone." And, turning to Crito: "Please, tell the attendant I am ready."

I cannot begin to describe the strength of my emotions as we entered the room next to Father's cell, and Crito signalled the slave to bring the poison. The fellow entered, carrying the fateful vessel. A tiny cup, painted green but otherwise unadorned, it contained no more than a sip or two of liquid.

That cup is engraved in my mind for all time. I could only think: *This is what he must drink? This is all that is required to end a life?*

Father said to the jailer, "You are experienced in these matters. Tell me what to do."

The man's expression was grave. "When you have consumed the hemlock, walk around until your legs grow heavy. Then lie down, and the poison will do its work."

My father took the cup. Holding it up, as if in a toast, he said, "I salute my wife, my sons, my grandson, Diotima, and my friends. May the sun shine on you all." He spoke the words calmly, without any sign of fear — after which he raised the cup to his lips and drank the hemlock.

We watched him, our hearts heavy with sorrow. I covered my face and wept, as did the rest of my family. One of Father's students — they were all weeping, too — startled us with a loud and passionate cry. Only Father stayed serene. "Please, remain calm," he said. "I want my last moments of life to be peaceful." It was very difficult to do as he asked, but somehow we restrained ourselves and held back our tears.

My father walked around the cell, taking great gulps of air, as if inhaling us all into his being. At length, he observed that his legs felt heavy, and he lay down on a plank that had been brought in for him. The jailer pinched one of his feet, and asked Father whether he felt it. He said he did not. Lifting himself slightly, he touched his thigh, and said he perceived a coldness about the groin. Falling back on the plank, he beckoned Crito to come closer. "I owe a rooster to Asclepius. Can you pay that debt for me?" he asked, his voice so soft that we all strained to hear him.

"The debt will be paid," Crito said, his voice breaking. "Is there anything else I can do for you?" But my father did not answer. He was gone.

A terrible silence filled the cell. We were all utterly shocked, unable to speak, barely able to breathe. As I stared at the inert form that had been my father, I overheard one of his students asking why Socrates, of all people, owed a rooster to Asclepius, the God of Healing. Had Socrates become pious at the end of his life? I knew the answer, although I did not have the strength to speak just then. Asclepius was the jailer who had smuggled in the ink and rolls of papyrus so my father could write. He would wake my father late every night and give him a lamp to work by. Father called him his rooster. Even as he breathed his last, Father had still managed a jest.

Heartbroken though we were, we had no time to mourn. After looking our last at the body of the man we all loved so dearly, we, his family, hurried out of the prison. A horse and cart, loaded with our possessions and our father's scrolls, waited at the Dipylon Gate to take us to Thebes. Although Lycon and Anytus had said they would leave us be after my father's death, we had no way of knowing for certain whether they would keep their word.

In the days that followed, I was filled with great anger and sadness. I had loved my father immensely; we all had. He had been a great father, and my brothers and I always knew that he loved us. As he used to say of his mother, my father was my sunshine. In my grief, I tried to find solace in his writings. I had never seen him as the person about whom I now read.

Although it is not always easy to know another person's state of mind, I do not recall many days when Father was not happy. Of course, he had his private doubts. All humans do, I suppose. It came to me, in time, that he wanted us, his sons, to realize that whatever thoughts and feelings we might experience, none are alien; others feel them, too. I believe it was important to him that we recognize that fact, and understand that the greatest battles are not with others, but with ourselves. In the end, I think he saw this as the true meaning of the words *know thyself*. He did not want us to agonize over the opinions of others; he wished us to be kind to ourselves.

A little more than a year after our father's death, Crito arrived in Thebes, bringing with him much news. For my brothers and me, the most interesting tidings were that Lycon had died of some painful malady, Anytus had been exiled from Athens and had been killed in Corinth, and Meletus had fallen to his death from the wall of the Acropolis. I admit to being suspicious that all three of Father's persecutors had died. Although I have no proof that any of his students were involved in wrongdoing, I learned that both Anytus and Meletus had died on the anniversary of Father's death.

It might have been safe for us to return to Athens now, but we decided to remain in Thebes. In time, most of the men who had been close to our father came in search of us. Some even took up residence in Thebes.

My brothers and I were invited to many dinner parties. It seemed as though Father's former students hoped to recapture the intellectual stimulation they had enjoyed with him — but not one of us is Socrates. We heard many interesting stories about Father on the battlefield and in the gymnasium, and about his arguments in the agora. He never bragged about himself, but others did. We heard of his brilliance, his capacity for hard work and his great talent for friendship. These stories made me appreciate, even more than I had before, my father's uniqueness as a person. If only I could tell him of my feelings. I wish he were here now, so we could converse together. I am so very proud to say that Socrates was my father.

To this day, strangers stop my brothers and me in the streets of Thebes, and tell us tales about our father. At first, we knew these accounts to be fairly accurate. But the more time goes by, the more outrageous the accounts become. We hear statements such as: "I saw Socrates stand upon Pnyx hill before the entire Assembly, and scold them like children."

Or: "I heard your father call Critias, the leader of The Thirty, the most dangerous man in Athens, a rutting pig." My father would be amused to know that his memory has endured so well, if not always correctly. Maybe his memory will endure a few more years, at least until all who knew him are gone from this earth.

Often the men who speak to us are searching for some kind of wisdom. They seem to believe that Father passed on some special knowledge to us, his children, to which only we are privy. Usually, they leave disappointed.

One such person was a young student of Father's, who had begun to write stories about him. He called my brothers and me dullards, maintaining that we would never amount to anything. So be it. I don't care what other men think of me. Indeed, I take pride in the accusation that I will amount to nothing. It means I have learned something from my father, for I am entirely content to be a father, a husband and a stonemason, as are my brothers. The sons of Socrates are happy men, and what greater legacy can a man leave than happy children?

And so I end with these words: I love you, Father. We all love you. And we will never forget you.

AUTHOR'S NOTE

It's called "the Socratic problem."

It's widely believed that Socrates himself didn't write anything — or at least nothing that has endured through more than 2,400 years of history. This makes it difficult, if not impossible, to determine the nature of his life, views and opinions. There really is no way for us to know the truth of Socrates' life.

Although much has been written about Socrates, only three authors — Aristophanes, Xenophon and Plato — knew him or were alive during his lifetime, and authored material about him that has survived to the present day.

Aristophanes, an Athenian playwright, lived from about 446 BCE to 386 BCE. He is credited with writing as many as 30 plays, 11 of which are still in existence. One of these surviving plays is called *The Clouds*. As depicted in this novel, Socrates was lampooned in this play. What we don't know is: Was Aristophanes' portrayal of Socrates accurate?

Xenophon, often characterized as a soldier-historian, was one of Socrates' students. He lived from about 430 BCE to 354 BCE and, years after his teacher's death, wrote four works associated with Socrates: *Memorabilia, Oeconomicus, Symposium* and *Apology of Socrates to the Jurors* (apology, in this case, meaning "defense"). But Xenophon was not present at Socrates' trial; he was away fighting in Persia at the time. He relied, therefore, on Hermogenes' account of the court case. So can we rely on Xenophon's interpretation of events?

The best-known source of information about Socrates is Plato, another of Socrates' students. Plato lived from about 427 BCE to 347 BCE and wrote numerous dialogues about subjects ranging from politics and ethics to family and education. In these dialogues, Socrates is portrayed as the main speaker, so Plato is considered a great source of information. This raises a question, however. Did Plato repeat what he learned from his teacher, or did he put his own words into Socrates' mouth, in the way of a ventriloquist?

So, since our information is limited, often conflicting and may not be completely trustworthy, how does one write about the life of Socrates? The answer: with a great deal of trepidation. Often during the writing of this book, I wondered what I had gotten myself into. If I, the author, was doubtful about trusting the only information available, how could I give an accurate portrayal of one of the most famous men in the Western world? The answer is, I couldn't. No way exists to factually recreate the life of a man who lived more than 2,400 years ago.

Accepting this, I focused on the reason I had wanted to write the novel in the first place: to explore ideas that I believe Socrates represented. These included such philosophical statements as: "I know that I know nothing," "Know thyself," and "The unexamined life is not worth living." Most importantly, Socrates' determination to *question everything* inspired me.

Although I structured the novel around these ideas, it would be incorrect to say I didn't use the sources previously mentioned. I used them extensively. Much as I distrust Plato (as well as Xenophon and Aristophanes), I must give credit where it's due. I have borrowed heavily from Plato's dialogues, in particular *Apology, Crito, Phædo, Alcibiades, Symposium, Meno,* and *Laches.*

Finally, the stories I have read about Socrates, written by other authors, all portray a man who was an infallible logician and an infinitely wise man. But this was not the Socrates I wanted to write about. I wanted to see my protagonist struggling for happiness and questioning his own motives. Above all, I desired that he be human. So, this is not an academic treatment of a revered historical figure. Rather, the novel should be read as a humanistic account.

In the end, I aspired to write an interesting story that would give readers access to some of the ideas for which Socrates is known to this day, and that would humanize a myth/legend.

Thank you for reading my novel.

HISTORICAL TIMELINE

776 BCE — The first Olympic Games were held in Olympia, Greece. The games originated as part of a religious festival dedicated to Zeus.

750 BCE — Homer wrote the *Iliad* and the *Odyssey*. Greek colonies were established in Sicily and southern Italy.

624 BCE — Birth of Thales. He is recognized as the first person to explain natural events without the need of mythology.

621 BCE — Draco established a code of laws by which Athenians were judged. Many of these crimes were punishable by death.

594 BCE — Solon replaced Draconian law in Athens and laid the foundation for democracy.

546 BCE — The Persians captured King Croesus of Lydia at Sardis.

508 BCE — Cleisthenes began to reform the Athenian code of law and established a democratic constitution.

500 BCE — Birth of Anaxagoras, who was credited as being the first person to bring philosophy to Athens. He was associated with Pericles.

495 BCE — Birth of Pericles.

490 BCE — The Athenian army defeated King Darius and his Persian army at the Battle of Marathon. Pheidippides ran from Marathon to Athens to deliver the news of the victory.

480 BCE — King Xerxes of Persia marched through Greece. The Persians burned Athens to the ground. The Athenian navy later defeated the Persian fleet at the Battle of Salamis.

479 BCE — The combined Greek army defeated the Persians at the Battle of Plataea.

469 BCE — Birth of Socrates.

465 BCE — Construction began on the Long Wall connecting Athens to Piraeus.

461 BCE — Pericles became the leading politician and general for Athens, remaining so for more than 30 years.

451 BCE — Birth of Alcibiades.

447 BCE — Building of the Parthenon began.

432 BCE — Battle of Potidaea. This was Socrates' first military engagement, during which he saved the life of Alcibiades. The Parthenon was completed.

431 BCE — War between Athens and Sparta began. This is commonly known as the Peloponnesian War.

430 BCE — Plague in Athens.

429 BCE — Death of Pericles. Socrates returned to Athens from Potidaea.

424 BCE — Battle of Delium. Socrates' second military engagement.

422 BCE — Battle of Amphipolis. Socrates' third military engagement.

421 BCE — Peace of Nicias brought a temporary cessation of hostilities between Athens and Sparta.

419 BCE — Athens and Sparta resumed hostilities.

415 BCE — Sicilian expedition. Mutilation of herms in Athens. Alcibiades defected to Sparta.

413 BCE — Syracuse defeated the Athenian expedition sent to Sicily.

411 BCE — The Four Hundred briefly took control of Athens.

407 BCE — Alcibiades returned to Athens from exile.

404 BCE — Alcibiades was murdered. Athens surrendered to Sparta. The Thirty, led by Critias, took control of Athens. The Long Wall fortifications were demolished.

403 BCE — The Thirty were removed from power. Democracy was restored to Athens.

399 BCE — Trial and execution of Socrates.

GLOSSARIES

GLOSSARY OF NAMES

ACHILLES — Greek hero who slew Hector. Central character in Homer's story the *Iliad*.

ACRON — One-eyed stonemason who worked with Socrates.

ALCIBIADES — Prominent general and politician. Student of Socrates.

ANAXAGORAS — Philosopher and counsellor to Pericles. Charged with impiety and forced to leave Athens.

ANTHEMION — Father of Anytus. Also the name of Anytus' first-born son.

ANYTUS — Athenian general and politician. Son of Anthemion. One of Socrates' three prosecutors (along with Lycon and Meletus).

APOLLO — God of Truth, Prophecy and Light.

ASCLEPIUS — God of Healing.

ASPASIA — Pericles' courtesan partner and mother of his youngest son.

ARES — God of War.

ARISTIDES — Athenian general known as "Aristides the Just." A general at the Battle of Salamis (480 BCE) and the Battle of Plataea (479 BCE).

ARTEMIS — Goddess of the Hunt, Wild Animals, Virginity and the Moon. Twin sister of Apollo.

ATLAS — Greek Titan condemned by Zeus to hold up the heavens.

ATHENA — Goddess of Wisdom and patron Goddess of Athens.

AUTOLYCUS — Son of Lycon.

CALLIOPE — Sister of Crito.

CHAEREPHON — Close friend of Socrates.

CLEON — Athenian general and warmonger.

CRITIAS — Wealthy Athenian and violent leader of The Thirty.

CRITO — Life-long friend of Socrates.

CRITOBULUS — Son of Crito.

CROESUS, KING — Wealthy king of Lydia until his defeat by the Persians.

DARIUS — One-time king of the Persian Empire. Father of King Xerxes. His army was defeated at the Battle of Marathon (490 BCE).

DEMETER — Goddess of Harvest and Agriculture.

DIAGORAS OF MELOS — Known as Diagoras the Atheist. Friend of Socrates.

DIAGORAS OF RHODES — Two-time Olympic boxing champion.

DIONYSUS — God of Wine and Ecstasy.

DIOTIMA — Slave and beloved friend of Socrates' family. Later freed.

ECPHANTUS — Patrocles assumed this name while an Athenian soldier.

EILEITHYIA — Goddess of Childbirth.

EROS — God of Love.

EURIPIDES — Contemporary of Socrates. Award-winning dramatic playwright.

HADES — God of the Underworld. Owned a three-headed dog named Cerberus.

HECTOR — Prince of Troy and Troy's greatest warrior. Slain by Achilles.

HELIO — Titan driver of the chariot of the sun.

HERA — Goddess of Women and Marriage. Wife of Zeus.

HERACLES — God of Strength and Sport. Famous for his 12 labours. Son of Zeus. Also the name of Socrates's childhood pet turtle.

HERMES — God of Roads, Borders and Luck. Protector of merchants and travellers. Son of Zeus.

HERMOGENES — Brother-in-law of Alcibiades. Student of Socrates.

HESIOD — Ancient Greek author and major source of Greek mythology.

HOMER — Ancient Greek author of the *Iliad* and the *Odyssey*.

ICARUS — A mythical man who constructed wings from feathers and wax that allowed him to fly like a bird.

LACHES — Athenian general. With Nicias, negotiated a short-lived peace with Sparta (the Peace of Nicias, 421 BCE).

LAMPROCLES — First-born son of Socrates.

LAMACHUS — Athenian general during the expedition to Sicily. Killed early during the expedition.

LYCON — Childhood classmate of Socrates. One of Socrates' three prosecutors (along with Anytus and Meletus).

MARDONIUS — Persian general and cousin to King Xerxes.

MELETUS — One of Socrates' three prosecutors (along with Lycon and Anytus).

MEMNON — Father of Lycon.

MENEXENUS — Third-born son of Socrates.

MILO OF CROTON — Winner of five Olympic wrestling titles. To build his strength, he carried full-grown bulls on his shoulders.

NICIAS — Wealthy Athenian politician and general. With Laches, successfully negotiated a short-lived peace with Sparta (the Peace of Nicias, 421 BCE).

ODYSSEUS — Central character in Homer's story, the *Odyssey*.

PARMENIDES — Philosopher and mentor of Zeno.

PATROCLES — Brother of Socrates. Used the name Ecphantus when he fought as a soldier.

PERICLES — The most prominent general and politician of his time.

PHIDIAS — Sculptor and friend of Pericles. Charged with impiety, he died in jail.

PLATO — Student of Socrates.

POSEIDON — God of the Sea and Earthquakes.

PROMETHEUS — Creator of mankind. Punished by Zeus for giving fire to mankind.

SIMON THE COBBLER — Friend and mentor to Socrates.

SOPHRONISCUS — Father of Socrates. Also the name of Socrates' second-born son.

STRATEGOS — Mythological Greek hero.

THESPIS — Father of Crito.

THEMISTOCLES — Prominent politician and general who advocated for a strong Athenian navy.

THALES — Philosopher who proposed non-mythological theories to explain natural events.

XANTHIPPE — Wife of Socrates.

XERXES — One-time king of the Persian Empire. Son of King Darius. Known for the massive expedition he mounted against Greece in 480 BCE.

ZEUS — God of Lightning and Thunder. King of the gods. Also the name of Socrates's pet dog.

ZENO — Philosopher and student of Parmenides. Known for his paradoxes.

GLOSSARY OF TERMS

ACROPOLIS — An area of elevated ground. In Athens it is a hill with steep rocky sides on which buildings such as the Parthenon are built.

AGORA — A central gathering place in ancient Greek cities. In Athens the agora consisted of a central marketplace where merchants kept stalls and sold their goods. The marketplace was surrounded by public buildings such as temples and stoas.

ANTHESTERIA FESTIVAL — Three-day festival in honor of Dionysus, to celebrate the beginning of spring.

ANDRON — The room in a Greek house that was reserved for men.

ASSEMBLY — Governing body of Athens that gathered on the Pnyx hill to discuss political issues and make decisions.

CAUL — The amniotic sac that sometimes covers a newborn's head and face at birth.

CORINTHIAN HELMET — A bronze helmet that covered the entire head and face, with slits for the eyes and mouth.

COUNCIL OF FIVE HUNDRED — Athenian administrative body made up of 500 citizens. It put into effect the decisions made by the Assembly.

CYCLOPS — Gigantic mythological male monster having only one eye, in the middle of his forehead.

DELIA FESTIVAL — A multi-day festival held in honour of Apollo. The festival took place on the Island of Delos. To preserve the purity of the Delia Festival, no executions were permitted in Athens between the time the sacred ship set sail for Delos and the time it returned to Athens.

DRACHMA — A silver coin. One drachma was equal to six obols. One drachma was the daily wage of a skilled labourer such as a stonemason.

GORGONS — Three horrifying mythological female creatures who had snakes for hair. A gaze from one of them could turn a person to stone.

GRAMMATISTE — Instructor who taught reading, writing, arithmetic and literature.

HERM — Rectangular stone pillar with a bust of Hermes's head on top and male genitalia carved at the appropriate height.

HOPLITE — Greek foot-soldier usually carrying a spear and sword and protected by various forms of armour, including the hoplon shield, from which these soldiers got their name.

HOPLON — Large round shield made of wood and bronze.

INGOT — Bar of relatively pure metal.

KERAMEIKOS — A district of Athens named after the community of potters who lived in the area. Also known for its brothels.

OBOL — Small silver coin. Six obols were equal to one drachma.

OLIGARCHY — Government run by a small, privileged (often tyrannical) group of people.

OMPHALOS — A stone in the Temple of Apollo at Delphi, the site that Greeks believed marked the centre of the earth.

ORACLE — A person through whom the gods communicated the future. The most famous of these is the Oracle of Delphi.

PAIDOTRIBE — Instructor who taught wrestling, discus and other forms of physical training.

PARTHENON — Temple located on the Athenian Acropolis, dedicated to the Goddess Athena.

PELTAST — Greek foot-soldier usually carrying a bow, javelin or sling, and a small pelte shield, from which this soldier got his name. The peltast soldier was not as well equipped (or respected) as his fellow foot-soldier, the hoplite.

PELTE — A small, crescent-shaped wicker shield.

PHALANX — Rectangular military formation made up of long parallel lines of hoplite soldiers. The hoplites were arranged very close to one another and moved together as a single unit.

PNYX — Rocky hill surrounded by trees where the Athenian assembly gathered.

STOA — Covered walkway, usually walled at the rear, having a row of pillars in the front.

STRATEGEION — Building located along the perimeter of the Athenian agora. Meeting place for the 10 generals elected each year to manage the military

TALENT — Block of silver weighing 26 kilograms or 57 pounds. A silver talent was equal to about 6000 drachmas.

THE FOUR HUNDRED — Short-lived oligarchy that briefly took over the administration of Athens in 411 BCE.

THE THIRTY — Group of men who governed Athens after its defeat by the Spartans, in 404/403 BCE. Led by Critias, The Thirty executed and exiled many Athenians.

THOLOS — Circular building where city officials met. Located in the southwest corner of the Athenian agora.

TITANS — Immortal giants who preceded the Olympian gods. After a 10-year battle, Zeus and his brothers and sisters defeated the Titans and imprisoned most of them in the deepest part of the underworld.

ALSO BY R. L. PRENDERGAST

A terrible car accident occurs. Richard and Sonia, a couple with a crumbling marriage, stop to help the critically injured victims. In the process, they find a 140-year-old journal by the side of the road. Six different people have written in the journal. Although the entries span three centuries, the writers share a quest: the search for meaning in their lives. These stories take Richard and Sonia on a personal and historic journey: across Canada, then to the jungles of India and eventually back to the Canadian Rocky Mountains, where a final mystery awaits.

A NATIONAL BESTSELLER
Available in print or eBook

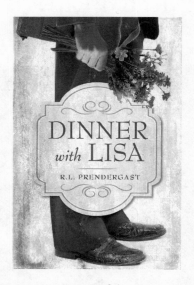

In the disastrous economic times of the 1930s, Joseph Gaston, a young widower with four children, arrives in the small town of Philibuster seeking security for his family. Instead, he faces barriers everywhere. He does his best despite great adversity, but the strain of feeding and protecting his family whittles away his strength. Finally, destitution forces him to consider giving up his children in order to save them. Enraged by his situation, he attempts one last desperate act — on the night he learns about the mysterious Lisa.

Heart wrenching, humorous and historically authentic, *Dinner with Lisa* incorporates the crucial issues of the depression: poverty, unemployment, drought and racism. In the midst of love and loyalty, trickery and despair, the ultimate message of the novel is one of hope and the courage to survive even the worst odds.

AWARD WINNER

Available in print or eBook

A MODERN DAY NURSERY RHYME
FOR SLEEP-DEPRIVED PARENTS

Please, little baby, please go to sleep,
Rest through the night and don't make a peep.
Mommy and daddy are sleep deprived,
And have been since you first arrived…

Find out what happens to our sleep-deprived parents!

ABOUT THE AUTHOR

R. L. (ROD) PRENDERGAST'S first novel, *The Impact of a Single Event*, was long-listed for literary fiction by the Independent Publisher Book Awards in 2009. The book became a bestseller in Canada. Rod's second novel, *Dinner with Lisa,* was awarded the 2012 Independent Publisher Book Awards Bronze Medal for Best Regional Fiction, Western Canada. Inspired by his son's inability to sleep through the night, Rod then wrote a children's story, *Baby, Please go to Sleep. The Confessions of Socrates* is his third novel and fourth book.

Rod lives with his wife and son in Edmonton, Alberta, Canada.

322

www.RLPrendergast.com